THE
DRAINING LAKE

Also by Arnaldur Indriðason

Jar City

Silence of the Grave

Voices

THE
DRAINING LAKE

Arnaldur Indriðason

Translated from the Icelandic by Bernard Scudder

Thomas Dunne Books
St. Martin's Minotaur ❧ New York

This is a work of fiction. All of the characters, organizations, and events portrayed in this novel are either products of the author's imagination or are used fictitiously.

THOMAS DUNNE BOOKS.
An imprint of St. Martin's Press.

Translation of poem by Jónas Hallgrímsson © Dick Ringler

www.thomasdunnebooks.com
www.minotaurbooks.com

Library of Congress Cataloging-in-Publication Data

Arnaldur Indriðason, 1961–
    [Kleifarvatn. English]
    The Draining lake / Arnaldur Indriðason ; translated from the Icelandic by Bernard Scudder.—1st U.S. ed.
        p. cm.
    ISBN-13: 978-0-312-35873-0 (alk. paper)
    ISBN-10: 0-312-35873-3 (alk. paper)
    I. Scudder, Bernard, 1954–2007. II. Title.

PT7511.A67 K5413 2008
839'.6934—dc22

                                                            2008021257

First published in Great Britain by Harvill Secker,
a Random House Group Company

First U.S. Edition: September 2008

10 9 8 7 6 5 4 3 2 1

Sleep, for I love you.
Traditional Icelandic verse

1

She stood motionless for a long time, staring at the bones as if it should not be possible for them to be there. Any more than for her.

At first she thought it was another sheep that had drowned in the lake, until she moved closer and saw the skull half-buried in the lake bed and the shape of a human skeleton. The ribs protruded from the sand and beneath them could be seen the outlines of the pelvis and thigh bones. The skeleton was lying on its left side so she could see the right side of the skull, the empty eye sockets and three teeth in the upper jaw. One had a large silver filling. There was a wide hole in the skull itself, about the size of a matchbox, which she instinctively thought could have been made by a hammer. She bent down and stared at the skull. With some hesitation she explored the hole with her finger. The skull was full of sand.

The thought of a hammer crossed her mind again and she shuddered at the idea of someone being struck over the head with one. But the hole was too large to have been left by a hammer. She decided not to touch the skeleton again. Instead, she took out her mobile and dialled emergency services.

She wondered what to say. Somehow this was so completely unreal. A skeleton so far out in the lake, buried on its sandy bed. Nor was she on her best form. Visions of hammers and matchboxes. She found it difficult to concentrate. Her thoughts were roaming all over the place and she had great trouble rounding them up again.

It was probably because she was hung-over. After planning to spend the day at home she had changed her mind and gone to the lake. She had persuaded herself that she must check the instruments. She was a scientist. She had always wanted to be a scientist and knew that the measurements had to be monitored carefully. But she had a splitting headache and her thoughts were far from logical. The National Energy Authority had held its annual dinner dance the night before and, as was sometimes the way, she had had too much to drink.

She thought about the man lying in her bed at home and knew that it was on his account that she had hauled herself off to the lake. She did not want to be there when he woke up and hoped that he would be gone when she returned. He had come back to her flat after the dance but was not very exciting. No more than the others she had met since her divorce. He hardly talked about anything except his CD collection and carried on long after she had given up feigning any interest. Then she fell asleep in a living-room chair. When she woke up she saw that he had got into her bed, where he was sleeping with his mouth open, wearing tiny underpants and black socks.

'Emergency services,' a voice said over the line.

'Hello – I'd like to report that I've found some bones,' she said. 'There's a skull with a hole in it.'

She grimaced. Bloody hangover! Who says that sort of thing? A skull with a hole in it. She remembered a phrase from a children's rhyme about a penny with a hole in it. Or was it a shilling?

'Your name, please,' said the neutral emergency-services voice.

She straightened out her jumbled thoughts and stated her name.

'Where is it?'

'Lake Kleifarvatn. North side.'

'Did you pull it up in a fishing net?'

'No. It's buried on the bed of the lake.'

'Are you a diver?'

'No, it's standing up out of the bed. Ribs and the skull.'

'It's on the bottom of the lake?'

'Yes.'

'So how can you see it?'

'I'm standing here looking at it.'

'Did you bring it to dry land?'

'No, I haven't touched it,' she lied instinctively.

The voice on the telephone paused.

'What kind of crap is this?' the voice said at last, angrily. 'Is this a hoax? You know what you can get for wasting our time?'

'It's not a hoax. I'm standing here looking at it.'

'So you can walk on water, I suppose?'

'The lake's gone,' she said. 'There's no water any more. Just the bed. Where the skeleton is.'

'What do you mean, the lake's gone?'

'It hasn't all gone, but it's dry now where I'm standing. I'm a hydrologist with the Energy Authority. I was recording the water level when I discovered this skeleton. There's a hole in the skull and most of the bones are buried in the sand on the bottom. I thought it was a sheep at first.'

'A sheep?'

'We found one the other day that had drowned years ago. When the lake was bigger.'

There was another pause.

'Wait there,' said the voice reluctantly. 'I'll send a patrol car.'

She stood still by the skeleton for a while, then walked over to the shore and measured the distance. She was certain the bones had not surfaced when she was taking measurements at the same place a fortnight earlier. Otherwise she would have seen them. The water level had dropped by more than a metre since then.

The scientists from the Energy Authority had been puzzling over this conundrum ever since they'd noticed that the water level in Lake Kleifarvatn was falling rapidly. The authority had set up its first

3

automatic surface-level monitor in 1964 and one of the hydrologists' tasks was to check the measurements. In the summer of 2000 the monitor seemed to have broken. An incredible amount of water was draining from the lake every day, twice the normal volume.

She walked back to the skeleton. She was itching to take a better look, dig it up and brush off the sand, but imagined that the police would be none too pleased at that. She wondered whether it was male or female and vaguely recalled having read somewhere, probably in a detective story, that their skeletons were almost identical: only the pelvises were different. Then she remembered someone telling her not to believe anything she read in detective stories. Since the skeleton was buried in the sand she couldn't see the pelvis, and it struck her that she would not have known the difference anyway.

Her hangover intensified and she sat down on the sand beside the bones. It was a Sunday morning and the occasional car drove past the lake. She imagined they were families out for a Sunday drive to Herdísarvík and on to Selvogur. That was a popular and scenic route, across the lava field and hills and past the lake down to the sea. She thought about the families in the cars. Her own husband had left her when the doctors ruled out their ever having children together. He remarried shortly afterwards and now had two lovely children. He had found happiness.

All that she had found was a man she barely knew, lying in her bed in his socks. Decent men became harder to find as the years went by. Most of them were either divorced like her or, even worse, had never been in a relationship at all.

She looked woefully at the bones, half-buried in the sand, and was close to tears.

About an hour later a police car approached from Hafnarfjördur. It was in no hurry, lazily threading its way along the road towards the lake. This was May and the sun was high in the sky, reflecting off the smooth surface of the water. She sat on the sand watching the road and when she waved to the car it pulled over. Two police officers got out, looked in her direction and walked towards her.

They stood over the skeleton in silence for a long time until one of them poked a rib with his foot.

'Do you reckon he was fishing?' he said to his colleague.

'On a boat, you mean?'

'Or waded here.'

'There's a hole,' she said, looking at each of them in turn. 'In the skull.'

One officer bent down.

'Well,' he said.

'He could have fallen over in the boat and broken his skull,' his colleague said.

'It's full of sand,' said the first one.

'Shouldn't we notify CID?' the other asked.

'Aren't most of them in America?' his colleague said, looking up into the sky. 'At a crime conference?'

The other officer nodded. Then they stood quietly over the bones for a while until one of them turned to her.

'Where's all the water gone?' he asked.

'There are various theories,' she said. 'What are you going to do? Can I go home now?'

After exchanging glances they took down her name and thanked her, without apologising for having kept her waiting. She didn't care. She wasn't in a hurry. It was a beautiful day by the lake and she would have enjoyed it even more in the company of her hangover if she had not chanced upon the skeleton. She wondered whether the man in the black socks had left her flat and certainly hoped so. Looked forward to renting a video that evening and snuggling up under a blanket in front of the television.

She looked down at the bones and at the hole in the skull.

Maybe she would rent a good detective film.

2

The police officers notified their duty sergeant in Hafnarfjördur about the skeleton in the lake; it took them some time to explain how it could be out in the middle of the lake yet still on dry land. The sergeant phoned the chief inspector at the Police Commissioner's office and informed him of the find, wanting to know whether or not they would take over the case.

'That's something for the identification committee,' the chief inspector said. 'I think I have the right man for the job.'

'Who's that?'

'We sent him off on holiday – he's got about five years' leave owing to him, I think – but I know he'll be pleased to have something to do. He's interested in missing persons. Likes digging things up.'

The chief inspector said goodbye, picked up the phone again and asked for Erlendur Sveinsson to be contacted and sent off to Lake Kleifarvatn with a small team of detectives.

Erlendur was absorbed in a book when the telephone rang. He had tried to shut out the relentless May sun as best he could. Thick curtains covered the living-room windows and he had closed the door to the kitchen, where there were no proper curtains. He had made it dark enough around him to have to switch on the lamp by his chair.

Erlendur knew the story well. He had read it many times before. It was an account of a journey in the autumn of 1868 from Skaftártunga along the mountain trail north of the Mýrdalsjökull glacier. Several people had been travelling together to a fishing camp in Gardar, in the south-west of Iceland. One was a young man aged seventeen whose name was Davíd. Although the men were seasoned travellers and familiar with the route, a perilous storm got up soon after they set off and they never returned. An extensive search was mounted but no trace of them was found. It was not until ten years later that their skeletons were discovered by chance beside a large sand dune, south of Kaldaklof. The men had spread blankets over themselves and were lying huddled against each other.

Erlendur looked up in the gloom and imagined the teenager in the group, fearful and worried. He had seemed to know what was in the offing before he set out; local farmers remarked how he had shared out his childhood toys among his brothers and sisters, saying that he would not be back to reclaim them.

Putting down his book, Erlendur stood up stiffly and answered the telephone. It was Elínborg.

'Will you be coming?' was the first thing she said.

'Do I have any choice?' Erlendur said. Elínborg had for many years been compiling a book of recipes which was now finally being published.

'Oh my God, I'm so nervous. What do you think people will make of it?'

'I can still barely switch on a microwave,' Erlendur said. 'So maybe I'm not...'

'The publishers loved it,' Elínborg said. 'And the photos of the dishes are brilliant. They commissioned a special photographer to take them. And there's a separate chapter on Christmas food...'

'Elínborg.'

'Yes.'

'Were you calling about anything in particular?'

'A skeleton in Lake Kleifarvatn,' Elínborg said, lowering her voice when the conversation moved away from her cookery book. 'I'm supposed to fetch you. The lake's shrunk or something and they found some bones there this morning. They want you to take a look.'

'The lake's shrunk?'

'Yes, I didn't quite get that bit.'

Sigurdur Óli was standing by the skeleton when Erlendur and Elínborg arrived at the lake. A forensics team was on the way. The officers from Hafnarfjördur were fiddling around with yellow plastic tape to cordon off the area, but had discovered they had nothing to attach it to. Sigurdur Óli watched their efforts and thought he could understand why village-idiot jokes were always set in Hafnarfjördur.

'Aren't you on holiday?' he asked Erlendur as he walked over across the black sand.

'Yes,' Erlendur said. 'What have you been up to?'

'Same old,' Sigurdur Óli said in English. He looked up at the road where a large jeep from one of the TV stations was parking at the roadside. 'They sent her home,' he said with a nod at the policemen from Hafnarfjördur. 'The woman who found the bones. She was taking some measurements here. We can ask her afterwards why the lake's dried up. Under normal circumstances we ought to be up to our necks on this spot.'

'Is your shoulder all right?'

'Yes. How's Eva Lind doing?'

'She hasn't done a runner yet,' Erlendur said. 'I think she regrets the whole business, but I'm not really sure.'

He knelt down and examined the exposed part of the skeleton. He put his finger in the hole in the skull and rubbed one of the ribs.

'He's been hit over the head,' he said and stood up again.

'That's rather obvious,' Elínborg said sarcastically. 'If it is a *he*,' she added.

'Rather like a fight, isn't it?' Sigurdur Óli said. 'The hole's just above the right temple. Maybe it only took one good punch.'

'We can't rule out that he was alone on a boat here and fell against the side,' Erlendur said, looking at Elínborg. 'That tone of yours, Elínborg, is that the style you use in your cookery book?'

'Of course, the smashed piece of bone would have been washed away a long time ago,' she said, ignoring his question.

'We need to dig out the bones,' Sigurdur Óli said. 'When do forensics get here?'

Erlendur saw more cars pulling up by the roadside and presumed that word about the discovery of the skeleton had reached the newsdesks.

'Won't they have to put up a tent?' he said, still eyeing the road.

'Yes,' Sigurdur Óli said. 'They're bound to bring one.'

'You mean he was fishing on the lake alone?' Elínborg asked.

'No, that's just one possibility,' Erlendur said.

'But what if someone hit him?'

'Then it wasn't an accident,' Sigurdur Óli said.

'We don't know what happened,' Erlendur said. 'Maybe someone hit him. Maybe he was out fishing with someone who suddenly produced a hammer. Maybe there were only the two of them. Maybe they were three, five.'

'Or,' Sigurdur Óli chipped in, 'he was hit over the head in the city and brought out to the lake to dispose of his body.'

'How could they have made him sink?' Elínborg said. 'You need something to weight a body down in the water.'

'Is it an adult?' Sigurdur Óli said.

'Tell them to keep their distance,' Erlendur said as he watched the reporters clambering down to the lake bed from the road. A light aircraft approached from the direction of Reykjavík and flew low over the lake; they could see someone holding a camera.

Sigurdur Óli went over to the reporters. Erlendur walked down to the lake. The ripples lapped lazily against the sand as he watched the afternoon sun glittering on the water's surface and wondered what was happening. Was the lake draining through the actions of man or was it nature at work? It was as if the lake itself wanted to uncover a crime. Did it conceal more misdeeds where it was deeper and still dark and calm?

He gazed up at the road. Forensics technicians wearing white overalls were hurrying across the sand in his direction. They were carrying a tent and bags full of mysteries. He looked skywards and felt the warmth of the sun on his face. Maybe it was the sun that was drying up the lake.

The first discovery that the forensics team made when they began clearing the sand from the skeleton with their little trowels and fine-haired brushes was a rope that had slipped between the ribs and lay by the spinal column then under the skeleton, where it vanished into the sand.

The hydrologist's name was Sunna and she had snuggled up under a blanket on the sofa. The tape was in the video player, the American thriller *The Bone Collector*. The man in the black socks had gone. He had left behind two telephone numbers which she flushed down the toilet. The film was just starting when the doorbell rang. She was forever being disturbed. If it wasn't cold-callers it was people selling dried fish door-to-door, or boys asking for empty bottles who lied that they were collecting for the Red Cross. The bell clanged again. Still she hesitated. Then with a sigh she threw off the blanket.

When she opened the door two men were standing before her. One looked a rather sorry sight, round-shouldered and wearing a peculiarly mournful expression on his face. The other one was younger and much nicer – handsome, really.

Erlendur watched her staring with interest at Sigurdur Óli and could not suppress a smile.

'It's about Lake Kleifarvatn,' he said.

Once they had sat down in her living room Sunna told them what she and her colleagues at the Energy Authority believed had happened.

'You remember the big south Iceland earthquake on the seventeenth of June 2000?' she said, and they nodded. 'About five seconds afterwards a large earthquake also struck Kleifarvatn, which doubled the natural rate of drainage from it. When the lake started to shrink people at first thought it was because of unusually low precipitation, but it turned out that the water was pouring down through fissures that run across the bed of the lake and have been there for ages. Apparently they opened up in the earthquake. The lake measured ten square kilometres but now it's only about eight. The water level has fallen by at least four metres.'

'And that's how you found the skeleton,' Erlendur said.

'We found the bones of a sheep when the surface had dropped by two metres,' Sunna said. 'But of course it hadn't been hit over the head.'

'What do you mean, hit over the head?' Sigurdur Óli said.

She looked at him. She had tried to be inconspicuous when she looked at his hands. Tried to spot a wedding ring.

'I saw a hole in the skull,' she said. 'Do you know who it is?'

'No,' Erlendur said. 'He would have needed to use a boat, wouldn't he? To get so far out onto the lake.'

'If you mean could someone have walked to where the skeleton is, the answer's no. It was at least four metres deep there until quite recently. And if it happened years back, which of course I know nothing about, the water would have been even deeper.'

'So they were on a boat?' Sigurdur Óli said. 'Are there boats on that lake?'

'There are houses in the vicinity,' Sunna said, staring into his eyes. He had beautiful eyes, dark blue under delicate brows. 'There might be some boats there. I've never seen a boat on the lake.'

If only we could row away somewhere, she thought to herself.

Erlendur's mobile began ringing. It was Elínborg.

'You ought to get over here,' she said.

'What's happened?'

'Come and see. It's quite remarkable. I've never seen anything like it.'

3

He stood up, switched on the television news and groaned. There was a lengthy report on the skeleton found at Lake Kleifarvatn, including an interview with a detective who said that there would be a thorough investigation of the case.

He walked over to the window and looked out towards the sea. On the pavement in front of him he saw the couple who walked past his house every evening, the man a few steps ahead as usual, the woman trying to keep up with him. While walking they were in conversation; the man talking over his shoulder and she at his back. They had been passing the house for years and had long since ceased to pay attention to their surroundings. In the past they would occasionally look up at the house and at the other buildings on the street by the sea, and into the gardens. Sometimes they even stopped to admire a new swing or work being carried out on fences and terraces. No matter what the weather or the time of year, they always took their walk in the afternoon or the evening, always together.

On the horizon he saw a large cargo ship. The sun was still high in the sky although it was well into the evening. The brightest period of the year lay ahead, before the days began growing shorter again and then shrinking to nothing. It had been a beautiful spring. He had noticed the first golden plovers outside his house in mid-April. They had followed the spring wind in from the continent.

It had been late summer when he had first sailed abroad. Cargo ships were not so enormous in those days and were not containerised. He remembered the deckhands lugging fifty-kilo sacks around the hold. Remembered their smuggling stories. They knew him from his spell in a summer job at the harbour and enjoyed telling him how they duped the Customs officers. Some stories were so fantastic that he knew they were making them up. Others were so tense and exciting that they had no need to invent any details. And there were stories he was never allowed to hear. Even though they knew he would never tell. Not the communist from that posh school!

Never tell.

He looked back to the television. He felt as though he had spent his whole life waiting for this report on the news.

He had been a socialist for as far back as he could remember, like everyone on both sides of his family. Political apathy was unheard of and he grew up loathing the conservatives. His father had been involved in the labour movement since the early decades of the twentieth century. Politics was a constant topic of discussion at home; they particularly despised the American base at Keflavík which the Icelandic capitalist class cheerfully accepted. It was Icelandic capitalists who benefited the most from the military.

Then there was the company he kept, his friends from similar backgrounds. They could be very radical and some were eloquent speakers. He remembered the political meetings well. Remembered the passion. The fervent debates. He attended the meetings with his friends who, like him, were finding their feet in the party's youth movement; he listened to their leader's thunderous haranguing of the rich who exploited the proletariat, and the American forces who had them in their pocket. He had heard this repeated over and again with the same unwavering and heartfelt conviction. Everything he heard inspired him, because he had been raised as an Icelandic nationalist and hardline socialist who never doubted his views for one moment. He knew the truth was on his side.

A recurrent theme at their meetings was the American presence at Keflavík and the tricks that Icelandic money-grubbers had pulled to allow a foreign military base to be established on Icelandic soil. He knew how the country had been sold to the Americans for the capitalists to grow fat on, like parasites. As a teenager, he was outside Parliament House when the ruling class's lackeys stormed out of it with tear gas and truncheons and beat up those protesting against Iceland's entry into NATO. The traitors are lapdogs of US imperialism! We're under the jackboot of American capitalism! The young socialists had no shortage of slogans.

He belonged to the oppressed masses himself. He was swept along by the fervour and the eloquence and the just notion that all men should be equal. The bosses should work alongside the labourers in the factory. Down with the class system! He had a genuine and steadfast faith in socialism. He felt the need to serve the cause, to persuade others and to fight for all the underprivileged, the workers and the oppressed.

Arise ye workers from your slumbers . . .

He took full part in discussions at the meetings and read what the youth movement recommended. There was plenty to be found in libraries and bookshops. He wanted to leave his mark. In his heart he knew that he was right. Much of what he had heard from the young socialist movement filled him with a sense of justice.

Gradually he learned the answers to questions about dialectical materialism, the class struggle as the vehicle of history, about capitalism and the proletariat, and he trained himself to garnish his vocabulary with phrases from the great revolutionary thinkers as he read more and became increasingly inspired. Before long he had surpassed his comrades in Marxist theory and rhetoric and caught the eye of the youth-movement leaders. Elections to party posts and the drafting of resolutions were important activities and he was asked whether he wanted to join the party council. He was then eighteen. They had founded a society at his school called 'The Red Flag'. His father decided that he should have the benefit of an education, the only one of the four children. For that, he was forever grateful to his father.

In spite of everything.

The youth movement published a broadsheet and held regular meetings. The chairman was even invited to Moscow and came back full of tales about the workers' state. Such magnificent development. People were so happy. Their every need catered for. The cooperatives and centralised economy promised unprecedented progress. Postwar reconstruction outstripped all expectations. Factories sprouted up, owned and run by the state, by the people themselves. New residential districts were being built in the suburbs. All medical services were free. Everything they had read, everything they had heard, was true. Every word of it. O, what times!

Others had been to the Soviet Union and described a different experience. The young socialists remained unmoved. The critics were servants of capitalism. They had betrayed the cause, the struggle for a fair society.

The Red Flag meetings were well attended and they managed to draft in more and more members. He was unanimously elected chairman of the society and was soon noticed by the Socialist Party's top brass. In his final year at school it was clear that he was future leadership material.

He turned from the window and walked over to the photograph hanging above the piano, taken at the school-leaving ceremony. He looked at the faces under the traditional white caps. The male students in front of the school building wearing black suits, the girls in dresses. The sun was shining and their white caps glittered. He was second-best student of the year. Only a hair's breadth from coming top of the school. He stroked his hand over the photograph. He missed those years. Missed the time when his conviction had been so strong that nothing could break it.

In his last year at school he was offered a job on the party paper. In his summer vacation he had worked as a docker, got to know the labourers and deckhands, and talked politics with them. Many of them were outright reactionaries and they called him 'the communist'. He was interested in journalism and knew that the paper was one of the pillars of the party. Before he started there, the chairman of the youth movement took him to the deputy leader's house. The deputy leader, a skinny man, sat in a deep armchair polishing his spectacles with a handkerchief and telling them about the establishment of a socialist state in Iceland. Everything that soft voice said was so true and so right that a chill ran down his spine as he sat in the little living room, devouring every word.

He was a good student. History, mathematics or any other subject came equally easily to him. Once a piece of knowledge entered his mind he retained it for instant recall. His memory and gift for study proved useful in journalism and he was a quick learner. He worked and thought fast, and could do long interviews without needing to jot down more than a few sentences. He knew that he was not an impartial reporter, but nor was anyone else in those days.

He had planned to enrol that autumn at the University of Iceland, but was asked to stay on at the paper for the winter. He didn't need to think twice. In the middle of the winter the deputy leader invited him home. The East German Communist Party was offering places for several Icelandic students at the University of Leipzig; if he accepted one he would have to make his own way there but would be provided with board and lodging.

He had wanted to go to Eastern Europe or the Soviet Union to see the post-war reconstruction for himself. To travel, discover different cultures and learn languages. He wanted to see socialism in action. He had been considering applying to the University of Moscow and had still not made up his mind when he visited the deputy leader. Wiping his spectacles, the deputy leader said that studying in Leipzig was a unique opportunity for him to observe the workings of a communist state and train to serve his own country even better.

The deputy leader put on his glasses.

'And serve the cause,' he added. 'You'll like it there. Leipzig's a historical city and has links with Icelandic culture. Halldór Laxness visited his friend the poet Jóhann Jónsson there. And Jón Árnason's collection of folk tales was published by Hinrich Verlag of Leipzig in 1862.'

He nodded. He had read everything Laxness had written about socialism in Eastern Europe and admired his powers of persuasion.

The idea that he could go by ship and work his passage occurred to him. His uncle knew someone at the shipping company. Securing the passage was no problem. His family were ecstatic. None of them had been abroad, to say nothing of studying in another country. It would be such an adventure. They wrote to each other and telephoned to discuss the wonderful news. 'He'll turn out to be something,' people said. 'It wouldn't surprise me if he ended up in government!'

The first port of call was in the Faroe Islands, then Copenhagen, Rotterdam and Hamburg. From there he took the train to Berlin and slept the night at the railway station. The following day, at noon, he boarded a train to Leipzig. He knew that nobody would be there to welcome him. He had an address written on a note in his pocket and asked for directions when he reached his destination.

Sighing heavily, he stood in front of the school photograph, looking at the face of his friend from Leipzig. They had been in the same class at school. If only he had known then what would happen.

He wondered whether the police would ever discover the truth about the man in the lake. He consoled himself with the thought that it was such a long time ago and that what had happened no longer mattered.

No one cared about the man in the lake any more.

4

Forensics had erected a large tent over the skeleton. Elínborg stood outside it as she watched Erlendur and Sigurdur Óli hurrying across the dry bed of the lake towards her. It was late in the evening and the media had left. Traffic had increased around the lake after the find was reported, but had died down and the area was quiet again.

'Nice of you to find the time,' Elínborg said as they approached.

'Sigurdur had to stop for a hamburger on the way,' Erlendur grunted. 'What's going on?'

'Come with me,' Elínborg said, opening the tent. 'The pathologist is here.'

Erlendur looked down towards the lake in the evening calm and thought about the fissures in its bed. The sun was still up, so it was completely daylight. Staring up at the white puffs of cloud directly above him, he was still pondering how strange it was that there had once been a lake four metres deep where he was standing.

The forensics team had unearthed the skeleton, which could now be seen in its entirety. There was not a single piece of flesh or scrap of clothing left on it. A woman aged about forty knelt beside it, picking at the pelvis with a yellow pencil.

'It's a male,' she said. 'Average height and probably middle-aged, but I need to check that more carefully. I don't know how long he's been in the water, perhaps forty or fifty years. Maybe longer. But that's just a guess. I can be more precise once I get him down to the morgue to study him properly.'

She stood up and greeted them. Erlendur knew her name was Matthildur and that she had recently been recruited as a pathologist. He longed to ask her what drove her to investigate crimes. Why she didn't just become a doctor like all the others and milk the health service?

'He's been hit over the head?' Erlendur asked.

'Looks like it,' Matthildur said. 'But it's difficult to establish what kind of instrument was used. All the marks around the hole have gone.'

'We're talking about wilful murder?' Sigurdur Óli said.

'All murders are wilful,' Matthildur said. 'Some are just more stupid than others.'

'There's no question that it's murder,' said Elínborg, who had been listening.

She scrambled over the skeleton and pointed down to a large hole that the forensics team had dug. Erlendur went over to her and saw that inside the hole was a bulky black metal box, tied by a rope to the bones. It was still mostly buried in the sand but what appeared to be broken instruments with black dials and black buttons were visible. The box was scratched and dented, it had opened up and there was sand inside.

'What's that?' Sigurdur Óli asked.

'God knows,' Elínborg said, 'but it was used to sink him.'

'Is it some kind of measuring device?' Erlendur said.

'I've never seen anything like it,' Elínborg said. 'Forensics said it was an old radio transmitter. They went off for something to eat.'

'A transmitter?' Erlendur said. 'What kind of transmitter?'

'They didn't know. They've still got to dig it up.'

Erlendur looked at the rope tied around the skeleton and at the black box used to sink the body. He imagined men lugging the corpse out of a car, tying it to the transmitter, rowing out onto the lake with it and throwing the whole lot overboard.

'So he was sunk?' he said.

'He hardly did it himself,' Sigurdur Óli blurted out. 'He wouldn't really go out onto the lake, tie himself to a radio transmitter, pick it up, fall over on his head and still take care to end up in the lake so he'd be sure to disappear. That would be the most ridiculous suicide in history.'

'Do you suppose the transmitter's heavy?' Erlendur asked, trying to contain his irritation with Sigurdur Óli.

'It looks really heavy to me,' Matthildur said.

'Is there any point in combing the bottom of the lake for a murder weapon?' Elínborg asked. 'With a metal detector, if it was a hammer or the like? It might have been thrown in with the body.'

'Forensics will handle that,' Erlendur said, kneeling down by the black box. He rubbed away the sand from it.

'Maybe he was a radio ham,' Sigurdur Óli said.

'Are you coming?' Elínborg asked. 'To my book launch?'

'Don't we have to?' Sigurdur Óli said.

'I'm not going to force you.'

'What's the book called?' Erlendur asked.

'*More Than Just Desserts*,' Elínborg said. 'It's a pun. Justice – get it – and desserts, and it's not just desserts . . .'

'Very droll,' Erlendur said, casting a look of astonishment at Sigurdur Óli, who was trying to smother his laughter.

Eva Lind sat facing him, wearing a white dressing gown with her legs curled up under her on the seat, twiddling her hair around her index finger, circle after circle as if hypnotised. As a rule in-patients were not allowed to receive guests but the staff knew Erlendur well and made no objection when he asked to see her. They sat in silence for a good while. They were in the in-patients' lounge and there were posters on the walls warning against alcohol and drug abuse.

'You still seeing that old bag?' Eva said, fiddling with her hair.

'Stop calling her an old bag,' Erlendur said. 'Valgerdur's two years younger than me.'

21

'Right, an old bag. You still seeing her?'

'Yes.'

'And . . . does she come round to yours, this Valgerdur woman?'

'She has done, once.'

'And then you meet at hotels.'

'Something like that. How are you doing? Sigurdur Óli sends his regards. He says his shoulder's getting better.'

'I missed. I wanted to hit him over the head.'

'You really can be a bloody idiot sometimes,' Erlendur said.

'Has she left her bloke? She's still married, isn't she, that Valgerdur?'

'It's none of your business.'

'So she's cheating on him? Which means you're shagging a married woman. How do you feel about that?'

'We haven't slept together. Not that it's any of your business. And cut out that filthy language!'

'Like hell you haven't slept together!'

'Aren't you supposed to get medication here? To cure your temper?'

He stood up. She looked up at him.

'I didn't ask you to put me in here,' she said. 'I didn't ask you to interfere in my life. I want you to leave me alone. Completely alone.'

He walked out of the lounge without saying goodbye.

'Say hello to the old bag from me,' Eva Lind called out after him, twiddling her hair as collected as ever. 'Say hello to that fucking old bag,' she added under her breath.

Erlendur parked outside his block of flats and entered the stairwell. When he reached his floor he noticed a lanky young long-haired man loitering by the door, smoking. The upper part of his body was in the shadows and Erlendur could not make out his face. At first he thought it was a criminal who had unfinished business with him. Sometimes they called him when they were drunk and threatened him for encroaching in some way or other upon their miserable lives. The occasional one turned up at his door to argue. He was expecting something like that in the corridor.

The young man stood up straight when he saw Erlendur approach.

'Can I stay with you?' he asked, having trouble deciding what to do with his cigarette butt. Erlendur noticed two dog-ends on the carpet.

'Who are . . . ?'

'Sindri,' the man said, stepping from the shadows. 'Your son. Don't you recognise me?'

'Sindri?' Erlendur said in surprise.

'I've moved back into town,' Sindri said. 'I thought I'd look you up.'

Sigurdur Óli was in bed beside Bergthóra when the telephone rang. He looked at the caller ID. Realising who it was, he decided not to answer. On the sixth ring, Bergthóra gave him a nudge.

'Answer it,' she said. 'It'll do him good to talk to you. He thinks you help him.'

'I'm not going to let him think he can call me at home in the middle of the night,' Sigurdur Óli said.

'Come on,' Bergthóra said, reaching over from her side of the bed for the telephone.

'Yes, he's here,' she said. 'Just a minute.'

She handed Sigurdur Óli the telephone.

'It's for you,' she said, smiling.

'Were you asleep?' a voice said at the other end of the line.

'Yes,' Sigurdur Óli lied. 'I've asked you not to call me at home. I don't want you to.'

'Sorry,' the voice said. 'I can't sleep. I'm taking medication and tranquillisers and sleeping tablets but none of them work.'

'You can't just call whenever you please,' Sigurdur Óli said.

'Sorry,' the man said. 'I don't feel too good.'

'Okay,' Sigurdur Óli said.

'It was a year ago,' the man said. 'To the day.'

'Yes,' Sigurdur Óli said. 'I know.'

'A whole year of hell,' the man said.

'Try to stop thinking about it,' Sigurdur Óli said. 'It's time you stopped tormenting yourself like this. It doesn't help.'

'That's easy enough to say,' the man on the telephone said.

'I know,' Sigurdur Óli said. 'But just try.'

'What was I thinking of with those bloody strawberries?'

'We've been through this a thousand times,' Sigurdur Óli said, shaking his head as he glanced at Bergthóra. 'It wasn't your fault. Stop torturing yourself.'

'Of course it was,' the man said. 'Of course it was my fault. It was all my fault.'

Then he rang off.

5

The woman looked at them in turn, gave a weak smile and invited them in. Elínborg went first and Erlendur closed the door behind them. They had telephoned in advance and the woman had placed crullers and soda cake on the table. The aroma of coffee wafted in from the kitchen. This was a town house in Breidholt suburb. Elínborg had spoken to the woman on the telephone. She had remarried. Her son from the previous marriage was doing a doctorate in medicine in the States. She had had two children with her second husband. Surprised by Elínborg's call, she had taken the afternoon off work to meet her and Erlendur at home.

'Is it him?' the woman asked as she offered them a seat. Her name was Kristín, she was past sixty and had put on weight with age. She had heard on the news about the skeleton that had been found in Lake Kleifarvatn.

'We don't know,' Erlendur said. 'We know it's a male but we're waiting for a more precise age on it.'

A few days had passed since the skeleton had been found. Some bones had been sent for carbon analysis but the pathologist had also used a different method, which she thought could speed up the results.

'Speed up the results how?' Erlendur had asked Elínborg.

'She uses the aluminium smelter in Straumsvík.'

'The smelter?'

'She's studying the history of pollution from it. It involves sulphur dioxide and fluoride and that sort of gunge. Have you heard about it?'

'No.'

'A certain amount of sulphur dioxide is emitted into the atmosphere and falls onto the land and the sea; it's found in lakes near the smelter, such as Kleifarvatn. They've reduced the quantity now with improved pollution control. She said she found a trace in the bones and at a very provisional estimate says the body was put in the lake before 1970.'

'Give or take?'

'Five years either way.'

At this stage the investigation into the skeleton from Kleifarvatn focused on males who had gone missing between 1960 and 1975. There were eight cases in the whole of Iceland. Five had lived in or around Reykjavík.

Kristín's first husband had been one of them. The detectives had read the files. She had reported his disappearance herself. One day he had not come home from work. She'd had his dinner ready for him. Their son was playing on the floor. She bathed the boy, put him to bed and tidied up in the kitchen. Then sat down and waited. She would have watched television, but in those days there were no broadcasts on Thursdays.

This was the autumn of 1969. They lived in a small flat they had recently bought. He was an estate agent and had been given a good deal on it. She had just finished Commercial College when they met. A year later they were married with due ceremony and a year after that their son was born. Her husband worshipped him.

'That's why I couldn't understand it,' Kristín said, her gaze flicking between them.

Erlendur had a feeling that she was still waiting for the husband who had so suddenly and inexplicably vanished from her life. He visualised her waiting alone in the autumn gloom. Calling people who knew him and their friends, telephoning the family, who would quietly gather in the flat over the following days to give her strength and support her in her grief.

'We were happy,' she said. 'Our little boy Benni was the apple of our eye, I'd got a job with the Merchants' Association and as far as I knew my husband was doing well at work. It was a big estate agency and he was a great salesman. He wasn't so good at school, dropped out after two years, but he worked hard and I thought he was happy with life. He never suggested otherwise to me.'

She poured coffee into their cups.

'I didn't notice anything unusual on the last day,' Kristín went on, passing them the dish of crullers. 'He said goodbye to me in the morning, phoned at lunchtime just to say hello and again to say he would be a little late. That was the last I heard from him.'

'But wasn't he having trouble at work, even if he didn't tell you?' Elínborg asked. 'We read the reports and . . .'

'Redundancies were on the way. He'd spoken about it a few days earlier but didn't know who. Then he was called in that day and told that they no longer needed him. The owner told me that later. He said my husband had showed no response to being made redundant, didn't protest or ask for an explanation, just went back out and sat down at his desk. Didn't react.'

'He didn't phone you to tell you?' Elínborg asked.

'No,' the woman said, and Erlendur could sense the sorrow still enveloping her. 'Like I told you, he phoned but didn't say a word about losing his job.'

'Why was he made redundant?' Erlendur asked.

'I never had a satisfactory answer to that. I think the owner wanted to show me compassion or consideration when we spoke. He said they needed to cut back because sales were down, but later I heard that Ragnar had apparently lost interest in the job. Lost interest in what he was doing. After a school reunion he had talked about enrolling again and finishing. He was invited to the reunion even though he had quit school and all his old friends had become doctors and lawyers and engineers. That was the way he talked. As if it brought him down, dropping out of school.'

'Did you link this to his disappearance in any way?' Erlendur asked.

'No, not particularly,' Kristín said. 'I can just as easily put it down to a little tiff we had the day before. Or that our son was difficult at night. Or that he couldn't afford a new car. Really I don't know what to think.'

'Was he depressive?' Elínborg said, noticing Kristín slip into the present tense, as if it had all just happened.

'No more than most Icelanders. He went missing in the autumn, if that means anything.'

'At the time you ruled out the possibility that there was anything criminal about his disappearance,' Erlendur said.

'Yes,' she said. 'I couldn't imagine that. He wasn't involved in anything of that sort. If he met someone who murdered him, it would have been pure bad luck. The thought that anything like that happened never crossed my mind, nor yours at the police. You never treated his disappearance as a criminal matter either. He stayed behind at work until everyone had left and that was the last time he was seen.'

'Wasn't his disappearance ever investigated as a criminal matter?' Elínborg said.

'No,' Kristín said.

'Tell me something else: was your husband a radio ham?' Erlendur asked.

'A radio ham? What's that?'

'To tell the truth I'm not quite sure myself,' Erlendur said, looking to Elínborg for help. She sat and said nothing. 'They're in radio contact with people all around the world,' Erlendur continued. 'You need, or used to need, a quite powerful transmitter to broadcast your signal. Did he have any equipment like that?'

'No,' the woman said. 'A radio ham?'

'Was he involved in telecommunications?' Elínborg asked. 'Did he own a radio transmitter or . . . ?'

Kristín looked at her.

'What did you find in that lake?' she asked with a look of astonishment. 'He never owned a radio transmitter. What kind of transmitter, anyway?'

'Did he ever go fishing in Kleifarvatn?' Elínborg continued without answering her. 'Or know anything about it?'

'No, never. He wasn't interested in angling. My brother's a keen salmon fisherman and tried to get him to go along, but he never would. He was like me in that. We never wanted to kill anything for sport or fun. We never went to Kleifarvatn.'

Erlendur noticed a beautifully framed photograph on a shelf in the living room. It showed Kristín with a young boy, whom he took to be her fatherless son, and he started thinking about his own son, Sindri. He had not realised at once why he had dropped by. Sindri had always avoided his father, unlike Eva Lind who wanted to make him feel guilty for ignoring her and her brother in their childhood. Erlendur had divorced their mother after a short marriage and as the years wore on he increasingly regretted having had any contact with his children.

They shook hands embarrassedly on the landing like two strangers; he let Sindri in and made coffee. Sindri said he was looking for a flat or a room. Erlendur said he didn't know of any vacant places but promised to tell him if he heard of anything.

'Maybe I could stay here for the time being,' Sindri said, looking at the bookcase in the living room.

'Here?' Erlendur said in surprise, appearing in the kitchen doorway. The purpose behind Sindri's visit dawned on him.

'Eva said you had a spare room that's just full of old junk.'

Erlendur looked at his son. There was indeed a spare room in his flat. The old junk Eva had mentioned was his parents' effects, which he kept because he could not bring himself to throw it out. Items from his childhood home. A chest full of letters written by his parents and forebears, a carved shelf, piles of magazines, books, fishing rods and a heavy old shotgun that his grandfather had owned, broken.

'What about your mother?' Erlendur said. 'Can't you stay with her?'

'Of course,' Sindri said. 'I'll just do that, then.'

They fell silent.

'No, there's no space in that room,' Erlendur said eventually. 'So . . . I don't know . . .'

'Eva's stayed here,' Sindri said.

His words were followed by a deep silence.

'She said you've changed,' Sindri said in the end.

'What about you?' Erlendur asked. 'Have you changed?'

'I haven't touched a drop for months,' Sindri said. 'If that's what you mean.'

Erlendur snapped out of his thoughts and sipped his coffee. He looked away from the photograph on the shelf and over at Kristín. He wanted a cigarette.

'So the boy never knew his father,' he said. Out of the corner of his eye he saw Elínborg glaring at him, but pretended not to notice. He was well aware that he was prying into the private life of a woman whose husband's mysterious disappearance more than thirty years before had never been satisfactorily resolved. Erlendur's question was irrelevant to the police investigation.

'His stepfather has treated him well and he has a very good relationship with his brothers,' she said. 'I can't see what that has to do with my husband's disappearance.'

'No, sorry,' Erlendur said.

'I don't think there's anything else, then,' Elínborg said.

'Do you think it's him?' Kristín asked, standing up.

'I don't think it's very likely,' Elínborg said. 'But we need to look into it more closely.'

They stood still for an instant as if something remained to be said. As if something was in the air that needed to be put into words before their meeting would be over.

'A year after he went missing,' Kristín said, 'a body was washed ashore on Snaefellsnes. They thought it was him but it turned out not to be.'

She clasped her hands.

'Sometimes, even today, I think he might be alive. That he didn't die at all. Sometimes I think he left us and moved to the countryside – or abroad – without telling us, and started a new family. I've even caught glimpses of him here in Reykjavík. About five years ago I thought I saw him. I followed this man around like an imbecile. It was in the shopping centre. Spied on him until I saw that of course it wasn't him.'

She looked at Erlendur.

'He went away, but all the same . . . he'll never go away,' she said with a sad smile playing across her lips.

'I know,' Erlendur said. 'I know what you mean.'

When they got into the car Elínborg scolded Erlendur for his callous question about Kristín's son. Erlendur told her not to be so sensitive.

His mobile rang. It was Valgerdur. He'd been expecting her to get in touch. They had met the previous Christmas when Erlendur had been investigating a murder at a hotel in Reykjavík. She was a bio-technician and they had been in a very on-off relationship since then. Her husband had admitted to having an affair but when it came to the crunch he did not want to end their marriage; instead he had humbly asked her to forgive him and promised to mend his ways. She maintained that she was going to leave him, but it had not happened yet.

'How's your daughter doing?' she asked, and Erlendur told her briefly about his visit to Eva Lind.

'Don't you think it's helping her, though?' Valgerdur asked. 'That therapy?'

'I hope so, but I really don't know what will help her,' Erlendur said. 'She's back in exactly the same frame of mind as just before her miscarriage.'

'Shouldn't we try to meet up tomorrow?' Valgerdur asked him.

'Yes, let's meet up then,' Erlendur agreed, and they said goodbye.

'Was that her?' Elínborg asked, aware that Erlendur was in some kind of relationship with a woman.

'If you mean Valgerdur, yes, it was her,' Erlendur said.

'Is she worried about Eva Lind?'

'What did forensics say about that transmitter?' Erlendur asked, to change the subject.

'They don't know much,' Elínborg said. 'But they do think it's Russian. The name and serial number were filed off but they can make out the outline of the odd letter and think it's Cyrillic.'

'Russian?'

'Yes, Russian.'

There were a couple of houses at the southern end of Kleifarvatn and Erlendur and Sigurdur Óli gathered information about their owners. They telephoned them and asked in general terms about missing persons who could be linked to the lake. It was fruitless.

Sigurdur Óli mentioned that Elínborg was busy preparing for the publication of her book of recipes.

'I think it'll make her famous,' Sigurdur Óli said.

'Does she want to be?' Erlendur asked.

'Doesn't everyone?' Sigurdur Óli said.

'Cobblers,' Erlendur said.

6

Sigurdur Óli read the letter, the last testimony of a young man who had walked out of his parents' house in 1970 and had never come back.

The parents were now both aged 78 and in fine fettle. They had two other sons, both younger, now in their fifties. They knew that their eldest son had committed suicide. They did not know how he went about it, nor where his remains were. Sigurdur Óli asked them about Kleifarvatn, the radio transmitter and the hole in the skull, but they had no idea what he was talking about. Their son had never quarrelled with anyone and had no enemies; that was out of the question.

'It's an absurd idea that he was murdered,' the mother said with a glance at her husband, still anxious after so many years about the fate of their son.

'You can tell from the letter,' the husband said. 'It's obvious what he had in mind.'

Sigurdur Óli reread the letter.

dear mum and dad forgive me but i can't do anything else it's unbearable and i can't think of living any longer i can't and i won't and i can't

The letter was signed *Jakob.*

'It was that girl's fault,' the wife said.

'We don't know anything about that,' her husband said.

'She started going out with his friend,' she said. 'Our boy couldn't take it.'

'Do you think it's him, it's our boy?' the husband asked. They were sitting on the sofa, facing Sigurdur Óli and waiting for answers to the questions that had haunted them ever since their son went missing. They knew that he could not answer the toughest question, the one they had grappled with during all those years, concerning parental actions and responsibilities, but he could tell them whether or not he had been found. On the news they had only said that a male skeleton had been found in Kleifarvatn. Nothing about a radio transmitter and a smashed skull. They did not understand what Sigurdur Óli meant when he started probing about. They had only one question: Was it him?

'I don't think that's likely,' Sigurdur Óli said. He looked back and forth at them. The incomprehensible disappearance and death of a loved one had left its mark on their lives. The case had never been closed. Their son had still not come home and that was the way it had been all those years. They did not know where he was or what had happened to him, and this uncertainty spawned discomfort and gloom.

'We think he went into the sea,' the wife said. 'He was a good swimmer. I've always thought that he swam out to sea until he knew he had gone too far out or until the cold took him.'

'The police told us at the time that because the body couldn't be found, he'd most probably thrown himself in the sea,' the husband said.

'Because of that girl,' the wife said.

'We can't blame her for it,' the husband said.

Sigurdur Óli could tell that they had slipped into an old routine. He stood up to take his leave.

'Sometimes I get so angry with him,' the wife said, and Sigurdur Óli did not know whether she was referring to her husband or her son.

Valgerdur was waiting for Erlendur at the restaurant. She was wearing the same full-length leather coat that she had worn on their first date.

They had met by chance and in a moment of madness he'd invited her out for dinner. He had not known then if she was married but had discovered later that she was, with two grown-up sons who had moved out and a marriage that was failing.

At their next meeting she admitted that she had intended to use Erlendur to get even with her husband.

Valgerdur contacted Erlendur again soon afterwards and they had met several times since. Once she had gone back to his flat. He'd tried to tidy up as best he could, throwing away old newspapers, arranging books on the shelves. He rarely had visitors and was reluctant to let Valgerdur call on him. She insisted, saying that she wanted to see how he lived. Eva Lind had called his apartment a hole that he crawled into to hide.

'Look at all those books,' Valgerdur said, standing in his living room. 'Have you read them all?'

'Most of them,' Erlendur said. 'Do you want some coffee? I bought some Danish pastries.'

She went over to the bookcase and ran her finger along the spines, browsed through a few titles and took one book off the shelf.

'Are these about ordeals and dangerous highland voyages?' she asked.

She had been quick to notice that Erlendur took a particular interest in missing persons and that he read whole series of accounts of people who had got lost and disappeared in the wilds of Iceland. He had told her what he had told no one else apart from Eva Lind, that his brother had died at the age of eight up in the highlands in eastern Iceland at the beginning of winter, when Erlendur was ten. There were three of them, the two boys and their father. Erlendur and his father found their way home safely, but his brother froze to death and his body was never found.

'You told me once that there was an account of you and your brother in one of these books,' Valgerdur said.

'Yes,' Erlendur said.

'Would you mind showing it to me?'

'I will,' Erlendur said, hesitantly. 'Later. Not now. I'll show you it later.'

Valgerdur stood up when he entered the restaurant and they greeted each other with their customary handshake. Erlendur was unsure what kind of a relationship this was but he liked it. Even after meeting regularly for almost half a year they had not slept together. At least their relationship was not a sexual one. They sat and talked about various aspects of their lives.

'Why haven't you left him?' he asked when they had eaten and drunk coffee and liqueur and talked about Eva Lind and Sindri and her sons and work. She repeatedly asked him about the skeleton in Kleifarvatn but there was little that he could tell her. Only that the police were talking to people whose loved ones had gone missing during a specific period around 1970.

Just before Christmas, Valgerdur had found out that her husband had been having an affair for the past two years. She already knew about an earlier incident which was not as 'serious', as he put it. She told him that she was going to leave him. He broke off the affair at once and nothing had happened since then.

'Valgerdur . . . ?' Erlendur began.

'You saw Eva Lind at her rehab, then,' she said hurriedly, as if sensing what would come next.

'Yes, I saw her.'

'Did she remember anything about being arrested?'

'No, I don't think she remembers being arrested. We didn't discuss it.'

'Poor girl.'

'Are you going to carry on with him?' Erlendur asked.

Valgerdur sipped her liqueur.

'It's so difficult,' she said.

'Is it?'

'I'm not prepared to put an end to it,' she said, looking into Erlendur's eyes. 'But I don't want to let go of you, either.'

When Erlendur went home that evening, Sindri Snaer was lying on the sofa, smoking and watching television. He nodded to his father and kept watching the programme. As far as Erlendur could see it was a cartoon. He had given his son a key to the flat and could expect him at any time, even though he had not agreed to let him stay.

'Would you mind switching that off?' he said as he took off his coat.

'I couldn't find the remote,' he said. 'Isn't this telly prehistoric?'

'It's only twenty years old or so,' Erlendur said. 'I don't use it much.'

'Eva phoned me today,' Sindri said, stubbing out his cigarette. 'Was it some friend of yours who arrested her?'

'Sigurdur Óli. She hit him. With a hammer. Tried to knock him out, but caught him on the shoulder instead. He wanted to charge her with assault and resisting arrest.'

'So you made a deal that she'd go into rehab instead.'

'She's never wanted therapy. Sigurdur Óli dropped the charges for my sake and she went into rehab.'

A dealer called Eddi had been involved in a drugs case and Sigurdur Óli and two other detectives had tracked him down to a den just up from Hlemmur bus station, close to the police station on Hverfisgata. Someone who knew Eddi had phoned the police. The only resistance they'd met had been from Eva Lind. She was completely out of her mind. Eddi lay half-naked on the sofa and did not stir. Another girl, younger than Eva Lind, lay naked beside him. When she saw the police Eva went berserk. She knew who Sigurdur Óli was. Knew that he worked with her father. She snatched up a hammer that was lying on the floor and tried to knock him out. Although she missed, she fractured his collarbone. Racked with pain, Sigurdur Óli fell to the floor. As she'd wound up for a second shot, the other officers had pounced and had floored her.

37

Sigurdur Óli did not talk about the incident but Erlendur heard from the other officers that he had hesitated when he saw Eva Lind going for him. She was Erlendur's daughter and he did not want to hurt her. That was how she had been able to deliver the blow.

'I thought she'd clean up her act when she had that miscarriage,' Erlendur said. 'But she's twice as difficult. It's as if nothing matters to her any more.'

'I'd like to go and see her,' Sindri said. 'But they don't allow visitors.'

'I'll have a word with them.'

The telephone rang and Erlendur picked it up.

'Erlendur?' said a weak voice on the other end. Erlendur recognised it at once.

'Marion?'

'What was it you found at Kleifarvatn?' Marion Briem asked.

'Bones,' Erlendur said. 'Nothing that need concern you.'

'Oh, really,' said Marion, who had retired but found it difficult not to get involved in any especially interesting cases that Erlendur might be investigating.

There was a long silence on the line.

'Did you want anything in particular?' Erlendur asked.

'You ought to check out Kleifarvatn better,' Marion said. 'But don't let me disturb you. Wouldn't dream of it. I don't want to disturb an old colleague who's got plenty on his plate already.'

'What about Kleifarvatn?' Erlendur asked. 'What are you talking about?'

'No. Goodbye,' Marion said, and hung up on Erlendur.

7

Sometimes, when he thought back, he could smell the headquarters on Dittrichring, the smothering stench of dirty carpet, sweat and fear. He also remembered the acrid stink of the coal smog that blanketed the city, even blocking out the sun.

Leipzig was not at all as he had imagined. He had swotted up before leaving Iceland and knew that it was located on the confluence of the Elster, Parthe and Pleisse rivers, and was an old centre of the German publishing and book trades. Bach was buried there and it was home to the famous *Auerbachkeller*, the beer cellar on which Goethe modelled a scene in *Faust*. The composer Jón Leifs studied music in Leipzig and lived there for years. In his mind's eye he had seen an ancient cultural German city. What he found was a sorry, gloomy post-war place. The Allies had occupied Leipzig but later handed it over to the Soviets, and the bullet holes could still be seen in the walls of buildings and half-collapsed houses, the ruins left by war.

The train arrived in Leipzig in the middle of the night. He was able to store his suitcase at the railway station and he walked the streets until the city began to awaken. There was an electricity shortage and the city centre was dark but he felt good at having arrived and he enjoyed the adventure of being alone so far from his native haunts. He walked up to Nikolaikirche and when he reached Thomaskirche he sat down on a bench. He recalled the account of the writer Halldór

Laxness and poet Jóhann Jónsson walking together through the city so many years before. Dawn was breaking and he imagined them looking up at Thomaskirche just as he was, admiring the sight before continuing their stroll.

A girl selling flowers walked past him and offered him a bouquet, but he had no money to spare and gave her an apologetic smile.

He was looking forward to everything that lay ahead. Standing on his own two feet and being the master of his own fate. Although he had no idea what awaited him, he intended to face it with an open mind. He knew that he would not feel homesick because he had set off on an adventure that would shape his life permanently. And while he realised that his course would be demanding, he was not afraid of applying himself. He had a passionate interest in engineering and knew that he would meet new people and make new friends. He was impatient to get down to studying.

He walked around the ruins and the streets in the light drizzle and a faint smile crossed his face when he thought again of the two writer friends walking the same streets long before.

At daybreak he fetched his suitcase, went to the university and found the registration office without any trouble. He was shown to a student residence not far from the main building. The dormitory was an elegant old villa that had been taken over by the university. He would be sharing a room with two other students. One was Emil, his classmate from school. The other was Czechoslovakian, he was told. Neither of them was in the room when he arrived. It was a three-storey house with a shared bathroom and kitchen on the middle floor. Old wallpaper was peeling from the walls, the timber floors were dirty and a musty smell permeated the building. In his room were three futons and an old desk. A bare light bulb hung down from the ceiling, whose old plaster had flaked off to reveal rotting timber panelling. There were two windows in the room, one of which was boarded up because the glass was broken.

Drowsy students were emerging from their rooms. A queue had

already formed outside the bathroom. Some went outdoors to urinate. In the kitchen a large pot had been filled with water and was being heated on an ancient cooker. There was an old-fashioned stove beside it. He looked around for his friend, but could not see him. And as he was looking at the group in the kitchen, he suddenly realised that it was a mixed residence.

One of the young women came over to him and said something in German. Although he had studied German at school, he did not understand her. In halting German, he asked her to speak more slowly.

'Are you looking for someone?' she asked.

'I'm looking for Emil,' he said. 'He's from Iceland.'

'Are you from Iceland too?'

'Yes. What about you? Where are you from?'

'Dresden,' the girl said. 'I'm Maria.'

'My name's Tómas,' he said and they shook hands.

'Tómas?' she repeated. 'There are a few Icelanders at the university. They often visit Emil. Sometimes we have to throw them out because they sing all night. Your German's not so bad.'

'Thanks. Schoolboy German. Do you know about Emil?'

'He's on rat duty,' she said. 'Down in the basement. It's swarming with rats here. Do you want a cup of tea? They're setting up a canteen on the top floor, but until then we have to cater for ourselves.'

'Rat duty?!'

'They come out at night. That's the best time to catch them.'

'Are there a lot?'

'If we kill ten, twenty take their place. But it's better now than it was during the war.'

Instinctively he looked around the floor as if expecting to see the creatures darting between people's feet. If anything repulsed him it was rats.

He felt a tap on his shoulder and when he turned round he saw his friend standing behind him, smiling. Holding them by their tails, he lifted up two gigantic rats. He had a spade in his other hand.

'A spade's the best thing to kill them with,' Emil said.

He was quick to adjust to his surroundings: the smell of rising damp, the appalling smell from the bathroom on the middle floor, a stink that spread through the whole building, the rotten futons, the creaking chairs and the primitive cooking facilities. He simply put them out of his mind and knew that the post-war reconstruction would be a lengthy process.

The university was excellent despite its frugal facilities. The teaching staff were highly qualified, the students were enthusiastic and he did well on his course. He got to know the engineering students who were either from Leipzig or other German cities, or from neighbouring countries, especially from Eastern Europe. Like him, several were on grants from the East German government. In fact, the students at the Karl Marx University seemed to be from all over the world. He soon met Vietnamese and Chinese students, who tended to keep themselves to themselves. There were Nigerians too, and in the room next door to his in the old villa lived a pleasant Indian by the name of Deependra.

The small group of Icelanders in the city stuck very closely together. Karl came from a little fishing village and was studying journalism. His faculty, nicknamed the Red Cloister, was said to admit only party hardliners. Rut was from Akureyri. She had chaired the youth movement there and now studied literature, specialising in Russian. Hrafnhildur was studying German language and literature, while Emil, from western Iceland, was an economics undergraduate. One way or another most of them had been picked out by the Socialist Party of Iceland for study grants in East Germany. They would meet up in the evenings and play cards or listen to Deependra's jazz records, or go to the local bar and sing Icelandic songs. The university ran an active film club and they watched *Battleship Potemkin* and discussed film as a vehicle for propaganda. They talked politics with other students. Attendance was compulsory at the meetings and talks held by the students' organisation *Freie Deutsche Jugend* – abbreviated as FDJ – the only society allowed to operate at the university. Everyone wanted to forge a new and better world.

All apart from one. Hannes had been in Leipzig the longest of all the Icelanders and avoided the others. Two months passed before Tómas first met him. He knew about Hannes from Reykjavík: the party had big plans for him. The chairman had mentioned his name at an editorial meeting and referred to him as material for the future. Like Tómas, Hannes had worked as a journalist on the party paper and he heard stories about him from the reporters. Tómas had seen Hannes speaking at meetings in Reykjavík and was impressed by his zeal, his phrases about how warmongering cowboys could buy out democracy in Iceland, how Icelandic politicians were puppets in the hands of American imperialists. 'Democracy in this country is not worth a shit for as long as the American army spreads its filth over Icelandic soil!' he had shouted to thunderous applause. In his first years in East Germany, Hannes had written a regular column called *Letter from the East*, describing the wonders of the communist system, until the articles had ceased to appear. The other Icelanders in the city had little to say about Hannes. He had gradually distanced himself from them and had gone his own way. Occasionally they discussed this but shrugged as if it were none of their business.

One day he came across Hannes in the university library. Evening had fallen, there were few people at the desks and Hannes had his head buried in his books. It was cold and blustery outside. Sometimes it was so cold in the library that people's breath steamed when they talked. Hannes was wearing a long overcoat and a cap with ear muffs. The library had suffered badly in the air raids and only part of it was in use.

'Aren't you, Hannes?' he asked in a friendly tone. 'We've never met.'

Hannes looked up from his books.

'I'm Tómas.' He held out his hand.

Hannes stared at him and the outstretched hand, then buried his head back in his books.

'Leave me alone,' he said.

Tómas was surprised. He had not expected such a reception from his compatriot, least of all from this man, who enjoyed great respect and had impressed him so deeply.

'Sorry,' he said. 'I didn't mean to disturb you. Of course, you're studying.'

Instead of answering, Hannes went on jotting notes from the open books on the table in front of him. He wrote quickly in pencil and was wearing fingerless gloves to keep his hands warm.

'I was just wondering if we could have a coffee sometime,' Tómas went on. 'Or a beer.'

Hannes did not reply. Tómas stood over him, waiting for some kind of response, but when none came he slowly backed off from the table and turned away. He was halfway behind a rack of books when Hannes looked up from his tomes and at last answered him.

'Did you say Tómas?'

'Yes, we've never met but I've heard . . .'

'I know who you are,' Hannes said. 'I was like you once. What do you want from me?'

'Nothing,' he said. 'Just to say hello. I was sitting over on that side and I've been watching you. I only wanted to say hello. I went to a meeting once where you—'

'What do you think of Leipzig?' Hannes interrupted.

'Brass-monkey weather and bad food but the university's good and the first thing I'm going to do when I get back to Iceland is to campaign for legalising beer.'

Hannes smiled.

'That's true, the beer's the best thing about this place.'

'Maybe we could have a jar together sometime,' Tómas said.

'Maybe,' Hannes said, and delved back into his books. Their conversation was over.

'What do you mean, you were like me once?' Tómas asked hesitantly. 'What's that supposed to mean?'

'Nothing,' Hannes said, looking up and scrutinising him. He hesitated.

'Take no notice of me,' he said. 'It'll do you no good.'

Confused, he walked out of the library and into the piercing winter wind. On the way to the dormitory he met Emil and Rut. They had been to collect a package posted from Iceland for her. It was a food parcel and they were gloating over it. He did not mention his encounter with Hannes because he did not understand what he had meant.

'Lothar was looking for you,' Emil said. 'I told him you were at the library.'

'I didn't see him,' he said. 'Do you know what he wanted?'

'No idea,' Emil said.

Lothar was his liaison, his *Betreuer*. Every foreigner at the university had a liaison who was available for help. Lothar had befriended the Icelanders at the dormitory. He offered to take them around the city and show them the sights. He assisted them at the university and sometimes paid the bill when they went to *Auerbachkeller*. He wanted to go to Iceland, he said, to study Icelandic, and he spoke the language well, could even sing the latest hit songs. He said he was interested in the old Icelandic sagas, had read *Njal's Saga* and wanted to translate it.

'Here's the building,' Rut said all of a sudden, and stopped. 'That's the office. There are prison cells inside.'

They looked up at the building. It was a gloomy stone edifice of four storeys. Plywood boarding had been nailed over all the ground-floor windows. He saw the name of the street: Dittrichring. Number 24.

'Prison cells? What is this place?' he asked.

'The security police are in there,' Emil said in a low voice, as if someone might hear him.

'Stasi,' Rut said.

He looked up along the building again. The pallid street lights cast a murky shadow onto its stone walls and windows, and a slight shiver ran through him. He felt clearly that he never wanted to enter that place but had no way of knowing then how little his own wishes counted for.

He sighed and looked out to sea where a little sailboat was cruising by.

Decades later, when the Soviet Union and communism had fallen, he had returned to the headquarters and noticed at once the old nauseating smell. It produced the same effect on him as when the rat had got trapped behind the dormitory stove and they had unwittingly roasted it over and again, until the stench in the old villa became unbearable.

8

Erlendur watched Marion sitting in the chair in the living room, breathing through an oxygen mask. The last time he had seen his former CID boss was at Christmas and he did not know that Marion had since fallen ill. Enquiring at work, he had discovered that decades of smoking had ruined Marion's lungs and a thrombosis had caused paralysis of the right side, arm and part of the face. The flat was dim despite the sun outside, with a thick layer of dust on the tables. A nurse visited once a day and she was just leaving when Erlendur called.

He sat down in the deep sofa facing Marion and thought about the sorry state to which his old colleague had been reduced. There was almost no flesh left on the bones. That huge head nodded slowly above a weak body. Every bone in Marion's face was visible, the eyes sunken under yellowy, scraggy hair. Erlendur dwelled on the tobacco-stained fingers and shrivelled nails resting on the chair's worn arm. Marion was asleep.

The nurse had let Erlendur in and he sat in silence waiting for Marion to wake. He was remembering the first time he'd turned up for work at the CID all those years ago.

'What's up with you?' was the first thing Marion said to him. 'Don't you ever smile?'

He did not know what to say in reply. Did not know what to expect from this stunted specimen for whom a Camel was a permanent fixture, forever enveloped in a stinking haze of blue smoke.

'Why do you want to investigate crimes?' Marion continued when Erlendur did not answer. 'Why don't you get on with directing traffic?'

'I thought I might be able to help,' Erlendur said.

It was a small office crammed with papers and files; a large ashtray on the desk was full of cigarette butts. The air was thick and smoky inside but Erlendur did not mind. He took out a cigarette.

'Do you have a particular interest in crime?' Marion asked.

'Some of them,' Erlendur said, fishing out a box of matches.

'Some?'

'I'm interested in missing persons,' Erlendur said.

'Missing persons? Why?'

'I always have been. I . . .' Erlendur paused.

'What? What were you going to say?' Marion chain-smoked and lit a fresh Camel from a tiny butt, still glowing when it landed in the ashtray. 'Get to the point! If you dither around like that at work I won't have anything to do with you. Out with it!'

'I think they might have more to do with crimes than people think,' Erlendur said. 'I've got nothing to back me up. It's just a hunch.'

Erlendur snapped out of this flashback. He watched Marion inhaling the oxygen. He looked out of the living-room window. Just a hunch, he thought.

Marion Briem's eyes opened slowly and noticed Erlendur on the sofa. Their gazes met and Marion removed the oxygen mask.

'Has everyone forgotten those bloody communists?' Marion said in a hoarse voice, drawling through a mouth twisted by the thrombosis.

'How are you feeling?' Erlendur asked.

Marion gave a quick smile. Or maybe it was a grimace.

'It'll be a miracle if I last the year.'

'Why didn't you tell me?'

'What's the point? Can you sort me out a new pair of lungs?'

'Cancer?'

Marion nodded.

'You smoked too much,' Erlendur said.

'What I wouldn't do for a cigarette,' Marion said.

Marion put the mask back on and watched Erlendur, as if expecting him to produce his cigarettes. Erlendur shook his head. In one corner the television was switched on and the cancer patient's eyes flashed over at the screen. The mask came back down.

'How's it going with the skeleton? Has everyone forgotten the communists?'

'What's all this talk about communists?'

'Your boss came to say hello to me yesterday, or maybe to say goodbye. I've never liked that upstart. I can't see why you don't want to be one of those bosses. What's the explanation? Can you tell me that? You should have been doing half as much for twice the money ages ago.'

'There is no explanation,' Erlendur said.

'He let it slip that the skeleton was tied to a Russian radio transmitter.'

'Yes. We think it's Russian and we think it's a radio transmitter.'

'Aren't you going to give me a cigarette?'

'No.'

'I haven't got long left. Do you think it matters?'

'You won't get a cigarette from me. Was that why you phoned? So I could finally finish you off? Why don't you just ask me to put a bullet through your head?'

'Would you do that for me?'

Erlendur smiled, and Marion's face lit up for an instant.

'Having a stroke is worse. I talk like an idiot and I can't really move my hand.'

'What's all this guff about communists?'

49

'It was a few years before you joined us. When was that again?'

'1977,' Erlendur said.

'You said you were interested in missing persons, I remember that,' Marion Briem said, wincing. Marion replaced the oxygen mask and leaned back, with eyes closed. A long while passed. Erlendur looked around the room. The flat reminded him uncomfortably of his own.

'Do you want me to call someone?'

'No, don't call anyone,' Marion said, taking the mask off. 'You can help me make us coffee afterwards. I just need to gather my strength. But surely you remember it? When we found those devices.'

'What devices?'

'In Lake Kleifarvatn. Does nobody remember anything any more?'

Marion looked at him and in a weak voice began recounting the story of the devices from the lake; it suddenly dawned on Erlendur what his old boss was talking about. He only vaguely recalled the matter and had not linked it at all to the skeleton in the lake, although he should have realised at once.

On 10 September 1973 the telephone had rung at Hafnarfjördur police station. Two frogmen from Reykjavík – 'they're not called frogmen any more', Marion chuckled painfully – had chanced upon a heap of equipment in the lake. It was at a depth of ten metres. It soon became clear that most of it was Russian and the Cyrillic lettering had been filed off. Telephone engineers were called in to examine it and established that it was an assortment of telecommunications and bugging devices.

'There was loads of the stuff,' Marion Briem said. 'Tape recorders, radio sets, transmitters.'

'Were you on the case?'

'I was at the lake when they fished it all out but I wasn't in charge of the investigation. The case got a lot of publicity. It was at the height of the Cold War and it was well known that Russian espionage in Iceland took place. Of course, the Americans spied too, but they were a friendly nation. Russia was the enemy.'

'Transmitters?'

'Yes. And receivers. It turned out that some were tuned to the wavelength of the American base at Keflavík.'

'So you want to link the skeleton in the lake with that equipment?'

'What do you think?' Marion Briem said, eyes closed again.

'Perhaps that's not implausible.'

'You bear it in mind,' Marion said, pulling a weary face.

'Is there anything I can do for you?' Erlendur said. 'Anything I can get you?'

'I sometimes watch westerns,' Marion said after a long pause, still sitting with eyes closed.

Erlendur was unsure whether he had heard correctly.

'Westerns?' he said. 'Are you talking about cowboy films?'

'Could you bring me a good western?'

'What's a good western?'

'John Wayne,' Marion said in a fading voice.

Erlendur sat by Marion's side for some time, in case his old boss woke up again. Noon was approaching. He went into the kitchen, made coffee and poured two cups. He remembered that Marion drank coffee black with no sugar, as he did, and placed one beside the armchair. He did not know what else he should do.

That afternoon Sigurdur Óli sat down in Erlendur's office. The man had rung again in the middle of the night, announcing that he was going to commit suicide. Sigurdur Óli had sent a police car to his house, but no one was at home. The man lived alone in a small detached house. On Sigurdur Óli's orders the police broke in but found no one.

'He called me again this morning,' Sigurdur Óli said after describing the episode. 'He was back home by then. Nothing happened but I'm getting a little tired of him.'

'Is he the one who lost his wife and child?'

'Yes. Inexplicably, he blames himself and refuses to listen to anything different.'

'It was sheer coincidence, wasn't it?'

'Not in his mind.'

Sigurdur Óli had been temporarily assigned to investigating road accidents. A Range Rover had driven into a car at a junction on the Breidholt Road, killing a mother along with her five-year-old daughter who was in the back, wearing a safety belt. The driver of the Range Rover had gone through a red light while drunk. The victims' car was the last in a long queue going over the junction at the very moment the Range Rover raced through the red light. If the mother had waited for the next green light, the Range Rover would have gone through without causing any damage and proceeded on its way. The drunken driver would probably have caused an accident somewhere, but it would not have been at that junction.

'But that's just how most accidents happen,' Sigurdur Óli said to Erlendur. 'Incredible coincidences. That's what the man doesn't understand.'

'His conscience is killing him,' Erlendur said. 'You ought to show some understanding.'

'Understanding?! He calls me at home in the middle of the night. How can I show him any more understanding?'

The woman had been shopping with their daughter at the supermarket in Smáralind. She was at the checkout when her husband called her mobile to ask her to get him a punnet of strawberries. She did, but it delayed her by a few minutes. The man was convinced that if he hadn't telephoned her she would not have been at the junction at the time when the Range Rover hit her. So he blamed himself. The crash had happened because he'd called her.

The scene of the accident was awful. The woman's car was torn apart, a write-off. The Range Rover had rolled off the road. The driver suffered a serious head injury and multiple fractures, and was unconscious when the ambulance took him away. The mother and daughter died instantly. They had to be cut from the wreckage. Blood ran down the road.

Sigurdur Óli went to visit the husband with a clergyman. The car was registered in the husband's name. He was beginning to worry about his wife and daughter and went into shock when he saw Sigurdur Óli and the vicar on his doorstep. When he was told what had happened he broke down and they called a doctor. Every so often since then he had telephoned Sigurdur Óli, who had become a kind of confidant, entirely against his will.

'I don't want to be his damned confessor,' Sigurdur Óli groaned. 'But he won't leave me alone. Rings at night and talks about killing himself! Why can't he go on at the vicar? He was there too.'

'Tell him to consult a psychiatrist.'

'He sees one regularly.'

'Of course, it's impossible to put yourself in his shoes,' Erlendur said. 'He must feel terrible.'

'Yes,' Sigurdur Óli said.

'And he's contemplating suicide?'

'So he says. And he could easily do something stupid. I just can't be bothered with it all.'

'What does Bergthóra reckon?'

'She thinks I can help him.'

'Strawberries?'

'I know. I'm always telling him. It's ridiculous.'

9

Erlendur sat listening to an account of someone who had gone missing in the 1960s. Sigurdur Óli was with him. This time it was a man in his late thirties.

A preliminary examination of the skeleton suggested that the body in Kleifarvatn was that of a man aged between 35 and 40. Based on the age of the accompanying Russian device, it had been left in the lake some time after 1961. A detailed study had been made of the black box discovered under the skeleton. It was a listening device – known in those days as a microwave receiver – which could intercept the frequency used by NATO in the 1960s. It was marked with the year of manufacture, 1961, badly filed off, and such inscriptions as remained to be deciphered were clearly Russian.

Erlendur examined newspaper reports from 1973 about the Russian equipment being found in Lake Kleifarvatn and most of what Marion Briem had told him fitted the journalists' accounts. The devices had been discovered at a depth of ten metres just off Geirshöfdi cape, some distance from where the skeleton had been found. He told Sigurdur Óli and Elínborg about this and they discussed whether it might be linked to their skeleton. Elínborg thought it was obvious. If the police had explored more thoroughly when they'd found the Russian equipment, they might have found the body as well.

According to contemporary police reports, the divers had seen a black limousine on the road to Kleifarvatn when they went there the previous week. They immediately thought it was a diplomatic car. The Soviet embassy did not answer enquiries about the case, nor did other Eastern European representatives in Reykjavík. Erlendur found a brief report stating that the equipment was Russian. It included listening devices with a range of 160 kilometres which were probably used to intercept telephone conversations in Reykjavík and around the Keflavík base. The devices probably dated from the 1960s, and used valves that had been rendered obsolete by transistor technology. They were battery-powered and would fit inside an ordinary suitcase.

The woman sitting opposite them was approaching seventy but had aged well. She and her partner had not had children by the time of his sudden disappearance. They were unmarried but had discussed going to the registrar. She had not lived with anyone since, she told them rather coyly but with a hint of regret in her voice.

'He was so nice,' the woman said, 'and I always thought he'd come back. It was better to believe that than to think he was dead. I couldn't accept that. And never have accepted it.'

They had found themselves a small flat and planned to have children. She worked in a dairy shop. This was in 1968.

'You remember them,' she said to Erlendur, 'and maybe you too,' she said, looking at Sigurdur Óli. 'They were special dairy shops that only sold milk, curds and the like. Nothing but dairy products.'

Erlendur nodded calmly. Sigurdur Óli had already lost interest.

Her partner had said he would collect her after work as he did every day, but she stood alone in front of the shop and waited.

'It's more than thirty years ago now,' she said, with a look at Erlendur, 'and I feel like I'm still standing in front of the shop waiting. All these years. He was always punctual and I remember thinking how late he was after ten minutes had gone by, then the first quarter of an hour and half an hour. I remember how infinitely long it was. It was like he'd forgotten me.'

She sighed.

'Later it was like he'd never existed.'

They had read the reports. She reported his disappearance early the following morning. The police went to her home. He was reported missing in the newspapers and on radio and television. The police told her he would surely turn up soon. Asked whether he drank or whether he had ever disappeared like this before, whether she knew about another woman in his life. She denied all these suggestions but the questions made her consider the man in completely different terms. Was there another woman? Had he ever been unfaithful? He was a salesman who drove all over the country. He sold agricultural equipment and machinery, tractors, hay blowers, diggers and bull-dozers, and travelled a lot. Maybe several weeks at a time on the longest trips. He had just returned from one when he disappeared.

'I don't know what he could have been doing up at Kleifarvatn,' she said, glancing from one detective to the other. 'We never went there.'

They had not told her about the Soviet spying equipment or the smashed skull, only that a skeleton had been found where the lake had drained and that they were investigating persons reported missing during a specific period.

'Your car was found two days later outside the coach station,' Sigurdur Óli said.

'No one there recognised my partner from the descriptions,' the woman said. 'I had no photos of him. And he had none of me. We hadn't been together that long and we didn't own a camera. We never went away together. Isn't that when people mostly use cameras?'

'And at Christmas,' Sigurdur Óli said.

'Yes, at Christmas,' she agreed.

'What about his parents?'

'They'd died long before. He'd spent a lot of time abroad. He'd worked on merchant ships and lived in Britain and France too. He spoke with a slight accent, he'd been away that long. About thirty coaches left the station heading all over Iceland between the time he disappeared and when the car was found, but none of the drivers could say if he had been on board one. They didn't think so. The police were certain that someone would have noticed him if he'd been on a coach, but I know they were just trying to console me. I think they supposed he was on a bender in town and would turn up in the end. They said worried wives sometimes called the police when their husbands were out drinking.'

The woman fell silent.

'I don't think they investigated it very carefully,' she eventually said. 'I didn't feel they were particularly interested in the case.'

'Why do you think he took the car to the coach station?' Erlendur asked. He noticed Sigurdur Óli jotting down the remark about the police work.

'I haven't got the faintest idea.'

'Do you think someone else could have driven it there? To throw you off the track, or the police? To make people think he'd left town?'

'I don't know,' the woman said. 'Of course I wondered endlessly whether he had simply been killed, but I don't understand who was supposed to have done it and even less why. I just can't understand it.'

'It's often plain coincidence,' Erlendur said. 'There needn't always be an explanation. In Iceland there's rarely a real motive behind a murder. It's an accident or a snap decision, not premeditated and in most cases committed for no obvious reason.'

According to police reports, the man had gone on a short sales trip early that day and intended to go home afterwards. A dairy farmer just outside Reykjavík was interested in buying a tractor and he was planning to drop by to try to clinch the sale. The farmer said the man had never called. He had waited for him all day, but he had never showed up.

'Everything seems hunky-dory, then he makes himself disappear,' Sigurdur Óli said. 'What do you personally think happened?'

'He didn't make himself disappear,' the woman retorted. 'Why do you say that?'

'No, sorry,' Sigurdur Óli said. 'Of course not. He disappeared. Sorry.'

'I don't know,' the woman said. 'He could be a bit depressive at times, silent and closed. Perhaps if we'd had children . . . maybe it would all have turned out differently if we'd had children.'

They fell silent. Erlendur imagined the woman waiting outside the dairy shop, anxious and disappointed.

'Was he in contact with any embassies in Reykjavík at all?' Erlendur asked.

'Embassies?'

'Yes, the embassies,' Erlendur said. 'Did he have any connections with them, the Eastern European ones in particular?'

'Not at all,' the woman said. 'I don't follow . . . what do you mean?'

'He didn't know anyone from the embassies, work for them or that sort of thing?'

'No, certainly not, or at least not after I met him. Not that I knew of.'

'What kind of car did you have?' Erlendur asked. He could not remember the model from the files.

The woman pondered. These strange questions were confusing her.

'It was a Ford,' she said. 'I think it was called a Falcon.'

'From the case files, it doesn't look as if there were any clues to his disappearance in the car.'

'No, they couldn't find anything. One of the hubcaps had been stolen, but that was all.'

'In front of the coach station?' Sigurdur Óli asked.

'That's what they thought.'

'A hubcap?'

'Yes.'

'What happened to the car?'

'I sold it. I needed the money. I've never had much money.'

She remembered the licence plate and mechanically repeated the number to them. Sigurdur Óli wrote it down. Erlendur gestured to him, they stood up and thanked her for her time. The woman stayed put in her chair. He thought she was bitterly lonely.

'Where did all the machinery he sold come from?' Erlendur asked, for the sake of saying something.

'The farm machinery? It came from Russia and East Germany. He said it wasn't as good as the American stuff, but much cheaper.'

Erlendur could not imagine what Sindri Snaer wanted from him. His son was completely different from his sister Eva, who felt Erlendur had not pressed hard enough for the right to see his children. They would never have known he existed if their mother had not been forever bad-mouthing him. When Eva grew up she tracked down her father and vented her anger mercilessly. Sindri Snaer did not seem to have the same agenda. He neither grilled Erlendur about destroying their family nor condemned him for taking no interest in him and Eva when they were just children who believed their father was bad for walking out on them.

When Erlendur got home Sindri was boiling spaghetti. He had tidied up the kitchen, which meant he had thrown away a few microwave-meal packets, washed a couple of forks and cleaned inside and around the coffee machine. Erlendur went into the living room and watched the television news. The skeleton from Lake Kleifarvatn was the fifth item. The police had taken care not to mention the Soviet equipment.

They sat in silence, eating the spaghetti. Erlendur chopped it up with his fork and spread it with butter while Sindri pursed his lips and sucked it up with tomato ketchup. Erlendur asked how his mother was doing and Sindri said he had not heard from her since he'd come to the city. A chat show was starting on the television. A pop star was recounting his triumphs in life.

'Eva told me at New Year that you had a brother who died,' Sindri said suddenly, wiping his mouth with a piece of kitchen roll.

59

'That's right,' Erlendur said after some thought. He had not been expecting this.

'Eva said it had a big effect on you.'

'That's right.'

'And explains a bit what you're like.'

'Explains what I'm like?' Erlendur said. 'I don't know what I'm like. Nor does Eva!'

They went on eating, Sindri sucking up spaghetti and Erlendur struggling to balance the strands on his fork. He thought to himself that he would buy some porridge and pickled haggis the next time he happened to pass a shop.

'It's not my fault,' Sindri said.

'What?'

'That I hardly know who you are.'

'No,' Erlendur said. 'It's not your fault.'

They ate in silence. Sindri put down his fork and wiped his mouth with kitchen roll again. He stood up, took a coffee mug, filled it with water from the tap and sat back down at the table.

'She said he was never found.'

'Yes, that's right, he was never found,' Erlendur said.

'So he's still up there?'

Erlendur stopped eating and put down his fork.

'I expect so, yes,' he said, looking into his son's eyes. 'Where's this all leading?'

'Do you sometimes look for him?'

'Look for him?'

'Are you still searching for him?'

'What do you want from me, Sindri?' Erlendur said.

'I was working out in the east. In Eskifjördur. They didn't know we . . .' Sindri groped for the right word . . . 'knew each other, but after Eva told me about that business with your brother I started asking the locals, older people, who were working in the fish factory with me.'

'You started asking about me?'

'Not directly. Not about you. I asked about the old days, about the people who used to live there and the farmers. Your dad was a farmer, wasn't he? My grandad.'

Erlendur did not answer.

'Some of them remember it well,' Sindri said.

'Remember what?'

'The two boys who went up to the mountains with their father, and the younger boy who died. And the family moved to Reykjavík afterwards.'

'Which people were you talking to?'

'People who live out east.'

'And you were spying on me?' Erlendur said grumpily.

'I wasn't spying on you at all,' Sindri said. 'Eva Lind told me about it and I asked people about what happened.'

Erlendur pushed away his plate.

'So what happened?'

'The weather was crazy. Your dad got home and the rescue team was called out. You were found buried in a snowdrift. Your dad didn't take part in the search. People said he sank into self-pity and went off the rails afterwards.'

'Went off the rails?' Erlendur said angrily. 'Bollocks.'

'Your mum was much tougher,' Sindri went on. 'She went out searching every day with the rescue team. And long after that. Until you moved away two years later. She was always going up onto the moors to look for her son. It was an obsession for her.'

'She wanted to be able to bury him,' Erlendur said. 'If you call that an obsession.'

'People told me about you too.'

'You shouldn't listen to gossip.'

'They said the elder brother, the one who was rescued, came back to the area regularly and walked the mountains and moors. There could be years between his visits and he hadn't been for several years now, but they always expect him there. He comes alone, with a tent, rents some horses and heads off for the mountains. He returns a week or ten days later, maybe a fortnight, then drives away. He never talks to anyone except when he rents the horses, and he doesn't say much then.'

'Are people out east still talking about that?'

'I don't think so,' Sindri said. 'Not so much. I was just curious and talked to people who remembered it. Remembered you. I talked to the farmer who rents you the horses.'

'Why did you do all this? You've never . . .'

'Eva Lind said she understood you better after you told her about it. She always wants to talk about you. I've never bothered thinking about you at all. I can't figure out what you represent to her. You don't matter to me in the least. That's fine with me. I'm glad I don't need you. Never have. Eva needs you. She always has.'

'I've tried to do what I can for Eva,' Erlendur said.

'I know. She's told me. Sometimes she thinks you're interfering, but I think she understands what you're trying to do for her.'

'Human remains can be found a whole generation later,' Erlendur said. 'Even hundreds of years. By sheer chance. There are lots of stories of that happening.'

'I'm sure,' Sindri said, looking over at the bookshelves. 'Eva said you felt responsible for what happened to him. That you lost hold of him. Is that why you go to the east to look for him?'

'I think . . .'

Erlendur stopped short.

'Your conscience?' Sindri asked.

'I don't know whether it's my conscience,' Erlendur said, with a vague smile.

'But you've never found him,' Sindri said.

'No,' Erlendur said.

'That's why you keep going back.'

'I like going to the east. Change of surroundings. Being by myself a bit.'

'I saw the house you lived in. It was abandoned ages ago.'

'Yes,' Erlendur said. 'Way back. It's half-collapsed. Sometimes I make plans to turn it into a summer house but . . .'

'It's in the middle of nowhere.'

Erlendur looked at Sindri.

'It's nice sleeping there,' Erlendur said. 'With the ghosts.'

When he lay down to go to sleep that night he thought about his son's words. Sindri was right. He had been to the east during several summers to look for his brother. He could not say why, apart from the obvious reason: to find his mortal remains and close the matter, even though he knew deep down that finding anything at this stage was a forlorn hope. On the first and last night he always slept in the old abandoned farmhouse. He slept on the living-room floor, looking out through the broken windows at the sky and thinking about the old times when he had sat in that same room with his family and relatives or the locals. He looked at the carefully painted door and saw his mother coming in with a jug of coffee and filling the guests' cups in the soft glow of the living-room lights. His father standing in the doorway, smiling at something that had been said. His brother came up to him, shy because of the guests, and asked if he could have another cruller. Himself, he stood by the window gazing out at the horses. Some riders had stopped by, cheerful and noisy.

Those were his ghosts.

10

Marion Briem seemed a little livelier when Erlendur called by the next morning. He had managed to dig up a John Wayne western. It was called *The Searchers* and seemed to cheer up Marion, who asked him to put it in the video player.

'Since when have you watched westerns?' Erlendur asked.

'I've always liked westerns,' Marion said. The oxygen mask lay on the table beside the chair in the living room. 'The best ones tell simple stories about simple people. I'd have thought you'd enjoy that kind of thing. Western stories. A country bumpkin like you.'

'I never liked the cinema,' Erlendur said.

'Making any headway with Kleifarvatn?' Marion asked.

'What does it tell us when a skeleton, probably dating from the 1960s, is found tied to a Russian listening device?' Erlendur asked.

'Isn't there only one possibility?' Marion said.

'Espionage?'

'Yes.'

'Do you think it might be a genuine Icelandic spy in the lake?'

'Who says he's Icelandic?'

'Isn't that a fairly straightforward assumption?'

'There's nothing to say he's Icelandic,' Marion said, suddenly bursting into a fit of coughing and gasping for breath. 'Hand me the oxygen, I feel better when I've got oxygen.'

Erlendur reached for the mask, put it over Marion's face and turned on the oxygen cylinder. He wondered whether to call a nurse or even a doctor. Marion seemed to read his thoughts.

'Relax. I don't need any more help. A nurse will be round later.'

'I shouldn't be tiring you out like this.'

'Don't go yet. You're the only visitor I can be bothered to talk to. And the only one who could conceivably give me a cigarette.'

'I'm not going to give you a cigarette.'

There was silence until Marion removed the mask again.

'Did any Icelanders spy during the Cold War?' Erlendur asked.

'I don't know,' Marion said. 'I know that people tried to get them to. I remember one bloke who came to us and said the Russians never left him alone.' Marion's eyes closed. 'It was an exceptionally cheesy spy story, but very Icelandic, of course.'

The Russians had contacted the man to ask if he would help them. They needed information about the Keflavík base and its buildings. The Russians took the matter seriously and wanted to meet the man in an isolated place outside the city. He found them very pushy and could not get rid of them. Although he refused to do what they asked, they would not listen and in the end he gave in. He contacted the police and a simple sting was set up. When the man drove off to meet the Russians by Lake Hafravatn there were two police officers in the car with him, hiding under a blanket. Other policemen had taken up positions nearby. The Russians suspected nothing until the police officers got out of the man's car and arrested them.

'They were expelled,' Marion said, with a pained smile at the thought of the Russians' amateurish attempts at spying. 'I always remember their names: Kisilev and Dimitriev.'

'I wanted to see if you remembered someone from Reykjavík who went missing in the 1960s,' Erlendur said. 'A man who sold farm machinery and diggers. He failed to turn up for a meeting with a farmer just outside town and he's never been heard of since.'

'I remember that well. Níels handled that case. The lazy bastard.'

65

'Yes, quite,' said Erlendur, who knew Níels. 'The man owned a Ford Falcon that was found outside the coach station. One hubcap had been removed.'

'Didn't he just want to give his old girl the slip? As far as I recall that was our conclusion. That he killed himself.'

'Could be,' Erlendur said.

Marion's eyes closed again. Erlendur sat on the sofa in silence for a while, watching the film while Marion slept. The video-box blurb described how John Wayne played a Confederate Civil War veteran hunting down the Indians who had killed his brother and sister-in-law and kidnapped their daughter. The soldier spent years searching for the girl and when he found her at last she had forgotten where she came from and become an Indian herself.

After twenty minutes Erlendur stood up and said goodbye to Marion, who was still sleeping under the mask.

When he arrived at the police station, Erlendur sat down with Elínborg, who was writing her speech for the book launch. Sigurdur Óli was in her office too. He said he had traced the sales history of the Falcon right up to the most recent owner.

'He sold the car to a spare-parts dealer in Kópavogur some time before 1980,' Sigurdur Óli said. 'The company's still in business. They just won't answer the phone. Maybe they're on holiday.'

'Anything new from forensics about the listening device?' Erlendur asked, and he noticed that Elínborg was moving her lips while she stared at the computer screen, as if she was trying out how the speech sounded.

'Elínborg!' he barked.

She lifted a finger to tell him to wait.

'. . . And I hope that this book of mine,' she read out loud from the screen, 'will bring you endless pleasure in the kitchen and broaden your horizons. I have tried to keep it plain and simple, tried to emphasise the household spirit, because cookery and the kitchen are the focal point . . .'

'Very good,' Erlendur said.

'Wait,' Elínborg said. '. . . The focal point of every good household where the family gathers every day to relax and enjoy happy times together.'

'Elínborg,' Sigurdur Óli said.

'Is it too sentimental?' Elínborg asked, pulling a face.

'It makes me puke,' Sigurdur Óli said.

Elínborg looked at Erlendur.

'What did forensics say about the equipment?' he asked.

'They're still looking at it,' Elínborg said. 'They're trying to get in touch with experts from Iceland Telecom.'

'I was thinking about all that equipment they found in Kleifarvatn years ago,' Sigurdur Óli said, 'and this one tied to the skeleton. Shouldn't we talk to some old codger from the diplomatic service?'

'Yes, find out who we can speak to,' Erlendur said. 'Someone who remembers the Cold War.'

'Are we talking about spying in Iceland?' Elínborg asked.

'I don't know,' Erlendur said.

'Isn't that pretty absurd?' Elínborg said.

'No more than "where the family gathers every day to relax and enjoy happy times together",' Sigurdur Óli parroted her.

'Oh, shut up,' Elínborg said, and deleted what she had written.

Wrecked cars were kept behind a large fence, stacked six high in some places. Some had been written off, others were just old and worn out. The spare-parts dealer looked the same, a weary man approaching sixty, in a filthy, ripped pair of overalls that had once been light blue. He was tearing the front bumper off a new Japanese car that had been hit from behind and had concertinaed right up to the front seats.

Erlendur stood sizing up the debris until the man looked up.

'A lorry went into the back of it,' he said. 'Lucky there was no one in the back seat.'

'A brand new car too,' Erlendur said.

'What are you looking for?'

'I'm after a black Ford Falcon,' Erlendur said. 'It was sold or given away to this yard around 1980.'

'A Ford Falcon?'

'It's hopeless, of course – I know,' Erlendur said.

'It would have been old when it came here,' the man said, pulling out a rag to wipe his hands. 'They stopped making Falcons around 1970, maybe earlier.'

'You mean you didn't have any use for it?'

'Most Falcons were off the streets long before 1980. Why are you looking for it? Do you need spares? Are you doing it up?'

Erlendur told him that he was from the police and that the car was connected with an old case of a missing person. The man's interest was aroused. He said he had bought the business from a man called Haukur in the mid-1980s but did not recall any Ford Falcon in the stock. The previous owner, who had died years ago, had kept a record of all the wrecks he'd bought, said the dealer, and showed Erlendur into a little room filled to the ceiling with files and boxes of papers.

'These are our books,' the man said with an apologetic smile. 'We, er, never throw anything away. You're welcome to take a look. I couldn't be bothered to keep records of the cars, never saw the point, but he did it conscientiously.'

Erlendur thanked him and began examining the files, which were all marked on the spine with a year. Spotting a stack from the 1970s, he started there. He did not know why he was looking for this car. Even if it did exist, he had no idea how it could help him. Sigurdur Óli had asked why he was interested in this particular missing person over the others he had heard about in the past few days. Erlendur had no proper answer. Sigurdur Óli would never have understood what he meant if he had told him that he was preoccupied by a lonely woman who believed she had found happiness at last, fidgeting outside a dairy shop, looking at her watch and waiting for the man she loved.

Three hours later, when Erlendur was on the verge of giving up and the owner had asked him repeatedly whether he had turned up anything, he found what he was looking for: an invoice for the car. The dealer had sold a black Ford Falcon on 21 October 1979, engine defunct, interior in reasonable condition, good lacquering. No licence plates. Stapled to the sheet of paper describing the sale was a pencilled invoice: Falcon 1967. 35,000 krónur. Buyer: Hermann Albertsson.

11

The First Secretary at the Russian embassy in Reykjavík was the same age as Erlendur but thinner and considerably healthier-looking. When he received them he seemed to make a special effort to be casual. He was wearing khaki trousers and said, with a smile, that he was on his way to the golf course. He showed Erlendur and Elínborg to their seats in his office, then sat down behind a large desk and smiled broadly. He knew the reason for their visit. The meeting had been arranged well in advance so Erlendur was surprised to hear the golfing excuse. He had the impression that they were supposed to rush through the meeting and then disappear. They spoke English and, although the First Secretary was aware of the reason for the enquiry, Elínborg briefly repeated the need for the meeting. A Russian listening device had been found tied to the skeleton of a man probably murdered and thrown into Lake Kleifarvatn some time after 1961. The discovery of the Russian equipment had still not leaked to the press.

'There have been a number of Soviet and Russian ambassadors in Iceland since 1960,' the Secretary said, smiling self-confidently as if none of what they had related was any of his business. 'Those who were here in the 1960s and early 1970s are long since dead. I doubt that they knew anything about Russian equipment in that lake. Any more than I do.'

He smiled. Erlendur smiled back.

'But you spied here in Iceland during the Cold War? Or at least tried to.'

'That was before my time,' the Secretary said. 'I couldn't say.'

'Do you mean you don't spy any more?'

'Why would we spy? We just go on the Internet like everyone else. Besides, your military base isn't so important any more. If it matters at all. The conflict zones have shifted. America doesn't need an aircraft carrier like Iceland any more. No one can understand what they're doing here with that expensive base. If this were Turkey I could understand.'

'It's not *our* military base,' Elínborg said.

'We know that some embassy staff were expelled from Iceland on suspicion of spying,' Erlendur said. 'When things were very tense in the Cold War.'

'Then you know more than I do,' the Secretary said. 'And of course it is your military base,' he added, looking at Elínborg. 'If we did have spies in this embassy then there were certainly twice as many CIA agents at the US embassy. Have you asked them? The description of the skeleton you found suggests to me – how should one put it – a mafia killing. Had that occurred to you? Concrete boots and deep water. It's almost like an American gangster movie.'

'It was Russian equipment,' Erlendur said. 'Tied to the body. The skeleton . . .'

'That tells us nothing,' the Secretary said. 'There were embassies or offices from other Warsaw Pact countries that used Soviet equipment. It need not be connected with *our* embassy.'

'We have a detailed description of the device with us, and photographs,' Elínborg said, handing them to him. 'Can you tell us anything about how it was used? Who used it?'

'I am not familiar with this equipment,' the Secretary said as he looked at the photographs. 'Sorry. I will enquire, though. But even if we did recognise it, we can't help you very much.'

'Couldn't you give it a try?' Erlendur asked.

The Secretary smiled.

'You'll just have to believe me. The skeleton in the lake has nothing to do with this embassy or its staff. Neither in the present, nor in the past.'

'We believe it's a listening device,' Elínborg said. 'It is tuned to the old wavelength of the American troops in Keflavík.'

'I can't comment on that,' the Secretary said, looking at his watch. His round of golf was waiting.

'If you had spied in the old days, which you didn't,' Erlendur said, 'what would you have been interested in?'

The Secretary hesitated for an instant.

'If we *had* been doing anything then obviously we would have wanted to observe the base, the transportation of military hardware, movements of warships, aircraft, submarines. We would have wanted to know about America's capability at any time. That's obvious. We would have wanted to know about what was going on at the base and other military installations in Iceland. They were all over the place. Not just in Keflavík. There were activities all over Iceland. We would also have monitored the activities of other embassies, domestic politics, political parties and that sort of thing.'

'A lot of equipment was found in Lake Kleifarvatn in 1973,' Erlendur said. 'Transmitters, microwave equipment, tape recorders, even radios. All from Warsaw Pact countries. Mostly from the Soviet Union.'

'I'm not aware of the incident,' the Secretary said.

'No, of course not,' Erlendur said. 'But what reason could there have been for throwing that equipment in the lake? Did you use a particular method for getting rid of old stuff?'

'I'm afraid I cannot assist you with that,' the Secretary said, no longer smiling. 'I've tried to answer you as best I can but there are some things I simply don't know. And that's that.'

Erlendur and Elínborg stood up. There was a smugness about the man that Erlendur disliked. Your base! What did he know about military bases in Iceland?

'Was the equipment obsolete, so there was no point in sending it home in a diplomatic bag?' he asked. 'Couldn't you throw it away like any other rubbish? These devices clearly demonstrate that spying went on in Iceland. When the world was much simpler and the lines were clearly drawn.'

'You can say what you like about it,' the Secretary said, standing up. 'I have to be somewhere else.'

'The man whose body was found in Kleifarvatn, could he have been at the embassy?'

'I think that's out of the question.'

'Or from another Eastern bloc embassy?'

'I don't think there's the slightest chance. And now I must ask you to—'

'Are there any persons missing from this period?'

'No.'

'You just know that? You don't need to look it up?'

'I have looked it up. No one is missing.'

'No one who disappeared and you don't know what became of them?'

'Goodbye,' the Secretary said, with a smile. He had opened the door.

'Definitely no one who disappeared?' Erlendur said as he walked out into the corridor.

'No one,' the Secretary said, and closed the door in their faces.

Sigurdur Óli was refused a meeting with the US ambassador or his staff. Instead he received a message from the embassy marked 'confidential' which stated that no US citizen in Iceland had been reported missing during the period in question. Sigurdur Óli wanted to take the matter further and insist on a meeting, but his request was denied by the top CID officials. The police would need something tangible to link the body in the lake to the US embassy, the base or American citizens in Iceland.

Sigurdur Óli telephoned a friend of his, a head of section at the Defence Department of the Ministry of Foreign Affairs, to ask whether he could locate any past employee to tell the police about foreign embassy officials in the 1960s and 1970s. He tried to give away as little as possible about the investigation, just enough to arouse his interest, and his friend promised to get back to him.

Erlendur stood awkwardly, a glass of white wine in his hand, scouring the crowd at Elínborg's book launch. He had found it quite difficult to make up his mind whether to put in an appearance, but in the end he had decided to go. Gatherings annoyed him, the few that came his way. He sipped the wine and grimaced. It was sour. He thought ruefully of his bottle of Chartreuse back home.

He smiled at Elínborg, who was standing in the crowd and waved to him. She was talking to the press. The fact that a woman from the Reykjavík CID had written a cookery book had prompted quite a lot of publicity and Erlendur was pleased to see Elínborg basking in the attention. She had once invited him, Sigurdur Óli and his wife Bergthóra for dinner to test a new Indian chicken dish that she had said would be in the book. It was a particularly spicy and tasty meal and they had praised Elínborg until she blushed.

Erlendur did not recognise many people apart from the police officers and was relieved to see Sigurdur Óli and Bergthóra walk over in his direction.

'Do try to smile for once when you see us,' Bergthóra said, kissing him on the cheek. He drank a toast of white wine, then they toasted Elínborg specially afterwards.

'When do we get to meet this woman you're seeing?' Bergthóra asked, and Erlendur noticed Sigurdur Óli tensing beside her. Erlendur's relationship with a woman was the talk of the CID, but few dared pry into the matter.

'One day, perhaps,' Erlendur said. 'On your eightieth birthday.'

'Can't wait,' Bergthóra said.

Erlendur smiled.

'Who are all these people?' Bergthóra said, looking around the gathering.

'I only know the officers,' Sigurdur Óli said. 'And I think all those fatsos over there are with Elínborg.'

'There's Teddi,' Bergthóra said, with a wave at Elínborg's husband.

Someone tapped a spoon against a glass and the murmuring stopped. In a far corner of the room a man began talking and they could not hear a word, but everyone laughed. They saw Elínborg push her way over to him and take out the speech that she had written. They inched closer to hear her and managed to catch her closing thanks to her family and colleagues in the force for their patience and support. A round of applause followed.

'Are you going to stay long?' Erlendur asked, sounding ready to leave.

'Don't be so uptight,' Bergthóra said. 'Relax. Enjoy yourself a bit. Get drunk.'

She snatched a glass of white wine from the nearest tray.

'Get this inside you!'

Elínborg appeared from the crowd, greeted them all with a kiss and asked if they were bored. She looked at Erlendur, who took a swig of the sour white wine. She and Bergthóra started talking about a female television celebrity who was there and who was having an affair with some businessman. Sigurdur Óli shook the hand of someone whom Erlendur did not recognise and he was about to sneak out when he bumped into an old colleague. He was nearing retirement, something that Erlendur knew he feared.

'You've heard about Marion,' the man said, sipping his white wine. 'Buggered lungs, I'm told. Just sits at home suffering.'

'That's right,' Erlendur said. 'And watches westerns.'

'Were you making enquiries about the Falcon?' the man asked, emptied his glass and grabbed another from a tray as it glided past them.

'The Falcon?'

'They were talking about it at the station. You were looking into missing persons in connection with the Kleifarvatn skeleton.'

'Do you remember anything about the Falcon?' Erlendur asked.

'No, not exactly. We found it outside the coach station. Níels was in charge of the investigation. I saw him here just now. Nifty book that girl's written,' he added. 'I was just looking at it. Good photos.'

'I think the girl's in her forties,' Erlendur said. 'And yes, it's a really good book.'

He scouted around for Níels and found him sitting on a wide windowsill. Erlendur sat down beside him and recalled how he had once envied him. Níels had a long police career behind him and a family that anyone would be proud of. His wife was a well-known painter, they had four promising children, all university graduates and now providing them with a succession of grandchildren. The couple owned a large house in the suburb of Grafarvogur, splendidly designed by the artist, and two cars, and had nothing to cast a shadow on their eternal happiness. Erlendur sometimes wondered whether a happier and more successful life was possible. They were not the best of friends. Erlendur had always found Níels lazy and absolutely unsuited for detective work. Nor did his personal success diminish the antipathy Erlendur felt towards him.

'Marion's really ill, I hear,' Níels said when Erlendur sat down beside him.

'I'm sure there's a while left yet,' Erlendur said against his better judgement. 'How are you doing?'

He asked simply out of politeness. He always knew how Níels was doing.

'I've given up trying to figure it out,' Níels said. 'We arrested the same man for burglary five times in one weekend. Every time he confesses and is released because the case is solved. He breaks in somewhere again, gets arrested, is released, burgles somewhere else. It's brainless. Why don't they set up a system here for sending idiots like that straight to prison? They clock up twenty or so crimes before they're given the minimum custodial sentence, then the minute they're out on probation you're arresting the same buggers again. What's the point of such madness? Why aren't these bastards given a proper sentence?'

'You won't find a more hopeless set-up than the Icelandic judicial system,' Erlendur said.

'Those scum make fools of the judges,' Níels said. 'And then those paedophiles! And the psychos!'

They fell silent. The debate on leniency struck a nerve among police officers, who brought criminals, rapists and paedophiles into custody only to hear later that they had been given light sentences or even suspended ones.

'There's another thing,' Erlendur said. 'Do you remember the man who sold agricultural machinery? He owned a Ford Falcon. Vanished without a trace.'

'You mean the car outside the coach station?'

'Yes.'

'He had a nice girlfriend, that bloke. What do you reckon happened to her?'

'She's still waiting,' Erlendur said. 'One of the hubcaps was missing from the car. Do you remember that?'

'We assumed it must have been stolen from outside the coach station. There was nothing about the case to suggest criminal activity – apart from that hubcap being stolen, perhaps. If it *was* stolen. He could have hit the kerb. Anyway, it was never found. No more than its owner was.'

'Why should he have killed himself?' Erlendur said. 'He had everything going for him. A pretty girlfriend. Bright future. He'd bought a Ford Falcon.'

'You know how none of that counts when people commit suicide,' Níels said.

'Do you think he caught a coach somewhere?'

'We thought that it was likely, if I recall correctly. We talked to the drivers but they didn't remember him. Still, that doesn't mean he didn't take a coach out of town.'

'You think he killed himself.'

'Yes,' said Níels. 'But . . .'

Níels hesitated.

'What?' Erlendur said.

'He was playing some kind of a game, that bloke,' Níels said.

'How so?'

'She said his name was Leopold but we couldn't find anyone by that name of the age she said he was; there was no one on our files or in the national register. No birth certificate. No driving licence. There was no Leopold who could have been that man.'

'What do you mean?'

'Either all the records about him had gone missing or . . .'

'Or he was deceiving her?'

'He couldn't have been called Leopold, at least,' Níels said.

'What did she say to that? What did his girlfriend say when you asked her about it?'

'We had the feeling he'd been pulling a fast one on her,' Níels said eventually. 'We felt sorry for her. She didn't even have a photograph of him. What does that tell you? She didn't know a thing about that man.'

'So?'

'We didn't tell her.'

'You didn't tell her what?'

'That we had no files about this Leopold of hers,' Níels said. 'It looked cut and dried to us. He lied to her, then walked out on her.'

Erlendur sat in silence while he tried to work out the implications of what Níels had told him.

'Out of consideration for her,' Níels said.

'And she still doesn't know?'

'I don't think so.'

'Why did you keep it a secret?'

'Probably for the sake of kindness.'

'She's still sitting waiting for him,' Erlendur said. 'They were going to get married.'

'That was what he convinced her of before he left.'

'What if he was murdered?'

'We considered it very unlikely. It's a rare scenario, but admittedly not unknown: men lie their way into women's lives, get . . . how should I put it, comfortable, then disappear. I think she knew deep down. We didn't need to tell her.'

'What about the car?'

'It was in her name. The loan for it was in her name. She owned the car.'

'You should have told her.'

'Perhaps. But would she have been any better off? She would have learned that the man she loved was a confidence trickster. He told her nothing about his family. She knew nothing about him. He had no friends. Forever on sales trips all over the countryside. What does that tell you?'

'She knew that she loved him,' Erlendur said.

'And that's how he paid her back.'

'What did the farmer say, the one he was going to meet?'

'That's all in the files,' Níels said, with a nod and a smile at Elínborg, who was deep in conversation with her publisher. Elínborg had once mentioned that his name was Anton.

'Come on, not everything goes into the files.'

'He never met the farmer,' Níels said, and Erlendur could see how he was trying to recall the details of the case. They all remembered the big cases, the murders or disappearances, every single major arrest, every single assault and rape.

'Couldn't you tell from the Falcon whether or not he met the farmer?'

'We didn't find anything in the car to indicate that he'd been to the farm.'

'Did you take samples from the floor by the front seats? Under the pedals?'

'It's in the files.'

'I didn't see it. You could have established whether he visited the farmer. He would have picked stuff up on his shoes.'

'It wasn't a complicated case, Erlendur. Nobody wanted to turn it into one. The man made himself vanish. Maybe he bumped himself off. We don't always find the bodies. You know that. Even if we had found something under the pedals, it could have been from anywhere. He travelled around the country a lot. Selling agricultural machinery.'

'What did they say at his work?'

Níels thought about the question.

'It was such a long time ago, Erlendur.'

'Try to remember.'

'He wasn't on the payroll, I remember that much, which was rare in those days. He was on commission and worked on a freelance basis.'

'Which means he would have had to pay his taxes himself.'

'As I said, there was no mention of him in the records under the name Leopold. Not a thing.'

'So you reckon he kept that woman when he was in Reykjavík but, what, lived somewhere else?'

'Or even had a family,' Níels said. 'There are blokes like that.'

Erlendur sipped his wine and looked at the perfect tie knot under Níels's shirt collar. He was not a good detective. To him, no case was ever complicated.

'You should have told her the truth.'

'That may well be, but she had happy memories of him. We concluded that it wasn't a criminal matter. The disappearance was never investigated as a murder because no clues were found to warrant it.'

They stopped talking. The guests' murmuring had become a solid wall of noise.

'You're still into these missing persons,' Níels said. 'Why this interest? What are you looking for?'

'I don't know,' Erlendur said.

'It was a routine disappearance,' Níels said. 'Something else was needed to turn it into a murder investigation. No clues ever emerged to give grounds for that.'

'No, probably not.'

'Don't you ever get tired of all this?' Níels asked.

'Sometimes.'

'And your daughter, she's always involved in the same old shit,' said Níels, with his four educated children who had all started beautiful families and lived perfect, impeccable lives, just like him.

Erlendur knew that the whole force was aware of Eva Lind's arrest and how she had attacked Sigurdur Óli. She sometimes ended up in police custody and received no special treatment for being his daughter. Níels had clearly heard about Eva. Erlendur looked at him, his tasteful clothing and his manicured nails, and wondered whether a happy life made people even more boring than they were to start with.

'Yes,' Erlendur said. 'She's as screwed up as ever.'

12

When Erlendur got home that evening there was no Sindri to welcome him. He had still not turned up when Erlendur went to bed just before midnight. There was no message, nor a telephone number where he could be reached. Erlendur missed his company. He dialled directory enquiries, but Sindri's mobile number was not listed.

He was falling asleep when the telephone rang. It was Eva Lind.

'You know they dope you up in here,' she said in a slurred voice.

'I was asleep,' Erlendur lied.

'They give you tablets to bring you down,' Eva said. 'I've never been so stoned in my life. What are you doing?'

'Trying to sleep,' Erlendur said. 'Were you causing trouble?'

'Sindri stopped by today,' Eva said without answering him. 'He said you'd had a talk.'

'Do you know where he is?'

'Isn't he with you?'

'I think he's left,' Erlendur said. 'Maybe he's at your mother's. Are you allowed to make phone calls from that place whenever you like?'

'Nice to hear from you too,' Eva snarled. 'And I'm not causing any fucking trouble.' She slammed the telephone down on him.

Erlendur lay staring up into the darkness. He thought about his two children, Eva Lind and Sindri Snaer, and their mother, who hated him. He thought about his brother, for whom he had been searching in vain all these years. His bones were lying somewhere. Perhaps deep in a fissure, or higher up in the mountains than he could ever imagine. Even though he had gone far up the mountainsides, trying to work out how high a boy of eight could stray in bad conditions and a blinding blizzard.

'Don't you ever get tired of all this?'

Tired of this endless search.

Hermann Albertsson opened the door to him just before noon the following day. He was a thin man aged around sixty, nimble, wearing scruffy jeans and a red check cotton shirt, and with a broad smile that never seemed to leave his face. From the kitchen came the smell of boiled haddock. He lived alone and always had done, he told Erlendur without being asked. He smelled of brake fluid.

'Do have some haddock,' he said when Erlendur followed him into the kitchen.

Erlendur declined firmly but Hermann ignored him and set a place at the table, and before he knew it he was sitting down with a complete stranger, eating soft-boiled haddock and buttered potatoes. They both ate the skin of the haddock and the skin of the potatoes, and for an instant Erlendur's thoughts turned to Elínborg and her cookery book. When she'd been working on it she had used him as a guinea pig for fresh monkfish with lime sauce, yellow from the quarter-kilo of butter she had put in it. It took Elínborg all day and night to boil down the fish stock until only four tablespoons remained on the bottom, essence of monkfish; she had stayed up all night to skim off the froth from the water. The sauce is everything, was Elínborg's motto. Erlendur smiled to himself. Hermann's haddock was delicious.

'I did that Falcon up,' Hermann said, putting a large piece of potato in his mouth. He was a car mechanic and for a hobby he restored old cars and then tried to sell them. It was becoming increasingly difficult, he told Erlendur. No one was interested in old cars any more, only new Range Rovers that never faced tougher conditions than a traffic jam on the way to the city centre.

'Do you still own it?' Erlendur asked.

'I sold it in 1987,' Hermann said. 'I've got a 1979 Chrysler now, quite a limo really. I've been under its bonnet for, what, six years.'

'Will you get anything for it?'

'Nothing,' said Hermann, offering him some coffee. 'And I don't want to sell it either.'

'You didn't register the Falcon when you owned it.'

'No,' Hermann said. 'It never had plates when it was here. I fiddled about with it for a few years and that was fun. I drove it around the neighbourhood and if I wanted to take it to Thingvellir or somewhere I borrowed the plates from my own car. I didn't think it was worth paying the insurance.'

'We couldn't find it registered anywhere,' Erlendur said, 'so the new owner hasn't bought licence plates for it either.'

Hermann filled two cups.

'That needn't be the case,' Hermann said. 'Maybe he gave up and got rid of it.'

'Tell me something else. The hubcaps on the Falcon, were they special somehow, in demand?'

Erlendur had asked Elínborg to check the Internet for him and on ford.com they had found photographs of old Ford Falcons. One was black and when Elínborg printed out the image for him, the hubcaps stood out very clearly.

'They were quite fancy,' Hermann said thoughtfully. 'Those hubcaps on American cars.'

'One hubcap was missing,' Erlendur said. 'At the time.'

'Really?'

'Did you buy a new hubcap when you got it?'

'No, one of the previous owners had bought a new set a long time before. The originals weren't on when I bought it.'

'Was it a remarkable car, the Falcon?'

'The remarkable thing about it was that it wasn't big,' Hermann said. 'It wasn't a monster like most American cars. Like my Chrysler. The Falcon was small and compact and good to drive. Not a luxury car at all. Far from it.'

The current owner turned out to be a widow a few years older than Erlendur. She lived in Kópavogur. Her husband, a furniture maker with a fad for cars, had died of a heart attack a few years before.

'It was in good condition,' she said, opening the garage for Erlendur, who was unsure whether she was talking about the car or her husband's heart. The car was covered with a thick canvas sheet which Erlendur asked if he could remove. The woman nodded.

'My husband took a great deal of care over that car,' she said in a weak voice. 'He spent all his time out here. Bought really expensive parts for it. Travelled all over the place to find them.'

'Did he ever drive it?' Erlendur asked as he struggled to untie a knot.

'Only around the block,' the woman said. 'It looks nice but my boys aren't interested in it and they haven't managed to sell it. There aren't many veteran-car enthusiasts these days. My husband was going to put plates on it when he died. He died in his workshop. He used to work alone and when he didn't come home for dinner and wouldn't answer the phone I sent my son round; he found him lying on the floor.'

'That must have been difficult,' Erlendur said.

'There's heart trouble in his family,' the woman said. 'His mother went that way and so did his cousin.'

She watched Erlendur fiddling with the canvas. She did not give the impression of missing her husband much. Perhaps she had overcome her grief and was trying to make a new start.

'What is it with this car, anyway?' she asked.

She had asked the same question when Erlendur telephoned and he could still not find a way to tell her why he was interested in the car without saying what the case involved. He wanted to avoid going into details. Not say too much for the time being. He hardly knew why he was chasing after the car, or whether it would prove useful.

'It was once connected with a police matter,' Erlendur said reluctantly. 'I just wanted to know if it was still around, in one piece.'

'Was it a famous case?' she asked.

'No, not at all. Not famous in the least,' Erlendur said.

'Do you want to buy it or . . . ?' the woman asked.

'No,' Erlendur said. 'I don't want to buy it. Old cars don't interest me as such.'

'As I say, it's in good condition. Valdi, my husband, said the main trouble was the underseal. It had gone rusty and he had to fix it. Otherwise it was all right. Valdi stripped the engine down, scrubbed every bit of it and bought new parts if he needed them.'

She paused.

'He didn't mind spending money on the car,' she said eventually. 'Never bought me anything. But men are like that.'

Erlendur tugged at the sheet, which slipped off the car and onto the floor. For a moment he stood looking along the beautiful sleek lines of the Ford Falcon that had been owned by the man who had disappeared outside the coach station. He knelt down beside one of the front wheels. Assuming that the hubcap was missing when the car was discovered, he wondered where it could possibly have ended up.

His mobile rang in his pocket. It was forensics with information about the Russian equipment in Kleifarvatn. Skipping all the formalities, the head of forensics told him that the device did not appear to have been functional when it was put in the lake.

'Oh?' Erlendur said.

'Yes,' the head of forensics said. 'It was certainly useless before it went into the water. The lake bed is porous sand and the contents of the container are too damaged to be explained by it having lain in water. It wasn't working when it got there.'

'What does that tell us?' Erlendur asked.

'Don't have the foggiest,' the head of forensics said.

13

The couple walked along the pavement, the man slightly ahead of the woman. It was a glorious spring evening. Rays of sunshine fell on the surface of the sea and in the distance showers of rain tumbled down. It was as if the couple were impervious to the evening's beauty. They strode forward, the man seemingly agitated. He talked incessantly. His wife followed silently, trying not to be left behind.

He watched them pass his window, looked at the evening sun and thought back to when he was young and the world was beginning to become so infinitely complex and unmanageable.

When the tragedy began.

He completed his first year at the university with flying colours and went back to Iceland in the summer. During the vacation he worked for the party newspaper, writing articles about the reconstruction of Leipzig. At meetings he described being a student there and discussed Iceland's historical and cultural links with the city. He met leading party members. They had big plans for him. He looked forward to going back. He felt he had a role to play, perhaps a greater one than others. It was said that he was highly promising.

That autumn he returned to East Germany; his second Christmas at the residence was approaching. The Icelanders looked forward to it because some would be sent food parcels from home: traditional Icelandic Christmas delicacies such as smoked lamb, salted fish, dried fish, confectionery, even books too. Karl had already received his parcel and when he began boiling a huge leg of lamb from Húnavatnssýsla where his uncle was a farmer the aroma filled the old villa. In the box there was also a bottle of Icelandic schnapps, which Emil requisitioned.

Only Rut could afford to go home to Iceland for Christmas. She was also the only one who felt seriously homesick after she returned from summer vacation, and when she left for the Christmas break some said she might not be back. The old villa was emptier than usual because most of the German students had gone home, as had some of the Eastern Europeans who were permitted to travel and were entitled to cheap rail transport.

So it was only a small group that gathered in the kitchen around the leg of smoked lamb and the bottle of schnapps that Emil had placed in the middle of the table. Two Swedish students had supplied potatoes, others brought red cabbage and Karl had somehow managed to produce a decent white sauce for the meat. Lothar Weiser, the liaison who had especially befriended the Icelanders, dropped by and was invited to join the feast. They all liked Lothar. He was talkative and entertaining. He seemed profoundly interested in politics and sometimes probed them for their views on the university, Leipzig, the German Democratic Republic, First Secretary Walter Ulbricht and his planned economy. He wondered whether they thought Ulbricht was too closely aligned to the Soviet government, and asked repeatedly about the events in Hungary and the American capitalists' attempts to drive a wedge into its friendship with the Soviet Union through their radio broadcasts and endless anti-communist propaganda. In particular he felt that young people were too gullible towards the propaganda and blind to the real intentions of the Western capitalist governments.

'Can't we just have a bit of fun?' Karl said when Lothar began talking about Ulbricht, and downed a shot of spirit. Grimacing terribly, he said that he had never liked Icelandic schnapps.

'Ja, ja, natürlich,' Lothar laughed. 'Enough of politics.'

He spoke Icelandic, which he said he had learned in Germany, and they thought he must be a linguistic genius because he spoke the language almost as well as they did, without ever having visited the country. When they asked how he had gained such a command of it he said he had listened to recordings and radio broadcasts. Nothing amused them more than when he sang old lullabies.

'Approaching rain,' was another phrase that he repeated endlessly, from the Icelandic weather forecasts.

In the box there were two letters to Karl which delivered the main news from Iceland since the autumn, along with some newspaper cuttings. They talked about the news from home and someone remarked that Hannes was absent as usual.

'Ja, Hannes,' Lothar said, with a smirk.

'I told him about this,' Emil said, downing a glass.

'Why is he so mysterious?' Hrafnhildur asked.

'Ah yes, mysterious,' Lothar said.

'It's so strange,' Emil said. 'He never turns up to the FDJ meetings or their lectures. I've never seen him doing volunteer work. Is he too good to work in the ruins? Aren't we good enough for him? Does he think he's better than us? Tómas, you've talked to him.'

'I think Hannes just wants to finish his course,' he said, with a shrug. 'He's just got this year left.'

'Everyone always spoke of him as a future star of the party,' Karl said. 'He was always described as leadership material. He doesn't look very promising here. I think I've only seen him twice this winter and he hardly said a word to me.'

'You barely see him,' Lothar said. 'He's rather glum,' he added, shaking his head, then sipped the schnapps and pulled the same sort of face that Karl had.

Down on the ground floor they heard the front door open,

followed by quick footsteps up the stairs. Two males and a female appeared at the gloomy far end of the corridor. They were students, passing acquaintances of Karl's.

'We heard you were having an Icelandic Christmas party,' the girl said when they entered the kitchen and saw the spread. There was plenty of lamb left and the others made room for them at the table. One of the men produced two bottles of vodka, to riotous applause. They introduced themselves: the men were from Czechoslovakia and the girl was Hungarian.

She sat beside him and he felt himself go weak. He tried not to stare at her after she emerged from the darkness of the corridor, but when he saw her there for the first time a wave of feelings rushed through him that he would never have thought himself capable of and found difficult to understand. Something strange happened and he was suddenly overwhelmed by a peculiar joy and euphoria, mixed with shyness. No girl had ever had such an effect on him.

'Are you from Iceland too?' She turned to him and asked her question in good German.

'Yes, I'm from Iceland,' he stammered, also in German, which he could speak well by now. He dragged his gaze away from her when it dawned on him that he had been staring at her ever since she'd sat down beside him.

'What monstrosity is that?' she asked, pointing to a boiled sheep's head on the table, still uneaten.

'A sheep's head, sawn in half and charred,' he said, and saw her wince.

'What sort of people do that?' she asked.

'Icelanders,' he said. 'Actually it's very good,' he added rather hesitantly. 'The tongue and the cheeks . . .' He stopped when he realised that it did not sound particularly appetising.

'So, you eat the eyes and lips too?' she asked, not trying to conceal her disgust.

'The lips? Yes, those too. And the eyes.'

'You can't have had much food if you had to resort to that,' she said.

'We were a very poor nation,' he said, nodding.

'I'm Ilona,' she said, holding out her hand. They exchanged greetings and he told her that his name was Tómas.

One of her companions called out to her. He had a plate full of smoked lamb and potatoes and urged her to try it, telling her that it was delicious. She stood up, found a plate and cut a slice of the meat.

'We never get enough meat,' she said as she sat down beside him again.

'Umm, wonderful,' she said with her mouth full of smoked lamb.

'Better than sheep's eyes,' he said.

They went on celebrating into the early hours. More students heard about the party and the house filled up. An old gramophone was taken out and someone put some Sinatra records on. Late in the night the different nationalities took turns singing songs about their countries. Karl and Emil, both definitely feeling the effects of the consignment from Iceland, began by singing a melancholy ode by Jónas Hallgrímsson. Then the Hungarians took over, followed by the Czechs, the Swedes and the Germans, and a student from Senegal who pined for the hot African nights. Hrafnhildur insisted on hearing the most beautiful words in all their mother tongues, and after some confusion it was agreed that one representative from each country would stand and recite the most beautiful passage in it. The Icelanders were unanimous. Hrafnhildur rose and declaimed the finest piece of Icelandic poetry ever written:

> The star of love
> over Steeple Rock
> is cloaked in clouds of night.
> It laughed, once, from heaven
> on the lad grieving
> deep in the dark valley.

Her delivery was shot through with emotion and even though only a few of them understood it, the group was stunned into momentary silence, until a mighty round of applause broke out and Hrafnhildur took a deep bow.

He was still sitting with Ilona at the kitchen table; she looked at him inquisitively. He told her about the character in the poem that had been recited, who was reflecting on a long journey through the Icelandic wilderness with a young girl for whom he yearned. He knew that they could never be lovers and with those morose thoughts he returned alone to his valley, weighed down by sorrow. Above him twinkled the star of love that had once lit his way but had now disappeared behind a cloud, and he thought to himself that their love, although unfulfilled, would last for ever.

She watched him while he was talking and whether it was his story of the sorrowful young lover, or the way he told it, or just the Icelandic schnapps, she suddenly kissed him right on the lips, so tenderly that he felt like a little child again.

Rut did not return from her Christmas vacation. She sent a letter to each of her friends in Leipzig, and in his she mentioned the facilities and various other complaints, and he understood that she had had enough. Or perhaps she was just too homesick. In the dormitory kitchen, the Icelanders talked it over. Karl said he missed her and Emil nodded. Hrafnhildur said she was soft.

The next time he met Hannes he asked why he had not wanted to join them at the residence. This was after a lecture on structural stress which had taken a strange turn. Hannes had attended it too. Twenty minutes after the lecture began, the door had opened and in walked three students who said they were from the FDJ and would like to say a few words. With them was a young man he had sometimes seen at the library and had assumed was a student of German literature. The student looked down at the floor. The leader of the group, who introduced himself as the secretary of the FDJ, began speaking about student solidarity and reminded them of the four aims of the university's work: to teach them Marxist theory, make them socially active, have them work in the service of society within a programme organised by young communists, and establish a class of intellectuals who would later become professionals in their respective fields.

He turned to the student with them and described how he had admitted listening to western radio broadcasts and then had promised to mend his ways. The student looked up, took one step forward, confessed his crime and said he would not tune in to western programmes again. Said they were corrupted by imperialism and capitalist profiteering, and urged everyone in the hall to listen only to Eastern European radio in future.

The secretary thanked him, then asked the students to join him in a pledge that no one in the room would listen to western radio. After everyone had repeated the oath, the secretary turned to the teacher and apologised for disturbing him, and the group left the room.

Hannes, sitting two rows in front, turned round and looked at him with an expression that combined deep sadness with anger.

When the lecture was over Hannes beat a hasty retreat, so he ran after him, grabbed him and asked quite brashly if everything was all right.

'All right?' Hannes repeated. 'Do you think what happened in there just now was all right? Did you see that poor bloke?'

'Just now,' he said, 'no, I . . . but, of course . . . we need—'

'Leave me alone,' Hannes interrupted. 'Just leave me alone.'

'Why didn't you come round for Christmas dinner? The others think you're rather full of yourself,' he said.

'That's bollocks,' Hannes said, quickening his pace as if wanting to shake him off.

'What's wrong?' he asked. 'Why are you acting like this? What's happened? What have we done to you?'

Hannes stopped in the corridor.

'Nothing. You haven't done anything to me,' he said. 'I just want to be left alone. I'll graduate in the spring and then it's over. That's it.

I'll go back to Iceland and it's over. This farce. Didn't you see it? Didn't you see how they treated that bloke? Is that what you want in Iceland?'

Then he strutted away.

'Tómas,' he heard a voice calling from behind him. He turned round and saw Ilona waving. He smiled at her. They were planning to meet up after the lecture. She had been to the dormitory to ask for him the day after the feast. From then on they met regularly. On this day they went for a long walk around the city and sat down outside Thomaskirche. He told her stories about the two Icelandic writer friends who had once stayed in Leipzig and had sat where they were sitting now. One died of tuberculosis. The other became the greatest writer his nation had ever produced.

'You're always so sad when you talk about those Icelanders of yours,' she said with a smile.

'I just think it's a brilliant story. Them walking the same streets as me in this city. Two Icelandic poets.'

By the church, he had noticed that she was uneasy and seemed on her guard. She glanced around as if looking for someone.

'Are you all right?' he asked.

'There's a man . . .'

She stopped.

'What man?'

'That man over there,' Ilona said. 'Don't look, don't turn your head, I saw him yesterday too. I just can't remember where.'

'Who is he? Do you know him?'

'I'd never seen him before, but now I've seen him twice in two days.'

'Is he from the university?'

'No, I don't think so. He's older.'

'Do you think he's watching you?'

'No, it's nothing. Come on.'

Instead of living on campus, Ilona rented a room in the city, and they went there. He tried to be sure whether the man from Thomaskirche was tracking them, but could not see him anywhere.

The room was in a little flat belonging to a widow who worked in a printshop. Ilona said she was very kindly and allowed her to waltz around the flat as she pleased. The woman had lost her husband and two sons in the war. He saw photographs of them on the walls. The two sons wore German army uniforms.

In Ilona's room were stacks of books and German and Hungarian newspapers and magazines, a dilapidated portable typewriter on the desk and a futon. While she went into the kitchen he browsed through her books and struck a few keys on the typewriter. On the wall above the futon were photographs of people he presumed were her relatives.

Ilona returned with two cups of tea and kicked the door to with her heel. She set the cups down carefully beside the typewriter. The tea was piping hot.

'It'll be just right by the time we've finished,' she said.

Then she walked over to him and gave him a long, deep kiss. Overcoming his surprise, he hugged her and kissed her passionately until they fell onto the futon and she began hitching up his sweater and undoing his belt. He was very inexperienced. He had had sex before, the first time after the school's farewell dance and once after that at the party paper's annual get-together, but those had been fairly clumsy efforts. He was not particularly skilled, but she seemed to be and he gladly let her take control.

She was right. When he slumped down beside her and she smothered a long groan the tea was just the right temperature.

Two days later in the *Auerbachkeller* they talked politics and argued for the first and only time. She began by describing how the Russian revolution had spawned a dictatorship, and that dictatorships were always dangerous no matter what form they took.

He did not want to argue with her although he knew perfectly well that she was wrong.

'It was thanks to Stalin's programme of industrialisation that the Nazis were defeated,' he said.

'He also made a pact with Hitler,' she said. 'Dictatorship fosters fear and servility. We're bearing the brunt of that in Hungary now. We're not a free nation. They've systematically established a communist state under Soviet control. No one asked us, the nation, what we wanted. We want to govern our own affairs but can't. Young people are thrown in prison. Some disappear. It's said that they're sent to the Soviet Union. You have an American army in your country. How would you feel if it ran everything by its military might?'

He shook his head.

'Look at the elections here,' she said. 'They call them free, but there's only one real party standing. What's free about that? If you think differently you're thrown in prison. What's that? Is that socialism? What else are people supposed to vote for in these free elections? Has everyone forgotten the uprising here the year before last that the Soviets crushed by shooting civilians on the streets, people who wanted change!'

'Ilona . . .'

'And interactive surveillance,' Ilona continued, seriously agitated. 'They say it's to help us. We're supposed to spy on our friends and family and inform on anti-socialist attitudes. If you know that one of your fellow students listens to western radio you're supposed to report him, and he's dragged from one lecture to the next to confess his crime. Children are encouraged to inform on their parents.'

'The party needs time to adapt,' he said.

When the novelty of being in Leipzig had worn off and reality confronted them, the Icelanders had discussed the situation. He had reached a firm conclusion on the surveillance society, about what was called 'interactive surveillance', whereby every citizen kept an eye on everyone else. Also on the dictatorship of the communist party, prohibition of freedom of speech and the press, and compulsory attendance at meetings and marches. He felt that instead of being secretive about the methods it employed, the party should admit that certain methods were needed during this phase of the transformation to a socialist state. They were justifiable if they were only temporary. In the course of time such methods would cease to be necessary. People would realise that socialism was the most appropriate system.

'People are scared,' Ilona said.

He shook his head and they started arguing. He had not heard much about events in Hungary and she was hurt when he doubted her word. He tried to employ arguments from the party meetings in Reykjavík, from the party leadership and youth movement and from the works of Marx and Engels, all to no avail. She just looked at him and said over and again: 'You mustn't close your eyes to this.'

'You let western imperialist propaganda turn you against the Soviet Union,' he said. 'They want to break the solidarity of the communist countries because they fear them.'

'That's wrong,' she said.

They fell silent. They had finished their glasses of beer. He was angry with her. He had never heard or seen anyone describe the Soviet Union and Eastern European countries in such terms, apart from the conservative press in Iceland. He knew about the strength of the western powers' propaganda machine, which worked well in Iceland, and he admitted that it was one reason for needing to restrict freedom of speech and press freedom too in Eastern Europe. This he could understand while socialist states were being constructed in the aftermath of the war. He did not regard it as repression.

'Let's not argue,' she said.

'No,' he said, putting some money on the table. 'Let's get going.'

On the way out, Ilona tugged lightly at his arm and he looked at her. She was trying to communicate something by her expression. Then she nodded furtively towards the bar.

'There he is,' she said.

He looked over and saw the man Ilona had said she thought was pursuing her. Dressed in an overcoat, he sipped his beer and acted as if they were not there. It was the same man from outside Thomaskirche.

'I'll have a word with him,' he said.

'No,' Ilona said. 'Don't. Let's go.'

A few days later he saw Hannes sitting at his table in the library, and sat down beside him. Hannes went on writing in pencil in his exercise book without looking up.

'Is she winding you up?' Hannes asked, still writing in the book.

'Who?'

'Ilona.'

'Do you know Ilona?'

'I know who she is,' Hannes said, and looked up. He was wearing a thick scarf and fingerless gloves.

'Do you know about us?' he asked.

'Everything gets around,' Hannes said. 'Ilona's from Hungary so she's not as green as us.'

'As green as us?'

'Forget it,' Hannes said, burying his head back in his exercise book.

He reached across the table and snatched the book away. Hannes looked up in surprise and tried to grab the book back, but it was out of his reach.

'What's going on?' he said. 'Why are you behaving like this?'

Hannes looked at the book that Tómas was holding, then stared at him.

'I don't want to get involved in what's going on here, I just want to go home and forget it,' he said. 'It's completely absurd. I hadn't been here as long as you when I got sick of it.'

'But you're still here.'

'It's a good university. And it took me a while to understand all the lies and lose my patience with them.'

'What is it that I can't see?' he asked, fearing the answer. 'What have you discovered? What am I missing?'

Hannes stared him in the eye, looked around the library and then at the book that Tómas was still holding, then back into his eyes.

'Just carry on,' he said. 'Stick to your convictions. Don't go off the tracks. Believe me, you won't gain anything by it. If you're comfortable with it, then it's all right. Don't delve any deeper. You can't imagine what you might find.'

Hannes held out his hand for his exercise book.

'Believe me,' he said. 'Forget it.'

'And Ilona?' he said.

'Forget her too,' Hannes said.

'What do you mean?'

'Nothing.'

'Why do you talk in riddles?'

'Leave me alone,' Hannes said. 'Just leave me alone.'

Three days later he was in a forest outside the city. He and Emil had enrolled in the Gesellschaft für Sport und Technik. It advertised itself as an all-round sports club that offered horse riding, rally driving and much more. Students were encouraged to take part in club activities, just like the volunteer work organised by the FDJ. It involved a week's harvesting in the autumn, one day a term or in the vacations clearing air-raid rubble, factory work, coal production or the like. Attendance was voluntary, but anyone who did not enrol was liable to be punished.

He was pondering this arrangement while standing in the forest with Emil and his other comrades, a week's camp in front of them which, as it turned out, largely involved military training.

Such was life in Leipzig. Very little was exactly what it seemed. Foreign students were under surveillance and took care not to say anything in public that might offend their hosts. They were taught socialist values at compulsory meetings and voluntary work was voluntary in name only.

As time went by they grew accustomed to all this and referred to it as 'the charade'. He believed the present situation would be temporary. Others were not so optimistic. He laughed to himself when he found out that the sports and technology club was merely a thinly veiled military unit. Emil was not so amused. He saw nothing funny in it and, unlike the others, never called it 'the charade'. Nothing about Leipzig struck him as funny. They were lying stretched out in their tent on their first night with their new companions. All evening Emil had talked with fervour about a socialist state in Iceland.

'All that injustice in such a tiny country where everyone could so easily be equal,' Emil said. 'I want to change that.'

'Would you want a socialist state like this one?' Tómas asked.

'Why not?'

'With all the trappings? The surveillance? The paranoia? Restrictions on freedom of expression? The charade?'

'Is she starting to get through to you?'

'Who?'

'Ilona.'

'What do you mean, get through to me?'

'Nothing.'

'Do you know Ilona?'

'Not at all,' Emil said.

'You've had girlfriends too. Hrafnhildur told me about one from the Red Cloister.'

'That's nothing,' Emil said.

'No, quite.'

'Maybe you'll tell me more about Ilona sometime,' Emil said.

'She's not as orthodox as we are. She sees problems with this system and wants to put them right. It's exactly the same situation here as in Hungary, except that young people there are doing something about it. Fighting the charade.'

'Fighting the charade!' Emil snarled. 'Fucking bollocks. Look at the way people live back in Iceland. Shivering in old American Nissen huts. Children are starving. People can hardly clothe themselves. And all the time the bloated elite gets richer and richer. Isn't that a charade? Who cares if you need to keep people under surveillance and restrict freedom of speech for a while? Eradicating injustice can mean making sacrifices. Who cares?'

They stopped talking. Silence had descended on the camp and it was pitch black.

'I'd do anything for the Icelandic revolution,' Emil said. 'Anything to eradicate injustice.'

He stood at the window watching the sunbeams and a distant rainbow and smiled to himself when he remembered the sports club. He could see Ilona laughing at the smoked-lamb feast and thought about the soft kiss that he could still feel on his lips, the star of love and the young man grieving, deep in his dark valley.

14

The Foreign Ministry's officials were more than willing to assist the police. Sigurdur Óli and Elínborg were having a meeting with the under-secretary, a smooth man Sigurdur Óli's age. They were acquaintances from their student years in America and reminisced about their time there. The under-secretary said the ministry had been surprised by the police request and he wanted to know why they required information about the former employees of foreign embassies in Reykjavík. They were as silent as the grave. Just a routine investigation, Elínborg said, and smiled.

'And we're not talking about all the embassies,' Sigurdur Óli said, smiling too. 'Just old Warsaw Pact countries.'

The under-secretary looked at them in turn.

'Are you talking about the ex-communist countries?' he asked, his curiosity clearly in no way satisfied. 'Why just them? What about them?'

'Just a routine investigation,' Elínborg repeated.

She was in an unusually good mood. The book launch had been a huge success and she was still over the moon about a review that had appeared in the largest-circulation newspaper praising her book, the recipes and photographs, which concluded by saying that hopefully this would not be the last to be heard from Elínborg, the detective-cum-gourmet.

'The communist states,' the under-secretary said thoughtfully. 'What was it that you found in the lake?'

'We don't know yet whether it's linked to any embassies,' Sigurdur Óli said.

'I suppose you should come with me,' the under-secretary said, standing up. 'Let's talk to the director general if he's in.'

The director general invited them into his office and listened to their request. He tried to wheedle out the reason for wanting this particular information, but they gave nothing away.

'Do we have a record of these employees?' the director general asked. He was a particularly tall man who wore a worried expression and had large rings under his weary eyes.

'As it happens we do,' the under-secretary said. 'It'll take a while to compile the list, but it's no problem.'

'Let's do that, then,' the director general said.

'Was there any espionage to speak of in Iceland during the Cold War?' Sigurdur Óli asked.

'Do you think it's a spy in the lake?' the under-secretary asked.

'We can't go into details of the investigation but it would appear that the skeleton has been in the lake since before 1970,' Elínborg said.

'It would be naive to assume that no spying took place,' the director general said. 'It was going on all around us, and Iceland was strategically vital then, much more so than it is today. There were several embassies here from Eastern European countries, plus of course the Nordic countries, the UK, US and West Germany.'

'When we say spying,' Sigurdur Óli said, 'what exactly is it that we're talking about?'

'I think it mainly involved keeping an eye on what the others were up to,' the director general said. 'In some cases there were attempts to establish contact. To get someone from the other side to work for you, that sort of thing. And of course there was the base, the details of operations there and military exercises. I don't think this had anything much to do with Icelanders themselves. But there are stories of attempts to get them to collaborate.'

The director general became lost in his thoughts.

'Are you looking for an Icelandic spy?' he asked.

'No,' Sigurdur Óli said, although he had no idea. 'Were there any? Icelandic spies? Isn't that a ridiculous notion?'

'Maybe you should talk to Ómar,' the chief of department said.

'Who's Ómar?' Elínborg said.

'He was director general here for most of the Cold War,' the chief of department said. 'Very old but clear as a bell,' he added, tapping his head with his index finger. 'Still comes to our annual dinner and he's the life and soul of the party. He knew all those chaps in the embassies. Maybe he could help you somehow.'

Sigurdur Óli wrote down the name.

'Actually it's a misunderstanding to talk about real embassies,' the director general said. 'Some of these countries only had delegations back then, trade delegations or trade offices or whatever you want to call them.'

The three detectives met in Erlendur's office at noon. Erlendur had spent the morning locating the farmer who had been waiting for the driver of the Falcon and had told the police that he failed to turn up for their meeting. His name was in the files. Erlendur discovered that some of the old farmland had been sold to property developers for the town of Mosfellsbaer. The man had stopped farming around 1980. He was now registered as living at an old people's home in Reykjavík.

Erlendur called in a forensics expert who brought his equipment to the garage, vacuumed up every speck of dust from the floor of the car and searched it for bloodstains.

'You're just messing about,' Sigurdur Óli said as he took a large bite from a baguette. He chewed fast and had clearly still not finished speaking. 'What are you trying to find?' he said. 'What are you going to do with the case? Are you planning to reopen the investigation? Do you think we have nothing better to do than fiddle about with old missing-persons cases? There are a million other things we could be doing.'

Erlendur eyed Sigurdur Óli.

'A young woman,' he said, 'stands outside the dairy shop where she works, waiting for her boyfriend. He doesn't come. They're going to get married. Nicely settled. The future's bright, as they say. Nothing to suggest that they won't live happily ever after.'

Sigurdur Óli and Elínborg said nothing.

'Nothing in their lives suggests anything is wrong,' Erlendur went on. 'Nothing suggests that he's depressed. He's going to fetch her after work. Then he doesn't arrive. He leaves work to meet someone but doesn't show up and disappears for ever. There are hints that he may have caught a coach out of the city. There are other signs that he committed suicide. That would be the most obvious explanation for his disappearance. Many Icelanders suffer serious depression, although most keep it well concealed. And there's always the possibility that someone did him in.'

'Isn't it just a suicide?' Elínborg asked.

'We have no official record of a man by the name of Leopold who went missing at that time,' Erlendur said. 'It seems he was lying to his girlfriend. Níels, who was in charge of the case, thought nothing of his disappearance. He even believed that the man lived somewhere else but had been having an affair in Reykjavík. If it wasn't just a straightforward suicide.'

'So he had a family out in the countryside and the woman in Reykjavík was his mistress?' Elínborg said. 'Isn't that reading a bit too much into his car being found outside the coach station?'

'You mean he might have got himself back home to the other end of the country and stopped shagging in Reykjavík?' Sigurdur Óli said.

'Shagging in Reykjavík!' Elínborg fumed. 'How can poor Bergthóra stand you?'

'That theory needn't be any more daft than any of the others,' Erlendur said.

'Can you get away with bigamy in Iceland?' Sigurdur Óli asked.

'No,' Elínborg said firmly. 'There are too few of us.'

'In America they make public announcements about guys like that,' Sigurdur Óli said. 'They have special programmes about that type of missing person, criminals and bigamists. Some murder their family, disappear, then start a new one.'

'Naturally, it's easier to hide in America,' Elínborg said.

'That may well be,' Erlendur said. 'But isn't it simple enough to lead a double life even for a while in a small community? He spent a lot of time in rural places, this man, weeks on end sometimes. He met a woman in Reykjavík and maybe he fell in love or maybe she was just a fling. When the relationship became serious he decided to break it off.'

'A sweet little urban love story,' Sigurdur Óli said.

'I wonder if the woman from the dairy shop had considered that possibility,' Erlendur said thoughtfully.

'Didn't they announce that this Leopold had gone missing?' Sigurdur Óli asked.

Erlendur had already checked and found a brief announcement in the newspapers describing the man's disappearance, along with a request for anyone who had seen him to contact the police. It gave a description of what he was wearing, his height and the colour of his hair.

'It led nowhere,' Erlendur said. 'He'd never been photographed. Níels said to me that they never told the woman they couldn't find any record of him.'

'They didn't tell her that?' Elínborg said.

'You know what Níels is like,' Erlendur said. 'If he can avoid trouble, he does. He had the feeling that the woman had been duped and I'm sure he felt she'd been through enough. I don't know. He's not particularly . . .'

Erlendur did not finish the sentence.

'Maybe he'd found a new girlfriend,' Elínborg suggested, 'and

107

didn't dare tell her. There's no greater coward than a cheating male.'

'Here we go,' Sigurdur Óli said.

'Didn't he travel around the country selling, what, agricultural machinery?' Elínborg said. 'Wasn't he always roaming the farms and villages? Perhaps we can't rule out that he met someone and started a new life. Didn't dare tell his girlfriend in Reykjavík.'

'And has been in hiding ever since?' Sigurdur Óli interjected.

'Of course things were completely different in 1970,' Erlendur said. 'It took a whole day to drive to Akureyri – the main road around Iceland hadn't been finished. Transportation was much worse and regional communities were much more isolated.'

'You mean there were all kinds of nowhere places that nobody ever visited,' Sigurdur Óli said.

'I once heard a story about a woman,' Elínborg said, 'who had this terrific boyfriend and everything was just fine until one day when he phoned her and said he was breaking it off, and after beating about the bush a bit he admitted he was going to marry someone else the next week. His girlfriend never heard any more of him. Like I say: there's no limit to what creeps men can be.'

'So why was Leopold in Reykjavík under false pretences?' Erlendur asked. 'If he didn't dare tell his girlfriend that he'd met someone outside the city and started a new life? Why this game of hide-and-seek?'

'What does anyone know about these characters?' Elínborg said in a resigned tone.

They all fell silent.

'What about the body in the lake?' Erlendur finally asked.

'I think we're looking for a foreigner,' Elínborg said. 'It's ridiculous to think it's an Icelander with Russian spy equipment tied around him. I just can't imagine it.'

'The Cold War,' Sigurdur Óli said. 'Weird times.'

'Yes, weird times,' Erlendur said.

'To me, the Cold War was always the fear of the end of the world,'

Elínborg said. 'I always remember thinking that. Somehow you could never escape it. Doomsday constantly looming over you. That's the only Cold War I knew.'

'One little fuse blows and ka-boom!' Sigurdur Óli said.

'That fear has to come out somewhere,' Erlendur said. 'In what we do. In what we are.'

'You mean in suicides, like the man who drove the Falcon?' Elínborg said.

'Unless he's alive and well and happily married in Sheepsville,' Sigurdur Óli said. He rolled up his baguette wrapping and threw it on the floor beside a nearby rubbish bin.

When Sigurdur Óli and Elínborg had left, Erlendur's phone rang. On the other end was a man he did not recognise.

'Is that Erlendur?' the voice said, deep and angry.

'Yes – who is this?' Erlendur said.

'I want to ask you to leave my wife alone,' the voice said.

'Your wife?'

The words caught Erlendur completely off guard. It did not occur to him that the voice was talking about Valgerdur.

'Understand?' the voice said. 'I know what you're up to and I want you to stop.'

'It's up to her what she does,' Erlendur said when it finally registered that this was Valgerdur's husband. He remembered what Valgerdur had said about his affair and how meeting Erlendur had initially been an attempt on her part to get even with him.

'You leave her alone,' the voice said, more menacingly.

'Get lost,' Erlendur said and slammed down the phone.

15

Ómar, the retired director general of the Foreign Ministry, was about eighty, completely bald, nimble and clearly pleased to have visitors; he had a broad face with a large mouth and chin. He complained bitterly to Erlendur and Elínborg about having been forced to retire when he turned seventy, still in fine fettle and with his capacity for work unimpaired. He lived in a large flat in Kringlumýri which he said he had swapped his house for after his wife died.

Several weeks had passed since the hydrologist from the Energy Authority had stumbled across the skeleton. It was now June and unusually warm and sunny. The city had unwound after the gloom of winter, people dressed more lightly and seemed somehow happier. Cafés had put out tables and chairs on the pavements in the continental fashion and people sat in the sunshine drinking beer. Sigurdur Óli was taking his summer holiday and barbecued whenever the chance arose. He invited Erlendur and Elínborg over. Erlendur was reluctant. He had not heard from Eva Lind but thought she was no longer in therapy. As far as he knew she had completed it. Sindri Snaer had not been in touch.

Ómar was very fond of talking, especially about himself, and Erlendur began at once to try to stem the flow of words.

'As I told you over the phone . . .' Erlendur began.

'Yes, yes, quite, I saw it all on the news, about the skeleton in Kleifarvatn. You think it's a murder and—'

'Yes,' Erlendur interrupted, 'but what hasn't been reported on the news and what no one knows and you must keep to yourself, is that a Russian listening device from the 1960s was tied to the skeleton. The equipment had clearly been tampered with to conceal its origin, but there's no doubt that it came from the Soviet Union.'

Ómar looked at them both and they saw how this aroused his interest. He seemed to turn more cautious and slip into his old ministry manner.

'How can I assist you with that?' he asked.

'The questions we're considering mainly involve whether there was spying on any scale in Iceland at the time and whether it is likely to be an Icelander or a foreign embassy official.'

'Have you looked up the missing persons from this time?' Ómar said.

'Yes,' Elínborg said. 'It's not possible to link any of them to Russian bugging devices.'

'I don't think any Icelanders went in for serious spying,' Ómar said after a long pause for thought, and they both sensed that he was choosing his words very carefully. 'We know that the Warsaw Pact and NATO countries both tried to get them to, and we know that there was espionage in one form or another in neighbouring countries.'

'The other Nordic countries, for instance?' Erlendur said.

'Yes,' Ómar said. 'But of course there's one obvious problem. If Icelanders were spying for either side we wouldn't know about it if it was successful. No Icelandic spy of any note has ever been uncovered.'

'Is there any other possible explanation for that Russian equipment lying there with the skeleton?' Elínborg asked.

'Of course,' Ómar said. 'It needn't have had anything to do with spying. But your inference is probably correct. It's a reasonable enough explanation that such an unusual discovery is somehow related to the ex-Warsaw Pact embassies.'

'Could such a spy have come from, let's say, the Foreign Ministry?' Erlendur asked.

'No official from the Foreign Ministry went missing, to my knowledge,' Ómar said.

'What I mean is, where would it have been most useful for the Russians, for instance, to plant spies?'

'Probably anywhere in government,' Ómar said. 'The civil service is small and the officials are all closely acquainted, so they keep very few secrets from each other. Dealings with the US defence force largely took place through us in the Foreign Ministry, so it would have been worth having someone there. But I can imagine it would have been enough for foreign spies or embassy officials to read the Icelandic newspapers – which they did, of course. It was all there. In a democracy like ours there's always a lot of public debate and things are difficult to conceal.'

'And then there were the cocktail parties,' Erlendur said.

'Yes, we mustn't forget them. The embassies were quite clever at compiling their guest lists. We're a small community, everyone knows everybody else and is related to everyone else, and they took advantage of that.'

'Did you never have the feeling that information was leaking out of the civil service?' Erlendur asked him.

'Never as far as I knew,' Ómar said. 'And if there was any espionage here on any scale, it would probably have come to light by now, after the Soviet system collapsed and the old-style secret services were disbanded in Eastern Europe. Former spies in those countries have been busily publishing their memoirs and there's never been any mention of Iceland. Most of their archives were opened and people could remove the files they found about themselves. The old communist countries gathered a huge amount of personal information and those records were destroyed before the Berlin Wall came down. Shredded.'

'Some spies in the West were uncovered after the Wall fell,' Elínborg said.

'Certainly,' Ómar said. 'I can imagine that it sent tremors through the whole espionage community.'

'But not all the archives were made public,' Erlendur said. 'It's not all waiting for anyone who cares to look.'

'No, of course not, there are still official secrets in those countries, just as there are here. But actually I'm no expert on espionage, neither abroad nor in Iceland. I know little more than you do, I expect. I've always found it a bit absurd to talk about spying in Iceland. Somehow it's so unreal for us.'

'Do you remember when those divers found some equipment in Kleifarvatn?' Erlendur asked. 'That was some distance from where we found the skeleton but the equipment provides an obvious link between the cases.'

'I remember when that was discovered,' Ómar said. 'Of course the Russians denied everything and so did the other Eastern bloc embassies. They claimed ignorance of the devices but the theory was, if I remember correctly, that they had simply been disposing of old listening devices and radio equipment. It wasn't worth the expense of sending them home in diplomatic bags and they couldn't dispose of them in the city dump so . . .'

'They tried to hide them in the lake.'

'I imagine it was something like that but, as I say, I'm no expert. The equipment proved that spying went on in Iceland. No question of that. But no one was surprised, either.'

They fell silent. Erlendur looked around the room. It was crowded with souvenirs from around the world after a long career in the ministry. Ómar and his wife had travelled widely and visited the four corners of the globe. There were Buddhas and photographs of Ómar at the Great Wall of China and at Cape Canaveral with a space shuttle in the background. Erlendur also saw photographs of him with a succession of cabinet ministers.

Ómar cleared his throat. He had, they felt, been mulling over whether to help them further or just send them away. After mentioning the Russian equipment in the lake, they sensed a hint of caution about him, and had the feeling that he was watching every word he said.

'It might not be, I don't know, such a bad idea for you to talk to Bob,' he eventually said, stumbling over his own words.

'Bob?' Elínborg repeated.

'Robert Christie. Bob. Head of security at the US embassy in the 1960s and 1970s, a fine man. We got to know each other well and we keep in touch. I always visit him when I go to America. He lives in Washington, retired ages ago like me, has a brilliant memory, a lively character.'

'How could he help us?' Erlendur asked.

'The embassies spied on each other,' Ómar said. 'He told me that much. I don't know on what scale and I don't think any Icelanders were involved, but the embassy staff, from NATO and the Warsaw Pact countries, had spies in their employ. He told me this after the end of the Cold War, and history corroborates that, of course. One of the embassies' tasks was to monitor the movements of diplomats from enemy countries. They knew exactly who came here and who left, what their jobs were, where they came from and where they went, their names, their personal circumstances and family situation. Most of the effort went into gathering that kind of information.'

'What was the point?' Elínborg asked.

'Some staff were known spies,' Ómar said. 'They came here, stayed briefly and left again. There was a hierarchy, so if someone of a certain rank arrived, you could be reasonably certain that something was going on. You recall the news reports in the old days about diplomats being expelled? That happened here too and it was a regular event in neighbouring countries. The Americans would expel some Russians for spying. The Russians would deny all the accusations and respond immediately by expelling a few Americans. It went on like that all over the world. Everyone knew the rules. Everyone knew everything about everyone else. They tracked each other's movements. They kept precise records about who joined the embassies and who left.'

Ómar paused.

'One of their priorities was recruitment,' he continued. 'Recruiting new spies.'

'You mean training diplomats to spy?' Erlendur said.

'No, recruiting spies from the enemy.' Ómar smiled. 'Getting staff from other embassies to spy for them. Of course, they tried to get people from all walks of life to spy and gather information, but embassy officials were particularly sought after.'

'And?' Erlendur said.

'Bob might be able to help you with that.'

'With what?' Elínborg asked.

'The diplomats,' Ómar said.

'I don't understand what . . .' Elínborg said.

'You mean he would know if something unusual or abnormal had gone on in the network?' Erlendur said.

'He certainly wouldn't tell you anything in detail. He never tells anyone that. Not me and certainly not you. I've asked him often enough but he just laughs and jokes about it. But he might tell you something innocent that aroused superficial interest and was difficult to explain, something odd.'

Erlendur and Elínborg looked at Ómar with slightly puzzled expressions.

'For instance, if someone came to Iceland but never left,' Ómar said. 'Bob could tell you that.'

'You're thinking about the Russian bug?' Erlendur asked.

Ómar nodded.

'What about you? The ministry must have kept tabs on who joined the embassies and what kind of people they were.'

'Yes, we did. We were always informed of organisational changes, new staff and the like. But we didn't have the opportunity or the capacity – or, as a rule, even the desire – to maintain surveillance of the embassies on the scale they did.'

'So that if, for example, a man joined the staff of one of the communist embassies in Reykjavík,' Erlendur said, 'and worked here without the American embassy ever noticing him leave the country, would your friend Bob know about that?'

'Yes,' Ómar said. 'I think Bob could help you with that kind of question.'

Marion Briem lugged the oxygen cylinder back into the sitting room after answering the door to Erlendur. Erlendur followed, wondering if this would be his fate when he grew old, withering away at home on his own, lost to the world and hauling an oxygen cylinder behind him. As far as he knew Marion had no siblings and few friends, yet the old fogey in the oxygen mask had never regretted not starting a family.

'What for?' Marion had said once. 'Families are just a nuisance.'

The subject of Erlendur's family had cropped up, which did not happen often because Erlendur disliked talking about himself. Marion had asked after his children, whether he kept in touch with them. This had been many years ago.

'Aren't there two of them?' Marion had asked.

Erlendur was sitting in his office writing a report on a fraud case when Marion suddenly appeared and started asking about his family. The scam involved two sisters who had defrauded their mother and left her penniless. This had prompted Marion to label families a nuisance.

'Yes, there are two of them,' Erlendur said. 'Can't we talk about this case here? I think that . . .'

'And when was the last time you saw them?' Marion asked.

'I don't think that's any of your b—'

'No, it's none of my business, but it's your business, isn't it? Isn't it your business? Having two children?'

The memory ebbed from Erlendur's mind when he sat down opposite Marion, who slumped into the tatty armchair. There was a reason that Erlendur did not like his ex-boss. He expected it was the same reason why the cancer patient had few visitors. Marion did not attract friends. On the contrary. Even Erlendur, who visited now and again, was no great friend.

Marion watched Erlendur and put on the oxygen mask. Some time went by without a word being said. At last Marion pulled down the mask. Erlendur cleared his throat.

'How are you feeling?'

'I'm dreadfully tired,' Marion said. 'Always dozing off. Maybe it's the oxygen.'

'Probably too healthy for you,' Erlendur said.

'Why do you keep hanging around here?' Marion said weakly.

'I don't know,' Erlendur said. 'How was the western?'

'You ought to watch it,' Marion said. 'It's a tale of obstinacy. How's it going with Kleifarvatn?'

'It's going,' Erlendur said.

'And the driver of the Falcon? Have you located him?'

Erlendur shook his head but said he had found the car. The current owner was a widow who did not know much about Ford Falcons and wanted to sell it. He told Marion how the man, Leopold, had been a mysterious figure. Not even his girlfriend knew much about him. There was no photograph of him and he was not in the official records. It was as if he had never existed, as if he had been a figment of the imagination of the woman who worked in the dairy shop.

'Why are you looking for him?' Marion asked.

'I don't know,' Erlendur said. 'I've been asked that quite a lot. I have no idea. Because of a woman who once worked in a dairy shop. Because a hubcap was missing from the car. Because a new car was left outside the coach station. There's something in all this that doesn't fit.'

Marion sank back deeper into the armchair, eyes closed now.

'We have the same name,' Marion said in an almost inaudible voice.

'What?' Erlendur said, leaning forwards. 'What was that you said?'

'Me and John Wayne,' Marion said. 'The same name.'

'What are you raving about?' Erlendur said.

'Don't you find it strange?'

Erlendur was about to reply when he saw that Marion had fallen asleep. He picked up the video case and read the title: *The Searchers*. A tale of obstinacy, he thought to himself. He looked at Marion, then back at the cover, which showed John Wayne on horseback, brandishing a rifle. He looked over at the television in an alcove in the sitting room, put the cassette in the player, switched on the TV, sat back in the sofa and watched *The Searchers* while Marion slept a gentle sleep.

16

Sigurdur Óli was on his way out of his office when the telephone rang. He hesitated. He would have liked to slam the door behind him, but instead he sighed and answered the call.

'Am I disturbing you?' the man on the phone said.

'You are actually,' Sigurdur Óli said. 'I'm on my way home. So . . .'

'Sorry,' the man said.

'Stop apologising for everything – and stop phoning me, too. I can't do anything for you.'

'I don't have many people I can talk to,' the man said.

'And I'm not one of them. I'm just someone who turned up at the scene of the accident. That's all. I'm not an agony aunt. Talk to the vicar.'

'Don't you think it's my fault?' the man asked. 'If I hadn't called . . .'

They had already gone back and forth through this conversation innumerable times. Neither believed in an inscrutable god who demanded sacrifices such as the man's wife and daughter. Neither was a fatalist. They did not believe that all things were predetermined and impossible to influence. Both believed in simple coincidences. Both were realists and accepted the fact that had the man not phoned his wife and delayed her, she would not have been at the crossing at the moment that the drunken driver in the Range Rover went through the red light. However, Sigurdur Óli did not blame the man for what happened, and thought his reasoning was absurd.

'The accident was not your fault,' Sigurdur Óli said. 'You know that, so stop tormenting yourself about it. You're not the one on the way to prison for manslaughter, it's the prat in the Range Rover.'

'That doesn't make any difference,' the man sighed.

'What does the psychiatrist say?'

'All she talks about is pills and side effects. If I take these drugs I'll get fat again. If I take those I'll lose my appetite. If I take others I'll vomit all the time.'

'Consider this scenario,' Sigurdur Óli said. 'A group of people have gone camping every year for twenty-five years. One member of the group originally suggested it. Then one year there's a fatal accident. One of the group is killed. Is the person who had the idea in the first place to blame? Of course that's rubbish! How far can you take speculations? Coincidences are coincidences. No one can control them.'

The man did not reply.

'Do you understand what I mean?' Sigurdur Óli said.

'I know what you mean but it doesn't help me.'

'Yes, well, I must be on my way,' Sigurdur Óli said.

'Thank you,' the man said, and rang off.

Erlendur was sitting in his chair at home, reading. He was lit up by lantern with a party of travellers beneath the slopes of Óshlíd at the beginning of the twentieth century. There were seven in the party, travelling past Steinófaera gully on their way from Ísafjördur. On one side was the sheer mountainside, bulging with snow, and on the other the icy sea. They were walking in a tight group to benefit from the single lantern they had with them. Some of them had been to see a play in Ísafjördur that evening, *Sheriff Leonard*. It was mid-winter and as they crossed Steinófaera, someone mentioned that there was a crack in the snow pack above them, as if a rock had rolled down. They talked about how it might be a sign that the snow farther up the mountainside was moving. They stopped, and at that very instant an avalanche crashed down, sweeping them out to sea. One person survived, badly crippled. All that was found of the others was a package that one of them had been carrying, and the lantern that had lit their way.

The telephone rang and Erlendur looked up from his book. He thought about letting it ring. But it might be Valgerdur, even Eva Lind, though he hardly expected that.

'Were you asleep?' Sigurdur Óli said when he eventually answered.

'What do you want?' Erlendur asked.

'Are you going to bring that woman with you to my barbecue tomorrow? Bergthóra wants to know. She needs to know how many guests to expect.'

'What woman are you talking about?' Erlendur said.

'The one you met at Christmas,' Sigurdur Óli said. 'Aren't you still seeing each other?'

'What business of yours is that?' Erlendur said. 'And what barbecue are you talking about? When did I say I wanted to come to your barbecue?'

There was a knock on the door. Sigurdur Óli had entered into a rigmarole about how Erlendur had said he would go to the barbecue that he and Bergthóra were giving, and how Elínborg was going to do the cooking, when Erlendur hung up on him and answered the door. Valgerdur gave a quick smile when he opened it and asked if she could come in. After a moment's hesitation he said that of course she could, and she walked into the living room and sat down on his battered sofa. He said he would make coffee, but she told him not to bother.

'I've left him,' she said.

He sat down on a chair facing her and remembered the telephone call from her husband telling him to leave her alone. She looked at him and saw the concern on his face.

'I should have left long ago,' she said. 'You were right. I should have settled all this way back.'

'Why now?' he asked.

'He told me that he called you,' Valgerdur said. 'I don't want you getting dragged into our business. I don't want him phoning you. This is between me and him. It's not about you.'

Erlendur smiled. Remembering the green Chartreuse in the cupboard, he stood and fetched the bottle and two glasses. He filled them and handed her one.

'I don't mean like that, but you know what I mean,' she said, and they sipped their liqueurs. 'All we have done is talk together. Which is more than he can claim.'

'But you didn't want to leave him until now,' Erlendur said.

'It's difficult after all these years. After all that time. Our boys and . . . it's just very difficult.'

Erlendur said nothing.

'I saw this evening how dead everything is between us,' Valgerdur continued. 'And I suddenly realised that I *want* it to be dead. I talked to the boys. They have to know exactly what's going on, why I'm leaving him. I'm meeting them tomorrow. I've been trying to spare them too. They adore him.'

'I slammed the phone down on him,' Erlendur said.

'I know, he told me. Suddenly I saw through it all. He no longer has any control over what I do or what I want. None. I don't know who he thinks he is.'

Valgerdur had been reluctant to reveal much about her husband, except that he had been cheating on her for two years with a nurse at the hospital and had had other affairs before. He was a doctor at the National Hospital, where she also worked, and Erlendur had sometimes wondered, when he was thinking about Valgerdur, what it must have been like for her to work at a place where everyone but her knew for a fact that her husband was chasing other women.

'What about work?' he asked.

'I'll get by,' she said.

'Do you want to sleep here tonight?'

'No,' Valgerdur said, 'I've spoken to my sister and I'll stay with her for the time being. She's been very supportive.'

'When you say it's not about me . . . ?'

'I'm not leaving him for your sake – it's for my own good,' Valgerdur said. 'I don't want him controlling my every move any more. And you and my sister are right, I should have left him ages ago. As soon as I found out about that affair.'

She paused and looked at Erlendur.

'He claimed just now that I'd driven him to it,' she said. 'Because I wasn't . . . wasn't . . . didn't find sex exciting enough.'

'They all say that,' Erlendur said. 'It's the first thing they say. You should ignore it.'

'He was quick to blame me,' Valgerdur said.

'What else can he say? He's trying to justify it to himself.'

They fell silent and finished their liqueurs.

'You're—' she said, but stopped in mid-sentence. 'I don't know what you are,' she said finally. 'Or who you are. I don't have the vaguest idea.'

'Nor do I,' Erlendur said.

Valgerdur smiled.

'Would you like to come to a barbecue with me tomorrow?' Erlendur suddenly asked. 'My friends are meeting up. Elínborg has just published a cookery book, maybe you've heard about it. She'll do the barbecue. She cooks very well,' Erlendur added, looking at his desk on which sat the wrapper from a packet of microwaveable meatballs.

'I don't want to rush into anything,' she said.

'Neither do I,' Erlendur said.

Plates clattered in the canteen at the old people's home as Erlendur walked down the corridor towards the old farmer's room. The staff were tidying up after breakfast and cleaning the rooms. Most of the doors were open and the sun shone in through the windows. But the door to the farmer's room was shut, so Erlendur knocked.

'Leave me alone,' he heard a strong, hoarse voice say from inside. 'Bloody disturbances all the time!'

Erlendur turned the handle, the door opened and he stepped inside. He knew precious little about the occupant. Only that his name was Haraldur and that he had moved off his land twenty years ago. When he gave up farming, before moving to the old people's home, he had lived in a block of flats in the Hlídar quarter of Reykjavík. Erlendur gleaned some information about him from one member of staff, who told him that Haraldur was a crotchety old troublemaker. He had recently hit another resident with a walking stick and was rude to the staff. Most could not stand him.

'Who are you?' Haraldur asked when he saw Erlendur standing in the doorway. He was eighty-four years old, white-haired and with big hands turned stiff by physical labour. He sat on the edge of his bed in his woollen socks, his back bent and his head sunk deep between his shoulder blades. A scraggy beard covered half his face. The room smelled and Erlendur wondered whether Haraldur took snuff.

He introduced himself, saying that he was from the police. This seemed to fire Haraldur's interest; he straightened up and looked Erlendur in the eye.

'What do the police want from me?' he asked. 'Is it because I took a swing at Thórdur at dinnertime?'

'Why did you hit Thórdur?' Erlendur asked. He was curious.

'Thórdur's a wanker,' Haraldur said. 'I don't have to tell you about that. Get out and shut the door behind you. They're always staring in at you all day long. Poking their noses into other people's business.'

'I wasn't going to talk to you about Thórdur,' Erlendur said as he entered the room and closed the door behind him.

'Listen,' Haraldur said, 'I don't care for you strolling in here. What's this supposed to mean? Get out. Just get out and leave me in peace!'

The old man straightened up, raised his head as far as he could and glared at Erlendur, who calmly sat down opposite him on the bed. It was still made and Erlendur imagined there was no point in offering anyone a room to share with grumpy old Haraldur. There were few personal articles in the room. On the bedside table were two dog-eared books of Einar Benediktsson's poetry that had clearly been read over and again.

'Aren't you comfortable here?' Erlendur asked.

'Me? What bloody business of yours is that? What do you want from me? Who are you? Why don't you get out of here like I've been telling you?'

'You were connected with an old case of a missing person,' Erlendur said, and started to describe the man who sold farm machinery and diggers and owned a black Ford Falcon. Haraldur listened in silence to his account, without interrupting. Erlendur could not be sure whether Haraldur remembered what he was talking about. He mentioned how the police had asked Haraldur whether the man had been at the farm and he had flatly denied having met him.

'Do you remember this?' Erlendur asked.

Haraldur did not answer. Erlendur repeated the question.

'Uhhh,' Haraldur groaned. 'He never came, the bugger. It was more than thirty years ago. I don't remember any of it any more.'

'But you remember that he didn't come?'

'Yes, what the hell, didn't I just say that? Come on, piss off out! I don't like having people in my room.'

'Did you keep sheep?' Erlendur asked.

'Sheep? When I was a farmer? Yes, I had a few sheep and horses, and about ten cows. Happy now?'

'You got a good price for the land,' Erlendur went on. 'So close to the city.'

'Are you from the tax office?' Haraldur snarled. He looked down at the floor. Bent by manual labour and old age, it was an effort to lift his head.

'No, I'm from the police,' Erlendur said.

'They're getting lots more for it now,' Haraldur said. 'Those gangsters. Now the city extends right up to it, or as good as. They were bloody sharks who got the land off me. Bloody sharks. Get out of here!' he added angrily, raising his voice. 'You ought to talk to those bloody sharks!'

'What sharks?' Erlendur asked.

'Those sharks,' Haraldur said. 'They took my land for shit and sixpence.'

'What were you going to buy from him? The salesman who drove that black car?'

'Buy from him? A tractor. I needed a good tractor. I went to Reykjavík to check out their tractors and liked the look of them. I met that bloke there. He took my phone number and was always pestering me. They're all the same, salesmen. Once they can tell you're interested they never leave you alone. I told him I'd hear him out if he could be bothered to come out to see me. He said he had a few brochures. So I waited for him like an idiot but he never arrived. The next thing I knew, some clown like you phoned me to ask if I'd seen him. I told him what I'm telling you now. And that's all I know, so you can bugger off.'

'He had a brand new Ford Falcon,' Erlendur said. 'The man who was going to sell you the tractor.'

'I don't know what you're talking about.'

'The funny thing is, that car's still around and it's even up for sale if they can find a buyer,' Erlendur said. 'When the car was originally found, one of the hubcaps was missing. Do you know what could have happened to that hubcap?'

'What are you going on about?' Haraldur said, his head darting up to glare at Erlendur. 'I don't know a thing about him. And what are you going on about that car for? Where do I come into the picture?'

'I'm hoping that it can help us,' Erlendur said. 'Cars like that can preserve evidence almost for ever. For instance, if this man did come to your farm and walked around the yard and inside the farmhouse, he might have carried away something on his shoes which is now in the car. After all those years. It might be something trivial. A grain of sand is enough if it's the same type as in your farm. You understand what I'm saying?'

The old man looked silently at the floor.

'Is the farm still there?' Erlendur asked.

'Shut up,' Haraldur said.

Erlendur inspected the room. He knew virtually nothing about the man sitting on the edge of the bed in front of him, except that he was nasty and foul-mouthed and that his room smelled. He read Einar Benediktsson but Erlendur thought to himself that, unlike the poet, he had probably never in his lifetime 'turned darkness into the light of day'.

'Did you live alone out there on the farm?'

'Get out, I said!'

'Did you have a housekeeper?'

'We were two brothers. Jói's dead. Now leave me alone.'

'Jói?' Erlendur did not recall any mention of anyone other than Haraldur in the police reports. 'Who was he?' he asked.

'My brother,' Haraldur said. 'He died twenty years ago. Now get out. For God's sake, bugger off out of here and leave me alone!'

17

He opened the box of letters and removed them one by one, read some of the envelopes and put them to one side, opened others and slowly read them through. He had not looked at the letters for years. They had come from Iceland, from his parents and sister and comrades in the party's youth movement who wanted to know about life in Leipzig. He remembered the letters he wrote in reply describing the city, the reconstruction and the morale there, and how it had all been in positive terms. He wrote about the collective spirit of the proletariat and socialist solidarity, all that dead, cliché-ridden rhetoric. He wrote nothing about the doubts that were beginning to stir within him. He never wrote about Hannes.

He delved deeper into the pile. There was a letter from Rut and beneath it the message from Hannes.

And there, at the bottom of the pile, were the letters from Ilona's parents.

He hardly thought about anything other than Ilona during the first weeks and months that they were together. Having little money, he lived frugally and tried to please her with small presents. One day, when his birthday was approaching, he received a package from Iceland, including a pocket edition of Jónas Hallgrímsson's poems. He gave the volume to her and told her that it was by the poet who had written the most beautiful words in the Icelandic language. She said she looked forward to learning Icelandic from him so that she could read them. She said she had nothing to give him in return. He smiled and shook his head. He had not told her it was his birthday.

'I just like having you,' he said.

'O-ho,' she said.

'What?'

'Naughty boy!'

She put down the book, pushed him back onto the bed he was sitting on, and straddled him. She gave him a long, deep kiss. It turned out to be the most pleasurable birthday of his life.

That winter he became closer friends with Emil and they spent a lot of time together. He liked Emil, who became more hardline the longer they stayed in Leipzig and the better he knew the system. Emil was unruffled by the other Icelanders' criticism of personal spying and surveillance, the shortage of consumer goods, compulsory attendance at FDJ meetings and the like. Emil scoffed at all that. Given the ultimate goal, such short-term considerations were trivial. He and Emil got on well together and backed each other up.

'But why don't they produce more goods that people need?' Karl asked once when they were sitting in the new cafeteria discussing Ulbricht's government. 'People have such an obvious point of comparison in West Germany which is swamped with consumer goods and everything anyone could desire. Why should East Germany put such a huge emphasis on industrial development when there are food shortages? The only thing they have plenty of is lignite, which isn't even proper coal.'

'The planned economy will deliver in the end,' Emil said. 'Reconstruction has hardly started and they don't have the same stream of dollars from the US. It all takes time. What matters is that the Socialist Unity Party is on the right track.'

Tómas and Ilona were not the only couple in their circle in Leipzig. Karl and Hrafnhildur both met Germans who fitted in well with their group. Karl was increasingly seen with a petite, brown-eyed student from Leipzig; her name was Ulrika. Her ill-tempered mother disapproved of the match and Karl's descriptions of their awkward dealings sent everyone into hysterics. He said they had discussed living together, even getting married. They were compatible, both cheerful and easygoing types, and she talked about going to Iceland, even living there. Hrafnhildur started going out with a shy and rather nondescript chemistry student from a little village outside Leipzig, who sometimes supplied moonshine for their parties.

It was February. He saw Ilona every day. They no longer discussed politics, but everything else was smooth and they had plenty to talk about. He told her about the land of boiled sheep heads and she told him about her family. She had two elder brothers, which did not make things easier for her. Both her parents were doctors. She was studying literature and German. One of her favourite poets was Friedrich Hölderlin. She read a lot and asked him about Icelandic literature. Books were a common interest.

Lothar spent more and more time with the Icelanders. He amused them with his mechanical, formal Icelandic and incessant questions about everything to do with Iceland. Tómas got along well with Lothar. They were both hardline communists and could discuss politics without arguing. Lothar practised his Icelandic on him and Tómas spoke German back. Lothar was from Berlin, which he said was a wonderful place. He had lost his father in the war but his mother still lived there. Lothar urged him to visit the city with him sometime – it was not far by train. In other respects the German was not very forthcoming about himself, which Tómas put down to the hardship that he had suffered as a boy during the war. He asked all the more about Iceland and seemed to have an unquenchable interest in the country. Wanted to know about the university there, political conflict, political and business leaders, how people lived, the US base at Keflavík. Tómas explained that Iceland had profited enormously from the war, Reykjavík had mushroomed and the country had been transformed almost overnight from a poor farming community to a modern bourgeois society.

Sometimes he spoke to Hannes at the university. Normally they ran into each other at the library or in the cafeteria in the main building. They became good friends in spite of everything, in spite of Hannes's pessimism. He tried to talk Hannes round, but in vain. Hannes had lost interest. His only thoughts were about finishing his studies and going home.

One day he sat down beside Hannes in the cafeteria. It was snowing outside. He had been sent a warm overcoat from Iceland at Christmas. He had mentioned in one of his letters how cold it was in Leipzig. Hannes made a point of asking about the overcoat and he could detect a hint of jealousy in his voice.

What he did not know was that this would be the last time they would speak together in Leipzig.

'How's Ilona?' Hannes asked.

'How do you know Ilona?' he replied.

'I don't know her,' Hannes said, looking around the cafeteria as if to make sure that no one could hear them. 'I just know that she's from Hungary. And she's your girlfriend. Isn't she? Aren't you going out?'

He sipped his turgid coffee without replying. There was a strange tone to Hannes's voice. Tougher and more obstinate than usual.

'Does she ever talk to you about what's going on in Hungary?' Hannes asked.

'Sometimes. We try not to talk much about . . .'

'You know what's going on there?' Hannes interrupted. 'The Soviets will use military force. I'm surprised they haven't already. They can't avoid it. If they allow what's happening in Hungary to escalate, the rest of Eastern Europe will follow and there'll be a full-scale revolt against Soviet authority. Doesn't she ever talk about that?'

'We talk about Hungary,' he said. 'We just don't agree on it.'

'No, of course, you know more about what's going on there than she, the Hungarian, does.'

131

'I'm not saying that.'

'So what *are* you saying?' Hannes said. 'Have you ever wondered seriously about that? When the red glow has faded from your eyes?'

'What happened to you, Hannes? Why are you so angry? What happened after you came here? You were the Great Hope back in Iceland.'

'The Great Hope,' Hannes snorted. 'I'm probably not that any more,' he said.

They fell silent.

'I just saw through all this crap,' Hannes said after a while in a low voice. 'The whole fucking lie. We've been spoon-fed the workers' paradise, equality and brotherhood until we sing the Internationale like the needle's stuck. One big hallelujah chorus without a word of criticism. Back home we go to campaign meetings. Here there's nothing but eulogies. Where do you see debate? Long live the party and nothing else! Have you spoken to people who live here? Do you know what they're thinking? Have you talked to a single ordinary person in this city? Did they want Walter Ulbricht and the Communist Party? Do they want a single party and a centralised economy? Did they want to ban freedom of speech and freedom of the press and real political parties? Did they want to be shot on the streets in the 1953 uprising? Back in Iceland, at least we can argue with our opponents and write articles in the newspapers. That's banned here. There's just one line, finito. Then, when people are herded up to vote for the only party that's allowed to operate in the country, they call it elections! The locals think it's a total farce. They know this is no democracy!'

Hannes paused. He was seething.

'People don't dare say what they think because everything here is under surveillance. The whole fucking society. Everything you say and do can rebound on you and you're called in, arrested, expelled. Talk to people. The phones are bugged. They spy on the citizens!'

They sat in silence.

He knew that Hannes and Ilona had a point. And he thought it was better for the party to come clean and admit that free elections and free discussion were for the time being impossible. They would come later, when the goal had been achieved: a socialist economy. They had sometimes made fun of the Germans for agreeing to every proposal at meetings and then saying the exact opposite in private. People were afraid to be straightforward, hardly dared to advance an independent view for fear that it would be interpreted as anti-socialist and they would be punished.

'They're dangerous men, Tómas,' Hannes said after a long silence. 'They're not playing games.'

'Why are you always talking about freedom of opinion?' he said angrily. 'You and Ilona. Look at the witch hunt against communists in America. You can see how they drive people out of the country, out of their jobs. And what about the surveillance society there? Did you read about the cowards who informed on their comrades to the House Un-American Activities Committee? The communist party's outlawed there. Only one opinion's permitted there, too – the opinion of the capitalist cartels, the imperialists, the warmongers. They reject everything else. Everything.'

He stood up.

'You're here at the invitation of the proletariat of this country,' he said angrily. 'It pays for your education and you ought to be ashamed of yourself for talking like that. Ashamed of yourself! And you ought to fuck off back home!'

He stormed out of the cafeteria.

'Tómas,' Hannes called after him, but he did not answer.

He strode down the corridor away from the cafeteria and bumped into Lothar, who asked what the hurry was. Glancing back, he said it was nothing. They left the building together. Lothar offered to buy him a beer and he accepted. When they sat down in *Baum* next to Thomaskirche he told Lothar about the argument and how Hannes, for some reason, had turned completely against socialism and denigrated it. He told Lothar that he could not tolerate Hannes's hypocrisy in arguing against the socialist system but reaping its benefits by studying there.

'I don't understand it,' he said to Lothar. 'I don't understand how he can abuse his position like that. I could never do that,' he said. 'Never.'

That evening he met Ilona and told her about the argument. He mentioned that Hannes sometimes gave the impression that he knew her, but she shook her head. She had never heard his name and never spoken to him.

'Do you agree with him?' he asked hesitantly.

'Yes,' she said after a long pause. 'I agree with him. And not just me. There are many, many others. People of my age in Budapest. Young people here in Leipzig.'

'Why don't they speak out?'

'We're doing that in Budapest,' she said. 'But we face huge opposition. It's awesome. And there's fear. Fear everywhere about what could happen.'

'The army?'

'Hungary is one of the Soviet Union's trophies from the war. They won't give it up without a fight. If we manage to break free from them, you couldn't say what would happen in the rest of Eastern Europe. That's the big question. The chain reaction.'

Two days later, without warning, Hannes was expelled from the university and ordered to leave the country.

He heard that a police guard had been stationed outside Hannes's digs and that he had been escorted to the airport by two members of the security police. As he understood it, none of the courses that Hannes had taken would be recognised by any other university. It was as if Hannes had never been a student. He had been erased.

He could not believe his ears when Emil burst in and related the news. Emil did not know much. He had met Karl and Hrafnhildur, who told him about the police guard and how everyone was saying that Hannes had been taken to the airport. Emil had to repeat it all before it sank in. Their compatriot was being treated as if he had committed some appalling offence. Like a common criminal. That evening the dormitory buzzed with the news. No one knew for sure what had happened.

The following day, three days after their argument in the cafeteria, he received a message from Hannes. Hannes's room-mate delivered it. It was in a sealed envelope with only his name on the front. Tómas. He opened the envelope and sat on his bed with the note. It did not take long to read.

You asked me what had happened in Leipzig. What had happened to me. It's simple. They kept asking me to spy on my friends, to tell them what they said about socialism, about East Germany, about Ulbricht, what radio stations you listened to. Not just you, but everyone I knew. I refused to be their informer. I said I would not spy on my friends. They thought I could be persuaded. Otherwise, they said, I would be expelled from the university. I refused and they let me be. Until now.

Why couldn't you just leave me alone?

Hannes

He read the message over and again and still could not believe what it said. A shiver ran down his spine and his head spun.

Why couldn't you just leave me alone?

Hannes blamed him for his expulsion. Hannes believed that he had gone to the university authorities and reported his opinions, his opposition to the system. If he had left him alone, it would never have happened. He stared at the letter. It was a misunderstanding. What did Hannes mean? He had not spoken to the university authorities, only to Ilona and Lothar, and in the evening he had mentioned his surprise at Hannes's views to Emil, Karl and Hrafnhildur in the kitchen. That was nothing new. They agreed with him. They felt that the way Hannes had changed was at best excessive, at worst despicable.

It could only have been a coincidence that Hannes was expelled after their argument, and a misunderstanding on Hannes's part to link it to their meeting. Surely he could not think that it was Tómas's fault he was not allowed to finish his course. He hadn't done anything. He hadn't told anyone except his friends. Wasn't the man being paranoid? Could he seriously believe this?

Emil was in the room with him, and he showed him the note. Emil snorted. He thoroughly disliked Hannes and everything he stood for, and did not conceal it.

'He's nuts,' Emil said. 'Take no notice of it.'

'But why does he say that?'

'Tómas,' Emil said. 'Forget it. He's trying to blame his own mistakes on someone else. He should have been out of here long ago.'

Tómas leapt to his feet, grabbed his coat, put it on rushing down the corridor, ran all the way to Ilona's digs and banged on the door. Her landlady answered and showed him in to Ilona. She was putting on a cap and already had her jacket and shoes on. She was going out. Clearly surprised to see him, she realised that he was very agitated.

'What's wrong?' she asked, moving towards him.

He closed the door.

'Hannes thinks I had something to do with him getting expelled and deported. Like I gave something away!'

'What are you saying?'

'He blames me for his expulsion!'

'Who did you talk to?' Ilona asked. 'After you met Hannes?'

'Just you and the others. Ilona, what did you mean the other day when you were talking about young people in Leipzig? The ones who agreed with Hannes? Who are they? How do you know them?'

'You didn't talk to anyone else? Are you sure?'

'No, only Lothar. What do you know about young people in Leipzig, Ilona?'

'Did you tell Lothar what Hannes had said?'

'Yes. What do you mean? He knows all about Hannes.'

Ilona stared at him thoughtfully.

'Please tell me what's going on,' he asked her.

'We don't know exactly who Lothar is,' Ilona said. 'Do you think anyone followed you here?'

'Followed me? What do you mean? Who doesn't know who Lothar is?'

Ilona stared at him with a more serious expression than he had ever seen before, a look almost of terror. He had no idea what was going on. All he knew was that his conscience was gnawing him about Hannes, who thought he was to blame for all that had happened. But he had done nothing. Nothing at all.

'You know the system. It's dangerous to say too much.'

'Too much! I'm not a child, I know about the surveillance.'

'Yes. Of course.'

'I didn't say anything, except to my friends. That's not illegal. They're my friends. What's going on, Ilona?'

'Are you sure no one followed you?'

'No one followed me,' he said. 'What do you mean? Why should anyone follow me? What are you talking about?' Then he thought about it: 'I don't know whether anyone followed me. I wasn't watching for that. Why should I be followed? Who would be following me?'

'I don't know,' Ilona said. 'Come on, let's go out the back door.'

'Go where?' he said.

'Come with me,' she said.

Ilona took him by the hand and led him out through the little kitchen where the old woman was in a chair, knitting. She looked up and smiled, and they smiled back and said goodbye. They came out in a dark backyard, climbed over a fence and ended up in a narrow alleyway. He had no idea what was happening. Why was he chasing behind Ilona on a dark evening, looking over his shoulder to check whether anyone was following them?

She took detours, stopping every so often and standing still to listen for footsteps. Then she continued on, with him in pursuit. After a long trek they emerged in a new residential quarter where blocks of flats were being built on an otherwise empty site a fair distance from the city centre. Some of the buildings had no windows or doors but people had moved in to others. They went inside one of the partially occupied blocks and ran down to the basement. Ilona banged on a door. Voices could be heard on the other side: they fell silent suddenly at the knock. The door opened. About ten people were in a small flat, looking out at them in the doorway. They scrutinised him. Ilona walked in, greeted them and introduced him.

'He's a friend of Hannes,' she said, and they looked at him and nodded.

A friend of Hannes, he thought in astonishment. How did they know Hannes? He was caught completely off his guard. A girl stepped forward, held out her hand and welcomed him.

'Do you know what happened?' she asked. 'Do you know why he was expelled?'

He shook his head.

'I have no idea,' he said. He surveyed the group. 'Who are you?' he asked. 'How do you all know Hannes?'

'Did anyone follow you?' the girl asked Ilona.

'No,' Ilona said. 'Tómas doesn't know what's going on and I wanted him to hear it from you.'

'We knew they were watching Hannes,' the girl said. 'After he refused to work for them. They were just waiting for a chance. Waiting for the opportunity to expel him from the university.'

'What did they want him to do?'

'They call it serving the communist party and the proletariat.'

A man came over to him.

'He was always so careful,' the man said. 'He made sure never to say anything that could get him into trouble.'

'Tell him about Lothar,' Ilona said. The tension had eased slightly.

138

Some of the group sat back down. 'Lothar is Tómas's *Betreuer*.'

'Nobody followed you?' someone else from the group asked, casting an anxious look at Ilona.

'No one,' she said. 'I told you. I made sure of that.'

'What about Lothar?' he asked, incredulous about all that he heard and saw. He looked around the little flat, at the people staring at him in fear and curiosity. He realised that he was at a cell meeting, but in reverse. This was not like when the young socialists met back in Iceland. It was not a meeting to campaign for socialism but a clandestine gathering of dissidents. These people met in secret for fear of being punished for anti-socialist behaviour.

They told him about Lothar. He had not been born in Berlin as he claimed. He was from Bonn and had been educated in Moscow, where Icelandic was one of the subjects he studied. His mission was to recruit young people at the university into the communist party. He made a particular effort with foreign students in places such as Leipzig who could conceivably be of use when they went home. It was Lothar who had tried to get Hannes to work for him. It was without doubt Lothar who had eventually played a part in his expulsion.

'Why didn't you tell me that you knew Hannes?' he asked Ilona, perplexed.

'We don't talk about this,' Ilona said. 'Not to anyone. Hannes never mentioned it to you either, did he? Otherwise you would have leaked it all to Lothar.'

'To Lothar?' he said.

'You told him about Hannes,' Ilona said.

'I didn't know . . .'

'We have to guard what we say all the time. You certainly didn't help Hannes by talking to Lothar.'

'I didn't know about Lothar, Ilona.'

'It needn't be Lothar,' Ilona said. 'It could be anyone. You can never tell. You never know who it is. That's how the system works. That's how *they* work.'

He stared at Ilona and knew she was right. Lothar had used him, taken advantage of his anger. What Hannes had written in his message was right. He had said something to someone that should have remained unspoken. No one had warned him. No one had talked about secrets. But he also knew in his heart that no one should have needed to tell him. He felt awful. Consumed by guilt. He was well aware how the system worked. He knew all about interactive surveillance. He had let his rage lead him astray. His naivety had helped them take Hannes.

'Hannes had stopped hanging around with the rest of us Icelanders,' he said.

'Yes,' Ilona said.

'Because he . . .' He did not finish the sentence.

Ilona nodded.

'What's going on?' he asked. 'What's really going on here? Ilona?'

She glanced around the group as if waiting for a response. The man who had spoken earlier nodded to her and she revealed that they had contacted her on their own initiative. One member of the group – Ilona pointed to the girl who had greeted him with a handshake – was studying German with her at the university and wanted to know details of what was happening in Hungary, dissent against the communist party there and fear of the Soviet Union. After cautious overtures to probe her views, and once she was convinced that Ilona was in favour of the uprising in Hungary, she asked her to come and meet her companions. The group held clandestine meetings. Surveillance was being stepped up considerably and people were urged increasingly to notify the security police if they became aware of anti-socialist behaviour or attitudes. This was connected with the 1953 uprising and was to some extent a reaction to the situation in Hungary. Ilona had met Hannes at her first meeting with the young activists in Leipzig. They wanted to know about Hungary and whether similar resistance could be built up in East Germany.

'Why was Hannes in this group?' he asked. 'How does he come into all this?'

'Hannes was completely brainwashed, just like you,' Ilona said. 'You must have strong leadership in Iceland.' She looked towards the man who had spoken before. 'Martin and Hannes are friends from engineering,' she said. 'It took Martin a long time to get Hannes to understand what we were saying. But we trusted him. We had no reason not to.'

'If you know all this about Lothar, why don't you do something?' he asked.

'We can't do anything except avoid him, which is difficult because he's trained to be friends with everyone,' a man said. 'What we can do if he gets too inquisitive is to lead him astray. People don't cotton on to him. He says what we want to hear and agrees with our views. But he's false. And he's dangerous.'

'Wait a minute,' he said, looking at Ilona. 'If you knew about Lothar, didn't Hannes know who he is?'

'Yes, Hannes knew,' Ilona said.

'Why didn't he say anything? Why didn't he warn me? Why didn't he say anything?'

Ilona went up to him.

'He didn't trust you,' she said. 'He didn't know where you stand.'

'He said he wanted to be left alone.'

'He did want to be left alone. He didn't want to spy on us or his fellow countrymen.'

'He called after me when I walked out on him. He was going to say something else but he . . . I was angry, I stormed out. And bumped straight into Lothar.'

He looked at Ilona.

'So that wasn't a coincidence?'

'I doubt it,' Ilona said. 'But it was sure to have happened sooner or later. They were keeping a close watch on Hannes.'

'Are there more people like Lothar at the university?' he asked.

'Yes,' Ilona said. 'But we don't know who they are. We only know about some of them.'

'Lothar is your *Betreuer*,' said a man sitting in a chair who had been listening to the proceedings without saying a word.

'Yes.'

'What's your point?' Ilona said to the man.

'Liaisons are supposed to watch the foreigners,' the man said, standing up. 'They're supposed to report everything about the foreigners. We know that Lothar is also meant to get them to collaborate.'

'Tell him what you want to say,' Ilona said and took a step closer to the man.

'How do we know we can trust this friend of yours?'

'I trust him,' Ilona said. 'That's enough.'

'How do you know Lothar is dangerous?' he asked. 'Who told you that?'

'That's our business,' the man said.

'He's right,' Tómas said, looking towards the man who had doubted his integrity. 'Why should you trust me?'

'We trust Ilona,' came the reply.

Ilona smiled awkwardly.

'Hannes said you'd come round eventually,' she said.

He looked at the faded sheet of paper and read the old message from Hannes. Soon it would be evening and the couple would walk past his window. He thought about that night in the basement flat in Leipzig and how it had changed his life. He thought about Ilona and about Hannes and Lothar. And he thought about the terrified people in the basement.

It was the children of those people who had turned Nikolaikirche into their fortress and had rushed out onto the streets when, decades later, the situation finally reached boiling point.

18

Valgerdur was not with Erlendur at Sigurdur Óli's barbecue, nor was her name mentioned. Elínborg barbecued delicious loins of lamb which she had marinated in a special spicy sauce with shredded lemon peel, but first they ate a shrimp dish that Bergthóra made which Elínborg praised highly. The dessert was a mousse by Elínborg; Erlendur did not catch what was in it but it tasted good. He had never intended to go to the barbecue, but eventually gave in after relentless badgering by Sigurdur Óli and Bergthóra. It was not as bad as Elínborg's book launch, however. Bergthóra was so pleased he had come that she allowed him to smoke in the living room. Sigurdur Óli's face fell a mile when she brought him an ashtray. Erlendur watched him with a smile and felt he had earned his reward.

They did not discuss work, apart from one occasion when Sigurdur Óli began wondering why the Russian equipment had been kaput before it went into the lake with the body. Erlendur had told them about the forensics results. The three of them were standing together on the patio. Elínborg was preparing the grill.

'Doesn't that tell us something?' she asked.

'I don't know,' Erlendur said. 'I don't know whether it matters whether it worked or not. I can't see the difference. A listening device is a listening device. Russians are Russians.'

'Yes, I guess so,' Sigurdur Óli said. 'Maybe it was damaged in a struggle. Fell to the floor and smashed.'

'Conceivably,' Erlendur said. He looked up at the sun. He did not really know what he was doing out there on the terrace. He had not been to Sigurdur Óli and Bergthóra's house before even though they had worked together for a long time. It did not surprise him to find everything neat and tidy there: designer furniture, objets d'art and smart flooring. Not a speck of dust to be seen. Nor any books.

Indoors, Erlendur perked up when he learned that Teddi, Elínborg's husband, knew about Ford Falcons. Teddi was a chubby car mechanic who was in love with Elínborg's cooking, like most people who knew her. His father had once owned a Falcon and he was a great admirer of the model. Teddi told Erlendur that it had been very smooth to drive, with a bench for the front seat, automatic gearbox and a big ivory steering wheel. It was a smaller family car than other American models from the 1960s, which tended to be huge.

'It didn't do too well on the old Icelandic roads,' Teddi said as he scrounged a cigarette from Erlendur. 'Maybe it wasn't built strongly enough for Icelandic conditions. We had a lot of bother when the axle broke once out in the countryside. Dad had to get a lorry to transport it back to town. They weren't particularly powerful cars, but good for small families.'

'Were the hubcaps special in any way?' Erlendur asked, lighting Teddi's cigarette.

'The hubcaps on American cars were always quite flashy, and they were on the Falcon too. But they weren't really distinctive. Mind you, the Chevrolet . . .'

For small families, Erlendur thought to himself, and Teddi's voice faded out. The missing salesman had bought a nice car for the small family he intended to have with the woman from the dairy shop. That was the future. When he disappeared, one hubcap was missing from his car. He may have taken a bend too quickly or struck the kerb. Or maybe the hubcap was simply stolen outside the coach station.

'. . . Then came the oil crisis in the 1970s and they had to manufacture more economical engines,' Teddi ploughed on, sipping his beer.

Erlendur nodded absent-mindedly and stubbed out his cigarette. He saw Sigurdur Óli opening a window to let the smoke out. Erlendur was trying to cut down but always smoked more than he intended. He was thinking about giving up worrying about cigarettes. It had not done any good so far. He thought about Eva Lind, who had not been in touch since she left rehab. She didn't worry about her health. He looked out onto the little patio behind Sigurdur Óli and Bergthóra's townhouse, and watched Elínborg barbecuing; she seemed to be warbling a song to herself. He looked into the kitchen where Sigurdur Óli kissed Bergthóra on the back of the neck as he walked past her. He cast a sideways glance at Teddi relishing his beer.

Maybe that was enjoying life. Maybe it was that simple when the sun was shining on a pleasant summer's day.

Instead of going home that evening he drove out of the city, past Grafarholt in the direction of Mosfellsbaer. He took a slip road towards a large farmhouse and turned off it nearer the sea until he reached the land that Haraldur and his brother Jóhann had farmed. Haraldur had given him only limited directions and had tried to be as unhelpful as possible. He refused to tell Erlendur whether the old farm buildings were still standing, claiming to know nothing about them. His brother Jóhann had died suddenly from a heart attack, he said. Not everyone's as lucky as my brother Jói, he added.

The buildings were still standing. Summer chalets had been built here and there on the old farmland. Judging from the trees growing around some of them, they had been there some time. Others were recent. Erlendur saw a golf course in the distance. Although it was late in the evening, he could see a few souls hitting balls, then strolling after them in the warm sun.

The farm buildings were dilapidated. A small farmhouse and sheds near it. The house was clad with corrugated iron. At one time it had been painted yellow, but the colour had almost entirely faded. Rusty corrugated-metal sheets were hung on the outside of the house; others had surrendered to the wind and weather and fallen to the ground. Most of the roofing sheets had been blown out to sea, Erlendur imagined. All the windows were broken and the front door was missing. Nearby stood the ruins of a small toolshed adjoining a cattle shed and barn.

He stood in front of the ruined farmhouse. It was almost like his childhood home.

Stepping inside, he entered a small hallway, then a narrow corridor. On the right was a kitchen and a laundry room, and a little pantry was to the left. An antiquated Icelandic cooker was still in the kitchen, with three hotplates and a small oven, rusted through. At the end of the corridor were two bedrooms and a living room. The floorboards creaked in the quiet of the evening. He did not know what he was looking for. He did not know why he had come there.

He went down to the sheds. Looking along the row of stalls in the cattle shed and into the barn, he could see a dirt floor. When he walked around the corner he could make out traces of a dung heap behind the cattle shed. A door hung on the toolshed, but when he pulled at it, it came off its hinges, fell to the ground and broke with what sounded like a heavy groan. Inside the toolshed were racks with little compartments for screws, nuts and bolts, and nails on the walls to hang tools from. The tools were nowhere to be seen. The brothers had doubtless taken everything serviceable with them when they moved to Reykjavík. A broken workbench was propped at an angle against the wall. A tractor bonnet rested on a heap of indeterminate iron objects on the floor. A felloe from the rear wheel of a tractor lay over in one corner.

Erlendur walked farther inside the toolshed. Did he come here, the driver of the Falcon? Or did he take a coach to some rural destination? If he did come here, what was he thinking? It had been late in the day when he'd left Reykjavík. He'd known that he did not have much time. She would wait for him in front of the dairy shop and he did not want to be late. But he did not want to rush the brothers. They were interested in buying a tractor from him. It would not take much to clinch the sale. But he did not want to give the impression of being pushy. It could jeopardise the deal if he appeared overexcited. Yet he was in a hurry. He wanted to get it all finished.

If he did come here, why didn't the brothers say so? Why should they be lying? They had no vested interests. They did not know the man in the least. And why was one hubcap missing from his car? Had it fallen off? Was it stolen outside the coach station? Was it stolen here?

If he was the man in the lake with a broken skull, how did he end up there? Where did the device tied to him come from? Was it relevant that he sold tractors and machinery from the Eastern bloc? Was there a connection?

Erlendur's mobile rang in his pocket.

'Yes,' he answered curtly.

'You leave me alone,' said a voice he knew well. He knew the voice particularly well when it was in this state.

'I intend to,' he said.

'You do that, then,' the voice said. 'You leave me alone from here on. Just stop interfering in my life for—'

He rang off. It was more difficult to switch off the voice. It echoed in his head: stoned, angry and repulsive. He knew that she must be in a den somewhere with someone whose name might be Eddi and was twice her age. He tried not to think about the life she led in too much detail. He had repeatedly done everything in his power to help her. He did not know what else to try. He was completely at a loss about his junkie daughter. Once he would have tried to locate her. Run off and found her. Once he would have persuaded himself that when she said 'leave me alone' she actually meant 'come and help me'. Not any more. He did not want to any more. He wanted to tell her: 'It's over. You can take care of yourself.'

She had moved in with him that Christmas. By then, after a short break when she'd had a miscarriage and been confined to hospital, she had begun taking drugs again. In the New Year he could sense her restlessness and she would disappear for varying lengths of time. He went after her and took her back home, but the next morning she would be gone. It went on like that until he stopped chasing her, stopped pretending that it made any difference what he did. It was her life. If she chose to live it in that way, that was up to her. He was incapable of doing more. He had not heard of her for more than two months when she hit Sigurdur Óli on the shoulder with the hammer.

He stood out in the yard looking over the ruins of a life that once had been. He thought about the man who owned the Falcon. About the woman who was still waiting for him. He thought about his own daughter and son. He looked into the evening sun and thought about his dead brother. What had he been thinking about in the blizzard?

How cold it was?

How nice it would be to get back home into the warm?

The next morning, Erlendur went back to the woman waiting for the man who drove the Falcon. It was a Saturday and she was not working. He rang in advance and she had coffee ready for him, even though he had specifically asked her not to go to any trouble for him. They sat down in her living room as before. Her name was Ásta.

'Of course, you always work weekends,' she said, adding that she worked in the kitchen at the City Hospital in Fossvogur.

'Yes, things are often busy,' he said, taking care not to answer her in too much detail. He could have taken this weekend off. But the Falcon case had piqued his curiosity and he felt a strange, pressing need to get to the bottom of it. He did not know why. Perhaps for the sake of the woman sitting opposite him who had done menial work all her life, who still lived alone and whose weary expression reflected how life had passed her by. It was just as if she thought that the man she had once loved would come back to her, as he had before, kiss her, tell her about his day at work and ask how she had been doing.

'The last time we came you said you didn't believe that another woman was involved,' he said cautiously.

On the way to see her, he had had second thoughts. He did not want to ruin her memories. He did not want to destroy anything she clung to. He had seen that happen so often before. When they arrived at the home of a criminal whose wife just stared at them, unable to believe her own eyes and ears. The children behind her. Her fortress crumbling all around her. My husband! Selling drugs? You must be mad!

'Why are you asking about that?' the woman said, sitting in her chair. 'Do you know more than I do? Have you found out something? Have you uncovered something new?'

'No, nothing,' Erlendur said, flinching inwardly when he sensed the eagerness in her voice. He described his visit to Haraldur and how he had located the Falcon, still in good shape and stored away in a garage in Kópavogur. He also told her that he had visited an abandoned farm near Mosfellsbaer. Her partner's disappearance, however, remained as much a mystery as ever.

'You said you had no photographs of him, or of you together,' he said.

'No, that's right,' Ásta said. 'We'd known each other for such a short time.'

'So no photograph ever appeared in the papers or on television when he was declared missing?'

'No, but they gave a detailed description. They were going to use the photo from his driving licence. They said they always kept copies of licences, but then they couldn't find it. Like he hadn't handed it in, or they'd mislaid it.'

'Did you ever see his driving licence?'

'Driving licence? No, not that I remember. Why were you asking about another woman?'

The question was delivered in a harder tone, more insistent. Erlendur hesitated before he opened the door on what, to her mind, would surely be hell itself. Maybe he had proceeded too quickly. Certain points needed closer scrutiny. Maybe he should wait.

'There are instances of men who leave their women without saying goodbye and start a new life,' he said.

'A new life?' she said, as if the concept was beyond her comprehension.

'Yes,' he said. 'Even here in Iceland. People think that everyone knows everyone else, but that's a long way from the truth. There are plenty of towns and villages that few people ever visit, except perhaps at the height of summer, maybe not even then. In the old days they were even more isolated than today – some were even half cut-off. Transportation was much worse then.'

'I don't follow,' she said. 'What are you getting at?'

'I just wanted to know if you'd ever contemplated that possibility.'

'What possibility?'

'That he got on a coach and went home,' Erlendur said.

He watched her trying to fathom the unfathomable.

'What are you talking about?' she groaned. 'Home? Home where? What do you mean?'

He could see that he had overstepped the mark. That despite all the years that had gone by since the man disappeared from her life, an unhealed wound still remained, fresh and open. He wished he had not gone so far. He should not have approached her at such an early stage. Without having anything more tangible than his own fantasies and an empty car outside the coach station.

'It's just one of the hypotheses,' he said in an effort to cushion the impact of his words. 'Of course, Iceland's too small for anything like that,' he hurried to say. 'It's just an idea, with no real foundation.'

Erlendur had spent a long time wondering what could possibly have happened if the man had not committed suicide. When the notion of another woman began to take root in his mind he started losing sleep. At first the hypothesis could not have been simpler: on his travels around Iceland the salesman had met all sorts of people from different walks of life: farmers, hotel staff, residents of towns and fishing villages, women. Conceivably he had found a girlfriend on one of his trips and in time came to prefer her to the one in Reykjavík, but lacked the courage to tell her so.

The more Erlendur thought about the matter, the more he tended to believe that, if another woman was involved, the man must have had a stronger motive to make himself disappear; he had started to think about a word that entered his mind outside the abandoned farm in Mosfellsbaer that had reminded him of his own house in east Iceland.

Home.

They had discussed this at the office. What if they reversed the paradigm? What if the woman facing him now had been Leopold's girlfriend in Reykjavík, but he had a family somewhere else? What if he had decided to put an end to the dilemma he had got himself into, and settled for going home?

He sketched for the woman the broad outlines of these ideas and noticed how a dark cloud gradually descended over her.

'He wasn't in any trouble,' she said. 'That's just nonsense you're coming out with. How could you think of such a thing? Talking about the man like that.'

'His name isn't very common,' Erlendur said. 'There are only a handful of men with that name in the whole country. Leopold. You didn't know his ID number. You have very few of his personal belongings.'

Erlendur fell silent. He remembered that Níels had kept from her the indications that Leopold had not used his real name. That he had tricked her and claimed to be someone he was not. Níels had not told Ásta about these suspicions because he felt sorry for her. Now, Erlendur understood what he meant.

'Perhaps he didn't use his real name,' he said. 'Did that ever occur to you? He was not officially registered under that name. He can't be found in the records.'

'Someone from the police called me,' the woman said angrily. 'Later. Much later. By the name of Briem or something like that. Told me about your theory that Leopold might not have been who he claimed to be. Said I should have been told immediately, but that there had been a delay. I've heard your ideas and they're ridiculous. Leopold would never have sailed under a false flag. Never.'

Erlendur said nothing.

'You're trying to tell me he might have had a family that he went back to. That I was only his fiancée in the city? What kind of rubbish is that?'

'What do you know about this man?' Erlendur persisted. 'What do you really know about him? Is it very much?'

'Don't talk like that,' she said. 'Please don't put such stupid notions to me. You can keep your opinions to yourself. I'm not interested in hearing them.'

Ásta stopped talking and stared at him.

'I'm not—' Erlendur began, but she interrupted him.

'Do you mean he's still alive? Is that what you're saying? That he's still alive? Living in some village?'

'No,' Erlendur said. 'I'm not saying that. I just want to explore that possibility with you. None of what I've been saying is any more than guesswork. There needn't be any grounds for it, and at the moment there are no grounds for it. I only wanted to know if you could recall anything that might give us reason for supposing so. That's all. I'm not saying anything is the case because I don't know anything is the case.'

'You're just talking rubbish,' she said. 'As if he'd just been fooling around with me. Why do I have to listen to this?!'

While Erlendur tried to convince her, a strange thought slipped into his mind. From now on, after what he had said and could not retract, it would be much greater consolation for the woman to know that the man was dead, rather than to find him alive. That would cause her immeasurable grief. He looked at her, and she seemed to be thinking something similar.

'Leopold's dead,' she said. 'There's no point telling me otherwise. To me, he's dead. Died years ago. A whole lifetime ago.'

They both fell silent.

'But what do you know about the man?' Erlendur repeated after some while. 'In actual fact?'

Her look implied that she wanted to tell him to give up and go.

'Do you seriously mean that he was called something else and wasn't using his real name?' she said.

'Nothing of what I've said need necessarily have happened,' Erlendur emphasised once again. 'The most likely explanation, unfortunately, is that for some reason he killed himself.'

'What do we know about other people?' she suddenly said. 'He was a quiet type and didn't talk much about himself. Some people are full of themselves. I don't know if that's any better. He said a lot of lovely things to me that no one had ever told me before. I wasn't brought up in that kind of family. Where people said nice things.'

'You never wanted to start again? Find a new man. Get married. Have a family.'

'I was past thirty when we met. I thought I'd end up an old maid. My time would run out. That was never the plan, but somehow that was how it turned out. Then you reach a certain age and all you have is yourself in an empty room. That's why he . . . he changed that. And even though he didn't say much and was away a lot, he was still my man.'

She looked at Erlendur.

'We were together, and after he went missing I waited for several years, and I'm probably still waiting. When do you stop? Is there any rule about it?'

'No,' Erlendur said. 'There's no rule.'

'I didn't think so,' she said, and he felt painfully sorry for her when he noticed that she was starting to weep.

19

One day a message appeared on Sigurdur Óli's desk from the US embassy in Reykjavík stating that it had information that might prove useful to the police in their investigation regarding the skeleton from Kleifarvatn. The message was delivered by the gloved hand of an embassy chauffeur who said he was supposed to wait for a reply. With the help of Ómar, the ex-director general of the foreign ministry, Sigurdur Óli had made contact with Robert Christie in Washington, who had promised to assist them after hearing what the request involved. According to Ómar, Robert – or Bob, as he called him – had been interested in the case and the embassy would soon be in touch.

Sigurdur Óli looked at the chauffeur and his black leather gloves. He was wearing a black suit and wore a peaked cap with gold braid; he looked a complete fool in such a get-up. After reading the message, Sigurdur Óli nodded. He told the chauffeur that he would be at the embassy at two o'clock the same day and would bring with him a detective called Elínborg. The chauffeur smiled. Sigurdur Óli expected him to salute on departing, but he did not.

Elínborg almost bumped into the chauffeur at the door to Sigurdur Óli's office. He apologised and she watched him walk off down the corridor.

'What on earth was that?' she said.

'The US embassy,' Sigurdur Óli said.

They arrived at the embassy on the stroke of two. Two Icelandic security guards stood outside the building and eyed them suspiciously as they approached. They stated their business, the door was opened and they were allowed inside. Two more security guards, this time American, received them. Elínborg was braced for a weapons check when a man appeared in the lobby and welcomed them with a handshake. He said his name was Christopher Melville and asked them to follow him. He praised them for being 'right on time'. They spoke in English.

Sigurdur Óli and Elínborg followed Melville up to the next floor, along the corridor and to a door which he opened. A sign on the door said: Director of Security. A man of around sixty was waiting for them inside, his head crewcut although he was wearing civilian clothes, and he introduced himself as the said director, Patrick Quinn. Melville left and they sat down with Quinn on a small sofa in his spacious office. He said he had spoken to the Defence Department at Iceland's Ministry of Foreign Affairs and that the Americans would gladly help the Icelandic police if they could. They exchanged a few words about the weather and agreed it was a good summer by Reykjavík standards.

Quinn said he had been with the embassy ever since Richard Nixon visited Iceland in 1973 for his summit meeting with French President Georges Pompidou, which was held at Kjarvalsstadir Art Museum. He said he liked Iceland very much in spite of the cold, dark winters. At that time of year he tried to make it to Florida for a vacation. He smiled. 'Actually I'm from North Dakota, so I'm used to this kind of winter. But I miss the warmer summers.'

Sigurdur Óli smiled back. He thought they had made enough idle chat, much as he would have liked to tell Quinn that he had studied criminology for three years in the States and loved America and all things American.

'You studied in the US, didn't you?' Quinn said. 'Criminology. Three years, wasn't it?'

The smile froze on Sigurdur Óli's face.

'I understand you like the country,' Quinn added. 'It's good for us to have friends in these difficult times.'

'Do you . . . do you have a file on me here?' Sigurdur Óli asked, dumbfounded.

'A file?' Quinn laughed. 'I just phoned Bára from the Fulbright Foundation.'

'Bára, yes, I see,' Sigurdur Óli said. He knew the foundation's director well.

'You were on a scholarship, right?'

'That's right,' Sigurdur Óli said awkwardly. 'I thought for a moment that . . .' He shook his head at his own folly.

'No, but I've got the CIA file on you here,' Quinn said, reaching over for a folder from the desk.

The smile froze on Sigurdur Óli's face again. Quinn waved an empty folder at him and started laughing.

'Boy, is he uptight,' he said to Elínborg.

'Who is this colleague of yours?' she asked.

'Robert Christie occupied the post I now hold at the embassy,' Quinn said. 'But the job is totally different now. He was the embassy's director of security during the Cold War. The security issues I handle are those of a changed world where terrorism is the greatest threat to the United States and, as borne out by events, to the rest of the world.'

He looked at Sigurdur Óli, who was still recovering.

'Sorry,' he said. 'I didn't mean to freak you out.'

'No, it's fine,' Sigurdur Óli said. 'A little joke. Never harmed anyone.'

'Bob and I are good friends,' Quinn continued. 'He asked me to help you with this skeleton you found at, what do you call it, Klowffervatten?'

'Kley-varrr-vahtn.' Elínborg pronounced it for him.

'Right,' Quinn said. 'You don't have anyone reported missing who could be the skeleton you found, or what?'

'Nothing seems to fit the man from Kleifarvatn.'

'Only two out of forty-four missing-persons cases over the past fifty years have been investigated as criminal matters,' Sigurdur Óli said. 'This one is the sort we want to look into more closely.'

'Yes,' Quinn said, 'I also understand that the body was tied to a Russian radio device. We'd be happy to examine it for you. If you have trouble establishing the model and date and its potential applications. That's easily done.'

'I think forensics is working on it with Iceland Telecom,' Sigurdur Óli said cheerfully. 'They might contact you.'

'Anyway, a missing person, not necessarily an Icelander,' Quinn said, putting on his reading glasses. He took a black folder from his desk and browsed through some papers. 'As you may know, embassy staffing was under close surveillance in the old days. The Reds watched us and we watched the Reds. That was the way things were and no one thought it was strange.'

'Maybe you still don't today,' Sigurdur Óli said.

'We had a look in our archives,' Quinn said, no longer smiling. 'Bob remembered it well. Everyone thought it was a mystery at the time and what was actually going on was never uncovered. What happened, according to our records – and I've talked to Bob in detail about this as well – is that an East German attaché entered Iceland at a certain time but we never noticed him leaving again.'

They looked at him blankly.

'Perhaps you'd like me to repeat that,' Quinn said. 'An East German diplomat came to Iceland but did not leave. According to our information, which is fairly reliable, either he's still here – and doing something completely different from embassy work – or he was killed and the body either disposed of or sent out of the country.'

'So you lost him in Iceland?' Elínborg said.

'It's the only case of this sort that we know about,' Quinn said. 'In Iceland, that is,' he added. 'The man was an East German spy. He was known to us as such. None of our embassies in other parts of the

157

world picked him up after he came to Iceland. A special alert was sent out about him. He never appeared. We made a special check on whether he had returned to East Germany. It was like the earth had swallowed him. The Icelandic earth.'

Elínborg and Sigurdur Óli mulled over his words.

'Could he have gone over to the enemy – I mean to you, the British or the French?' Sigurdur Óli said, trying to recall films and books about spies that he had seen and read. 'And then gone underground?' he added, unsure of exactly what he was talking about. He was not a great fan of spy stories.

'Out of the question,' Quinn said. 'We would have known about that.'

'Or used a false identity when he left the country?' Elínborg suggested, groping and as much in the dark as Sigurdur Óli.

'We knew most of them,' Quinn said. 'And we kept a fairly good watch on their embassies on that score. We believe that this man never left the country.'

'What about in some other way from what you expected?' Sigurdur Óli said. 'By ship?'

'That was one possibility we checked,' Quinn said. 'And without going into too much detail about our procedures then and now, I can assure you that this man never emerged in East Germany, which was where he came from originally, nor in the Soviet Union or any other country in Eastern or Western Europe. He vanished.'

'What do you think happened? Or thought at the time?'

'That they killed him and buried him in the embassy garden,' Quinn said without batting an eyelid. 'Killed their own spy. Or, as has since transpired, sank him in Lake Kleifarvatn tied to one of their listening devices. I don't know why. It's perfectly clear that he didn't work for us, nor for any NATO country. He wasn't a counter-espionage agent. If he was, he was working so deep that nobody knew about it, and he would probably have hardly known it himself.'

Quinn flicked through the folder and told them that the man had first come to Iceland in the early 1960s and worked in the diplomatic corps for a few months. Then, in autumn 1962, he left, but returned briefly two years later. After that he had moved between posts in Norway, East Germany and Moscow for one year and ended up at the East German embassy in Argentina, with the title of 'trade attaché' – 'like most of them,' Quinn said, grinning. 'Our guys too. He spent a short spell at the embassy in Reykjavík in 1967, then went back to Germany and from there to Moscow. He returned to Iceland in 1968, in the spring. By the fall he had disappeared.'

'Fall 1968?' Elínborg said.

'That was when we noticed that he was no longer at the embassy. We investigated through specific channels and he was nowhere to be found. Admittedly, the East Germans did not operate a proper embassy in Reykjavík, only what was called a trade delegation, but that's a minor point.'

'What do you know about this man?' Sigurdur Óli asked. 'Did he have friends here? Or enemies at home? Did he do anything wrong to your knowledge?'

'No. As I say, we're not aware of that. And of course we don't know everything. We suspect that something happened to him here in 1968. We don't know what. He could just as easily have left the diplomatic service and made himself disappear. He knew how to do that, how to merge into the crowd. It's up to you how you interpret this information. This is all we know.'

He paused.

'Perhaps he slipped away from us,' he said then. 'Maybe there's a rational explanation for it all. This is all we've got. Now you must tell me one thing. Bob asked about it. How was he killed? The man in the lake.'

Elínborg and Sigurdur Óli exchanged glances.

'He was hit over the head and sustained a hole in the skull just by the temple,' Sigurdur Óli said.

'Hit over the head?' Quinn asked.

'He could have fallen, but it would have been from quite a height,' Elínborg said.

'So it's not a straightforward execution? A bullet in the back of the head?'

'Execution?' Elínborg said. 'We're Icelanders. The last execution in this country was done with an axe almost two hundred years ago.'

'Yes, of course,' Quinn said. 'I'm not saying that an Icelander killed him.'

'Does it tell you anything, him dying like that?' Sigurdur Óli asked. 'If it is this spy who was found in the lake?'

'No, nothing,' Quinn said. 'The man was a spy and his job entailed certain risks.'

He stood up. They could tell that the conversation was coming to an end. Quinn put the folder down on the table. Sigurdur Óli looked at Elínborg.

'What was his name?'

'His name was Lothar,' Quinn said.

'Lothar,' Elínborg parroted.

'Yes,' Quinn said, looking at the papers he was holding. 'His name was Lothar Weiser and he was born in Bonn. And, interestingly enough, he spoke Icelandic like a native.'

20

Later that day they requested a meeting at the German embassy, stating the reason to give the staff time to gather information about Lothar Weiser. The meeting was arranged for later in the week. They told Erlendur about what the meeting with Patrick Quinn had revealed, and discussed the possibility that the man in the lake was an East German spy. A number of signs pointed to that, they felt, notably the Russian device and the location. They agreed that there was something foreign about the murder. Something about the case that they had seldom, if ever, seen before. Admittedly it was ferocious, but all murders were ferocious. More importantly, it appeared to have been carefully planned, skilfully executed, and had remained covered up for so many years. Icelandic murders were not generally committed in this way. They were more coincidental, clumsy and squalid, and the perpetrators almost without exception left a trail of clues.

'If he didn't just fall on his head,' Elínborg said.

'No one falls on their head before being tied to a spying device and thrown into Kleifarvatn,' Erlendur said.

'Making any progress with the Falcon?' Elínborg asked.

'None at all,' Erlendur said, 'except that I've been putting the wind up Leopold's girlfriend, who can't understand what I'm going on about.' Erlendur had told them about the brothers from outside Mosfellsbaer and his half-baked hypothesis that the man who owned the Falcon might even still be alive or, for that matter, living in another part of Iceland. They had discussed this idea before and regarded it in much the same way as the missing man's girlfriend – they had nothing substantial to support it. 'Too far-fetched for Iceland,' Sigurdur Óli said. Elínborg agreed. 'Perhaps in a city of a million people.'

'Funny that this guy can't be found anywhere in the system, though,' Sigurdur Óli said.

'That's the point,' Erlendur said. 'Leopold, as he called himself – that much we do know – is quite a mysterious figure. Níels handled the case originally and never looked into his background properly, he never found any records. It wasn't investigated as a criminal matter.'

'No more than most missing persons in Iceland,' Elínborg chipped in.

'Only a few people had that name then and they can all be identified. I did a quick check. His girlfriend said he had spent a lot of time abroad. He may even have been born abroad. You never know.'

'Why do you think he was called Leopold in the first place?' Sigurdur Óli asked. 'Isn't that a rather odd name for an Icelander?'

'It was the name he used, at least,' Erlendur said. 'He may well have used another name elsewhere. That's quite likely actually. We know nothing about him until he suddenly surfaces selling bulldozers and farm machinery and as the boyfriend of a woman who somehow becomes the victim in the whole affair. She knows precious little about him but is still in mourning for him. We have no background. No birth certificate. Nothing about his schooling. We just know that he travelled widely, lived abroad and might have been born there. He lived abroad for so long that he spoke with a slight foreign accent.'

'Unless he just killed himself,' Elínborg said. 'The only foundation for your theory about Leopold's double life is in your own fantasies.'

'I know,' Erlendur said. 'The overwhelming odds are that he took his own life and that's the only mystery there is to it.'

'I think you were bloody crass, trying out that ludicrous idea on the woman,' Elínborg said. 'Now she thinks he might be alive.'

'She's believed that herself the whole time,' Erlendur said. 'Deep down. That he just walked out on her.'

They stopped talking. It was late in the day. Elínborg looked at her watch. She was testing a new marinade for chicken breasts. Sigurdur Óli had promised to take Bergthóra to Thingvellir. They were going to spend a summer night at the hotel there. The weather was at its best for June: warm, sunny and with the scent of flowers in the air.

'What are you doing tonight?' Sigurdur Óli asked Erlendur.

'Nothing,' Erlendur said.

'Maybe you'd like to come to Thingvellir with me and Bergthóra,' he said, making a bad job of concealing the answer he wanted to hear. Erlendur smiled. Their concern for him could get on his nerves. Sometimes, like now, it was merely politeness.

'I'm expecting a visitor,' Erlendur said.

'How's Eva Lind doing?' Sigurdur Óli asked, rubbing his shoulder.

'I haven't heard much from her,' Erlendur said. 'I just know she completed rehab, but I've hardly heard anything else.'

'What were you saying about Leopold?' Elínborg suddenly said. 'Did he speak with a foreign accent? Did you say that?'

'Lothar was bound to have had an accent,' Sigurdur Óli said.

'What do you mean?' Erlendur said.

'Well, the guy at the US embassy said that this German, Lothar, spoke fluent Icelandic. But he must have spoken it with an accent.'

'We'll have to bear that in mind, of course,' Erlendur said.

'That they're the same man?' Elínborg said. 'Leopold and Lothar?'

'Yes,' Erlendur said. 'I don't think it's an abnormal assumption to make. At least they both disappeared the same year, 1968.'

'So Lothar called himself Leopold?' Sigurdur Óli said. 'Why?'

'I don't know,' Erlendur said. 'I have no idea what was going on. Not the faintest.'

'Then there's the Russian equipment,' Erlendur said after a long silence.

'And?' Elínborg said.

'Leopold's last business was at Haraldur's farm. Where would Haraldur have got a Russian listening device to sink him in the lake with? You could begin to understand it if Lothar had been involved, if he was a spy and something happened that ended with his body being dumped in the lake. But Haraldur and Leopold are worlds apart.'

'Haraldur flatly denies that the salesman ever went to his farm,' Sigurdur Óli said. 'Whether his name was Leopold or Lothar.'

'That's the point,' Erlendur said.

'What is?' Elínborg said.

'I think he's lying.'

Erlendur went to three video rental shops before he found the western to take for Marion Briem. He had once heard Marion describe it as a favourite because it was about a man who faced a looming peril alone when the community, including all his best friends, turned its back on him.

He knocked on the door, but no one answered. Marion was expecting him, because Erlendur had telephoned in advance, so he opened the door, which was unlocked, and let himself in. Not planning to stay, he only intended to drop the video in. He was awaiting a visit that evening from Valgerdur, who had moved in with her sister.

'So you're here?' said Marion, who had fallen asleep on the sofa. 'I heard you knock. I feel so tired. I've slept all day. Do you mind pushing the oxygen tank over to me?'

Erlendur placed the cylinder by the sofa and an old memory of a lonely and absurd death suddenly crossed his mind when he saw Marion's hand reach for the oxygen.

The police had been called to a house in Thingholt. He had gone with Marion. He had only been in the CID a few months. Someone had died at home and it was classified as accidental death. A large elderly woman was sitting in an armchair in front of her television. She had been dead for a fortnight. Erlendur was almost overpowered by the stench in the flat. The woman's neighbour had called the police because of the smell. He had not seen her for some time and eventually noticed that her television could be heard softly through the wall around the clock. She had choked. A plate of salted meat and boiled turnips was on the table beside her. A knife and fork lay on the floor by the chair. A large lump of meat was lodged in her throat. She had not managed to get out of the deep armchair. Her face was dark blue. It turned out that she had no relatives who called on her. No one ever visited her. No one missed her.

'I know we all have to die,' Marion had said, looking down at the body, 'but I don't want to die like that.'

'Poor woman,' Erlendur said, covering his nose and mouth.

'Yes, poor woman,' Marion said. 'Was that why you joined the police force? To look at things like this?'

'No,' Erlendur said.

'Why, then?' Marion asked. 'What are you doing this for?'

'Have a seat,' he heard Marion say through his thoughts. 'Don't stand there like a dickhead.'

He returned to himself and sat down in a chair facing Marion.

'You don't have to visit me, Erlendur.'

'I know,' Erlendur said. 'I brought you another film. Starring Gary Cooper.'

'Have you seen it?' Marion asked.

'Yes,' Erlendur said. 'Ages ago.'

'Why are you so glum, what were you thinking about?' Marion asked.

' "We all have to die, but I don't want to die like that." '

'Yes,' Marion said, after a short pause. 'I remember her. That old girl in the chair. And now you're looking at me and thinking the same thing.'

Erlendur shrugged.

'You didn't answer my question,' Marion said. 'And you still haven't.'

'I don't know why I joined the police force,' Erlendur said. 'It was a job. A cushy office job.'

'No, there was something more to it,' Marion said. 'Something more than just a cushy office job.'

'Don't you have anyone?' Erlendur asked, trying to change the subject. He did not know how to phrase it. 'Anyone who can take care of things after . . . when it's all over?'

'No,' Marion said.

'What do you want done with you?' Erlendur asked. 'Don't we have to discuss that some time? The practical stuff. You're bound to have arranged it all, if I know you.'

'Are you starting to look forward to it?' Marion asked.

'I never look forward to anything,' Erlendur said.

'I've spoken to a lawyer, a young solicitor, who will sort out my affairs, thank you. Perhaps you could handle the practical side. The cremation.'

'Cremation?'

'I don't want to rot in a coffin,' Marion said. 'I'll have myself cremated. There won't be a ceremony. No fuss.'

'And the ashes?'

'You know what the film's really about?' said Marion, clearly trying to avoid giving an answer. 'The Gary Cooper film. It's about the witch hunts against communists in 1950s America. An outlaw gang arrives in town to attack Cooper and his friends turn their backs on him. He ends up alone and defenceless. *High Noon*. The best westerns are much more than just westerns.'

'Yes, you said that to me once.'

It was well into the evening but the sky was still bright. Erlendur looked out of the window. It would not get dark, either. He always missed that in the summer. Missed the darkness. Yearned for the cold black of night and the deep winter.

'What's this thing you've got about westerns?' Erlendur asked. He could not resist asking. He knew nothing of Marion's passion for westerns before. In fact he knew very little about Marion at all, and when he started to think about it, sitting in the living room, he recalled only very rarely ever having spoken to Marion on a personal level.

'The landscapes,' Marion said. 'The horses. The wide open spaces.'

Silence crept over the room. Marion appeared to be dozing off.

'The last time I was here I mentioned Leopold, the man who owned the Ford Falcon and went missing from the coach station,' Erlendur said. 'You told me you'd telephoned his girlfriend to tell her there was no record anywhere of a man by that name.'

'Does that matter? If I remember correctly, that twat Níels was trying to avoid telling her. I'd never heard anything so stupid.'

'What did she say when you raised it?'

Marion's mind drifted back in time. Erlendur knew that despite old age and various ailments, Marion Briem's memory was still infallible.

'Naturally she wasn't very pleased. Níels was handling the case and I didn't want to interfere too much.'

'Did you give her any hope that he could still be alive?'

'No,' Marion said. 'That would have been ridiculous. Totally absurd. I hope you haven't got that kind of bee in your bonnet.'

'No,' Erlendur said. 'I haven't.'

'And don't let her hear it!'

'No,' Erlendur said. 'That would definitely be ridiculous.'

Eva Lind called him when he got home. He had been away from his office almost all day, then went to buy some food. He had put a ready meal in the microwave, which rang at the same moment as the telephone. Eva Lind was much calmer now. Although she would not tell him where she was, she said she had met a man in rehab whom she was staying with for the time being, and told her father not to worry about her. She had met Sindri at a café in town. He was looking for a job.

'Is he going to live in Reykjavík?' Erlendur asked.

'Yes, he wants to move back to the city. Is that a bad thing?'

'Him moving to the city?'

'You seeing more of him.'

'No, I don't think it's a bad thing. I think it's good if he wants to move back. Don't always think the worst of me, Eva. Who is this man you're staying with?'

'No one,' Eva Lind said. 'And I don't always think the worst of you.'

'Are you doing drugs together?'

'Doing drugs?'

'I can hear it, Eva. The way you talk. I'm not reproaching you. I can't be bothered any more. You can do as you please, but don't lie to me. I won't have you lying.'

'I'm not . . . what do you know about the way I talk? You always have to . . .'

She hung up on him.

Valgerdur did not come as they had planned. She called to say that she had been delayed at work and had just got back to her sister's.

'Is everything all right?' he asked.

'Yes,' she said. 'We'll talk later.'

He went into the kitchen and took the meal from the microwave: meatballs in gravy with mashed potatoes. He thought about Eva and Valgerdur, and then about Elínborg. He threw the package, unopened, into the rubbish bin, and lit a cigarette.

The telephone rang for the third time that evening. He watched it ringing, hoping it would stop and leave him in peace, but when it didn't, he answered it. It was one of the forensics experts.

'It's about the Falcon,' he said.

'Yes, what about the Falcon? Did you find anything?'

'Nothing but dirt from the streets,' the forensics man said. 'We analysed it all and found substances that could have come from cow dung or the like, from a cattle shed. No blood anywhere.'

'Cow dung?'

'Yes, there's all kind of sand and muck like in most cars, but cow dung too. Didn't this man live in Reykjavík?'

'Yes,' Erlendur said, 'but he did a lot of travelling in the country.'

'It's nothing to go by,' the technician said. 'Not after all that time and so many owners.'

'Thank you,' Erlendur said.

They exchanged goodbyes and an idea crossed Erlendur's mind. He looked at the clock. It was past ten. No one goes to sleep at this time, he thought to himself, uncertain whether to go ahead. Not in the summer. Yet he held back. Eventually he made a move.

'Hello,' answered Ásta, Leopold's girlfriend. Erlendur grimaced. He could tell at once that she was not accustomed to receiving telephone calls so late in the evening. Even though it was the middle of summer. After he had introduced himself she asked in surprise what he wanted and why it couldn't wait.

'Of course it can wait,' Erlendur said, 'but I've just found out that there was cow dung on the floor of the car. I had a sample taken. How long had you and Leopold owned the car when he went missing?'

'Not long – only a few weeks. I thought I told you that.'

'Did he ever drive it out into the countryside?'

'The countryside?'

The woman considered this.

'No,' she said, 'I don't think so. He'd owned it such a short time. I also remember him saying that he didn't want to waste it on the country roads, which were in such bad condition. He was just going to use it to drive around town to begin with.'

'There's another thing,' Erlendur said, 'and forgive me for disturbing you so late at night, this case is just . . . I know the car was registered in your name. Do you remember how he paid for it? Did Leopold take a loan? Did he have any savings? Do you remember, by any chance?'

Another silence followed on the line while the woman went back in time and tried to recall details that few people would ever commit to memory.

'I didn't pay any of it,' she said eventually. 'I remember that. I think

169

he already had most of what it cost. He'd been saving up when he was working on the ships, he told me. What do you want to know that for? Why did you telephone me so late? Has anything happened?'

'Do you know why he wanted to have the car in your name?'

'No.'

'Didn't you find that odd?'

'Odd?'

'That he didn't register the car in his own name? That would have been the normal procedure. The men bought the cars and were registered as the owners. There were very few exceptions to that rule in those days.'

'I don't know anything about that,' Ásta said.

'He could have done it to cover his tracks,' Erlendur said. 'If the car had been registered in his name it would have meant providing certain information about himself, which he might not have wanted to do.'

There was a long silence.

'He wasn't in hiding,' the woman said at last.

'No, perhaps not,' Erlendur said. 'But he might have had a different name. Something different from Leopold. Don't you want to know who he was? Who he really was?'

'I know perfectly well who he was,' the woman said, and he could hear that she was on the verge of tears.

'Of course,' Erlendur said. 'I'm sorry to have bothered you. I didn't notice the time. I'll let you know if we find anything out.'

'I know perfectly well who he was,' the woman repeated.

'Of course,' Erlendur said. 'Of course you do.'

21

The cow dung provided no help. The car had had other owners before being sold for scrap and any one of them could have trodden in dung and carried it inside. Reykjavík had been so provincial thirty years ago that the owner would not even have needed to leave the city to come across cows.

Haraldur's temper had not improved since the last time Erlendur sat in his room. He was eating his lunch, some kind of thin porridge with a slice of soft liver sausage, his dentures sitting on the bedside table. Erlendur tried to avoid stealing a glance at the teeth. Hearing the slurping of porridge and seeing it running out of one side of his mouth was quite enough. Haraldur sucked up his porridge and relished the liver sausage that went with it.

'We know that the owner of the Falcon visited you and your brother at the farm,' Erlendur said when the liquid noises stopped and Haraldur had wiped his mouth. As before he had snorted when he saw Erlendur and told him to bugger off, but Erlendur had just smiled and sat down.

'Can't you leave me alone?' Haraldur had said with a greedy eye on his porridge. He had not wanted to start eating with Erlendur watching over him.

'Eat your porridge,' Erlendur had said. 'I can wait.'

Haraldur shot him a filthy look but soon gave up.

'Where's your proof?' Haraldur said. 'You've got no proof because he never came to us. Isn't there a law against this kind of harassment? Are you allowed to badger people day in and day out?'

'We now know that he visited you,' Erlendur said.

'Huh. Bloody nonsense. How do you think you know that?'

'We've examined his car more closely,' Erlendur said. In fact he had nothing concrete but thought it was worth putting pressure on the old man. 'We didn't take a comprehensive forensic profile of the car at the time. But microscopic technology has been revolutionised since then.'

He tried to use long words. Haraldur hung his head as before and stared at the floor.

'So we obtained some new evidence,' Erlendur went on. 'At the time, the case wasn't investigated as a criminal matter. Missing persons generally aren't, because it isn't considered significant in this country if people disappear. It could be the climate. Or Icelandic apathy. Perhaps we don't mind having a high suicide rate.'

'I don't know what you're talking about,' Haraldur said.

'His name was Leopold. You remember? He was a salesman and you'd led him on about buying a tractor and all he had left to do was to pop over to see you that day. I think he did.'

'I must have some rights,' Haraldur said. 'You can't just burst in here whenever you like.'

'I think Leopold came to visit you,' Erlendur repeated without answering Haraldur.

'Bollocks.'

'He came to see you and your brother and something happened. I don't know what. He saw something he wasn't supposed to see. You started arguing with him about something he said. Maybe he was too pushy. He wanted to agree the sale that day.'

'I don't know what you're talking about,' Haraldur repeated. 'He never came. He said he was going to, but he didn't.'

'How long do you think you have left to live?' Erlendur asked.

'Fuck knows. And if you had any evidence you'd have told me

about it. But you don't have a thing. Because he never came.'

'Won't you just tell me what happened?' Erlendur said. 'You can't have long to go. You'd feel better. Even if he did come to your farm, it doesn't mean that you killed him. I'm not saying that. He might just as easily have left you and then vanished.'

Haraldur raised his head and stared at him from beneath his bushy eyebrows.

'Get out,' he said. 'I never want to see you here again.'

'You had cows at the farm, you and your brother, didn't you?'

'Get out!'

'I went out there and saw the cattle shed and the dung heap behind it. You told me you had ten cows.'

'What are you getting at?' Haraldur said. 'We were farmers. Are you going to bang me up for that?'

Erlendur stood up. Haraldur was irritating him, although he knew he shouldn't have allowed him to. He ought to have walked out and continued with the investigation instead of allowing him to wind him up. Haraldur was nothing but a bad-tempered and annoying old fogey.

'We found cow dung in the car,' he said. 'That's why I've been thinking about your cows. Daisy and Buttercup or whatever you called them. I don't think the dung was brought into the car on his shoes. Of course there's a chance that he trod in it and drove away. But I think someone else brought the dung into the car. Someone who lived on the farm he visited. Someone who quarrelled with him. Someone who attacked him, then jumped into the car in his wellies straight from the cow shed and drove down to the coach station.'

'Leave me alone. I don't know anything about any cow dung.'

'Are you sure?'

'Yes, now go away. Leave me in peace.'

Erlendur looked down at Haraldur.

'There's just one flaw in this theory of mine,' Erlendur continued.

'Huh,' Haraldur grunted.

'That coach station business.'

'What about it?'

'There are two things that don't fit.'

'I'm not interested. Get your arse out of here.'

'It's too clever.'

'Huh.'

'And you're too stupid.'

The company for which Leopold was working when he went missing was still operating but now as one of three departments in a large car-import business. The original owner had left a good few years earlier. His son told Erlendur that he had struggled to keep the company afloat but it was a hopeless venture and in the end he had sold it, on the brink of bankruptcy. The son was part of the deal and became manager of the new company's agricultural and earth-moving machinery department. All this had happened more than a decade before. A few employees had gone with him, but none of them was working for the company any longer. The son gave Erlendur his father's details and those of the longest-serving salesman with the old company, who had been there at the same time as Leopold.

When Erlendur got back to his office he looked up the salesman in the telephone directory and called him. There was no answer. He telephoned the former owner. The same story.

Erlendur picked up the telephone again. He looked out of the window and watched the summer on the streets of Reykjavík. He didn't know why he was so engrossed in the case of the owner of the Falcon. Surely the man had committed suicide. Even though there was almost nothing to suggest otherwise, he sat there, telephone receiver in hand, poised to apply for permission to search the brothers' farmland for the body, with a team of fifty police officers, rescue workers and all the media rumpus that would entail.

Perhaps, after all, the salesman was Lothar who had been lying on the bottom of Lake Kleifarvatn. Maybe they were one and the same man.

Slowly he replaced the telephone. Was he so eager to solve cases of missing persons that it blurred his judgement? He knew in his bones that the most sensible thing to do would be to shut Leopold's case away in a drawer and allow it to fade away, like other disappearances for which no simple explanation could be found.

While he was absorbed in his thoughts the telephone rang. It was Patrick Quinn from the US embassy. They exchanged a few pleasantries, then the diplomat got to the point.

'Your people were given the information that we felt safe revealing at the time,' Quinn said. 'We've now been authorised to go a step further.'

'They're not really my people,' Erlendur said, thinking about Sigurdur Óli and Elínborg.

'Yes, whatever,' Quinn said. 'I understand you're in charge of the investigation into the skeleton in the lake. They weren't entirely convinced by what we told them about Lothar Weiser's disappearance. We had information that he came to Iceland but never left the country, but the way we presented it, it sounded a little, how should I say, insubstantial. I contacted Washington and got permission to go a bit further. We have the name of a man, a Czech, who may be able to confirm Weiser's disappearance. He's called Miroslav. I'll see what I can do.'

'Tell me another thing,' Erlendur said. 'Do you have a photograph of Lothar Weiser that you could lend us?'

'I don't know,' Quinn said. 'I'll look into it. It might take a while.'

'Thank you.'

'Don't expect too much, though,' Quinn said and they rang off.

Erlendur tried to contact the old salesman again and was about to put down the telephone when he answered. Hard of hearing by now, the man mistook Erlendur for a social worker and started complaining about the lunches that were delivered to his home. 'The food is always cold,' he said. 'And that's not all,' he went on.

Erlendur had the impression he was about to launch into a long speech about the treatment of the elderly in Reykjavík.

'I'm from the police,' Erlendur said in a loud, clear voice. 'I wanted to ask about a salesman who used to work with you at Machine and Plant in the old days. He went missing one day and hasn't been heard of since.'

'You mean Leopold?' the man said. 'What are you asking about him for? Have you found him?'

'No,' Erlendur said. 'He hasn't been found. Do you remember him?'

'A little,' the man said. 'Probably better than most of the others, just because of what happened. Because he disappeared. Didn't he leave a brand-new car somewhere?'

'Outside the coach station,' Erlendur said. 'What kind of a man was he?'

'Eh?'

Erlendur was on his feet now. He repeated the question, half-shouting into the telephone.

'That's difficult to say. He was a mysterious sort of bloke. Never talked about himself much. He'd worked on ships, might even have been born abroad. At least, he spoke with a bit of an accent. And he had a dark complexion, not lily white like us Icelanders. A really friendly bloke. Sad how it turned out.'

'He did sales trips around the country,' Erlendur said.

'Oh yes, you bet, we all did. Called at the farms with our brochures and tried to sell stuff to the farmers. He probably put the most effort into that. Took along booze, you see, to break the ice. Everyone did. It helped the deals along.'

'Did you have any particular sales patches, I mean, did you share out the regions?'

'No, not really. The richest farmers are in the south and north, of course, and we tried to divvy them up. But the bloody Co-op had them all by the balls anyway.'

'Did Leopold go to any particular places? That he visited more than others?'

There was a silence and Erlendur imagined the old salesman trying to dig up details about Leopold that he had forgotten long ago.

'Come to mention it,' he said eventually. 'Leopold spent quite a lot of time in the east fjords, the southern part. You could call that his favourite patch. The west too, the whole of west Iceland. And the West Fjords. And the south-west too. He went everywhere, really.'

'Did he sell a lot?'

'No, I wouldn't say so. Sometimes he was away for weeks on end, months even, without producing very much. But you ought to talk to old Benedikt. The owner. He might know more. Leopold wasn't with us for long and if I remember correctly there was some bother about fitting him in.'

'Bother about fitting him in?'

'I think they had to sack someone to make way for him. Benedikt insisted that he joined the firm but wasn't happy with his work. I never understood that. Talk to him instead. Talk to Benedikt.'

At home, Sigurdur Óli turned off the television. He had been watching the Icelandic football late-evening highlights. Bergthóra was at her sewing group. He thought it was her calling when he answered the telephone. It wasn't.

'Sorry I'm always phoning you,' the voice said.

Sigurdur Óli hesitated briefly before putting the telephone back down. It began ringing again immediately. He stared at it.

'Shit,' he said.

'Don't hang up,' the man said. 'I just want to talk to you. I feel I can talk to you. Ever since you came round with the news.'

'I'm . . . seriously, I'm not your therapist. You're going too far. I want you to stop. I can't help you. It was an awful coincidence and nothing more. You'll have to accept it. Try to understand that. Goodbye.'

'I know it was a coincidence,' the man said. 'But I made it happen.'

'No one makes coincidences happen,' Sigurdur Óli said. 'That's why they're coincidences. They begin the moment you're born.'

'If I hadn't delayed her, they would have made it home safely.'

'That's absurd. And you know it. You can't blame yourself. You simply can't. No one can blame themselves for that kind of thing.'

'Why not? Coincidences don't come from nowhere. They're consequences of the conditions we create. Like me that day.'

'This is so absurd I can't even be bothered discussing it.'

'Why?'

'Because if we let that sort of thinking control our actions, how would we ever make decisions? Your wife went to the shop at a particular time, you didn't come anywhere near that decision. So was it suicide? No! It was some drunken idiot in a Range Rover. Nothing more.'

'I made the coincidence happen when I phoned her.'

'We can go on like this until the end of time,' Sigurdur Óli said. 'Should we go for a drive out of town? Should we go to the cinema? Should we meet at a café? Who'd dare to suggest anything, for fear of something happening? You're ridiculous.'

'That's the point,' the man said.

'What?'

'How are we supposed to do anything?'

Sigurdur Óli heard Bergthóra come in through the door.

'I've got to stop this,' he said. 'It's just nonsense.'

'Yes, me too,' the man said. 'I've got to stop this.'

Then he put the telephone down.

22

He followed the radio, television and newspaper reports on the discovery of the skeleton, and saw how the story gradually paled in significance until eventually not a word was said about it. Occasionally a short statement appeared saying that there was nothing new to report, quoting a detective whose name was Sigurdur Óli. He knew that the lull in news about the skeleton meant nothing. The investigation must be in full swing and if a breakthrough happened someone would eventually knock on his door. He did not know when or who it would be. Maybe soon. Maybe that Sigurdur Óli. Maybe they would never find out what had happened. He smiled to himself. He was no longer sure that this was what he wanted. It had preyed on him for far too long. Sometimes he felt that he had no existence, no life, beyond living in fear of the past.

Before, he had sometimes felt a compulsion, an uncontrollable urge, to reveal what had happened, to come forward and tell the truth. He always resisted it. He would calm down and in the course of time this need faded and he became numb again to what had occurred. He regretted nothing. He would not have changed anything, given the way things had turned out.

Whenever he looked back he saw Ilona's face the first time he met her. When she sat down beside him in the kitchen, he explained Jónas Hallgrímsson's *End of the Journey* to her and she kissed him. Even now, when he was alone with his thoughts and revisited everything that was so precious to him, he could almost feel again the soft kiss on his lips.

He sat down in the chair by the window and recalled the day when his world had caved in.

Instead of going back to Iceland for the summer he had worked in a coal mine for a while and travelled around East Germany with Ilona. They had planned to go to Hungary, but he could not get a permit. As he understood it, foreigners were finding it increasingly difficult to obtain permission. He heard that travel to West Germany was also being severely restricted.

They went by train and coach and then mainly on foot, and enjoyed travelling on their own. Sometimes they slept outdoors. Sometimes in small guesthouses, school buildings or railway and coach stations. Occasionally they spent a few days on farms that they chanced upon in their travels. Their longest stay was with a sheep farmer who was impressed by having an Icelander knock on his door and repeatedly asked about his northern homeland, especially Snaefellsjökull glacier; it transpired that he had read Jules Verne's *Journey to the Centre of the Earth*. They spent two weeks with him and enjoyed working on his farm. Much the wiser about farming, they set off from him and his family with a rucksack packed with food, and taking their good wishes with them.

She described her childhood home in Budapest and her doctor parents. She had told them about him in her letters home. What did they plan to do? her mother wrote. She was the only daughter. Ilona told her not to worry, but she did nevertheless. Are you going to get married? What about your studies? What about the future?

These were all questions that they had considered, both together and separately, but they were not pressing. All that mattered was the two of them in the present. The future was mysterious and uncharted and all they could be sure about was that they would meet it together.

Sometimes in the evenings she would tell him about her friends – who would welcome him, she assured him – and how they sat in pubs and cafés forever discussing the necessary reforms that were on the horizon. He looked at Ilona and saw her become animated when she talked about a free Hungary. She talked about the liberty that he had known and enjoyed all his life as if it were a mirage, intangible and remote. Everything that Ilona and her friends desired he had always had and taken so much for granted that he had never given it any special consideration. She talked about friends who had been arrested and spent time in prison, about people who had disappeared and whose whereabouts were unknown. He noticed the fear in her voice but also the exhilaration brought about by having deep conviction and fighting for it regardless of the cost. He sensed her tension and excitement at the great events that were unfolding.

He thought a lot during the weeks they spent travelling that summer, and grew convinced that the socialism he had found in Leipzig was built on a lie. He began to understand how Hannes felt. Like Hannes, he had woken up to the realisation that the truth was not single, simple and socialist; rather, there was no simple truth. This complicated beyond all measure his view of the world, forcing him to tackle new and challenging questions. The first and most important hinged on how to react. He was in the same position as Hannes. Should he continue studying in Leipzig? Should he go back to Iceland afterwards? The assumptions behind studying in Leipzig had changed. What was he supposed to say to his family? From Iceland he heard that Hannes, the former youth movement leader, had written newspaper articles and addressed meetings about East Germany, criticising communist policy. He provoked both anger and uproar among Icelandic socialists and had weakened their cause, especially against the backdrop of what was happening in Hungary.

He knew that he was still a socialist and that that would not change, but the version of socialism he had seen in Leipzig was not what he wanted.

And what about Ilona? He did not want to do anything without her. Everything they would do after this, they would do together.

They discussed all this during the last days of their trip and reached a joint decision. She would continue studying and working in Leipzig, go to her clandestine cell meetings, distribute information and monitor developments in Hungary. He would continue studying and act as if nothing had changed. He remembered his diatribe against Hannes for abusing the East German communist party's hospitality. He now intended to do precisely the same, and had trouble justifying this to himself.

He felt uncomfortable. Never before had he been in such a dilemma – his life had always been so simple and secure. He thought of his friends back in Iceland. What was he going to tell them? He had lost his bearings. Everything he had believed in so steadfastly had become alien. He knew that he would always live according to the socialist ideal of equality and fair distribution of wealth, but socialism as practised in East Germany was no longer worth believing in or fighting for. His mind was only beginning to change. It would take time to understand it completely and to redefine the world, and in the meantime he did not intend to make any radical decisions.

When they returned to Leipzig he moved out of the ramshackle villa and into Ilona's room. They slept together on the old futon. At first, her landlady had doubts. As a strict Catholic she wanted to preserve decorum, but she gave in. She told him that she had lost her husband and both sons in the siege of Stalingrad. She showed him photographs of them. They got on well together. He did odd tasks for her in the flat, mended things, bought kitchen utensils and food, and cooked. His friends from the dormitory sometimes called round, but he felt himself growing away from them, and they found him more subdued and reticent than before.

Emil, his closest friend, mentioned this once when he sat down beside him in the library.

'Is everything okay?' Emil asked, sniffing. He had a cold. It was a gloomy, blustery autumn and the dormitory was freezing.

'Okay?' he said. 'Yes, everything's okay.'

'No, because,' Emil said, 'well . . . we get the feeling you're avoiding us. That's wrong, isn't it?'

He looked at Emil.

'Of course that's wrong,' he said. 'There's just so much that has changed for me. Ilona and, you know, lots of things have changed.'

'Yes, I know,' Emil said in a concerned voice. 'Of course. Ilona and all that. Do you know much about this girl?'

'I know everything about her,' he laughed. 'It's okay, Emil. Don't look so worried.'

'Lothar was talking about her.'

'Lothar? Is he back?'

He had not told his friends what Ilona's comrades had revealed about Lothar Weiser and his part in Hannes's expulsion from the university. Lothar was not at the university when it reconvened that autumn and he had not seen or heard of him until now. He had resolved to avoid Lothar, avoid everything connected with him, avoid talking to him and about him.

'He was in our kitchen the night before last,' Emil said. 'Brought a big bag of pork chops. He always has plenty of food.'

'What did he say about Ilona? Why was he talking about her?'

He made a bad job of concealing his eagerness. He glared agitatedly at Emil.

'Just that she was a Hungarian and that they were a law unto themselves,' Emil said. 'That sort of thing. Everyone's talking about what's going on in Hungary but no one seems to know exactly what it is. Have you heard anything through Ilona? What's happening in Hungary?'

'I don't know much,' he said. 'All that I know is people are discussing change. What exactly did Lothar say about Ilona? A law unto themselves? Why did he say that? What did he mean by it?'

Noticing his eagerness, Emil tried to remember Lothar's exact words.

'He said he didn't know where she stood,' Emil ventured after a long pause. 'He doubted that she was a genuine socialist and said she was a bad influence. She talked about people behind their backs. Us too, your comrades. He said she was nasty about us. He'd heard her do that.'

'Why did he say that? What does he know about Ilona? They're complete strangers. She's never spoken to him.'

'I don't know,' Emil said. 'It's just idle gossip. Isn't it?'

He said nothing, deep in thought.

'Tómas?' Emil said. 'Isn't that just idle gossip that Lothar's repeating?'

'Of course it's crap,' he said. 'He doesn't know Ilona in the slightest. She's never spoken badly of you. It's a fucking lie. Lothar—'

He was on the brink of telling Emil what he had been told about Lothar, when he suddenly realised that he could not. He realised that he could not trust Emil. His friend. Although he had no reason not to trust him, his life had suddenly begun to revolve around whom he could trust and who not. People he could open his heart to and those he could not talk to. Not because they were underhand, treacherous and conniving, but because they might allow something indiscreet to slip out, just as he had done about Hannes. This included Emil, Hrafnhildur and Karl, his dormitory friends. He had told them about his experience in the basement when it had happened, how Ilona and Hannes knew each other, how exciting everything was, even dangerous. He could not talk like that any longer.

As far as Lothar was concerned, he had to tread particularly carefully. He tried to figure out why Lothar spoke of Ilona like that in his friend's hearing. Tried to remember whether the German had ever described Hannes in such terms. He could not remember. Perhaps it was a message to him and Ilona. They knew precious little about Lothar. They didn't know who exactly he was working for. Ilona believed her friends who thought he worked for the security police. And this could well be the method the police used. Spreading slander in small groups to create friction.

'Tómas?'

Emil was trying to get his attention.

'What about Lothar?'

'Sorry,' he said. 'I was thinking.'

'You were going to say something about Lothar,' Emil said.

'No,' he said, 'it was nothing.'

'What about you and Ilona?' Emil asked.

'What about us?' he said.

'Are you going to stay together?' Emil asked falteringly.

'What do you mean? Of course. What makes you ask?'

'Just take care,' Emil said.

'What do you mean?'

'Well, after Hannes got thrown out, you never know what might happen.'

He told Ilona about his conversation with Emil, trying to play it down as best he could. Her expression turned anxious immediately and she asked him for every detail of what Emil had said. They tried to puzzle out Lothar's motivation. He was clearly slandering her in front of other students and her closest circle, his friends. Was this the start of something bigger? Could Lothar be keeping a special watch on her? Could he know about the meetings? They decided to lie low for a few weeks.

'They'll just send us home then,' Ilona said, trying to smile. 'What else could they do? We'll go the way of Hannes. It'll never be more serious than that.'

'No,' he said consolingly, 'it will never be more serious than that.'

'They could arrest me for subversion,' she said. 'Anti-communist propaganda. Conspiracy against the Socialist Union Party. They have phrases for it.'

'Can't you stop? Withdraw for a while? See what happens?'

She looked at him.

'What do you mean?' she said. 'I don't let prats like Lothar order me around.'

'Ilona!'

'I say what I think,' she said. 'Always. I'd tell everyone who's interested what's going on in Hungary and the reforms people are demanding. I've always been that way. You know that. I'm not going to stop.'

They both fell into an anxious silence.

'What's the worst they can do?'

'Send you home.'

'They'll send me home.'

They looked at each other.

'We'll have to be careful,' he said. 'You'll have to be careful. Promise me.'

Weeks and months went by. Ilona continued as before, but was more cautious than ever. He attended his classes but was beset by worries about Ilona, telling her time and again to take care. Then one day he met Lothar. He had not seen him for a long time and when he thought afterwards about what had happened he knew that their encounter was no coincidence. He was leaving lectures on his way to meet Ilona by Thomaskirche when Lothar appeared from nowhere. Lothar greeted him warmly. He did not return the greeting and was about to go his own way when Lothar grabbed him by the arm.

'Don't you want to say hello?' he said.

He tore himself free and was heading down the stairs when he felt a hand on his arm again.

'We ought to talk,' Lothar said when he turned round.

'We've got nothing to talk about,' he said.

Lothar smiled again, but his eyes were no longer smiling.

'On the contrary,' Lothar said. 'We've got plenty to talk about.'

'Leave me alone,' he said, continuing down the stairs to the floor where the cafeteria was located. He did not look back and hoped that

Lothar would leave him be, but Lothar stopped him again and glanced around him. He did not want to attract attention.

'What's all this about?' he snapped at Lothar. 'I don't have anything to say to you. Try to get that into your head. Leave me alone!'

He tried to walk past him, but Lothar blocked his path.

'What's wrong?' Lothar said.

He stared into the German's eyes without answering.

'Nothing,' he said eventually. 'Just leave me alone.'

'Tell me why you won't talk to me. I thought we were friends.'

'No, we're not friends,' he said, 'Hannes was my friend.'

'Hannes?'

'Yes, Hannes.'

'Is this because of Hannes?' Lothar said. 'Is it because of Hannes you're acting like this?'

'Leave me alone,' he said.

'What has Hannes got to do with me?'

'You—'

He stopped immediately. Where did Hannes come into the picture? He had not seen Lothar since Hannes's expulsion. After that Lothar had vanished into thin air. In the meanwhile he had heard Ilona and her friends describe Lothar as a puppet of the security police, a traitor and informer who tried to make people reveal what their friends were thinking and saying. Lothar did not know that he suspected anything. But he had been poised to tell him everything, tell him what Ilona had said about him. Suddenly it struck him that if there was one thing he must not do, it was to give Lothar a piece of his mind, or imply that he knew about him.

It dawned on him how much he still had to learn about the game he was beginning to play, not only with Lothar but also his fellow Icelanders and in fact everyone he met, apart from Ilona.

'I what?' Lothar said stubbornly.

'Nothing,' he said.

'Hannes didn't belong here any more,' Lothar said. 'He had no

187

business being here. You said that yourself. You said that to me. You came to me and we talked about it. We were sitting in the pub and you told me what a cheapskate you thought Hannes was. You and Hannes weren't friends.'

'No, that's right,' he said, an unsavoury taste in his mouth. 'We weren't friends.'

He felt he had to say that. He was not fully aware who he was covering for. He no longer knew exactly where he stood. Why he did not speak his mind as he had in the past. He was playing some game of bluff that he barely understood, trying to inch his way forward in total darkness. Maybe he was no braver than that. Maybe he was a coward. His thoughts turned to Ilona. She would have known what to say to Lothar.

'I never said he ought to be expelled,' he said, steeling himself.

'Actually, I recall you talking along exactly those lines,' Lothar said.

'I didn't,' he said and raised his voice. 'That's a lie.'

Lothar smiled.

'Calm down,' he said.

'Just leave me alone.'

He was about to walk away but Lothar stopped him. This time he was more menacing and gripped his arm tighter, pulling him close and whispering in his ear.

'We need to talk.'

'We have nothing to talk about,' he said and tried to tear himself loose. But Lothar held him fast.

'We just need to have a word about your Ilona.'

He felt his face flush suddenly. His muscles slackened, and Lothar felt his arm go powerless for an instant.

'What are you talking about?' he said, trying not to give himself away.

'I don't think she's good enough company for you,' Lothar said, 'and I say that as your *Betreuer* and your comrade. I hope you'll forgive me for intruding.'

'What are you talking about?' he repeated. 'Good enough company? I don't think it's any of your business what—'

'I don't think she associates with the likes of us,' Lothar interrupted him. 'I'm afraid she'll drag you down into the mire with her.'

Speechless, he stared at Lothar.

'What are you talking about?' he blurted out for the third time; he did not know what else he ought to say. His mind was a blank. All he could think about was Ilona.

'We know about the meetings she organises,' Lothar said. 'We know who goes to the meetings. We know that you've been at those meetings. We know about the pamphlets she circulates.'

He could not believe what he was hearing.

'Let us help you,' Lothar said.

He stared at Lothar, who fixed him with a serious expression. Lothar had dropped all the charades. His false smile was gone. He could see only unflinching harshness on his face.

'Us?' he said. 'What us? What are you talking about?'

'Come with me,' Lothar said. 'I want to show you something.'

'I'm not coming with you,' he said. 'I don't have to come anywhere with you!'

'You won't regret it,' Lothar said in the same steady voice. 'I'm trying to help you. Try to understand that. Let me show you something. So you understand exactly what I'm talking about.'

'What can you show me?'

'Come on,' Lothar said, half-pushing him along in front. 'I'm trying to help you. Trust me.'

He wanted to resist, but fear and curiosity drove him on and he yielded. If Lothar had something to show him it might be worth seeing it, rather than turning his back on him. They left the university building for the city centre, heading across Karl Marx Square and along Barfussgässchen. Soon he saw that they were approaching Dittrichring 24, which he knew was the city headquarters of the security police. He slowed, then stopped dead when he saw that Lothar intended to go up the steps into the building.

'What are we doing here?' he asked.

'Come on,' Lothar said. 'We need to talk to you. Don't make this more difficult for yourself.'

'Difficult? I'm not going in there!'

'Either you come now or they come and get you,' Lothar said. 'It's better this way.'

He stood still in his tracks. He would have liked to run away. What did the security police want of him? He hadn't done anything. From the street corner he looked in all directions. Would anyone see him go inside?

'What do you mean?' he said in a low voice. He was genuinely afraid.

'Come on,' Lothar said, and opened the door.

Hesitantly, he walked up the steps and followed Lothar into the building. They entered a small foyer with a grey stone staircase and brownish marble walls. A door at the top of the steps led to a reception room. He immediately noticed the smell of dirty linoleum, grimy walls, smoking, sweat and fear. Lothar nodded to the man at reception and opened a door onto a long corridor. The walls were painted green. Halfway down the corridor was an alcove, inside it an office with the door open and beside it a narrow steel door. Lothar went into the office where a weary middle-aged man was sitting at a desk. He looked up and acknowledged Lothar.

'Hell of a long time that took,' the man said to Lothar, ignoring the visitor.

The man smoked fat, pungent cigarettes. His fingers were stained yellow and the ashtray was crammed with minuscule cigarette butts. He had a thick moustache, discoloured by tobacco. He was swarthy, with greying sideburns. He pulled out one of the desk drawers, took out a file and opened it. Inside were a few typed pages and some black-and-white photographs. The man removed the photographs, looked at them, then tossed them across the desk to him.

'Isn't that you?' he asked.

Tómas picked up the photographs. It took him a while to realise what they were. They had been taken in the evening from some distance and showed people leaving a block of flats. A light above the door illuminated the group. Peering more closely at the photograph, he could suddenly see Ilona and a man who had been at the meeting in the basement flat, another woman from the same meeting and himself. He leafed through the photographs. Some were enlargements of faces – Ilona's face and his own.

After lighting a cigarette, the man with the thick moustache leaned back in his seat. Lothar had sat down on a chair in a corner of the office. On one wall was a street map of Leipzig and a photograph of Ulbricht. Three sturdy steel cupboards stood against another wall.

He turned to Lothar, trying to conceal the trembling in his hands. 'What's this?' he asked.

'You ought to tell us that,' Lothar retorted.

'Who took these photos?'

'Do you think that matters?' Lothar said.

'Are you spying on me?'

Lothar and the man with the burnt moustache exchanged glances, then Lothar began laughing.

'What do you want?' he said, addressing Lothar. 'Why are you taking these photographs?'

'Do you know what this gathering is?' Lothar asked.

'I don't know those people,' he said and was not lying. 'Apart from Ilona, of course. Why are you photographing them?'

'No, of course you don't know them,' Lothar said. 'Apart from pretty little Ilona. You know her. Know her better than most people do. You even know her better than your friend Hannes did.'

He did not know what Lothar was driving at. He looked at the man with the moustache. He looked out into the corridor where the steel door confronted him. There was a small hole in it with a shutter across. He wondered whether anyone was inside. Whether they had anyone in custody. He wanted to get out of the office at whatever cost. He felt like a trapped animal looking desperately for an escape route.

'Do you want me to stop going to those meetings?' he offered. 'That's no problem. I haven't been to many.'

He stared at the steel door. Suddenly he was overwhelmed by fear. He had already started to back down, already started to promise that he would mend his ways, despite not knowing exactly what he had done wrong or what he could do to appease them. He would do anything to get out of that office.

'Stop?' said the man with the moustache. 'Not at all. No one's asking you to stop. On the contrary. We'd like you to go to more meetings. They must be very interesting. What's their purpose?'

'Nothing,' he said, struggling to put on a brave face. They must be able to tell. 'No purpose. We just talk about university matters. Music. Books. Stuff like that.'

The man with the moustache grinned. Surely he recognised fear. Must see how obvious his fear was. Almost tangible. He had never been a good liar anyway.

'What were you saying about Hannes?' he asked hesitantly, looking at Lothar. 'That I know Ilona better than Hannes did? What are you talking about?'

'Didn't you know?' Lothar said, faking surprise. 'They were together, just like you and Ilona are together now. Before you appeared on the scene. Didn't she mention that?'

Lost for words, he gaped at Lothar.

'Why do you suppose she never told you?' Lothar said in the same tone of mock surprise. 'She must have a knack with you Icelanders. You know what I think? I don't think Hannes was willing to help her.'

'Help her?'

'She wants to marry one of you and move to Iceland,' Lothar said. 'It didn't work out with Hannes. Perhaps you can help her. She's wanted to leave Hungary for a long time. Hasn't she told you anything about that? She's made quite an effort to get away.'

'I don't have time for all this,' he said, trying to brace himself. 'I must be going. Thanks for telling me all this. Lothar, I'll discuss it better with you later.'

He walked towards the door, half-falteringly. The man with the moustache looked at Lothar, who shrugged.

'Sit down, you fucking idiot!' the man screamed as he leaped out of his chair.

He stopped by the door, stunned, and turned round.

'We don't tolerate subversion!' the moustachioed man shouted in his face. 'Especially not from fucking foreigners like you who come here to study under false pretences. Sit down, you fucking idiot! Shut the door and sit down!'

He closed the door, went back into the office and sat down on a chair by the desk.

'Now you've made him angry,' Lothar said, shaking his head.

He wished that he could go back to Iceland and forget the whole business. He envied Hannes for having escaped this nightmare. This was the first thought to cross his mind when they finally released him. They forbade him to leave the country. He had been instructed to hand in his passport the same day. Then his thoughts turned to Ilona. He knew he could never leave her and, when his fear had largely subsided, neither did he want to. He could never leave Ilona. They used her as a threat against him. If he didn't do what they said, something might happen to her. Although not explicit, the threat was clear enough. If he told her what had happened, something might happen to her. They did not say what. They left the threat hanging to allow him to imagine the worst.

It was as if they had had him in their sights for a long time. They knew precisely what they were going to do and how they wanted him to serve them. None of this had been decided on the spur of the moment. As far as he could tell they planned to install him as their man at the university. He was supposed to report to them, monitor antisocial activity, inform. He knew that he would be under surveillance from now on, because they had told him so. What interested them most were the activities of Ilona and her companions in Leipzig and the rest of Germany. They wanted to know what went on at the meetings. Who the leaders were. The guiding ideology. Whether there were links with Hungary or other Eastern European countries. How widespread the dissent was. What was said about Ulbricht and the communist party. They recited more points but he had long since ceased to listen. His ears were buzzing.

'What if I refuse?' he said to Lothar in Icelandic.

'Speak German!' the man with the moustache snapped.

'You will not refuse,' Lothar said.

The man told him what would happen if he did. He would not be deported. He would not get off as lightly as Hannes. In their eyes, he was worthless. He was like vermin. If he did not do as instructed, he would lose Ilona.

'But if I tell you everything I've lost her anyway,' he said.

'Not the way we've arranged it,' the man with the moustache said, stubbing out yet another cigarette.

Not the way we've arranged it.

This was the sentence that would haunt him after he had left the headquarters and it rang in his head all the way home.

Not the way we've arranged it.

He stared at Lothar. They had arranged something involving Ilona. Already. It simply had to be enacted. If he didn't do as he was told.

'What are you anyway?' he said to Lothar, rising nervously from his chair.

'Sit down!' shouted the man with the moustache, who also stood up.

Lothar looked at him, a vague smile playing across his lips.

'How do you sleep at night?'

Lothar did not answer.

'What if I tell Ilona about this?'

194

'You shouldn't,' Lothar said. 'Tell me another thing, how did she manage to win you over? According to our information, you were the hardest of the hardliners. What happened? How did she manage to turn you?'

He walked over to Lothar. He mustered the courage to tell him what he wanted to say. The man with the moustache walked around the desk and stood behind him.

'It wasn't her who won me over,' he said in Icelandic. 'It was you. Everything you stand for persuaded me. Your cynicism. Hatred. Lust for power. Everything you are won me over.'

'It's very simple,' Lothar said. 'Either you're a socialist or you're not.'

'No,' he said. 'You don't get it, Lothar. Either you're a human being or you're not.'

He hurried home, thinking about Ilona. He had to tell her what had happened, no matter what they demanded or had arranged. She had to flee the city. Could they go to Iceland together? He felt how infinitely far away Iceland was. Maybe she could escape back to Hungary. Maybe even cross over to West Germany. To West Berlin. The controls were not that strict. He could tell them everything they wanted to hear to keep them off Ilona's back while she set up her escape. She had to leave the country.

What was that about Hannes? What had Lothar said about Hannes and Ilona? Were they together once? Ilona had never told him that. Only that they were friends and had got to know each other at the meetings. Was Lothar playing mind games with him? Or was Ilona really using him to get away?

He had broken into a run. People flashed past without him noticing them. He went from one street to the next completely oblivious, his mind racing with thoughts about Ilona and himself and Lothar and the security police and the steel door with the hatch on it and the man with the moustache. He would be shown no mercy. That much he knew. Icelandic citizen or not. It made no difference to these men. They wanted him to spy for them. Submit reports about what went on at the meetings with Ilona. Inform on what he heard in the corridors of the university, among the Icelanders at the dormitory and other foreign students. They knew they had leverage. If he refused he would not get off as lightly as Hannes.

They had Ilona.

By the time he finally reached home he was in tears, and he hugged Ilona speechlessly. She was worried. She said she had spent ages waiting for him outside Thomaskirche. He told her everything, even though they had ordered him to tell her nothing. Ilona listened to him in silence, then began questioning him. He answered her as accurately as he could. The first thing she asked about was her group of friends, the Leipzigers, whether they could be identified from the photographs. He said he thought the police knew about every single one of them.

'Oh my God,' Ilona groaned. 'We have to tip them off. How did they find out about this? They must have followed us. Someone's blown the whistle. Someone who knew about the meetings. Who? Who's informed on us? We were always so cautious. No one knew about those meetings.'

'I don't know,' he said.

'I must contact them,' she said, pacing the floor of their little room. She stopped by the window overlooking the street and peeped outside. 'Are they watching us?' she asked. 'Now?'

'I don't know,' he said.

'Oh my God,' Ilona groaned again.

'They said that you and Hannes were together,' he said. 'Lothar said so.'

'That's a lie,' she said. 'Everything they say is a lie. Surely you know that. They're playing a game, playing a game with us. We need to decide what to do. I must warn the others.'

'They said you hung around with us in order to escape to Iceland.'

'Of course they say that, Tómas. What else would they say? Stop being so stupid.'

'I wasn't supposed to tell you anything, so we have to act carefully,' he said, knowing she was right. Everything they said was a lie. Everything. 'You're in great danger,' he said. 'They let me know that. We mustn't do anything stupid.'

They looked at each other in desperation.

'What have we got ourselves into?' he sighed.

'I don't know,' she said, hugging him and calming down slightly. 'They don't want another Hungary. *That's* what we've got ourselves into.'

Three days later, Ilona went missing.

Karl was with her when they came and arrested her. He went running to Tómas on the campus and gasped out the news. Karl had gone to collect a book she was going to lend him. Suddenly the police appeared in the doorway. He was slammed against the wall. They turned the room upside down. Ilona was led away.

Karl was only halfway through his account when Tómas ran off. They had been so cautious. Ilona had passed on a message to her companions and they had made arrangements to leave Leipzig. She wanted to go back to Hungary to stay with her family; he was going back to Iceland and would meet her in Budapest. His studies no longer mattered. Only Ilona mattered.

When he reached their house, his lungs were bursting. The door was open and he ran inside and into their room. Everything was in disarray, books and magazines and bedclothes on the floor, the desk overturned, the bed on its side. They had spared nothing. Some objects were broken. He stepped on the typewriter that lay on the floor.

He ran straight to the Stasi headquarters. Only when he was there did he realise that he did not know the name of the man with the moustache; the people at reception did not understand what he meant. He asked to go down the corridor and find him for himself, but the receptionist just shook his head. He barged against the door to the corridor, but it was locked. He shouted for Lothar. The receptionist had come from behind his desk and called for assistance. Three men appeared and dragged him away from the door. At that moment it opened and the man with the moustache entered.

'What did you do with her?!' he roared. 'Let me see her!' He shouted down the corridor: 'Ilona! Ilona!'

The man with the moustache slammed the door behind him and barked orders at the others, who seized him and led him outside. He pounded on the front door and cried out to Ilona, but to no avail. He was out of his mind with anxiety. They had arrested Ilona and he was convinced they were keeping her in that building. He had to see her, had to help her, get her released. He would do anything.

He remembered noticing Lothar on campus that morning and left in haste. A tram had stopped by the campus and he jumped aboard. He leaped out by the university while the tram was still moving and found Lothar sitting alone at a table in the cafeteria. There were few people inside. He sat down facing Lothar, panting and wheezing, his face red from running, worry and fear.

'Is everything all right?' Lothar said.

'I'll do anything for you if you let her go,' he said immediately.

Lothar took a long look at him, observing his sufferings almost philosophically.

'Who?' he said.

'Ilona – you know who I'm talking about. I'll do anything if you let her go.'

'I don't know what you're on about,' Lothar said.

'You arrested Ilona this lunchtime.'

'We?' Lothar said. 'Who's "we"?'

'The security police,' he said. 'Ilona was arrested this morning. Karl was with her when they came. Won't you talk to them? Won't you tell them I'll do whatever it takes for them to release her?'

'I don't think you matter any more,' Lothar said.

'Can you help me?' he said. 'Can you intervene?'

'If she's been arrested, there's nothing I can do. It's too late. Unfortunately.'

'What can I do?' he said, almost bursting into tears. 'Tell me what I can do.'

Lothar took a long look at him.

'Go back to Poechestrasse,' he said in the end. 'Go home and hope for the best.'

'What kind of a person are you?' he said, feeling the anger coursing through him. 'What kind of bastard are you? What makes you act like . . . like a monster? What is it? Where does this incredible urge to dominate come from, this arrogance? This inhumanity!'

Lothar looked around at the few souls sitting in the cafeteria. Then he smiled.

'People who play with fire get burned, but they're always surprised when they are. Always fucking innocent and surprised when it happens.'

Lothar stood up and bent over him.

'Go home,' he said. 'Hope for the best. I'll talk to them but I can't promise anything.'

Then Lothar walked away, taking slow steps, calmly, as if none of this was any concern of his. He stayed in the cafeteria and buried his face in his hands. He thought about Ilona and tried to persuade himself that they had only called her in for interrogation and she would soon be released. Maybe they were intimidating her, as they had done to him a few days before. They exploited fear. Fed off it. Maybe she was already back home. He stood up and left the cafeteria.

When he left the university building he found everything strangely unaltered wherever he looked. People were acting as if nothing had happened. They hurried along the pavements or stood talking. His world had collapsed, yet everything seemed unchanged. As if everything were still in order. He would return to their room and wait for her. Maybe she was already back home. Maybe she would be back later. She had to come. What were they detaining her for? For meeting people and talking to them?

He was at his wits' end when he rushed off home. It was such a short time since they'd been lying snuggled up against each other and she had told him that what she had suspected for some time had been confirmed. She whispered in his ear. It had probably happened at the end of the summer.

He lay paralysed, staring up at the ceiling, uncertain how to take the news. Then he hugged her and said he wanted to live with her for his whole life.

'Both of us,' she whispered.

'Yes, both of you,' he said, and laid his head on her stomach.

He was brought back to his senses by the pain in his hand. Often when he thought back to what had happened in East Germany he would clench his fists until his hands ached. He relaxed his muscles, wondering as usual whether he could have prevented it all. Whether he could have done something else. Something that would have changed the course of events. He never reached a conclusion.

He stood up stiffly from his chair and walked to the door down to the basement. Opening it, he switched on the light and carefully descended the stone steps. They were worn after decades of use and could be slippery. He entered the roomy basement and turned on the lights. Various oddments had accumulated there over the years. If he could avoid it, he never threw anything away. It was not untidy, however, because he kept it all in order – everything had its place.

Along one wall stood a workbench. Sometimes he made carvings. Produced small objects from wood and painted them. That was his only hobby. Taking a square block of wood and creating from it something living and beautiful. He kept some of the animals upstairs in his flat. The ones he was most satisfied with. The smaller he succeeded in making them, the more rewarding they were to carve.

He had even carved an Icelandic sheepdog with a curly tail and cocked ears, scarcely larger than a thumbnail.

He reached under the workbench and opened the box he kept there. He felt the butt, then removed the pistol from its place. The metal was cold to the touch. Sometimes his memories would draw him down to the basement to fondle the weapon or just to reassure himself that it was where it belonged.

He did not regret what had happened all those years later. Long after he returned from East Germany.

Long after Ilona disappeared.

He would never regret that.

23

The German ambassador in Reykjavík, Frau Doktor Elsa Müller, received them personally in her office at noon. She was an imposing woman, past sixty, and immediately started eyeing up Sigurdur Óli. Erlendur in his brown woollen cardigan under his tatty jacket attracted less attention from her. She said she was a historian by profession, hence the doctorate. She had German biscuits and coffee waiting for them. They sat down and Sigurdur Óli accepted the offer of coffee. He did not want to be impolite. Erlendur declined. He would have liked to smoke, but could not bring himself to ask permission.

They exchanged pleasantries, the detectives about the efforts that the German embassy had gone to, Dr Müller about how natural it was to try to assist the Icelandic authorities.

The Icelandic CID's enquiry about Lothar Weiser had gone through all the proper channels, she told them – or rather she told Sigurdur Óli, because she directed her words almost entirely towards him. They spoke English. She confirmed that a German by that name had worked as an attaché to the East German trade delegation in the 1960s. It had proved particularly difficult to acquire information about him, because he had been an agent for the East German secret service at the time and had connections with the KGB in Moscow. She told them that a large number of Stasi files had been destroyed after the fall of the Berlin Wall, and the scant information that survived was largely obtained from West German intelligence sources.

'He vanished without a trace in Iceland in 1968,' Frau Müller said. 'No one knew what happened to him. At the time it was thought most likely that he had done something wrong and . . .'

Frau Müller stopped and shrugged.

'Was bumped off,' Erlendur completed the sentence for her.

'That may be one possibility, but we have no confirmation of it yet. He may also have committed suicide and been sent home in a diplomatic bag.'

She smiled at Sigurdur Óli as if to signal that this was a humorous remark.

'I know you'll find it amusingly absurd,' she said, 'but in terms of the diplomatic service, Iceland is the back end of the world. The weather's dreadful. The incessant storms, the darkness and cold. There was hardly a worse punishment imaginable than to post people here.'

'So was he being punished for something when he was sent here?' Sigurdur Óli asked.

'As far as we can find out, he worked for the security police in Leipzig. When he was younger.' She flicked through some papers on the table in front of her. 'During the period 1953 to 1957 or 1958 he had the task of getting the foreign students at the university in the city, who were mostly if not all communists, to work for him or to become informers. This wasn't proper espionage. It was more keeping watch on what the students were doing.'

'Informers?' Sigurdur Óli said.

'Yes, I don't know what you would call it,' Frau Müller said. 'Spying on people around you. Lothar Weiser was said to be very good at getting young people to work for him. He could offer money and even good exam results. The situation was volatile then because of Hungary and all that. Young people kept a close eye on what was going on there. The security police kept a close eye on the youngsters.

203

Weiser infiltrated their ranks. And not just him. There were people like Lothar Weiser in every university in East Germany and in all the communist countries, as a rule. They wanted to monitor their own people, know what they were thinking. Foreign students could have a dangerous influence, although most were conscientious both as students and socialists.'

Erlendur recalled having heard about Lothar's command of Icelandic.

'Were there Icelandic students in Leipzig then?' he asked.

'I really don't know,' Frau Müller said. 'You must be able to find that out.'

'What about Lothar?' Sigurdur Óli asked. 'After he was in Leipzig?'

'This must all sound rather strange to you, I imagine,' Frau Müller said. 'Secret service and espionage. You only know about this from hearsay out here in the middle of the ocean, don't you?'

'Probably,' Erlendur smiled. 'I don't remember us having a single decent spy.'

'Weiser became a spy for the East German secret service. He'd stopped working for the security police by then. He did a lot of travelling and worked at embassies around the world. Among other postings he was sent here. He had a special interest in this country, as proven by the fact that he learned Icelandic when he was young. Lothar Weiser was a highly talented linguist. Like everywhere else, his role here was to get local people to work for him, so he had the same sort of function as in Leipzig. If their ideals were shaky, he could offer money.'

'Did he have any Icelanders in his charge?' Sigurdur Óli asked.

'He didn't necessarily make any headway here,' Frau Müller said.

'What about the embassy officials who worked with him in Reykjavík?' Erlendur said. 'Are any of them still alive?'

'We have a list of the staff from that time but haven't managed to identify anyone who is still alive and would have known Weiser or what happened to him. All we know at the moment is that his story seems to end here in Iceland. How, we don't know. It's as if he simply vanished into thin air. Admittedly, the old secret service files aren't very reliable. There are a lot of gaps, just as in the Stasi files. When they were made public after unification, or most of the personal records anyway, a lot were missing. To tell the truth, our information about what happened to Lothar Weiser is unsatisfactory, but we'll keep searching.'

They fell into silence. Sigurdur Óli nibbled at a biscuit. Erlendur still craved a cigarette. He could not see an ashtray anywhere and it was probably a forlorn hope that he would be able to light up.

'Actually, there's one interesting point in all this,' Frau Müller said, 'considering that it involves Leipzig. The Leipzigers are very proud of starting, in effect, the uprising that brought down Honecker and the Wall. There were massive protests in Leipzig against the communist government. The centre of the uprising was Nikolaikirche near the city centre. People gathered there to protest and to pray, and one night the protesters left the church and broke into the Stasi headquarters, which were nearby. In Leipzig at least, this is regarded as the start of the developments that brought down the Berlin Wall.'

'Indeed,' Erlendur said.

'Strange if a German spy went missing in Iceland,' Sigurdur Óli said. 'It's somehow . . .'

'Ridiculous?' Frau Müller smiled. 'In one way it was convenient for his killer – if he *was* killed – that Weiser was a secret agent. You can see that from the reaction of the East German trade delegation here; they didn't have a proper embassy then. They did nothing. It's a typical response for covering up a diplomatic scandal. Nobody says a thing. It's as if Weiser had never existed. We have no evidence of any investigation of his disappearance.'

She looked at them in turn.

'He wasn't reported missing to the police here,' Erlendur said. 'We've checked that.'

'Doesn't that suggest it was an internal matter?' Sigurdur Óli asked. 'That one of his colleagues killed him?'

'It could,' Frau Müller said. 'We still know so little about Weiser and his fate.'

'Don't you suppose the murderer's dead by now?' Sigurdur Óli said. 'It was such a long time ago. If Lothar Weiser was murdered, that is.'

'Do you think he's the man in the lake?' Frau Müller asked.

'We don't have any idea,' Sigurdur Óli said. They had not told the embassy any details regarding the discovery. He looked at Erlendur, who nodded.

'The skeleton we found,' Sigurdur Óli said, 'was tied to a Russian listening device dating from the 1960s.'

'I see,' Frau Müller said thoughtfully. 'A Russian device? So what? What significance does that have?'

'There are a number of possibilities,' Sigurdur Óli said.

'Could the device have come from the East German embassy or delegation or whatever you call it?' Erlendur asked.

'Of course,' Frau Müller said. 'The Warsaw Pact countries co-operated very closely, including in the field of espionage.'

'When Germany was unified,' Erlendur said, 'and the embassies here in Reykjavík were merged, did you find any devices like that in the hands of the East Germans?'

'We didn't merge,' Frau Müller said. 'The East German one was dissolved without our knowledge. But I'll check about the devices.'

'What do you read into finding a Russian listening device with the skeleton?' Sigurdur Óli asked.

'I can't say,' Frau Müller answered. 'It's not my job to speculate.'

'No, right,' Sigurdur Óli said. 'But all we have is speculation, so . . .'

Erlendur put his hand in his jacket pocket and clutched his cigarette packet. He did not dare take it out of his pocket.

'What did *you* do wrong?' he asked.

'What do you mean, what did I do wrong?' Frau Müller said.

'Why were you sent to this dreadful country? To the arsehole of the world?'

Frau Müller gave a smile which Erlendur thought was rather ambiguous.

'Do you think that's an appropriate question?' she asked. 'I *am* the German ambassador to Iceland, remember.'

Erlendur shrugged.

'Sorry,' Erlendur said, 'but you described a diplomatic job here as being some kind of punishment. But it's none of my business, of course.'

An awkward silence descended upon the office until Sigurdur Óli made a move, cleared his throat and thanked her for her assistance. Frau Müller said coldly that she would be in contact if anything came to light about Lothar Weiser that might prove useful. They could tell from the tone of her voice that she would not be running to the nearest telephone.

When they were outside the embassy they discussed whether there might have been Icelandic students in Leipzig who became acquainted with Lothar Weiser. Sigurdur Óli said he would look into it.

'Weren't you a bit rude to her?' he asked.

'That arsehole-of-the-world stuff gets on my nerves,' Erlendur said and lit a long-awaited cigarette.

24

When Erlendur got home from the office that evening, Sindri Snaer was waiting for him in his flat. He was sleeping on the sofa but when Erlendur came in he woke up.

'Where have you been hiding?' Erlendur asked.

'Around,' Sindri Snaer said, sitting up.

'Have you had anything to eat?'

'No, it's okay.'

Erlendur took out some rye bread, lamb pâté and butter, and made coffee. Sindri said he was not hungry but Erlendur noticed how he wolfed down the pâté and bread. He put some cheese on the table and that vanished too.

'Do you know anything about Eva Lind?' Erlendur asked over a cup of coffee when Sindri Snaer's hunger seemed to have been satisfied.

'Yes,' he said, 'I spoke to her.'

'Is she all right?'

'Sort of,' Sindri said and produced a packet of cigarettes. Erlendur did likewise. Sindri lit his father's cigarette with a cheap lighter. 'I think it's been a long time since Eva was all right,' he said.

They sat smoking and not speaking over their black coffee.

'Why is it so dark in here?' Sindri asked, looking into the living room where the thick curtains kept the evening sun at bay.

'It's too bright outside,' Erlendur said. 'In the evenings and at night,' he added, after a short pause. He did not go into the matter any further. He did not tell Sindri that he much preferred short days and pitch darkness to perpetual sunshine and the endless light it radiated. He did not know himself the reason for it. Did not know why he felt better in dark winters than during bright summers.

'Where did you dredge her up?' he asked. 'Where did you find Eva?'

'She texted me. I phoned her. We've always kept in touch, even when I was away from the city. We've always got on well.'

He stopped talking and looked at his father.

'Eva's a good soul,' he said.

'Yes,' Erlendur said.

'Seriously,' Sindri said. 'If you'd known her when she was . . .'

'You don't have to tell me anything about it,' Erlendur said, not realising how curt he sounded. 'I know all about that.'

Sindri sat in silence, watching his father. Then he stubbed out his cigarette. Erlendur did the same. Sindri stood up.

'Thanks for the coffee,' he said.

'Are you leaving?' Erlendur said, standing up too and following Sindri out of the kitchen. 'Where are you going?'

Sindri did not answer. He took his scruffy denim jacket from the chair and put it on. Erlendur watched him. He did not want Sindri to leave in a temper.

'I didn't mean to . . .' he began. 'It's just that . . . Eva's so . . . I know you're good friends.'

'What do you think you know about Eva?' Sindri asked. 'Why do you reckon you know anything about Eva?'

'Don't make a martyr out of her,' Erlendur said. 'She doesn't deserve it. And she wouldn't want you to either.'

'I'm not,' Sindri said, 'but don't kid yourself that you know Eva. Don't think that. And what do you know about what she deserves?'

'I know she's a bloody junkie,' Erlendur snarled. 'Is there anything else I need to know? She does nothing about sorting herself out. You know she had a miscarriage. The doctors said it was a mercy after all the dope she took during her pregnancy. Don't get on a high horse about your sister. That idiot's lost the plot yet again and I can't be bothered to go through all that crap any more.'

Sindri had opened the door and was halfway out onto the landing. He paused and looked back at Erlendur. Then he turned round, went back into the flat and closed the door. He walked over to him.

'Put myself on a high horse about my sister?' he said.

'You have to be realistic,' Erlendur said. 'That's all I'm saying. For as long as she doesn't want to do anything to help herself, there's bugger all we can do.'

'I remember Eva well when she wasn't on drugs,' Sindri said. 'Do you remember her?'

He had gone right up close to his father and Erlendur could see the anger in his movements, his face, his eyes.

'Do you remember Eva when she wasn't doing drugs?' he repeated.

'No,' Erlendur said. 'I don't. You know that perfectly well.'

'Yes, I know that perfectly well,' Sindri said.

'Don't start preaching any bollocks to me,' Erlendur said. 'She's done plenty of that.'

'Bollocks?' Sindri said. 'Are we just bollocks?'

'Jesus Christ,' Erlendur groaned. 'Stop it. I don't want to argue with you. I don't want to argue with her and I certainly don't want to argue *about* her.'

'You don't know anything, do you?' Sindri said. 'I saw Eva. The day before yesterday. She's with a bloke called Eddi who's ten, fifteen years older than her. He was out of his head. He was going to stab me because he thought I was a thug. Thought I'd come to collect a debt. They both deal but they do a lot of stuff too, then they need more and the heavies come round for the money. People are after them now. Maybe you know this Eddi, since you're a cop. Eva didn't want to tell me where she's crashing – she's scared shitless. They're in some den near the city centre. Eddi supplies her with dope and she loves him. I've never seen such true love. Get it? He's her dealer. She was dirty – no, she was *filthy*. And you know what she wanted to know?'

Erlendur shook his head.

'She wanted to know if I'd seen you,' Sindri said. 'Don't you think that's weird? The only thing she wanted to know was if I'd seen you. Why do you think that is? Why do you think she's worried about that? Amongst all that squalor and misery? Why do you think that is?'

'I don't know,' Erlendur said. 'I stopped trying to work Eva out long ago.'

He could have mentioned that he and Eva had been through thick and thin together. That although their relationship was difficult and fragile and by no means free from friction, it was a relationship nevertheless. Sometimes it was even a very good one. He thought back to Christmas when she was so depressed about the baby she had lost that he thought she might attempt something stupid. She spent the Christmas and New Year with him and they discussed the baby and the guilt about it that tormented her. Then, one morning in the New Year, she was gone.

Sindri stared at him.

'She was worried about how you were getting on. How *you* were getting on!'

Erlendur said nothing.

'If only you'd known her the way she used to be,' Sindri said. 'Before she got into dope, if you'd known her like I did, you'd have been shocked. I hadn't met her for a long time and when I saw her, the way she looked . . . I . . . wanted to . . .'

'I think I did all I could to help her,' Erlendur said. 'There are limits to what can be done. And when you feel there's no real desire to do anything in return . . .'

His words faded away.

'She had ginger hair,' Sindri said. 'When we were kids. Thick ginger hair that Mum said she must have got from your side of the family.'

'I remember the ginger,' Erlendur said.

'When she was twelve she had it cropped and dyed black,' Sindri said.

'Why did she do that?'

'Her relationship with Mum was tough a lot of the time,' Sindri said. 'Mum never treated me the way she did Eva. Perhaps because she was older and reminded her too much of you. Maybe because Eva was always up to something. She was definitely hyperactive. Ginger-haired and hyperactive. She got on the wrong side of her teachers. Mum sent her to another school but that really just made things worse. She was teased for being the new kid, so she pulled all sorts of pranks to get attention. And she bullied others because she thought that would help her fit in. Mum went to millions of meetings at school about her.'

Sindri lit a cigarette.

'She never believed what Mum said about you. Or she said she didn't believe it. They fought like cat and dog and Eva was brilliant at using you to wind Mum up. Said it was no surprise you left her. That no one could live with her. She defended you.'

Sindri scouted around with the cigarette in his hand. Erlendur pointed to an ashtray on the coffee table. After taking a drag, Sindri sat at the table. He had calmed down and the tension between them eased. He told Erlendur how Eva had invented stories about him when she was old enough to ask sensible questions about her father.

Erlendur's children could sense their mother's animosity towards him, but Eva did not believe what she said and pictured her father as she felt fit, images completely different to the ones her mother presented. Eva had run away from home twice, at the ages of nine and eleven, to look for him. She lied to her friends, saying that her real Dad – not the ones who used to hang around her mother – was always abroad. Whenever he came back he brought her wonderful presents. She could never show them any of the presents because her father did not want her boasting about them. Others were told that her father lived in a huge mansion where she sometimes went to stay and could have whatever she fancied because he was so rich.

When she began to grow up her tales about her father became more mundane. Once their mother said that as far as she knew he was still in the police force. Through all her troubles at school and at home, when she started smoking tobacco and hash, drinking at the age of thirteen or fourteen, Eva Lind always knew that her father was somewhere in the city. As time wore on she grew unsure about whether she wanted to find him any longer.

Maybe, she said to Sindri once, it's better to keep him in your head. She was convinced he would turn out to be a disappointment, like everything else in her life.

'No doubt I did,' Erlendur said.

He had sat down in his armchair. Sindri took out his cigarette packet again.

'And she didn't make a good impression with all those studs in her face,' Erlendur said. 'She always falls into the same old rut. Never has any money, latches on to some dealer and hangs around with him, and no matter how badly they treat her, she always stays.'

'I'll try to talk to her,' Sindri said. 'But what I really think is that she's waiting for you to come and rescue her. I think she's on her last legs. She's often been bad, but I've never seen her like that before.'

'Why did she cut her hair?' Erlendur asked. 'When she was twelve.'

'Someone touched her and stroked her hair and talked dirty to her,' Sindri said.

He said this straightforwardly, as if he could search his memory for such incidents and find a whole hoard of them.

Sindri looked along the bookshelves in the living room. There was almost nothing but books in the flat.

Erlendur's expression remained unchanged, his eyes cold as marble.

'Eva said you were always looking into missing persons,' Sindri said.

'Yes,' Erlendur said.

'Is it because of your brother?'

'Perhaps. Probably.'

'Eva said you told her you were her missing person.'

'Yes,' Erlendur said. 'Just because people disappear doesn't mean they're necessarily dead,' he added, and into his mind came the image of a black Ford Falcon outside Reykjavík coach station, one hubcap missing.

Sindri did not want to stay. Erlendur invited him to sleep on the sofa but Sindri declined and they said goodbye. For a long while after his son had left, Erlendur sat in his chair wondering about his brother and Eva Lind – the little he remembered of her from when she was small. She was two when they separated. Sindri's description of her childhood had struck a nerve and he saw his strained relationship with Eva in a different, sadder light.

When he fell asleep, shortly after midnight, he was still thinking about his brother and Eva and himself and Sindri, and he dreamed a bizarre dream. The three of them, him and his children, had gone out for a drive. The kids were in the rear and he was behind the wheel, and he could not tell where they were because there was bright light all around them and he couldn't make out the landscape. Yet he still felt the car was moving and that he needed to steer it more carefully than usual because he could not see. Looking in the rear-view mirror at the children sitting behind him, he could not distinguish their faces. They looked as if they might be Sindri and Eva, but their faces were somehow blurred or wreathed in fog. He thought to himself that the children could not be anyone else. Eva did not look more than four years old. He saw that they were holding hands.

The radio was on and a seductive female voice was singing:

I know tonight you'll come to me . . .

Suddenly he saw a gigantic lorry heading for him. He tried to sound the horn and slam on the brakes but nothing happened. In the rear-view mirror he noticed that the children had gone and felt an indescribable sense of relief. He looked out at the road ahead. He was approaching the lorry at full speed. A crash was inevitable.

When it was all too late, he felt a strange presence beside him. He glanced across at the passenger seat and saw Eva Lind sitting there, staring at him and smiling. She was no longer a little girl but grown up and looking terrible in a filthy blue anorak with clumps of dirt in her hair, rings under her eyes, sunken cheeks and black lips. He noticed that, in her broad smile, some of her teeth were missing.

He wanted to say something to her but could not get the words out. Wanted to shout at her to throw herself from the car, but something held him back. Some kind of calmness about Eva Lind. Total indifference and peace. She looked away from him to the lorry and began to laugh.

An instant before they struck the lorry he started from sleep and called his daughter's name. It took him a while to get his bearings, then he laid his head back on the pillow and a strangely melancholic song crept up on him and ushered him back to a dreamless sleep.

I know tonight you'll come to me . . .

25

Níels did not remember Haraldur's brother Jóhann very clearly or really understand why Erlendur was making a fuss that he went unmentioned in the reports about the missing person. Níels was on the telephone when Erlendur interrupted him in his office. He was talking to his daughter who was studying medicine in America – a postgraduate course in paediatric medicine, as a matter of fact, Níels said proudly when he got off the telephone, as if he had never told anyone this before. In fact he hardly spoke about anything else. Erlendur could not have cared less. Níels was approaching retirement and dealt mainly with petty crimes now, car theft and minor burglaries, invariably telling people to try to forget it, not press charges, that it was just a waste of time. If they found the culprits they would make a report, but to no real purpose. The offenders would be released immediately after interrogation and the case would never go to court. In the unlikely event that it did, when enough petty crimes had been accumulated, the sentence would be ridiculous and an insult to their victims.

'What do you remember about this Jóhann?' Erlendur asked. 'Did you meet him? Did you ever go to their farm near Mosfellsbaer?'

'Shouldn't you be investigating that Russian spying equipment?' Níels retorted, took a pair of nail clippers from his waistcoat pocket and began manicuring himself. He looked at his watch. It would soon be time for a long and leisurely lunch.

'Oh yes,' Erlendur said. 'There's plenty to do.'

Níels stopped trimming his nails and looked at him. There was something in Erlendur's tone that he disliked.

'Jóhann, or Jói as his brother called him, was a bit funny,' Níels said. 'He was backward, or a halfwit as you used to be allowed to say. Before the political-correctness police ironed out the language with all their polite phrases.'

'Backward how?' Erlendur asked. He agreed with Níels about the language. It had been rendered absolutely impotent out of consideration for every possible minority.

'He was just dim,' Níels said and resumed his manicure. 'I went up there twice and talked to the brothers. The elder one spoke for them both – Jóhann didn't say much. They were completely different. One was nothing but skin and bone with a whittled face, while the other was fatter with a sort of childish, sheepish expression.'

'I can't quite picture Jóhann,' Erlendur said.

'I don't remember him too well, Erlendur. He sort of clung on to his brother like a little boy and was always asking who we were. Could hardly talk, just stammered out the words. He was like you'd imagine a farmer from some remote valley with straw in his hair and wellington boots on his feet.'

'And Haraldur managed to persuade you that Leopold had never been to their farm?'

'They didn't need to persuade me,' Níels said. 'We found the car outside the coach station. There was nothing to suggest that he'd been with the brothers. We had nothing to work with. No more than you do.'

'You don't reckon the brothers took the car there?'

'There was no indication of that,' Níels said. 'You know these missing-persons cases. You would have done exactly the same with the information we had.'

'I located the Falcon,' Erlendur said. 'I know it was years ago and the car must have been all over since then, but something that could be cow dung was found in it. It occurred to me that if you'd bothered to investigate the case properly, you might have found the man and been able to reassure the woman who was waiting for him then and has been ever since.'

'What a load of old codswallop,' Níels groaned, looking up from trimming his nails. 'How can you imagine anything so stupid? Just because you found some cow shit in the car thirty years later. Are you losing it?'

'You had the chance to find something useful,' Erlendur said.

'You and your missing persons,' Níels said. 'Where are you going with this, anyway? Who put you on to it? Is it a real case? Says who? Why are you reopening a thirty-year-old non-case which no one can figure out anyway, and trying to make something of it? Have you raised that woman's hopes? Are you telling her you can find him?'

'No,' Erlendur said.

'You're nuts,' Níels said. 'I've always said so. Ever since you started here. I told Marion that. I don't know what Marion saw in you.'

'I want to make a search for him in the fields out there,' Erlendur said.

'Search for him in the fields?' Níels roared in astonishment. 'Are you crackers? Where are you going to look?'

'Around the farm,' Erlendur said, unruffled. 'There are brooks and ditches at the bottom of the hill which lead all the way out to sea. I want to see whether we can't find something.'

'What grounds have you got?' Níels said. 'A confession? Any new developments? Bugger all. Just a lump of shit in an old heap of scrap!'

Erlendur stood up.

'I just wanted to tell you that if you plan to make a song and dance about it, I must point out how shoddy the original investigation was because there are more holes in it than a—'

'Do as you please,' Níels interrupted him with a hateful glare. 'Make an arse of yourself if you want to. You'll never get a warrant!'

Erlendur opened the door and went out into the corridor.

'Don't cut your fingers off,' he said and closed the door behind him.

Erlendur had a brief meeting with Sigurdur Óli and Elínborg about the Lake Kleifarvatn case. The search for further information about Lothar Weiser was proving slow and difficult. All enquiries had to go through the German embassy, which Erlendur had managed to offend, and they had few leads. As a formality they sent an inquiry to Interpol and the provisional answer was that it had never heard of Lothar Weiser. Quinn from the US embassy was trying to persuade one of the Czech embassy officials from that period to talk to the Icelandic police. He could not tell what these overtures would deliver. Lothar did not seem to have associated with Icelanders very much. Enquiries among old government officials had led nowhere. The East German embassy's guest lists had been lost a long time ago. There were no guest lists from the Icelandic authorities for those years. The detectives had no idea how to find out whether Lothar had known any Icelanders. Nobody seemed to remember the man.

Sigurdur Óli had requested help from the German embassy and Icelandic ministry of education in providing a list of Icelandic students in East Germany. Not knowing which period to focus on, he started by asking about all students from the end of the war until 1970.

Meanwhile, Erlendur had ample time to absorb himself in his pet topic, the Falcon man. He realised full well that he had almost nothing to go on if he wanted a warrant to mount a full-scale search for a body on the brothers' land near Mosfellsbaer.

He decided to drop in on Marion Briem, whose condition was improving slightly. The oxygen tank was still at the ready but the patient looked better, talking about new drugs that worked better than the old ones and cursing the doctor for 'not knowing his arse from his elbow'. Erlendur thought Marion Briem was getting back on form.

'What are you doing sniffing around here all the time?' Marion asked, sitting down in the chair. 'Don't you have anything better to do?'

'Plenty,' Erlendur said. 'How are you feeling?'

'I'm not having any luck dying,' Marion said. 'I thought I might have died last night. Funny. Of course that can happen when you're lying around with nothing to do but wait for death. I was certain it was all over.'

Marion sipped from a glass of water with parched lips.

'I suppose it's what they call astral projection,' Marion said. 'You know I don't believe in that crap. It was a delirium while I dozed. No doubt brought on by those new drugs. But I was hovering up there,' Marion said, staring up at the ceiling, 'and looked down on my wretched self. I thought I was going and was completely reconciled to it in my heart. But of course I wasn't dying at all. It was just a funny dream. I went for a check-up this morning and the doctor said I was a bit brighter. My blood's better than it's been for weeks. But he didn't give me any hope for the future.'

'What do doctors know?' Erlendur said.

'What do you want from me anyway? Is it the Ford Falcon? Why are you snooping around on that case?'

'Do you remember if the farmer he was going to visit near Mosfellsbaer had a brother?' Erlendur asked on the off chance. He did not want to tire Marion, but he also knew that his old boss enjoyed all things mysterious and strange.

Eyes closed, Marion pondered.

'That lazy bugger Níels talked about the brother being a bit funny.'

'He says he was a halfwit, but I don't know what that means, exactly.'

'He was backward, if I remember correctly. Big and strong but with the mind of a child. I don't think he could really speak. Just babbled nonsense.'

'Why wasn't this investigation pursued, Marion?' Erlendur asked.

'Why was it allowed to peter out? It would have been possible to do so much more.'

'Why do you say that?'

'The brothers' land should have been combed. Everyone took it for granted that the salesman never went there. No doubts were ever raised. It was all cut and dried; they decided the man committed suicide or left the city and would come back when it suited him. But he never did come back and I'm not certain that he killed himself.'

'You think the brothers killed him?'

'I'd like to look into that. The backward one's dead but the elder brother's at an old people's home here in Reykjavík and I reckon he'd have been capable of attacking someone on the slightest pretext.'

'And what would that be?' Marion asked. 'You know you have no motive. He was going to sell them a tractor. They had no reason to kill him.'

'I know,' Erlendur said. 'If they did, it was because something happened out there when he called on them. A chain of events was set in motion, perhaps by sheer coincidence, which led to the man's death.'

'Erlendur, you know better than that,' Marion said. 'These are fantasies. Stop this nonsense.'

'I know I have no motive and no body and it was years ago, but there's something that doesn't fit and I'd like to find out what it is.'

'There's always something that doesn't gel, Erlendur. You can never balance all the columns. Life's more complicated than that, as you of all people ought to know. Where was the farmer supposed to have got the Russian spying equipment to sink the body in Kleifarvatn?'

'Yes, I know, but that might be another, unrelated case.'

Marion looked at Erlendur. There was nothing new about detectives becoming absorbed in cases that they were investigating and then getting completely obsessed by them. It had often happened to Marion, who knew that Erlendur tended to take the most serious cases to heart. He had a rare sensitivity, which was both his blessing and his curse.

'You were talking about John Wayne the other day,' Erlendur said. 'When we watched the western.'

'Have you dug that up?' Marion said.

Erlendur nodded. He had asked Sigurdur Óli, who knew about all things American and was a mine of information about celebrities.

'His name was Marion too,' Erlendur said. 'Wasn't it? You are namesakes.'

'Funny, isn't it?' Marion said. 'Because of the way I am.'

26

Benedikt Jónsson, the retired agricultural-machinery importer, greeted Erlendur at the door and invited him in. Erlendur's visit had been delayed. Benedikt had been to see his daughter who lived outside Copenhagen. He had just returned home and gave the impression he would have liked to stay longer. He said he felt very much at home in Denmark.

Erlendur nodded intermittently while Benedikt rambled on about Denmark. A widower, he appeared to live well. He was fairly short with small, fat fingers and a ruddy, harmless-looking face. He lived alone in a small, neat house. Erlendur noticed a new Mercedes jeep outside the garage. He thought to himself that the old businessman had probably been shrewd and saved up for his old age.

'I knew I'd end up answering questions about that man eventually,' Benedikt said when at last he got to the point.

'Yes, I wanted to talk about Leopold,' Erlendur said.

'It was all very mysterious. Someone was bound to start wondering in the end. I should probably have told you the truth at the time but . . .'

'The truth?'

'Yes,' Benedikt said. 'May I ask why you're enquiring about this man now? My son said you'd questioned him too and when I spoke to you on the phone you were rather cagey. Why the sudden interest?

I thought you investigated the case and cleared it up back then. Actually, I was hoping you had.'

Erlendur told him about the skeleton found in Lake Kleifarvatn and that Leopold was one of several missing persons being investigated in connection with it.

'Did you know him personally?' Erlendur asked.

'Personally? No, I can hardly say that. And he didn't sell much either, in the short time he worked for us. If I remember correctly he made a lot of trips outside the city. All my salesmen did regional work – we sold agricultural machinery and earth-moving equipment – but none travelled as much as Leopold and none was a worse salesman.'

'So he didn't make you any money?' Erlendur said.

'I didn't want to take him on in the first place,' Benedikt said.

'Really?'

'Yes, no, that's not what I mean. They forced me to, really. I had to sack a damn good man to make room for him. It was never a big company.'

'Wait a minute, say that again. Who forced you to hire him?'

'They told me I mustn't tell anyone so . . . I don't know if I should be blabbing about it. I felt quite bad about all that plotting. I'm not one for doing things behind people's backs.'

'This was decades ago,' Erlendur said. 'It can hardly do any harm now.'

'No, I guess not. They threatened to move their franchise elsewhere. If I didn't hire that bloke. It was like I'd got caught up in the Mafia.'

'Who forced you to take on Leopold?'

'The manufacturer in East Germany, as it was then. They had good tractors that were much cheaper than the American ones. And bulldozers and diggers. We sold a lot of them although they weren't considered as classy as Massey Ferguson or Caterpillar.'

'Did they have a say in which staff you recruited?'

224

'That was what they threatened,' Benedikt said. 'What was I supposed to do? I couldn't do a thing. Of course I hired him.'

'Did they give you an explanation? Why you ought to recruit that specific person?'

'No. None. No explanation. I took him on but never got to know him. They said it was a temporary arrangement and, like I told you, he wasn't in the city much, just spent his time rushing back and forth around the country.'

'A temporary arrangement?'

'They said he didn't need to work for me for long. And they set conditions. He wasn't to go on the payroll. He was to be paid as a contractor, under the table. That was pretty difficult. My accountant was continually querying that. But it wasn't much money, nowhere near enough to live on, so he must have had another income as well.'

'What do you think their motive was?'

'I don't have a clue. Then he disappeared and I never heard any more about Leopold, except from you lot in the police.'

'Didn't you report what you're now telling me at the time he went missing?'

'I haven't told anyone. They threatened me. I had my staff to think of. My livelihood depended on that company. Even though it wasn't big we managed to make a bit of money and then the hydropower projects started up. The Sigalda and Búrfell stations. They needed our heavy plant machinery then. We made a fortune out of the hydropower projects. It was around the same time. The company was growing. I had other things to think about.'

'So you just tried to forget it?'

'Correct. I didn't think it was any skin off my nose, either. I hired him because the manufacturer wanted me to, but he was nothing to do with me as such.'

'Do you have any idea what could have happened to him?'

'None at all. He was supposed to meet those people outside Mosfellsbaer but didn't turn up, as far as we know. Maybe he just abandoned the idea or postponed it. That's not inconceivable. Maybe he had some urgent business to attend to.'

'You don't think that the farmer he was supposed to meet was lying?'

'I honestly don't know.'

'Who contacted you about hiring Leopold? Did he do it himself?'

'No, it wasn't him. An official from their embassy on Aegisída came to see me. It was really a trade delegation, not a proper embassy, that they ran in those days. Later it all got so much bigger. Actually he met me in Leipzig.'

'Leipzig?'

'Yes, we used to go to annual trade fairs there. They arranged big exhibitions of industrial goods and machinery and a fairly large contingent of us who did business with the East Germans always went.'

'Who was this man who spoke to you?'

'He never introduced himself.'

'Do you recognise the name Lothar? Lothar Weiser. An East German.'

'Never heard the name. Lothar? Never heard of him.'

'Could you describe this embassy official?'

'It's such a long time ago. He was quite plump. Perfectly nice bloke, I expect, apart from forcing me to hire that salesman.'

'Don't you think you should have passed on this information to the police at the time? Don't you think it could have helped?'

Benedikt hesitated. Then he shrugged.

'I tried to act as if it wasn't any business of mine or my company. And I genuinely didn't think it was any of my business. The man wasn't one of my team. Really he wasn't anything to do with the company. And they threatened me. What was I supposed to do?'

'Do you remember his girlfriend, Leopold's girlfriend?'

'No,' Benedikt said after some thought. 'No, I can't say I do. Was she . . . ?'

He stopped short, as if he had no idea of what to say about a woman who had lost the man she loved and never received any answers about his fate.

'Yes,' Erlendur said. 'She was heartbroken. And still is.'

Miroslav, the former Czech embassy official, lived in the south of France. He was an elderly man but had a good memory. He spoke French, but also good English, and was prepared to talk to Sigurdur Óli over the telephone. Quinn from the US embassy in Reykjavík, who had put them on to the Czech, acted as a go-between. In the past, Miroslav had been found guilty of spying against his own country and had spent several years in prison. He was not considered a prolific or important spy, having spent most of his diplomatic career in Iceland. Nor did he describe himself as a spy. He said he had succumbed to temptation when he was offered money to inform American diplomats about any unusual developments at his embassy or those of the other Iron Curtain countries. He never had anything to say. Nothing ever happened in Iceland.

It was the middle of summer. The skeleton in Kleifarvatn had fallen completely off the radar in the summer holidays. The media had long since stopped mentioning it. Erlendur's request for a warrant to search for the Falcon man on the brothers' farmland had not yet been answered because the staff were on holiday.

Sigurdur Óli had taken a fortnight in Spain with Bergthóra and returned suntanned and content. Elínborg had travelled around Iceland with Teddi and spent two weeks at her sister's summer chalet in the north. There was still considerable interest in her cookery book and a glossy magazine had quoted her in its *People in the News* column as saying that she already had 'another one in the oven'.

And one day at the end of July Elínborg whispered to Erlendur that Sigurdur Óli and Bergthóra had finally succeeded.

'Why are you whispering?' Erlendur asked.

'At last,' Elínborg sighed with delight. 'Bergthóra just told me. It's still a secret.'

'What is?' Erlendur said.

'Bergthóra's pregnant!' Elínborg said. 'It's been so difficult for them. They had to go through IVF and now it's worked at last.'

'Is Sigurdur Óli going to have a baby?' Erlendur said.

'Yes,' Elínborg said. 'But don't talk about it. No one's supposed to know.'

'The poor kid,' said Erlendur in a loud voice, and Elínborg walked off muttering curses under her breath.

At first Miroslav turned out to be eager to help them. The conversation took place in Sigurdur Óli's office with both Erlendur and Elínborg present. A tape recorder was connected to the telephone. On the arranged day at the arranged time, Sigurdur Óli picked up the handset and dialled.

After a number of rings a female voice answered and Sigurdur Óli introduced himself and asked for Miroslav. He was asked to hold the line. Sigurdur Óli looked at Erlendur and Elínborg and shrugged as if not knowing what to expect. Eventually a man came to the telephone and said his name was Miroslav. Sigurdur Óli introduced himself again as a detective from Reykjavík and presented his request. Miroslav said at once that he knew what the matter involved. He even spoke some Icelandic, although he asked for the conversation to be conducted in English.

'Is gooder for me,' he said in Icelandic.

'Yes, quite. It was about that official with the East German trade delegation in Reykjavík in the 1960s,' Sigurdur Óli said in English. 'Lothar Weiser.'

'I understand you found a body in a lake and think it's him,' Miroslav said.

'We haven't come to any conclusions,' Sigurdur Óli said. 'It's only one of several possibilities,' he added after a short pause.

'Do you often find bodies tied to Russian spy equipment?' Miroslav laughed. Quinn had clearly put him in the picture. 'No, I understand. I understand you want to play safe and not say too much, and obviously not over the phone. Do I get any money for my information?'

'Unfortunately not,' Sigurdur Óli said. 'We don't have permission to negotiate that kind of thing. We were told you would be cooperative.'

'Cooperative, right,' Miroslav said. 'No monies?' he asked in Icelandic.

'No,' Sigurdur Óli said, also in Icelandic. 'No money.'

The telephone went silent and they all looked at each other, crammed into Sigurdur Óli's office. Some time elapsed until they heard the Czech again. He called out something that they thought was in Czech and heard a woman's voice in the background answer him. The voices were half-smothered as if he were holding his hand over the mouthpiece. More words were exchanged. They could not tell whether it was an argument.

'Lothar Weiser was one of East Germany's spies in Iceland,' Miroslav said straightforwardly when he returned to the telephone. The words gushed out as if his exchange with the woman had incited him. 'Lothar spoke very good Icelandic that he'd learned in Moscow – did you know that?'

'Yes, we did,' Sigurdur Óli said. 'What did he do here?'

'He was called a trade attaché. They all were.'

'But was he anything else?' Sigurdur Óli asked.

'Lothar wasn't employed by the trade delegation, he worked for the East German secret service,' Miroslav said. 'His specialism was enlisting people to work for him. And he was brilliant at it. He used all kinds of tricks and had a knack for exploiting weaknesses. He blackmailed. Set up traps. Used prostitutes. They all did. Took incriminating photographs. You know what I mean? He was incredibly imaginative.'

'Did he have, how should I say, collaborators in Iceland?'

'Not that I know of, but that doesn't mean he didn't.'

Erlendur found a pen on the desk and started jotting down an idea that had occurred to him.

'Was he friends with any Icelanders that you remember?' Sigurdur Óli asked.

'I don't know much about his contact with Icelanders. I didn't get to know him very well.'

'Could you describe Lothar to us in more detail?'

'All that Lothar was interested in was himself,' Miroslav said. 'He didn't care who he betrayed if he could benefit by it. He had a lot of enemies and a lot of people were sure to have wanted him dead. That's what I heard, at least.'

'Did you know personally about anyone who wanted him dead?'

'No.'

'What about the Russian equipment? Where could it have come from?'

'From any of the communist embassies in Reykjavík. We all used Russian equipment. They manufactured it and all the embassies used it. Transmitters and recorders and bugging devices, radios too and awful Russian television sets. They flooded us with that rubbish and we had to buy it.'

'We think we've found a listening device that was used to monitor the US military at the Keflavík base.'

'That was really all we did,' Miroslav said. 'We bugged other embassies. And the American forces were stationed all over the country. But I don't want to talk about that. I understood from Quinn that you only wanted to know about Lothar's disappearance in Reykjavík.'

Erlendur handed the note to Sigurdur Óli, who read out the question that had crossed his mind.

'Do you know why Lothar was sent to Iceland?' Sigurdur Óli asked.

'Why?' Miroslav said.

'We're led to believe that being stuck out here in Iceland wasn't very popular with embassy officials,' Sigurdur Óli said.

'It was fine for us Czechoslovakians,' Miroslav said. 'But I'm not aware that Lothar ever did anything to merit being sent to Iceland as a punishment, if that's what you mean. I know that he was expelled from Norway once. The Norwegians found out he was trying to get a high-ranking official in the foreign ministry to work for him.'

'What do you know about Lothar's disappearance?' Sigurdur Óli asked.

'The last time I saw him was at a reception in the Soviet embassy. That was just before we started hearing reports that he was missing. It was 1968. Those were bad times of course, because of what was happening in Prague. At the reception, Lothar was recalling the Hungarian uprising of 1956. I only heard snatches of it, but I remember it because what he said was so typical of him.'

'What was that?' Sigurdur Óli asked.

'He was talking about Hungarians he knew in Leipzig,' Miroslav said. 'Especially a girl who hung around with the Icelandic students there.'

'Can you remember what he said?' Sigurdur Óli asked.

'He said he knew how to deal with dissidents, the rebels in Czechoslovakia. They ought to arrest the lot of them and send them off to the gulag. He was drunk when he said it and I don't know what exactly he was talking about, but that was the gist of it.'

'And soon afterwards you heard that he'd gone missing?' Sigurdur Óli said.

'He must have done something wrong,' Miroslav said. 'At least that's what everyone thought. There were rumours that they took him out themselves. The East Germans. Sent him home in a diplomatic bag. They could easily do that. Embassy mail was never examined and we could take whatever we wanted in and out of the country. The most incredible things.'

'Or they threw him in the lake,' Sigurdur Óli said.

'All I know is that he disappeared and nothing more was ever heard of him.'

'Do you know what his crime was supposed to have been?'

'We thought he'd gone over.'

'Gone over?'

'Sold himself to the other side. That often happened. Just look at me. But the Germans weren't as merciful as us Czechs.'

'You mean he sold information . . . ?'

'Are you sure there's no money in this?' Miroslav interrupted Sigurdur Óli. The woman's voice in the background had returned, louder than before.

'Unfortunately not,' Sigurdur Óli said.

They heard Miroslav say something, probably in Czech. Then in English: 'I've said enough. Don't call me again.'

Then he hung up. Erlendur reached over to the tape recorder and switched it off.

'What a twat you are,' he said to Sigurdur Óli. 'Couldn't you lie to him? Promise ten thousand krónur. Something. Couldn't you try to keep him on the phone longer?'

'Cool it,' Sigurdur Óli said. 'He didn't want to say any more. He didn't want to talk to us any more. You heard that.'

'Are we any closer to knowing who was at the bottom of the lake?' Elínborg asked.

'I don't know,' Erlendur said. 'An East German trade attaché and a Russian spy device. It could fit the bill.'

'I think it's obvious,' Elínborg said. 'Lothar and Leopold were the same man and they sank him in Kleifarvatn. He fouled up and they had to get rid of him.'

'And the woman in the dairy shop?' Sigurdur Óli asked.

'She doesn't have a clue,' Elínborg said. 'She doesn't know a thing about that man except that he treated her well.'

'Perhaps she was part of his cover in Iceland,' Erlendur said.

'Maybe,' Elínborg said.

'I think it must be significant that the device wasn't functional when it was used to sink the body,' Sigurdur Óli said. 'Like it was obsolete or had been destroyed.'

'I was wondering whether the device necessarily came from one of the embassies,' Elínborg said. 'Whether it couldn't have entered the country by another channel.'

'Who would want to smuggle Russian spying equipment into Iceland?' Sigurdur Óli asked.

They fell silent, all thinking in their separate ways that the case was beyond their understanding. They were more accustomed to dealing with simple, Icelandic crimes without mysterious devices or trade attachés who weren't trade attachés, without foreign embassies or the Cold War, just Icelandic reality: local, uneventful, mundane and infinitely far removed from the battle zones of the world.

'Can't we find an Icelandic angle on this?' Erlendur asked in the end, for the sake of saying something.

'What about the students?' Elínborg said. 'Shouldn't we try to locate them? Find out if any of them remembers this Lothar? We still have that to check.'

By the following day Sigurdur Óli had obtained a list of Icelandic students attending East German universities between the end of the war and 1970. The information was supplied by the ministry of education and the German embassy. They began slowly, starting with students in Leipzig in the 1960s and working back. Since there was no hurry, they handled the case alongside other investigations that came their way, mostly burglaries and thefts. They knew when Lothar had been enrolled at the University of Leipzig in the 1950s, but also that he could have been attached to it for much longer than that, and they were determined to do a proper job. They decided to work backwards from when he disappeared from the embassy.

Instead of calling people and speaking to them over the telephone, they thought it would be more productive to make surprise visits to their homes. Erlendur believed that the first reaction to a police visit often provided vital clues. As in war, a surprise attack could prove crucial. A simple change of expression when they mentioned their business. The first words spoken.

So, one day in September, when their investigation of Icelandic students had reached the mid-1950s, Sigurdur Óli and Elínborg knocked on the door of a woman by the name of Rut Bernhards. According to their information, she had abandoned her studies in Leipzig after a year and a half.

She answered the door and was terrified to hear that it was the police.

27

Rut Bernhards stood blinking at Sigurdur Óli and then at Elínborg, unable to understand how they could be from the police. Sigurdur Óli had to tell her three times before it sank in and she asked what they wanted. Elínborg explained. This was around ten o'clock in the morning. They were standing on the landing of a block of flats, not unlike Erlendur's but dirtier, the carpet more worn and a stench of rising damp on every floor.

Rut was even more surprised once Elínborg had said her piece.

'Students in Leipzig?' she said. 'What do you want to know about them? Why?'

'Maybe we could come in for a minute,' Elínborg said. 'We won't be long.'

Still very doubtful, Rut thought for a moment before opening the door to them. They entered a small hallway which led to the living room. There were bedrooms on the right-hand side and beside the living room was the kitchen. Rut offered them a seat and asked whether they wanted tea or the like, apologising because she had never spoken to the police before. They saw that she was very confused as she stood in the kitchen doorway. Elínborg thought she would come to her senses if she made some tea, so she accepted the offer, to Sigurdur Óli's chagrin. He wasn't interested in attending a tea party and gave Elínborg an expression to signal that. She just smiled back at him.

*

The day before, Sigurdur Óli had received yet another telephone call from the man who had lost his wife and daughter in a car crash. He and Bergthóra had just come back from a visit to the doctor who told them that the pregnancy was progressing well, the foetus was flourishing and they had nothing to worry about. But the doctor's words were not so reassuring. They had heard him talk that way before. They were sitting at home in the kitchen, cautiously discussing the future, when the telephone rang.

'I can't talk to you now,' Sigurdur Óli said when he heard who was on the other end.

'I didn't mean to disturb you,' the man said, polite as ever. His mood never changed, nor did the pitch of his voice; he spoke with the same calm tone, which Sigurdur Óli attributed to tranquillisers.

'No,' Sigurdur Óli said, 'don't disturb me again.'

'I just wanted to thank you,' the man said.

'There's no need, I haven't done anything,' Sigurdur Óli said. 'You don't need to thank me at all.'

'I think I'm gradually getting over it,' the man said.

'That's good,' Sigurdur Óli said.

There was silence over the telephone.

'I miss her so terribly,' the man said eventually.

'Of course you do,' Sigurdur Óli said with a glance at Bergthóra.

'I'm not going to give up. For their sake. I'll try to put on a brave face.'

'That's good.'

'Sorry to bother you. I don't know why I'm always calling you. This will be the last time.'

'That's okay.'

'I've got to keep going.'

Sigurdur Óli was about to say goodbye when he suddenly rang off.

'Is he okay?' Bergthóra asked.

'I don't know,' Sigurdur Óli said. 'I hope so.'

Sigurdur Óli and Elínborg heard Rut making the tea in the kitchen, then she came out, holding cups and a sugar bowl, and asked whether they took milk. Elínborg repeated what she had said at the front door about their search for Icelandic students from Leipzig, adding that it was potentially connected – only potentially, she repeated – with a person who went missing in Reykjavík just before 1970.

Rut listened to her without answering until the kettle began to whistle in the kitchen. She left and returned with the tea and a few biscuits on a dish. Elínborg knew that she was past seventy and thought she had aged well. She was thin, of a similar height to her, her hair was dyed brown and her face was quite long with a serious expression underlined by wrinkles, but a pretty smile that she seemed to use sparingly.

'And you think this man studied in Leipzig?' she asked.

'We have no idea,' Sigurdur Óli said.

'What missing person are you talking about?' Rut asked. 'I don't remember anything from the news that . . .' Her expression turned thoughtful. 'Except Kleifarvatn in the spring. Are you talking about the skeleton from Kleifarvatn?'

'It fits.' Elínborg smiled.

'Is it connected with Leipzig?'

'We don't know,' Sigurdur Óli said.

'But you must know something if you came here to talk to an ex-student from Leipzig,' Rut said firmly.

'We have some clues,' Elínborg said. 'They're not convincing enough for us to say much about them, but we were hoping you might be able to assist us.'

'How does this link up with Leipzig?'

'The man doesn't have to link up with Leipzig at all,' Sigurdur Óli said, in a slightly sharper tone than before. 'You left after a year and a half,' he said to change the subject. 'Didn't you finish your course, or what?'

Without answering him, she poured the tea and added milk and sugar to her own. She stirred it with a little spoon, her thoughts elsewhere.

'Was it a man in the lake? You said "the man".'

'Yes,' Sigurdur Óli said.

'I understand that you're a teacher,' Elínborg said.

'I went to teacher training college when I came back to Iceland,' Rut said. 'My husband was a teacher too. Both primary school teachers. We've just got divorced. I've stopped teaching now. Retired. No need for me any more. It's like you stop living when you stop working.'

She sipped her tea, and Sigurdur Óli and Elínborg did the same.

'I kept the flat,' she added.

'It's always sad when . . .' Elínborg began, but Rut interrupted her as if to say that she was not asking for sympathy from a stranger.

'We were all socialists,' she said, looking at Sigurdur Óli. 'All of us in Leipzig.'

She paused while her mind roamed back to the years when she was young with her whole life ahead of her.

'We had ideals,' she said, moving her gaze to Elínborg. 'I don't know if anyone has them any more. Young people, I mean. Genuine ideals for a better and fairer society. I don't believe anyone thinks about that these days. Nowadays, everyone just thinks about getting rich. No one used to think about making money or owning anything. There wasn't this relentless commercialism then. No one had anything, except perhaps beautiful ideals.'

'Built on lies,' Sigurdur Óli said. 'Weren't they? More or less?'

'I don't know,' Rut said. 'Built on lies? What's a lie?'

'No,' Sigurdur Óli said in a peculiarly brash tone. 'I mean that communism has been abandoned all over the world except where gross violations of human rights take place such as China and Cuba. Hardly anyone admits to having been a communist any more. It's almost a term of abuse. So wasn't it like that in the old days, or what?'

Elínborg glared at him, shocked. She could not believe that Sigurdur Óli was being rude to the woman. But she might have expected it. She knew that Sigurdur Óli voted conservative and had sometimes heard him talk about Icelandic communists as if they ought to do penance for defending a system they knew was useless and had ultimately offered nothing but dictatorship and repression. As if communists still had to settle accounts with the past because they should have known the truth all along and were responsible for the lies. Perhaps he found Rut an easier target than most. Perhaps he had run out of patience.

'You had to give up your studies,' Elínborg hurried to say, to steer the conversation into safer waters.

'To our way of thinking, there was nothing more noble,' Rut said, still staring at Sigurdur Óli. 'And that hasn't changed. The socialism we believed in then and believe in now remains the same, and it played a part in establishing the labour movement, ensuring a decent living wage and free hospitals to care for you and your family, educated you to become a police officer, set up the national insurance system, set up the welfare system. But that's nothing compared with the implicit socialist values we all live by, you and me and her, so that society can function. It's socialism that makes us into human beings. So don't go making fun of me!'

'Are you absolutely sure that socialism actually established all this?' Sigurdur Óli said, refusing to budge. 'As far as I recall it was the conservatives who set up the national insurance system.'

'Rubbish,' Rut said.

'And the Soviet system?' Sigurdur Óli said. 'What about *that* lie?'

Rut did not reply.

'Why do you think you have some kind of score to settle with me?' she asked.

'I don't have a score to settle with you,' Sigurdur Óli said.

'People may well have thought they had to be dogmatic,' Rut said.

'It might have been necessary then. You could never understand that. Different times come along and attitudes change and people change. Nothing is permanent. I can't understand this anger. Where does it come from?'

She looked at Sigurdur Óli.

'Where does this anger come from?' she repeated.

'I didn't come here to argue,' Sigurdur Óli said. 'That wasn't the aim.'

'Do you remember anyone from Leipzig by the name of Lothar?' Elínborg asked awkwardly. She was hoping that Sigurdur Óli would invent some excuse to go out to the car, but he sat fast by her side, his eyes fixed on Rut. 'Lothar Weiser,' she added.

'Lothar?' Rut said. 'Yes, but not so well. He spoke Icelandic.'

'I gathered that,' Elínborg said. 'So you remember him?'

'Only vaguely,' Rut said. 'He sometimes came for dinner with us at the dormitory. But I never got to know him especially well. I was always homesick and . . . the conditions weren't that special, bad housing and . . . I . . . it didn't suit me.'

'No, obviously things weren't in very good shape after the war,' Elínborg said.

'It was just awful,' Rut said. 'West Germany was redeveloping ten times as fast, with the west's backing. In East Germany, things happened slowly, or not at all.'

'We understand that his role was to get students to work for him,' Sigurdur Óli said. 'Or monitor them somehow. Were you ever aware of that?'

'They watched us,' Rut said. 'We knew that and everyone else knew that. It was called interactive surveillance, another term for spying. People were supposed to come forward of their own accord and report anything that offended their socialist principles. We didn't, of course. None of us. I never noticed Lothar trying to enlist us. All the foreign students had a liaison they could turn to but who also watched them. Lothar was one of them.'

'Do you still keep in touch with your student friends from Leipzig?' Elínborg asked.

'No,' Rut said. 'It's a long time since I saw any of them. We don't keep in contact, or if they do, I don't know about it. I left the party when I came back. Or maybe I didn't leave, I just lost interest. It's probably called withdrawing.'

'We have the names of some other students from the time you were there: Karl, Hrafnhildur, Emil, Tómas, Hannes . . .'

'Hannes was expelled,' Rut interjected. 'I was told he stopped going to lectures and the Day of the Republic parades and generally didn't fit in. We were supposed to take part in all that. And we did socialist work in the summer. On farms and in the coal mines. As I understand it Hannes didn't like what he saw and heard. He wanted to finish his course but wasn't allowed to. Maybe you should talk to him. If he's still alive, I don't know.'

She looked at them.

'Was it him you found in the lake?' she said.

'No,' Elínborg said. 'It's not him. We understand he lives in Selfoss and runs a guest house there.'

'I remember that he wrote about his Leipzig experiences when he came back to Iceland, and they tore him to shreds for it. The party old guard. Denounced him as a traitor and liar. The conservatives welcomed him like a prodigal son and championed him. I can't imagine he would have cared for that. I think he just wanted to tell the truth as he saw it, but of course there was a price to pay. I met him once a few years later and he looked awfully depressed. Maybe he thought I was still active in the party, but I wasn't. You ought to talk to him. He might have known Lothar better. I was there such a short time.'

Back out in the car, Elínborg scolded Sigurdur Óli for allowing his political opinions to influence a police enquiry. He ought to keep his mouth shut and not attack people, she said, especially elderly women who lived by themselves.

'What's wrong with you, anyway?' she said as they drove away from the block of flats. 'I've never heard such crap. What were you thinking? I agree with what she asked you: where does all this anger come from?'

'Oh, I don't know,' Sigurdur Óli said. 'My dad was a communist like that, never saw the light,' he added eventually. This was the first time that Elínborg had ever heard him mention his father.

Erlendur had just got back home when the telephone rang. It took him a while to realise which Benedikt Jónsson was on the other end, then suddenly he remembered. The one who had given Leopold a job with his company.

'Am I bothering you, phoning home like this?' Benedikt asked politely.

'No,' Erlendur said. 'Is there something that . . . ?'

'It was to do with that man.'

'Which man?'

'From the East German embassy or trade delegation or whatever it was,' Benedikt said. 'The one who told me to hire Leopold and said the company in Germany would take action if I didn't.'

'Yes,' Erlendur said. 'The fat one. What about him?'

'As far as I recall,' Benedikt said, 'he knew Icelandic. Actually, I think he spoke it pretty well.'

28

Everywhere he turned he ran up against antipathy and total indifference on the part of the authorities in Leipzig. No one would tell him what had happened to her, where she had been taken, where she was being detained, the reason for her arrest, which police department was responsible for her case. He tried to enlist the help of two university professors but they said they could do nothing. He tried to get the university vice-chancellor to intervene but he refused. He tried to get the chairman of the FDJ to make enquiries but the students' society ignored him.

In the end he telephoned the foreign ministry in Iceland, which promised to enquire about the matter but nothing came of it: Ilona was not an Icelandic national, they were unmarried, Iceland had no vested interest in the matter and did not maintain diplomatic relations with East Germany. His Icelandic friends at university tried to pep him up, but were equally at a loss about what to do. They did not understand what was going on. Maybe it was a misunderstanding. She would turn up sooner or later and everything would be clarified. Ilona's friends and other Hungarians at the university, who were as determined as he was to find answers, said the same. They all tried to console him and told him to keep calm – everything would be explained eventually.

He discovered that Ilona had not been the only person arrested that day. The security police raided the campus and her friends from the meetings were among others taken into custody. He knew she had warned them after he found out they were being watched, that the police had photographs of them. A few were released the same day. Others were detained longer and some were still in prison when he was deported. No one heard anything of Ilona.

He contacted Ilona's parents, who had heard of her arrest, and they wrote moving letters asking whether he knew of her whereabouts. To the best of their knowledge she had not been sent back to Hungary. They had received no word from her since she wrote to them a week before her disappearance. Nothing suggested that she was in danger. Her parents described their fruitless efforts to persuade the Hungarian authorities to look into their daughter's fate in East Germany. The authorities were not particularly upset that she was missing. Given the situation in their own country, officials were not concerned about the arrest of an alleged dissident. Her parents said they had been refused permission to travel to East Germany to enquire into Ilona's disappearance. They seemed to have reached a dead end.

He wrote back telling them he was looking for answers himself in Leipzig. He longed to tell them all that he knew, how she had spread underground propaganda against the communist party, against the student society FDJ, which was an arm of the party, against the lectures and against restrictions on freedom of speech, association and the press. That she had mobilised young Germans and organised clandestine meetings. And that she could not have foreseen her arrest. No more than he did. But he knew he could not write that kind of letter. Everything he sent would be censored. He had to be careful.

Instead, he said he would not rest until he had found out what had happened to Ilona and secured her release.

He stopped attending lectures. During the day he went from one government office to the next, asked to meet officials and sought help and information. As time went by, he did this more out of habit, as he received no answers and realised he never would. At night he paced the floor of their little room in anguish. He hardly slept, dozing for a few hours at a time. Strode back and forth hoping that she would appear, that the nightmare would come to an end, that they would let her off with a warning and she would come back to him so that they could be together again. He woke up at every sound on the street. If a car approached he went to the window. If the house creaked he stopped and listened, thinking it might be her. But it never was. And then a new day dawned and he was so terribly alone.

Eventually he summoned up the courage to write a new letter to Ilona's parents telling them that she had been pregnant by him. He felt as though he could hear their cries with every key he struck on her old typewriter.

Now, all those years later, he was sitting with their letters in his hands, rereading them and sensing again the anger in what they wrote, then despair and incomprehension. They never saw their daughter again. He never saw his girlfriend again.

Ilona had disappeared from them once and for all.

He heaved as deep a sigh as ever when he allowed himself to delve into his most painful memories. No matter how many years passed, his grief was always as raw, his loss as incomprehensible. These days he avoided imagining her fate. Previously he would torture himself endlessly with thoughts of what might have happened to her after she was arrested. He envisaged the interrogations. He saw the cell beside the little office in the security police headquarters. Had she been locked away there? For how long? Was she afraid? Had she fought back? Did she cry? Had she been beaten? And of course the biggest question of all: what fate did she meet?

For years he had obsessed over these questions; there was room for little else in his life. He never married or had children. He tried to stay in Leipzig for as long as he could, but because he no longer went to lectures and was challenging the police and FDJ, his grant was withdrawn. He tried to persuade the student paper and local press to print a photograph of Ilona with a report about her unlawful arrest, but all his requests were turned down and in the end he was ordered to leave the country.

There were various possibilities, judging from what he read later when he probed into the treatment of dissidents across Eastern Europe at that time. She could have died at the hands of the police in Leipzig or East Berlin, where the headquarters of the security police were located, or been sent to a prison such as the Honecker castle to die there. That was the largest female prison for political prisoners in East Germany. Another infamous prison for dissidents was Bautzen II, nicknamed 'Yellow Misery' after the colour of its brick walls. Prisoners were sent there who were guilty of 'crimes against the state'. Many dissidents were released soon after their first arrest. That was regarded as a warning. Others were let out after a short internment without trial. Some were sent to prison and came out years later; some never. Ilona's parents received no notification of her death and for years they lived in the hope that she would come back, but that never happened. No matter how they implored the authorities in Hungary and East Germany, they received no information, not even whether she was alive. It was simply as if she had never existed.

As a foreigner in a country that he did not know well and understood even less, he had few recourses. He was well aware how little he could do against the might of the state, of his impotence as he went from office to office, from one police chief to the next, one official to another. He refused to give up. Refused to accept that someone like Ilona could be locked away for having opinions that didn't match the official line.

He repeatedly asked Karl what had happened when Ilona was arrested. Karl was the only witness to the police raid on their home. He had been to collect a manuscript of poems by a young Hungarian dissident which Ilona had translated into German and was going to lend him.

'And then what happened?' he asked Karl for the thousandth time as he sat facing him in the university cafeteria with Emil. Three days had passed since Ilona disappeared and there was still hope that she might be released; he expected to hear from her at any minute, even for her to walk into the cafeteria. He glanced regularly towards the door. He was out of his mind with worry.

'She offered me some tea,' Karl said. 'I said yes and she boiled the water.'

'What did you talk about?'

'Nothing really, just the books we were reading.'

'What did she say?'

'Nothing. It was just empty conversation. We didn't talk about anything special. We didn't know she'd be arrested a moment later.'

Karl could see how he was suffering.

'Ilona was a friend to all of us,' he said. 'I don't understand it. I don't understand what's going on.'

'And then what? What happened next?'

'There was a knock on the door,' Karl said.

'Yes.'

'The door to the flat. We were in her room, I mean in your room. They hammered on the door and shouted something we couldn't make out. She went to the door and they burst in the moment she opened it.'

'How many of them were there?'

'Five, maybe six, I don't remember exactly, something like that. They piled into the room. Some were in uniform like the police on the streets. Others were wearing ordinary suits. One of them was in charge. They obeyed his orders. They asked her name. If she was Ilona. They had a photograph. Maybe from the university files. I don't know. Then they took her away.'

'They turned everything upside down!' he said.

'They found some documents that they took away with them, and some books. I don't know what they were,' Karl said.

'What did Ilona do?'

'Naturally she wanted to know their business and kept asking them. I did too. They didn't answer her, nor me. I asked who they were and what they wanted. They didn't give me as much as a look. Ilona asked to make a phone call but they refused. They were there to arrest her and nothing else.'

'Couldn't you ask where they were taking her?' Emil asked. 'Couldn't you do something?'

'There was nothing that could be done.' Karl squirmed. 'You have to understand that. We couldn't do anything. I couldn't do anything! They meant to take her and they took her.'

'Was she scared?' he asked.

Karl and Emil gave him a sympathetic look.

'No,' Karl said. 'She wasn't scared. Defiant. She asked what they were looking for and if she could help them find it. Then they took her away. She asked me to tell you that everything would be okay.'

'What did she say?'

'I had to tell you that everything would be okay. She said that. Told me to pass it on to you. That everything would be okay.'

'Did she say that?'

'Then they put her in the car. They had two cars with them. I ran after them but it was hopeless, of course. They disappeared around the next corner. That was the last I saw of Ilona.'

'What do they want?' he sighed. 'What have they done with her? Why won't anyone tell me anything? Why don't we get any answers? What are they going to do with her? What can they do with her?'

He rested his elbows on the table and clutched his head.

'My God,' he groaned. 'What has happened?'

'Maybe it will be okay,' Emil said, trying to console him. 'Maybe she's back home already. Maybe she'll come tomorrow.'

He looked at Emil with broken eyes. Karl sat at the table in silence.

'Did you know that . . . no, of course you didn't know.'

'What?' Emil said. 'What didn't we know?'

'She told me just before she was arrested. No one knew.'

'No one knew what?' Emil said.

'She's pregnant,' he said. 'She's just found out. We're expecting a baby together. Do you get it? Do you realise how disgusting it is? That fucking bloody interactive fucking surveillance! What are they? What kind of people are they? What are they fighting for? Are they going to make a better world by spying on each other? How long do they plan to rule by fear and hatred?'

'Was she pregnant?' Emil groaned.

'I should have been with her, Karl, not you,' he said. 'I would never have allowed them to take her. Never.'

'Are you blaming me?' Karl said. 'There was nothing to be done. I was helpless.'

'No,' he said, burying his face in his hands to hide the tears. 'Of course not. Of course it wasn't your fault.'

Later, on his way out of the country after being ordered to leave Leipzig and East Germany, he sought out Lothar for the final time and found him in the FDJ office at the university. He still had no clue as to Ilona's whereabouts. The fear and anxieties that had driven him on for the first days and weeks had given way to an almost intolerable burden of hopelessness and sorrow.

In the office, Lothar was cracking jokes with two girls who were laughing at something he had said. They fell silent when he entered the room. He asked Lothar for a word.

'What is it now?' Lothar said without moving. The two girls looked at him seriously. All the joy was purged from their faces. Word of Ilona's arrest had spread around the campus. She had been denounced as a traitor and it was said she had been sent back to Hungary. He knew that was a lie.

'I just want a word with you,' he said. 'Is that okay?'

'You know I can't do anything for you,' Lothar said. 'I've told you that. Leave me alone.'

Lothar shifted round to entertain the girls further.

'Did you play any part in Ilona's arrest?' he asked, switching to Icelandic.

Lothar turned his back on him and did not answer. The girls watched the proceedings.

'Was it you who had her arrested?' he said, raising his voice. 'Was it you who told them she was dangerous? That she had to be removed from circulation? That she was distributing anti-socialist propaganda? That she ran a dissidents' cell? Was it you, Lothar? Was that your role?'

Pretending not to hear, Lothar said something to the two girls, who returned silly smiles. He walked up to Lothar and grabbed him.

'Who are you?' he said calmly. 'Tell me that.'

Lothar turned and pushed him away, then walked up to him, seized his jacket by the lapels and thrust him against the filing cabinets. They rattled.

'Leave me alone!' Lothar hissed between clenched teeth.

'What did you do with Ilona?' he asked in the same collected tone of voice, not attempting to fight back. 'Where is she? Tell me that.'

'I didn't do a thing,' Lothar hissed. 'Take a closer look, you stupid Icelander!'

Then Lothar threw him to the floor and stormed out of the office.

On the way back to Iceland he got the news that the Soviet army was crushing an uprising in Hungary.

He heard the old grandfather clock strike midnight, and he put the letters back in their place.

He had watched on television when the Berlin Wall fell and Germany was reunited. Seen the crowds scale the wall and hit it with hammers and pickaxes as if striking blows against the very inhumanity that built it.

When German reunification had been achieved and he felt ready, he travelled to the former East Germany for the first time since he had studied there. It now took him half a day to reach his destination. He flew to Frankfurt and caught a connection to Leipzig. From the airport he took a taxi to his hotel, where he dined alone. It was not far from the city centre and campus. There were only two old couples and a few middle-aged men in the dining room. Salesmen perhaps, he thought. One nodded at him when their gazes met.

In the evening he took a long walk and remembered the first time he had strolled around the city when he arrived there as a student, and he reflected on how the world had changed. He looked around the university quarter. His dormitory, the old villa, had been restored and now served as the headquarters of a multinational company. The old university building where he had studied was gloomier in the dark of night than he remembered it. He walked towards the city centre and looked inside Nikolaikirche, where he lit a candle in memory of the dead. Crossing the old Karl-Marx-Platz to Thomaskirche, he gazed at the statue of Bach that they had so often stood beneath.

An old woman approached him and invited him to buy some flowers. With a smile, he bought a small posy.

Shortly afterwards he went where his thoughts had so often returned. He was pleased to see that the house was still standing. It had been partly refurbished and there was a light in the window. Much as he longed to, he did not dare peek inside, but he had the impression that a family lived there. A television set gave off a flickering light from what had been the living room of the old landlady who had lost her family in the war. Everything inside would be different now, of course. Perhaps the eldest child was sleeping in their old room.

He kissed the posy of flowers, placed it at the door and made the sign of the cross over it.

A few years earlier he had flown to Budapest and met Ilona's elderly mother and two brothers. Her father was dead by then, never having discovered his daughter's fate.

He spent all day sitting with Ilona's mother, who showed him photographs of Ilona from when she was a baby through to her student years. The brothers, who like him were beginning to age, told him what he already knew: nothing had come of their search for answers about Ilona. He could sense their bitterness, the resignation that had taken root in them long ago.

The day after he arrived in Leipzig he went to the old security police headquarters, which were still in the same building on Dittrichring 24. Instead of police at the reception desk in the foyer, there was now a young woman who smiled as she handed him a brochure. Still able to speak passable German, he introduced himself as a visitor to the city and asked to look around. Other people had entered the building for the same purpose, and walked in and out through open and unlocked doors, free to go where they pleased. When she heard his accent the young woman asked where he was from. Then she told him that an archive was being set up in the old Stasi offices. He was welcome to listen to a talk that was about to begin, then tour the building. She showed him to the corridor leading to where chairs had been arranged, every one of them occupied. Some of the audience were standing up against the walls. The talk was about the imprisonment of dissident writers in the 1970s.

After the talk he went to the office in the alcove where Lothar and the man with the thick moustache had interrogated him. The cell next door was open and he went inside. He thought again that Ilona might have been there. There were graffiti and scratches all over the walls, made with spoons, he imagined.

He had put in a formal application to look at the files when the Stasi archive opened after the fall of the Berlin Wall. Its purpose was to help people delve into the fate of loved ones who had gone missing, or find information about themselves that had been collected by neighbours, colleagues, friends and family, under the system of interactive surveillance. Journalists, academics and people who suspected they had been documented in the files could apply for access, which he had done by letter and telephone from Iceland. Applicants had to explain in detail why they needed to study the files and what they were looking for. He knew there were thousands of large brown paper bags full of files that had been shredded in the last days of the East German regime; a huge team was employed on taping them back together. The scale of the records was incredible.

His trip to East Germany produced nothing. No matter how he searched, he could not find a scrap of information about Ilona. Her file had probably been destroyed, he was told. Possibly she had been sent to a labour camp or gulag in the old Soviet Union, so there was a slim chance that he could find some record of her in Moscow. It was also conceivable that she had died in police custody in Leipzig or in Berlin if she had been sent there.

Nor did he find any information in the Stasi files about whichever traitor had turned his beloved girlfriend over to the security police.

He sat and waited for the police to call. He had done that all summer; now it was autumn and nothing had happened yet. Certain that the police would knock on his door sooner or later, he sometimes wondered how he would react. Would he act nonchalantly, deny the accusations and feign surprise? It would depend on what evidence they had. He had no idea what this might be, but imagined that it would be substantial, if they had managed to trace a lead to him in the first place.

He stared into space and drifted back once again to his years in Leipzig.

Four words from his last encounter with Lothar had remained etched into his mind right up to the present day and would remain there for ever. Four words that said it all.

Take a closer look.

29

Erlendur and Elínborg arrived unannounced, knowing very little about the man they were going to see, except that his name was Hannes and he had once studied in Leipzig. He ran a guest house in Selfoss and grew tomatoes as a sideline. They knew where he lived, so they drove straight there and parked outside a bungalow identical to all the others in the little town, apart from not having been painted for a long time and having a concreted space in front of it where a garage was perhaps supposed to stand. The garden around the house was well kept, with hedges and flowers and a small birdhouse.

In the garden was a man they took to be in his seventies struggling with a lawnmower. The motor would not catch and he was clearly out of breath from tugging at the starting cord, which as soon as he released it darted back into its hole again like a snake. He did not notice them until they were standing right next to him.

'A heap of old junk, is it?' Erlendur asked as he looked down at the lawnmower and inhaled smoke from his cigarette. He had lit up the moment he got out of the car. Elínborg had forbidden him to smoke on the way. His car was awful enough anyway.

The man looked up and stared at them, two strangers in his garden. He had a grey beard and grey hair that was starting to thin, a tall and intelligent forehead, thick eyebrows and alert brown eyes. On his nose sat a pair of glasses that might have been in fashion a quarter of a century before.

'Who are you?' he asked.

'Is your name Hannes?' Elínborg asked back.

The man said yes and gave them a probing look.

'Do you want some tomatoes?' he asked.

'Maybe,' Erlendur said. 'Are they any good? Elínborg here is an expert.'

'Didn't you study in Leipzig in the 1950s?' Elínborg said.

The man regarded her blankly. It was almost as if he did not understand the question, and certainly not the reason it was being asked. Elínborg repeated it.

'What's going on?' the man said. 'Who are you? Why are you asking me about Leipzig?'

'You first went there in 1952, didn't you?' Elínborg said.

'That's right,' he said in surprise. 'So what?'

Elínborg explained to him that the investigation into the skeleton found in Kleifarvatn in the spring had led to Icelandic students in East Germany. This was merely one of many questions raised in connection with the case, she told him, without mentioning the Russian spying device.

'I . . . what . . . I mean . . .' Hannes stuttered. 'What does that have to do with those of us who were in Germany?'

'Leipzig, to be absolutely precise,' Erlendur said. 'We're enquiring in particular about a man called Lothar. Does that name ring a bell? A German. Lothar Weiser.'

Hannes stared at them in astonishment, as if he had just seen a ghost. He looked at Erlendur, then back at Elínborg.

'I can't help you,' he said.

'It shouldn't take very long,' Erlendur said.

'Sorry,' Hannes said. 'I've forgotten all that. It was so long ago.'

'If you could please . . .' Elínborg said, but Hannes interrupted her.

'Please leave,' he said. 'I don't think I have anything to say to you.

255

I can't help you. I haven't talked about Leipzig for a long time and I'm not going to start now. I've forgotten and I won't stand for being interrogated. You'll gain nothing from talking to me.'

He returned to the starter cord of his lawnmower and tinkered with the motor. Erlendur and Elínborg exchanged glances.

'What makes you think that?' Erlendur said. 'You don't even know what we want from you.'

'No, and I don't want to know. Leave me alone.'

'This isn't an interrogation,' Elínborg said. 'But if you want we can bring you in for questioning. If you'd prefer that.'

'Are you threatening me?' Hannes said, looking up from the lawnmower.

'What's wrong with answering a couple of questions?' Erlendur said.

'I don't have to if I don't want to and I don't intend to. Goodbye.'

Elínborg was on the verge of saying something which, judging from her face, would have been quite a scolding, but before she had the chance Erlendur took her by the arm and dragged her off towards the car.

'If he reckons he can get away with that kind of bullshit—' Elínborg began when they were sitting in the car, but Erlendur interrupted.

'I'll try to smooth things over and if that doesn't work it's up to him,' he said. 'Then we'll have him brought in.'

He got out of the car and went back to Hannes. Elínborg watched him walking off. Hannes had finally started the lawnmower and was cutting the grass. He ignored Erlendur, who stepped in front of him and switched off the machine.

'It took me two hours to start that,' Hannes shouted. 'What's all this supposed to mean?'

'We've got to do this,' Erlendur said calmly, 'even if it's no fun for either of us. Sorry. We can do it now and be quick about it, or we can send a patrol car round for you. And maybe you won't say anything then, so we'll send for you straight away the next day and the day after that, until you're one of our regulars.'

'I don't let people push me around!'

'Nor do I,' Erlendur said.

They stood facing each other with the lawnmower between them. Neither was going to yield. Elínborg sat watching the standoff from the car, shook her head and thought to herself: Men!

'Fine,' Erlendur said. 'See you in Reykjavík.'

He turned away and walked back towards the car. Frowning, Hannes watched him.

'Does it go in your reports?' he called out after Erlendur. 'If I talk to you.'

'Are you afraid of reports?' Erlendur said, turning round.

'I don't want to be quoted. I don't want any files about me or about what I say. I don't want any spying.'

'That's all right,' Erlendur said. 'Neither do I.'

'I haven't thought about this for decades,' Hannes said. 'I've tried to forget about it.'

'Forget about what?' Erlendur asked.

'Those were strange times,' Hannes said. 'I haven't heard Lothar's name for ages. What's he got to do with the skeleton in Kleifarvatn?'

For a good while Erlendur just stood looking at him, until Hannes cleared his throat and said they should maybe go inside. Erlendur nodded and waved Elínborg over.

'My wife died four years ago,' Hannes said as he opened the door. He told them that his children sometimes dropped by with his grandchildren on a Sunday drive in the countryside, but that in other respects he was left to himself and preferred it that way. They asked about his circumstances and how long he had lived in Selfoss; he said he had moved there about twenty years before. He had been an engineer with a large firm engaged on hydropower projects, but had lost interest in the subject, moved from Reykjavík and settled in Selfoss, where he liked living.

When he brought the coffee into the living room Erlendur asked him about Leipzig. Hannes tried to explain what it was like to be a student there in the mid-1950s and before he knew it he was telling them about the shortages, voluntary work, clearing of ruins, the Day of the Republic parades, Ulbricht, compulsory attendance at lectures on socialism, the Icelandic students' views on socialism, anti-party activities, the Freie Deutsche Jugend, Soviet power, the planned economy, collectives and the interactive surveillance which ensured that no one could get away with causing trouble and weeded out all criticism. He told them about the friendships that were formed among the Icelandic students, the ideals they discussed, and about socialism as a genuine alternative to capitalism.

'I don't think it's dead,' Hannes said, as if reaching some kind of conclusion. 'I think it's very much alive, but in a different way from what we may have imagined. It's socialism that makes it bearable for us to live under capitalism.'

'You're still a socialist?' Erlendur said.

'I always have been,' Hannes said. 'Socialism bears no relation to the blatant inhumanity that Stalin turned it into or the ridiculous dictatorships that developed across Eastern Europe.'

'But didn't everyone join in singing the praises of that deception?' Erlendur said.

'I don't know,' Hannes said. 'I didn't after I saw how socialism was put into practice in East Germany. Actually I was deported for not being submissive enough. For not wanting to go the whole hog in the spy network they ran and so poetically described as interactive. They thought it was acceptable for children to spy on their parents and report them if they deviated from the party line. That has nothing to do with socialism. It's the fear of losing power. Which of course they did in the end.'

'What do you mean, go the whole hog?' Erlendur asked.

'They wanted me to spy on my companions, the Icelanders. I refused. Other things I saw and heard there made me rebel. I didn't go to the compulsory lectures. I criticised the system. Not openly, of course, because you never criticised anything out loud, just discussed the flaws in the system with small groups of people you trusted. There were dissident cells in the city, young people who met secretly. I got to know them. Is it Lothar you found in Kleifarvatn?'

'No,' Erlendur said. 'Or rather, we don't know.'

'Who were "they"?' Elínborg asked. 'You said "they" asked you to spy on your companions.'

'Lothar Weiser, for one.'

'Why him?' Elínborg asked. 'Do you know?'

'He was nominally a student but didn't seem serious about it and went about his own business as he pleased. He spoke fluent Icelandic and we believed he was there explicitly on the orders of the party or student organisation, which was the same thing. Clearly, one of his functions was to keep an eye on the students and try to enlist their cooperation.'

'What kind of cooperation?' Elínborg asked.

'It took all kinds of forms,' Hannes said. 'If you knew someone listened to western radio, you were supposed to let an official from the FDJ know. If anyone said he couldn't be bothered to clear the ruins or do other voluntary work, you were meant to inform on him. Then there were more serious offences such as allowing yourself to air anti-socialist views. Not attending the Day of the Republic parade was also seen as a sign of opposition rather than simple laziness. Likewise if you skived those pointless FDJ lectures on socialist values. Everything was under close control and Lothar was one of the players. We were urged to report on others. Really you weren't showing the right spirit if you didn't inform.'

'Could Lothar have asked other Icelanders to give him information?' Erlendur asked. 'Could he have asked other people to spy on their companions?'

'There's no question about it. I'm sure he did,' Hannes said. 'I imagine he tried that on every one of them.'

'And?'

'And nothing.'

'Was there any particular reward for being cooperative or was it purely idealistic?' Elínborg asked. 'Spying on your neighbours?'

'There were systems to reward those who wanted to impress. Sometimes a bad student who was loyal to the party line and politically sound would get a bigger grant than a brilliant student who had much higher grades but was not politically active. The system worked like that. When an undesirable student was expelled, like I was in the end, it was important for the other students to show what they thought by siding with the party apparatchiks. Students could gain kudos by denouncing the offender to show loyalty to the general line, as it was called. The Freie Deutsche Jugend was in charge of discipline. It was the only student organisation that was allowed and it had a lot of power. Not belonging to it was frowned upon. As was not attending their talks.'

'You said there were dissident cells,' Erlendur said.

'I don't even know if you could call them dissident cells,' Hannes said. 'Mainly they were young people who got together and listened to western radio stations and talked about Bill Haley and West Berlin, where many of them had been, or even religion, which the officials didn't think highly of. Then there were other proper dissident groups that wanted to fight for reforms to the political structure, real democracy, freedom of speech and the press. They were crushed.'

'You said Lothar Weiser "for one" had asked you to spy. Do you mean there were others like him?' Erlendur asked.

'Yes, of course,' Hannes said. 'Society was strictly controlled, both the university and the public at large. And people feared surveillance. Orthodox communists took part in it wholeheartedly, the sceptics tried to avoid it and come to terms with living under it, but I think most people found it at odds with everything socialism stands for.'

'Did you know any Icelandic student who may have worked for Lothar?'

'Why do you want to know that?' Hannes asked.

'We need to know whether he was in contact with any Icelanders when he was here as a trade attaché in the 1960s,' Erlendur said. 'It's a perfectly normal check. We're not trying to spy on people, just gathering information because of the skeleton we found.'

Hannes looked at them.

'I don't know of any Icelander who paid any attention to that system, except Emil maybe,' he said. 'I think he was acting under cover. I told Tómas that once when he asked me the same question. Much later, in fact. He came to see me and asked exactly the same question.'

'Tómas?' Erlendur said. He remembered the name from the list of students in East Germany. 'Do you keep in touch with Leipzig alumni?'

'No, I don't have much contact with them and never have,' Hannes said. 'But Tómas and I had one thing in common: we were both expelled. Like me, he came back home before he finished his course. He was ordered to leave. He looked me up when he got back to Iceland and told me about his girlfriend, a Hungarian girl called Ilona. I knew her vaguely. She wasn't the type to toe the party line, to put it mildly. Her background was rather different. The climate was more liberal in Hungary then. Young people were starting to say what they thought about the Soviet hegemony that covered the whole of Eastern Europe.'

'Why did he tell you about her?' Elínborg asked.

'He was a broken man when he came to see me,' Hannes said. 'A shadow of his former self. I remembered him when he was happy and confident and full of socialist ideals. He fought for them. Came from a solid working-class family.'

'Why was he a broken man?'

'Because she disappeared,' Hannes said. 'Ilona was arrested in Leipzig and never seen again. He was totally destroyed by it. He told me Ilona was pregnant when she went missing. Told me with tears in his eyes.'

'And he came to see you again later?' Erlendur asked.

'That was quite strange actually. Him coming after all those years to reminisce. I'd forgotten the whole business really, but it was obvious that Tómas had forgotten nothing. He remembered it all. Every detail, as if it had happened yesterday.'

'What did he want?' Elínborg said.

'He was asking me about Emil,' Hannes said. 'If he'd worked for Lothar. If they'd been in close contact. I don't know why he wanted to know, but I told him I had proof that Emil needed to get into Lothar's good books.'

'What kind of proof?' Elínborg asked.

'Emil was a hopeless student. He didn't really belong at university, but he was a good socialist. Everything we said went straight to Lothar, and Lothar made sure that Emil received a good grant and good marks. Tómas and Emil were good friends.'

'What proof did you have?' Elínborg repeated.

'My engineering professor told me when I said goodbye to him. After I was expelled. He was hurt that I wasn't allowed to finish the course. All the teaching staff talked about it, he said. The teachers disliked students like Emil, but couldn't do a thing. They didn't all like Lothar and his ilk, either. The professor said that Emil must have been valuable to Lothar, because there was hardly a worse student around, but Lothar ordered the university authorities not to fail him. The FDJ sanctioned the move and Lothar was behind it.'

Hannes paused.

'Emil was the staunchest of us all,' he said after a while. 'A hardline communist and Stalinist.'

'Why . . .' Erlendur began, but Hannes continued as if his mind were elsewhere.

'It was all such a shock,' he said, staring ahead. 'The whole system. We witnessed absolute dictatorship by the party, fear and repression. Some tried to tell the party members here about it when they got back, but made no headway. I always felt that the socialism they practised in

East Germany was a kind of sequel to Nazism. This time they were under the Russian heel, of course, but I pretty quickly got the feeling that socialism in East Germany was essentially just another kind of Nazism.'

30

Hannes cleared his throat and looked at them. They could both tell that he found it difficult to talk about his student days. He did not appear to be in the habit of recalling his Leipzig years. Erlendur had forced him to sit down and open up.

'Is there anything else you need to know?' Hannes asked.

'So Tómas turns up years after he left Leipzig and asks you about Emil and Lothar, and you tell him you have proof that they were operating together,' Erlendur said. 'Emil performed for him the important task of monitoring and informing on the students.'

'Yes,' Hannes said.

'Why was Tómas asking about Emil, and who is Emil?'

'He didn't tell me why and I know very little about Emil. The last I heard, he was living abroad. I think he did ever since we studied in Germany. He never moved back as far as I know. I met one of the students from Leipzig a few years ago, Karl. We were both travelling in Skaftafell and we started talking about the old days, and he said he thought Emil had decided to settle abroad after university. He hadn't seen or heard of him since.'

'But Tómas, do you know anything about him?' Erlendur asked.

'Not really. He did engineering at Leipzig but I'm not aware that he worked in the field. He was expelled. I only met him once when he got back from Germany, that one time he came to ask about Emil.'

'Tell us about it,' Elínborg said.

'There's not much to tell. He dropped in and we reminisced about the old days.'

'Why was he interested in Emil?' Erlendur asked.

Hannes looked at them again.

'I should make some more coffee,' he said and stood up.

Hannes told them how he had been living in a new townhouse in the Vogar district of Reykjavík at the time. One evening the doorbell rang. When he opened it Tómas was standing on the steps. It was autumn and the weather was rough, the wind shook the trees in the garden and sheets of rain lashed against the house. Hannes did not recognise the visitor at first and was taken aback when he realised it was Tómas. He was so astonished that it did not occur to him at first to invite him in out of the rain.

'Sorry to disturb you like this,' Tómas said.

'No, it's fine,' Hannes said. Then he realised: 'What awful weather. Come on in, come on.'

Tómas took off his coat and greeted Hannes's wife; their children came out to look at the guest and he smiled at them. Hannes had a small study in the basement and when they had finished their coffee and chatted about the weather he invited Tómas down. He sensed that Tómas was ill at ease, that something was preying on him. He was jumpy and a little awkward about having called on people he really did not know at all. They had not been friends in Leipzig. Hannes's wife had never heard Tómas's name mentioned.

When they had settled down in the basement they reminisced about their Leipzig years for a while; between them they knew where some of the students were now, but not others. Hannes sensed how Tómas was inching towards the purpose of his visit, and he thought to himself that he would have liked him if he'd known him better. He remembered the first time he saw him at the university library. Recalled the impression of polite bashfulness that he gave.

Well aware of Ilona's disappearance, he remembered the previous time Tómas had visited him, just back from East Germany and a changed man, to tell him what had happened. He felt nothing but pity for Tómas. He had sent him a message written in a moment of anger, blaming him for his expulsion from Leipzig. But when his rage had died down and he was back in Iceland he realised that it was not Tómas's fault, but as much his own for defying the system. Tómas mentioned the note and said it was preying on his mind. He told him to forget it, that it had been written in a fit of pique and did not represent the truth. They were fully reconciled. Tómas told him he had contacted the party leaders about Ilona and they had promised to make inquiries in East Germany. He was severely reproached for being expelled, for abusing his position and the trust he had been shown. Tómas had admitted to it all, he said, and repented. He told them whatever they wanted to hear. His sole aim was to help Ilona. It was all in vain.

Tómas mentioned the rumour that Ilona and Hannes had been going out together at one time and that Ilona wanted to marry in order to leave the country. Hannes said that was news to him. He had been to a few meetings and seen Ilona there, then given up all involvement in politics.

And now Tómas was sitting there again, in his home. It was twelve years since they had last faced each other. He had begun talking about Lothar and finally seemed to be getting to the point.

'I wanted to ask you about Emil,' Tómas said. 'You know we were good friends in Germany.'

'Yes, I knew,' he said.

'Could Emil have, say, had a special connection with Lothar?'

He nodded. Although he disliked maligning people, he was no friend of Emil's and felt he understood what sort of character he was. Hannes repeated the professor's words about Emil and Lothar. How it confirmed his suspicions. That Emil had been actively engaged in interactive surveillance and had benefited from his loyalty to the student organisation and the party.

'Do you ever wonder if Emil played a part in your expulsion?' Tómas asked.

'That's impossible to say. Anyone could have grassed on me to the FDJ – more than one person, more than two. I blamed you, as you remember. I wrote you that note. It gets so complicated talking to people when you don't know what you're allowed to say. But I haven't been dwelling on it. It's over and done with long ago. Buried and forgotten.'

'Did you know that Lothar is in Iceland?' Tómas suddenly asked.

'Lothar? In Iceland? No, I didn't.'

'He's involved with the East German embassy, some kind of official there. I met him by chance – actually I didn't meet him, I saw him. He was on his way to the embassy. I was walking down Aegisída. I live in the west of town. He didn't notice me. I was some way off but it was him, large as life. I accused him back in Leipzig of being involved in Ilona's disappearance and he said to me: "Take a closer look." But I didn't understand what he meant. I think I understand now.'

They stopped talking.

He looked at Tómas and could tell how helpless and alone in the world his former fellow student was, and wanted to do something for him.

'If I can help you with . . . you know, if I can do anything for you . . .'

'Did the professor say that Emil was operating with Lothar and gained from it?'

'Yes.'

'Do you know what became of Emil?'

'Isn't he living abroad? I don't think he came back when he graduated.'

They fell silent again for a while.

'That story about me and Ilona, who told you it?' Hannes asked.

'Lothar,' Tómas said.

Hannes was unsure how to proceed.

'I don't know whether I should tell you this,' he said eventually, 'but I heard something else just before I left. You were so upset when you got back from Germany and I didn't want to spread gossip. There's plenty of that anyway. But I was told Emil had been trying to get off with Ilona before you started going out together.'

Tómas stared at him.

'That's what I heard,' Hannes said, seeing Tómas turn pale at the news. 'There's not necessarily any truth in it.'

'Are you saying they went out together before I . . . ?'

'No, more that he was trying. He used to snoop around her, did voluntary work with her and . . .'

'Emil and Ilona?' Tómas groaned in disbelief, as if unable to grasp the idea.

'He was only trying, that was all I heard,' Hannes hurried to say, immediately regretting his words. He could tell from Tómas's expression that he should never have mentioned it.

'Who told you this?' Tómas asked.

'I don't remember and it needn't be true.'

'Emil and Ilona? She didn't fancy him?'

'Not at all,' Hannes said. 'That was what I heard. She wasn't interested in him. But Emil was hurt.'

They paused.

'Ilona never mentioned this to you?'

'No,' Tómas said. 'She never did.'

'Then he left,' Hannes said, looking at Erlendur and Elínborg. 'I haven't seen him since and actually I have no idea whether he's dead or alive.'

'That must have been a nasty experience for you in Leipzig,' Erlendur said.

'The worst things were being spied on and the endless suspicion. But it was a good place to be in many ways. Maybe we weren't all happy to see the glorious face of socialism up close but most of us

268

tried to live with the drawbacks. Some of us found it easier than others. In terms of education it was a model institution. The overwhelming majority of students were the children of farmers and workers. Has that happened anywhere before or since?'

'Why did Tómas turn up after all those years and ask you about Emil?' Elínborg said. 'Do you think he went on to meet Emil again?'

'I don't know,' Hannes said. 'He never told me.'

'This girl Ilona,' Erlendur said, 'is anything known about her?'

'I don't think so. Times were strange because of Hungary, where everything later erupted. They weren't going to let that happen in other communist countries. There was no leeway for exchanging views, for criticism or debate. I don't think anyone knows what became of Ilona. Tómas never found out. I don't think so anyway, although it's not really anything to do with me. Nor is that period in my life. I put it behind me a long while ago and I don't like talking about it. They were awful times. Awful.'

'Who told you about Emil and Ilona?' Elínborg asked.

'His name's Karl,' Hannes said.

'Karl?' Elínborg said.

'Yes,' Hannes said.

'Was he in Leipzig too?' she asked.

Hannes nodded.

'Do you know of any Icelanders who could have been in possession of such a thing as a Russian listening device in the 1960s?' Erlendur asked. 'Who could have been dabbling in espionage?'

'A Russian listening device?'

'Yes, I can't go into details but does anyone occur to you?'

'Well, if Lothar was an attaché to the embassy he would be a candidate,' Hannes said. 'I can't imagine that . . . are you . . . you're not talking about an Icelandic spy, are you?'

'No, I think that would be bizarre,' Erlendur said.

'Like I say, I'm just not in the picture. I've hardly had any contact with the group from Leipzig. I don't know anything about Russian spying.'

'You wouldn't happen to have a photograph of Lothar Weiser, would you?' Erlendur asked.

'No,' Hannes said. 'I don't have many mementoes from those years.'

'Emil seems to have been a secretive character,' Elínborg said.

'That may well be. As I told you, I think he's lived abroad all his life. Actually I . . . the last time I saw him . . . was after Tómas paid me that weird visit. I saw Emil in the centre of Reykjavík. I hadn't seen him since Leipzig and I only caught a glimpse, but I'm sure it was Emil. But as I say, I don't know anything else about the man.'

'So you didn't talk to him?' Elínborg asked.

'Talk to him? No, I couldn't. He got into a car and drove away. I only saw him for a split second, but it was definitely him. I remember it because of the shock of suddenly recognising him.'

'Do you remember what kind of car it was?' Erlendur asked.

'What kind?'

'The model, colour?'

'It was black,' Hannes said. 'I don't know anything about cars. But I remember it was black.'

'Could it have been a Ford?'

'I don't know.'

'A Ford Falcon?'

'Like I said, I only remember it being black.'

31

He put the pen down on the desk. In his account of the events in Leipzig and later in Iceland, he had tried to be as clear and succinct as possible. It ran to more than seventy carefully written pages which had taken him several days to produce, and he had still not finished the conclusion. He had made up his mind. He was reconciled to what he was going to do.

He had reached the point in his narrative where he was walking along Aegisída and saw Lothar Weiser approach one of the houses. Although he had not seen Lothar for years, he recognised him at once. With age Lothar had put on weight and now walked with more of a plod; he did not notice the onlooker. Tómas had stopped dead and stared at Lothar in astonishment. Once the surprise wore off, his first reaction was to keep out of sight, so he half-turned away and very slowly retraced his steps. He watched Lothar go through the gate, shut it carefully behind him and disappear behind the house. He presumed that the German had gone in through the back door. He noticed a sign saying 'The Trade Delegation of the German Democratic Republic'.

Standing outside on the pavement, he stared at the house, transfixed. It was lunchtime and he had gone out for a stroll in the good weather. Normally he would use his lunch break for an hour at home. He worked for an insurance company in the town centre. He had been there for two years and enjoyed his job insuring families against setbacks. With a glance at his watch he realised he was due back.

Early that evening he went for another walk, as he sometimes did. As a man of routine he generally followed the same streets in the western quarter and alongside the seashore on Aegisída. He walked slowly and stared in through the windows of the house, expecting to catch a glimpse of Lothar, but saw nothing. Only two windows were lit and he could not discern anyone inside. He was about to go back home when a black Volga suddenly backed out of the drive beside the house and drove down Aegisída away from him.

He did not know what he was doing. He did not know what he expected to see or what would happen next. Even if he saw Lothar leave the house he would not have known whether to call out or simply follow him. What was he supposed to say to him?

For the next few evenings he would walk along Aegisída and past the house, and one evening he saw three people leaving it. Two got into a black Volga and drove away while the third, who was Lothar, said goodbye to them and walked up Hofsvallagata towards the city centre. It was about eight o'clock and he followed him. Lothar walked slowly up to Túngata, along Gardastraeti all the way to Vesturgata, where he entered the Naustid restaurant.

He spent two hours waiting outside the restaurant while Lothar dined. It was autumn and the evenings were beginning to turn noticeably colder, but he was dressed warmly in a winter coat with a scarf and a cap with ear flaps. Playing this childish game of spies made him feel rather silly. He mainly stayed on Fischersund, trying not to let the restaurant door out of his sight. When Lothar finally re-emerged, he went down Vesturgata and along Austurstraeti towards the Thingholt district. On Bergstadastraeti, he stopped outside a small shed in the back garden of a house not far from Hótel Holt. The door opened and someone let Lothar in. He did not see who it was.

He could not imagine what was going on and, driven by curiosity, he hesitantly approached the shed. The street lighting did not reach that far and he inched his way carefully forward in the near-dark. There was a padlock on the door. He crept up to a small window on the side of the shed and peered inside. A lamp was switched on over a workbench and in its light he could see the two men.

One of them reached out for something under the light. Suddenly he saw who it was and darted back from the window. It was as if he had been hit in the face.

It was his old student friend from Leipzig, whom he had not seen for all those years.

Emil.

He crept away from the shed and back onto the street, where he waited for a long time until Lothar emerged. Emil was with him. Emil vanished into the darkness beside the shed, but Lothar set off again for the west of town. He had no idea what kind of contact Emil and Lothar maintained. As far as he knew, Emil lived abroad.

He turned all this over in his mind without reaching a conclusion. In the end he decided to visit Hannes. He had done that once before, as soon as he returned from East Germany, to tell him about Ilona. Hannes might know something about Emil and Lothar.

Lothar went into the house on Aegisída. Tómas waited for a while a reasonable distance away before setting off home, and suddenly the German's strange and incomprehensible sentence at their last encounter entered his mind:

Take a closer look.

32

Driving back from Selfoss, Erlendur and Elínborg discussed Hannes's story. It was evening and there was not much traffic on Hellisheidi moor. Erlendur thought about the black Falcon. There would hardly have been many on the streets in those days. Yet the Falcon was popular, according to Elínborg's husband Teddi. He thought about Tómas, whose girlfriend had gone missing in East Germany. They would visit him at the first opportunity. He still could not work out the link between the body in the lake and the Leipzig students in the 1960s. And he thought about Eva Lind, who was destroying herself in spite of his attempts to save her, and about his son Sindri, whom he did not know in the slightest. He puzzled over all this without managing to organise his thoughts. Giving him a sideways glance, Elínborg asked what was on his mind.

'Nothing,' he said.

'There must be something,' Elínborg said.

'No,' Erlendur said. 'It's nothing.'

Elínborg shrugged. Erlendur thought about Valgerdur, from whom he had not heard for several days. He knew that she needed time and he was in no hurry either. What she saw in him was a riddle to Erlendur. He could not understand what attracted Valgerdur to a lonely, depressive man who lived in a gloomy block of flats. He asked himself sometimes whether he deserved her friendship at all.

However, he knew precisely what it was that he liked about Valgerdur. He had known from the first moment. She was everything he was not but would love to be. To all intents and purposes she was his opposite. Attractive, smiling and happy. In spite of the marital problems she had to deal with, which Erlendur knew had had a profound effect on her, she tried not to let them ruin her life. She always saw the upside to any problem and was incapable of feeling hatred or irritation about anything. She allowed nothing to darken her outlook on life, which was gentle and generous. Not even her husband, whom Erlendur regarded as a moron for being unfaithful to such a woman.

Erlendur knew perfectly what he saw in her. Being with her reinvigorated him.

'Tell me what you're thinking about,' Elínborg pleaded. She was bored.

'Nothing,' Erlendur said. 'I'm not thinking about anything.'

She shook her head. Erlendur had been rather gloomy that summer, even though he had spent an unusual amount of time after work with the other detectives. She and Sigurdur Óli had discussed this and thought he was probably depressed by having virtually no contact with Eva Lind any longer. They knew that he was in anguish about her and had tried to help her, but the girl seemed to have no control over herself. She's a loser, was Sigurdur Óli's stock response. Two or three times Elínborg had approached Erlendur to talk about Eva and ask how she was, but he had brushed her off.

They sat in deep silence until Erlendur drew up in front of Elínborg's townhouse. Instead of getting straight out of the car, she turned to him.

'What's wrong?' she asked.

Erlendur did not reply.

'What should we do about this case? Do we talk to this Tómas character?'

'We have to,' Erlendur said.

'Are you thinking about Eva Lind?' Elínborg asked. 'Is that why you're so quiet and serious?'

'Don't worry about me,' Erlendur said. 'I'll see you tomorrow.' He watched her walk up the steps to her house. When she went inside he drove away.

Two hours later, Erlendur was sitting in his chair at home reading when the doorbell rang. He stood up and asked who it was, then pressed the button to open the front door downstairs. After switching on the light in his flat he went to the hallway, opened the door and waited. Valgerdur soon appeared.

'Perhaps you want to be left alone?' she said.

'No, do come in,' he said.

She slipped past him and he took her coat. Noticing an open book by the chair, she asked what he was reading and he told her it was a book about avalanches.

'And everyone meets a ghastly death, I suppose,' she said.

They had often talked about his interest in Icelandic lore, historical accounts, biography and books about fatal ordeals at the mercy of the elements.

'Not everyone. Some survive. Fortunately.'

'Is that why you read these books about death in the mountains and avalanches?'

'What do you mean?' Erlendur said.

'Because some people survive?'

Erlendur smiled.

'Maybe,' he said. 'Are you still living with your sister?'

She nodded. She said she expected to need to consult a lawyer about the divorce and asked Erlendur if he knew any. She said she had never needed a lawyer's advice before. Erlendur offered to ask at work, where he said lawyers were nineteen to the dozen.

'Have you got any of that green stuff left?' she asked, sitting down on the sofa.

With a nod he produced the Chartreuse and two glasses.

Remembered hearing once that thirty different botanical ingredients were used to achieve the correct flavour. He sat down beside her and told her about them.

She told him she had met her husband earlier that day, how he had promised to turn over a new leaf and tried to persuade her to move back in. But when he realised that she was intent on leaving him, he had grown angry and in the end had lost control of himself, shouting and cursing at her. They were in a restaurant and he had showered her with abuse, paying no heed to the customers watching in astonishment. She had stood up and walked out without looking back.

Once she had related the day's events they sat in silence finishing their drinks. She asked for another glass.

'So what should we do?' she asked.

Erlendur downed the rest of his drink and felt it scorch his throat. He refilled the glasses, thinking about the perfume on her that he had noticed when she'd walked past him at the door. It was like the scent of a bygone summer and he was filled with a strange nostalgia that was rooted too far back for him to identify properly.

'We'll do whatever we like,' he said.

'What do you want to do?' she asked. 'You've been so patient and I was wondering if it is really patience, if it isn't just as much . . . that somehow you didn't want to get involved.'

They fell silent. The question hung in the air.

What do you want to do?

He finished his second glass. This was the question he had been asking himself since he first met her. He did not consider himself to have been patient. He had no idea what he had been, apart from trying to be a support to her. Perhaps he had not shown her sufficient attention or warmth. He did not know.

'You didn't want to rush into anything,' he said. 'Nor did I. There hasn't been a woman in my life for a long time.'

He stopped. He wanted to tell her that he had mostly been by himself, in this place, with his books, and that her sitting on his sofa brought him special joy. She was so completely different from everything he was accustomed to, a sweet scent of summer, and he did not know how to handle it. How to tell her this was all he had wanted and yearned for from the moment he saw her. Being with her.

'I didn't mean to be stand-offish,' he said. 'But this sort of thing takes time, especially for me. And of course you've . . . I mean, it's tough going through a divorce . . .'

She could see that he felt uncomfortable discussing this sort of thing. Whenever the conversation took that direction he became awkward and hesitant and clammed up. As a rule he did not say very much, which may have been why she felt comfortable in his presence. There was no pretence about him. He was never acting. He probably would have had no idea how to behave if he wanted to try to be different somehow. He was totally honest in everything he said and did. She sensed this and it offered her a security that she had lacked for so long. In him she found a man she knew she could trust.

'Sorry,' she smiled. 'I wasn't intending to turn this into some kind of negotiation. But it can be nice to know where you stand. You realise that.'

'Completely,' Erlendur said, feeling the tension between them easing slightly.

'It all takes time and we'll see,' she said.

'I think that's very sensible,' he said.

'Fine,' she said, standing up from the sofa. Erlendur stood up as well. She said something about having to meet her sons, which he did not catch. His thoughts were elsewhere. She walked over to the door and while he helped her put on her coat she could tell he was dithering about something. She opened the door to the corridor and asked if everything was all right.

Erlendur looked at her.

'Don't go,' he said.

She stopped in the doorway.

'Stay with me,' he said.

Valgerdur hesitated.

'Are you sure?' she said.

'Yes,' he said. 'Don't go.'

She stood motionless and took a long look at him. He walked up to her, led her back inside, closed the door and began taking off her coat without her offering any objection.

They made love slowly, smoothly and tenderly, both of them feeling a little hesitation and uncertainty which they gradually overcame. She told him that he was the second man she had ever slept with.

As they lay in bed he looked up at the ceiling and told her that he sometimes went to the east of Iceland, to his childhood haunts, where he stayed in his old house. There was nothing but bare walls, a half-collapsed roof and little indication that his family had ever lived there. Yet relics of a vanished life remained. Patches of a patterned carpet that he remembered well. Broken cupboards in the kitchen. Window-sills that little hands had once leaned upon. He told her it was nice to go there, to lie down with his memories and rediscover a world that was full of light and tranquillity.

Valgerdur squeezed his hand.

He started to tell her a story about the ordeals of a young girl who left her mother's house with no exact idea of where she was going. She had suffered setbacks and was weak-willed – understandably perhaps, because she had never been given what she longed for most of all. She felt something lacking in her life. Felt a sense of betrayal. She ploughed on headlong, driven by a strange self-destructive urge, and sank deeper and deeper until she could go no farther, bound up in her self-annihilation. When she was found she was taken back and nursed to health, but as soon as she had recuperated she disappeared again without warning. She roamed around in storms and sometimes sought shelter where her father lived. He tried his best to keep her out of the tempestuous weather, but she never listened and set off again as if fate held nothing in store for her but destruction.

Valgerdur looked at him.

'No one knows where she is now. She's still alive, because I would have heard if she had died. I'm waiting for that news. I've ventured into that storm time and again, found her and dragged her back home and tried to help her, but I doubt whether anyone really can.'

'Don't be too sure,' Valgerdur said after a long silence.

The telephone on his bedside table rang. Erlendur looked at it and was not going to answer, but Valgerdur told him that it must be important for someone to call so late at night. Muttering that it must be Sigurdur Óli with some stupid brainwave, he reached over.

It took him a while to realise that the man on the other end was Haraldur. He was calling from the old people's home and said he had sneaked into the office and wanted to talk to Erlendur.

'What do you want?' Erlendur asked.

'I'll tell you what happened,' Haraldur said.

'Why?' Erlendur asked.

'Do you want to hear it or not?' Haraldur said.

'Calm down,' Erlendur said. 'I'll drop by tomorrow. Is that all right?'

'You do that, then,' Haraldur said, and slammed down the telephone.

33

He put the pages that he had written into a large envelope, addressed it and laid it on his desk. Running his hand over the envelope, he thought about the story it contained. He had wrestled with himself about whether to describe the events at all, then decided it could not be avoided. The body had been found in Kleifarvatn. Sooner or later the trail would lead to him. He knew that there was really barely any link between him and the body in the lake, and the police would have their work cut out to establish the truth without his assistance. But he did not want to lie. If all he left behind was the truth, that would be enough.

He enjoyed both his visits to Hannes. Ever since their first meeting he had liked him, despite their occasional disagreements. Hannes had helped him. He had shed new light on Emil's relationship with Lothar and revealed that Emil and Ilona had known each other before he arrived in Leipzig, although in very vague terms. Perhaps this helped to explain what happened later. Or perhaps that connection complicated the matter. He did not know what to think about it.

He finally came to the conclusion that he had to talk to Emil. Had to ask him about Ilona and Lothar and the chicanery in Leipzig. He could not be sure that Emil would be able to tell him the answers, but he needed to hear what he did know. Nor could he snoop around

Emil's shed. That was beneath his dignity. He did not want to play hide-and-seek.

Another motive drove him on. A thought that had struck him after visiting Hannes, connected with his own involvement and how naive, gullible and innocent he had been. If there was no other explanation for what had happened, then he would have been the cause of it. He had to know which.

This was why he was back on Bergstadastraeti one afternoon a few days after he had trailed Lothar and peered into the shed. He had gone round to confront Emil straight from work. It was starting to get dark and the weather was cold. He felt winter approaching.

He walked into the backyard where the shed stood. As he approached, he noticed that the door was unlocked. The padlock was undone. He pushed the door open and peeped inside. Emil was sitting hunched over the workbench. He crept in. The shed was filled with an assortment of old rubbish that he could not identify in the dark. A single bare light bulb hung above the bench.

Emil did not notice him until he was standing right next to him. His jacket lay over the chair and looked as though it had been ripped in a fight. Emil was muttering something to himself and sounded angry. Suddenly Emil seemed to sense a presence in the shed. He glanced up from his maps, turned his head slowly and looked at him. He saw that it took Emil a while to work out who it was.

'Tómas,' he said with a sigh. 'Is that you?'

'Hello, Emil,' he said. 'The door was open.'

'What are you doing?' Emil said. 'What . . .' He was speechless. 'How did you know . . .'

'I followed Lothar here,' he said. 'I followed him from Aegisída.'

'You followed Lothar?' Emil said in disbelief. He stood up without taking his eyes off the visitor. 'What are you doing?' he repeated. 'Why did you follow Lothar?' He looked out through the door as if expecting more uninvited guests. 'Are you on your own?' Emil asked him.

'Yes, I'm alone.'

'What did you come here for?'

'You remember Ilona,' he said. 'In Leipzig.'

'Ilona?'

'We were going out together, me and Ilona.'

'Of course I remember Ilona. What about her?'

'Can you tell me what happened to her?' he asked. 'Can you tell me now after all these years? Do you know?'

Not wanting to appear overzealous, he tried to remain calm, but it was futile. He could be read like a book, his years of agonising over the girl he had loved and lost plain to see.

'What are you talking about?' Emil said.

'Ilona.'

'Are you still thinking about Ilona? Even now?'

'Do you know what happened to her?'

'I don't know anything. I don't know what you're talking about. You shouldn't be here. You ought to leave.'

He looked around inside the shed.

'What are you doing?' he asked. 'What's this shed for? When did you come home?'

'You ought to get out,' Emil said again, peering anxiously through the door. 'Does anyone else know I'm here?' he added after a moment. 'Does anyone else know about me here?'

'Can you tell me?' he repeated. 'What happened to Ilona?'

Emil looked at him, then suddenly lost his temper.

'Piss off, I said. Get out! I can't help you with that shit.'

Emil pushed him, but he stood firm.

'What did you get for informing on Ilona?' he asked. 'What did they give you, their golden boy? Did they give you money? Did you get good marks? Did you get a good job with them?'

'I don't know what you're on about,' Emil said. He had been half-whispering, but now he raised his voice.

Emil seemed to have changed a lot since Leipzig. He was as skinny as ever but looked unhealthier, with dark rings beneath his eyes, his fingers stained yellow from smoking, his voice hoarse. His protruding Adam's apple moved up and down when he spoke, his hair was starting to thin. He had not seen Emil for a long time and remembered him only as a young man. Now he seemed tired and haggard, with several days' beard on his face; he looked like a drinker.

'It was my fault, wasn't it?' he said.

'Will you stop being so stupid,' Emil said, moving closer to push him again. 'Get out!' he said. 'Forget it.'

He stepped out of the way.

'I was the one who told you what Ilona was doing there, wasn't I? I put you on to her. If I hadn't told you she might have got away. They wouldn't have known about the meetings. They wouldn't have photographed us.'

'Get out of here!'

'I talked to Hannes. He told me about you and Lothar and how Lothar and the FDJ got the university to reward you with good marks. You were never much of a student, were you, Emil? I never saw you open a book. What did you get for grassing on your comrades? On your friends? What did they give you for spying on your friends?'

'She didn't manage to convert me with her preaching, but you fell flat for it,' Emil snarled. 'Ilona was a traitor.'

'Because she betrayed you?' he said. 'Because she wouldn't have anything to do with you? Was it that painful? Was it so painful when she rejected you?'

Emil stared at him.

'I don't know what she saw in you,' he said, a tiny smile playing across his lips. 'I don't know what she saw in the smart idealist who wanted to make a socialist Iceland but changed his mind the moment she got him into the sack. I don't know what it was she saw in you!'

'So you wanted revenge,' he said. 'Was that it? Vengeance against her?'

'You deserved each other,' Emil said.

He stared at Emil and a strange coldness ran through him. He no longer knew his old friend, did not know who or what Emil had become. He knew that he was looking at the same unflinching evil that he had seen in his student years, and knew that he should be consumed by hatred and anger and attack Emil, but suddenly felt no urge to. Felt no need to take out years of worry, insecurity and fear on him. And not only because he had never had a violent streak or never got into fights. He despised violence in all forms. He knew that he ought to have been seized with such mighty rage that he would want to kill Emil. But instead of swelling up with anger, his mind emptied of everything except coldness.

'And you're right,' Emil went on as they stood face to face. 'It was you. You have only yourself to blame. It was you who first told me about her meetings, her views and her ideas about helping people to attack socialism. It was you. If that was what you wanted to know, I can confirm it. It was what you said that got Ilona arrested! I didn't know how she worked. You told me. Do you remember? After that they started watching her. After that they called you in and warned you. But it was too late then. It had moved on. The matter was out of our hands.'

He remembered the occasion well. Time and again he had wondered whether he had told someone something he should not have. He had always believed that he could trust his fellow Icelanders. Trust them not to spy on each other. That the small band of friends was immune to interactive surveillance. That the thought police had nothing to do with the Icelanders. It was in that faith that he told them about Ilona, her companions and their ideas.

Looking at Emil, he recognised his inhumanity and how whole societies could be built on brutality alone.

'There was one thing I started thinking about when it was all over,' he went on as if talking to himself, as if removed from time and space to a place where nothing mattered any more. 'When it was all over and nothing could be put right. Long after I came back to Iceland. I was the one who told you about Ilona's meetings. I don't know why, but I did. I suppose I was just encouraging you and the others to go to the meetings. There were no secrets between us Icelanders. We could discuss it all without worrying. I didn't reckon on someone like you.'

He paused.

'We stood together,' he went on. 'Someone informed on Ilona. The university was a big place and it could have been anyone. It wasn't until long afterwards that I started to consider the possibility that it was one of us Icelanders, one of my friends, who did it.'

He looked Emil in the eye.

'I was an idiot to think we were friends,' he said in a low voice. 'We were just kids. Barely twenty.'

He turned to leave the shed.

'Ilona was a fucking slut,' Emil snarled behind him.

At the moment these words were spat out he noticed a spade standing on top of a dusty old cabinet. He grabbed it by its shaft, turned a half-circle and let out a mighty roar as he brought the spade down on Emil with all his might. It struck him on the head. He saw how the light flickered off in Emil's eyes as he dropped to the floor.

He stood looking down at Emil's limp body as if in a world of his own, until a long-forgotten sentence returned to his mind.

'It's best to kill them with a spade.'

A dark pool of blood began to form on the floor and he knew at once that he had dealt Emil a fatal blow. He was completely detached. Calm and collected as he watched Emil motionless on the floor and the pool of blood growing. Looked on as if it were nothing to do with him. He had not gone to the shed to kill him. He had not planned to murder him. It had happened without a moment's thought.

He had no idea how long he had been standing there before he registered someone beside him, speaking to him. Someone who tugged at him and slapped his cheek lightly and said something indistinct. He looked at the man but did not recognise him at once. He saw him bend over Emil. Put a finger to his jugular as if to check for a pulse. He knew that it was hopeless. He knew that Emil was dead. He had killed Emil.

The man stood up from the body and turned to him. He now saw who it was. He had followed that man through Reykjavík; he had led him to Emil.

It was Lothar.

34

Karl Antonsson was at home when Elínborg knocked on his door. His curiosity was aroused the moment she told him that the discovery of the skeleton in Kleifarvatn had prompted them to make inquiries about Icelandic students in Leipzig. He invited Elínborg into the living room. He and his wife were on their way to the golf course, he told her, but it could wait.

Earlier that morning Elínborg had telephoned Sigurdur Óli and asked how Bergthóra was feeling. He said she was fine. Everything was going well.

'And that man, has he stopped phoning you at night?'

'I hear from him now and again.'

'Wasn't he suicidal?'

'Pathologically,' Sigurdur Óli said, and added that Erlendur was waiting for him. They were going to meet Haraldur at the old people's home as a part of Erlendur's ridiculous quest for Leopold. The application for a full-scale search of the land in Mosfellsbaer had been turned down, much to Erlendur's disgust.

Karl lived on Reynimelur in a pretty house divided into three flats with a neatly kept garden. His wife Ulrika was German and she shook Elínborg's hand firmly. The couple wore their age well and were both fit. It might be the golf, Elínborg thought to herself. They were very surprised by this unexpected visit and looked blankly at each other when they heard the reason.

'Is it someone who studied in Leipzig that you found in the lake?' Karl asked. Ulrika went into the kitchen to make coffee.

'We don't know,' Elínborg said. 'Do either of you remember a man by the name of Lothar in Leipzig?'

Karl looked at his wife, who was standing in the kitchen doorway.

'She's asking about Lothar,' he said.

'Lothar? What about him?'

'They think it's him in the lake,' Karl said.

'That's not quite right,' Elínborg said. 'We aren't suggesting that's the case.'

'We paid him to clear everything,' Ulrika said. 'Once.'

'Clear everything?'

'When Ulrika came back to Iceland with me,' Karl said. 'He had influence and was able to assist us. But for a price. My parents scraped it together – and Ulrika's parents in Leipzig too, of course.'

'And Lothar helped you?'

'Very much,' Karl said. 'He charged for it so it wasn't just a favour, and I think he helped other people too, not just us.'

'And all it involved was paying money?'

Karl and Ulrika exchanged glances and she went into the kitchen.

'He mentioned that we might be contacted later, you know. But we never were and never would have entertained the idea. Never. I was never in the party after we came back to Iceland, never went to meetings or the like. I gave up all involvement in politics. Ulrika was never political, she had an aversion to that sort of thing.'

'You mean you would have been given tasks?' Elínborg said.

'I have no idea,' Karl said. 'It never came to that. We never met Lothar again. Thinking back, it's sometimes hard to believe what we actually experienced in those years. It was a completely different world.'

'The Icelanders called it "the charade",' Ulrika said, having rejoined them. 'I always thought that was an apt way to describe it.'

'Are you in contact with your university friends at all?' Elínborg asked.

'Very little,' Karl said. 'Well, we bump into each other in the street sometimes, or at birthday parties.'

'One of them was called Emil,' Elínborg said. 'Do you know anything about him?'

'I don't think he ever came back to Iceland,' Karl said. 'He always lived in Germany. I haven't seen him since . . . is he still alive?'

'I don't know,' Elínborg said.

'I never liked him,' Ulrika said. 'He was a bit sleazy.'

'Emil was always a loner. He didn't know many people. He was said to do the authorities' bidding. I never saw that side of him.'

'And you don't know anything else about this Lothar character?'

'No, nothing,' Karl said.

'Do you have any photographs of the students from Leipzig?' Elínborg asked. 'Of Lothar or anyone else?'

'Not Lothar and definitely not Emil, but I do have one of Tómas and his girlfriend. Ilona. She was Hungarian.'

Karl stood up and walked across the living room to a large cupboard. He took out an old album and flicked through it until he found the photograph, which he handed to Elínborg. It was a black-and-white snap of a young couple holding hands. The sun was shining on them and they were smiling into the camera.

'It's taken in front of Thomaskirche,' Karl said. 'A few months before Ilona disappeared.'

'I heard about that,' Elínborg said.

'I was there when they came to get her,' Karl said. 'It was awful. The brutality. No one found out what happened to her and I don't think Tómas ever recovered.'

'She was very brave,' Ulrika said.

'She was a dissident,' Karl said. 'That was frowned upon.'

*

Erlendur knocked on Haraldur's door at the old people's home. Breakfast had just finished and the clatter of plates could still be heard from the canteen. Sigurdur Óli was with him. They heard Haraldur shout something from inside and Erlendur opened the door. Haraldur was sitting up in bed, his head lowered, staring down at the floor. He looked up when they entered the room.

'Who's that with you?' he asked when he saw Sigurdur Óli.

'He works with me,' Erlendur said.

Instead of greeting Sigurdur Óli, Haraldur shot him a warning look. Erlendur sat on a chair facing Haraldur. Sigurdur Óli remained standing and leaned against the wall.

The door opened and another grey-haired resident put his head in.

'Haraldur,' he said, 'there's choir practice in room eleven tonight.'

Without waiting for an answer, he closed the door again.

Erlendur gaped at Haraldur.

'Choir practice?' he said. 'Surely you don't go in for that?'

'"Choir practice" is code for a booze-up,' Haraldur grunted. 'I hope I don't disappoint you.'

Sigurdur Óli grinned to himself. He was having trouble concentrating. What he had said to Elínborg that morning was not entirely true. Bergthóra had been to the doctor, who had told her that it was fifty-fifty. Bergthóra had tried to be positive when she related this, but he knew that she was in torment.

'Let's get a move on,' Haraldur said. 'Maybe I didn't tell you the whole truth, but I can't see why you need to go around sticking your nose into other people's affairs. But . . . I wanted . . .'

Erlendur sensed an unusual hesitation in Haraldur when the old man lifted his head to be able to look him in the face.

'Jói didn't get enough oxygen,' he said, looking back at the floor. 'That was why. At birth. They thought it was all right, he grew properly, but he turned out different. He wasn't like the other kids.'

Sigurdur Óli indicated to Erlendur that he had no idea what the old man was talking about. Erlendur shrugged. Something about

Haraldur had changed. He was not his usual self. He was in some way milder.

'It turned out that he was a bit funny,' Haraldur continued. 'Simple. Backward. Kind inside but couldn't cope, couldn't learn, never knew how to read. It took a long time to emerge and we took a long time to accept it and come to terms with it.'

'That must have been difficult for your parents,' Erlendur said after a long silence, once Haraldur seemed unlikely to say anything else.

'I ended up looking after Jói when they died,' Haraldur said at last, his eyes trained on the floor. 'We lived out there on the farm, barely scraping a living towards the end. Had nothing to sell but the land. It was worth quite a lot because it was so close to Reykjavík and we made a fair bit on the deal. We could buy a flat and still have money left over.'

'What was it you were going to tell us?' Sigurdur Óli said impatiently. Erlendur glared at him.

'My brother stole the hubcap from the car,' Haraldur said. 'That was the whole crime and now you can leave me alone. That's the long and the short of it. I don't know how you can make such a fuss about it. After all these years. He stole a hubcap! What kind of a crime is that?'

'Are we talking about the black Falcon?' Erlendur asked.

'Yes, it was the black Falcon.'

'So Leopold *did* visit your farm,' Erlendur said. 'You're admitting that now.'

Haraldur nodded.

'Do you think you were right to sit on this information for your whole life?' Erlendur asked angrily. 'Causing everyone unnecessary trouble?'

'Don't you go preaching to me,' Haraldur said. 'It won't get you anywhere.'

'There are people who have been suffering for decades,' Erlendur said.

'We didn't do anything to him. Nothing happened to him.'

'You ruined the police investigation.'

'Put me in the nick, then,' Haraldur said. 'It won't make much difference.'

'What happened?' Sigurdur Óli asked.

'My brother was a bit simple,' Haraldur said. 'But he never harmed that man. There wasn't a violent bone in him. He thought the bloody hubcaps were pretty so he stole one. He thought it was enough for that bloke to have three.'

'And what did the man do?' Sigurdur Óli asked.

'You were looking for a missing man,' Haraldur went on, staring at Erlendur. 'I didn't want to complicate things. You would have complicated it if I'd told you that Jói took the hubcap. Then you would have wanted to know if he killed him, which he didn't, but you'd never have believed me and you'd have taken Jói away.'

'What did this man do when Jói took the hubcap?' Sigurdur Óli repeated.

'He seemed very tense.'

'So what happened?'

'He attacked my brother,' Haraldur said. 'He shouldn't have done that, because even though Jói was stupid, he was strong. Threw him off like a sack of feathers.'

'And killed him,' Erlendur said.

Haraldur raised his head.

'What did I just tell you?'

'Why should we believe you now, after you've been lying all these years?'

'I decided to pretend that he never came. That we'd never met him. That was the obvious thing to do. We never touched him, apart from Jói defending himself. He left and he was fine then.'

'Why should we believe you now?' Sigurdur Óli said.

'Jói didn't kill anyone. He never could have. He never hurt a fly, Jói. But you wouldn't have believed that. I tried to get him to give the hubcap back, but he wouldn't say where he'd hidden it. Jói was like a raven. He liked pretty things and they were nice, shiny hubcaps. He wanted to own one. As simple as that. The bloke got really worked up and threatened us both, and then he went for Jói. We had a fight and then he left and we never saw him again.'

'Why should I believe this?' Erlendur asked again.

Haraldur snorted.

'I don't give a monkey's what you believe,' he said. 'Take it or leave it.'

'Why didn't you tell the police this touching tale about you and your brother when they were searching for the man?'

'The police didn't seem interested in anything much,' Haraldur said. 'They didn't ask for any explanations. They took a statement from me and that was it.'

'And the man left you after the fight?' Erlendur said, thinking of lazy Níels.

'Yes.'

'With one hubcap missing?'

'Yes. He stormed off without bothering about the hubcap.'

'What did you do with it? Or did you ever find it?'

'I buried it. After you started asking about that bloke. Jói told me where he'd put it and I dug a little hole behind the house and buried it in the ground. You'll find it there.'

'All right,' Erlendur said. 'We'll poke around behind the house and see if we can't find it. But I still think you're lying to us.'

'I don't care,' Haraldur said. 'You can think what you like.'

'Anything else?' Erlendur said.

Haraldur sat without saying a word. Perhaps he felt he had said enough. There wasn't a sound in his little room. Noises were heard from the canteen and the corridor: old people wandering around, waiting for their next meal. Erlendur stood up.

'Thank you,' he said. 'This will be useful. We should have been told this more than thirty years ago, but . . .'

'He dropped his wallet,' Haraldur said.

'His wallet?'

'In the fight. The salesman. He dropped his wallet. We didn't find it until after he'd gone. It was where his car had been parked. Jói saw it and hid it. He wasn't *that* stupid.'

'What did you do with it?' Sigurdur Óli asked.

'I buried it with the hubcap,' Haraldur said, a sudden vague smile on his face. 'You'll find that there, too.'

'You didn't want to return it?'

'I tried, but I couldn't find the name in the phone book. Then you lot started asking about that bloke, so I hid it with the hubcap.'

'You mean Leopold wasn't in the directory?'

'No, and nor was the other name.'

'The other name?' Sigurdur Óli said. 'Did he have another name?'

'I couldn't figure out why, but some documents in the wallet had the name he introduced himself by, Leopold, and on others there was a different name.'

'What name?' Erlendur asked.

'Jói was funny,' Haraldur said. 'He was always hanging around the spot I buried the hubcap. Sometimes he'd lie on the ground or sit down where he knew it was. But he never dared dig it up. Never dared touch it again. He knew he'd done something wrong. He cried in my arms after that fight. The poor boy.'

'What name was it?' Sigurdur Óli asked.

'I can't remember,' Haraldur said. 'I've told you all you need to know, so bugger off. Leave me alone.'

Erlendur drove to the abandoned farm just outside Mosfellsbaer. A cold northerly wind was getting up and autumn was descending over the land. He felt chilly when he walked behind the house. He pulled his coat tighter around him. At one time there had been a fence around the yard, but it had broken up long before and the yard was now mostly overgrown with grass. Before they left, Haraldur had given Erlendur a fairly detailed description of where he had buried the hubcap.

He took a shovel from the farmhouse, paced out the distance from the wall and began to dig. The hubcap would not be buried very deep. The digging made him hot, so he took a rest and lit a cigarette. Then he carried on. He dug down about one metre but found no sign of the hubcap. He began widening the hole. He took another break. It was a long time since he had done manual work. He smoked another cigarette.

About ten minutes later there was a chink when he thrust the shovel's blade down, and he knew he had found the hubcap from the black Falcon.

He dug carefully around it, then got down on his knees and scraped the dirt away with his hands. Soon the entire hubcap was visible and he lifted it carefully from the earth. Although rusty, the hubcap was clearly from a Ford Falcon. Erlendur stood up and knocked it against the wall, and the dirt fell away. The hubcap made a ringing sound when it struck the wall.

Erlendur put it down and peered into the hole. He still had to find the wallet that Haraldur had described. It was not yet visible, so he knelt down again, leaned over the hole and dug away at the earth with his hands.

Everything that Haraldur had told him was true. Erlendur found the wallet in the ground nearby. After carefully extracting it he stood up. It was a regular, long, black leather wallet. The moisture in the ground meant that the wallet had begun to rot and he had to handle it carefully because it was in tatters. When he opened it he saw a cheque book, a few Icelandic banknotes long since withdrawn from circulation, a few scraps of paper and a driving licence in Leopold's name. The damp had seeped through and the photograph was ruined. In another compartment he found another card. It looked like a foreign driving licence and the photograph on it was not so badly damaged. He peered at it, but did not recognise the man.

As far as Erlendur could tell the licence had been issued in Germany, but it was in such a bad condition that only the odd word was legible. He could see the owner's name clearly, but not his surname. Erlendur stood holding the wallet and looked up.

He recognised the name on the driving licence.

He recognised the name Emil.

35

Lothar Weiser shook him, shouted at him and slapped him repeatedly around the face. Gradually he came to his senses and saw how the pool of blood under Emil's head had spread across the dirty concrete floor. He looked into Lothar's face.

'I killed Emil,' he said.

'What the hell happened?' Lothar hissed. 'Why did you attack him? How much did you know about him? How did you track him down? What are you doing here, Tómas?'

'I followed you,' he said. 'I saw you and followed you. And now I've killed him. He said something about Ilona.'

'Are you still thinking about her? Aren't you ever going to forget that?'

Lothar went over to the door and closed it carefully. He looked around the shed as if searching for something. Tómas stood riveted to the spot, watching Lothar as if in a trance. His eyes had adjusted to the darkness and he could now see better inside the shed. It was full of piles of old rubbish: chairs and gardening tools, furniture and mattresses. Scattered across the bench he noticed various pieces of equipment, some of which he did not recognise. There were telescopes, cameras of different sizes and a large tape recorder that seemed to be connected to something resembling a radio transmitter. He also noticed photographs lying around, but could not see clearly what they showed. On the floor by the bench was a large black box with dials and buttons whose function eluded him. Beside it was a brown suitcase that the black box could fit inside. It appeared to be damaged – the dials were smashed and the back had dropped open onto the floor.

He was still mesmerised. In a strange, dreamlike state. What he had done was so unreal and remote that he could not begin to face it. He looked at the body on the floor and at Lothar tending to it.

'I thought I recognised him . . .'

'Emil could be a real bastard,' Lothar said.

'Was it him? Who told you about Ilona?'

'Yes, he drew our attention to her meetings. He worked for us in Leipzig. At the university. He didn't care who he betrayed or what secrets he spilled. Even his best friends weren't safe. Like you,' Lothar said and stood up again.

'I thought we were safe,' he replied. 'The Icelanders. I never suspected . . .' He stopped in mid-sentence. He was coming back to his senses. The haze was lifting. His thoughts were clearer. 'You weren't any better,' he said. 'You weren't any better yourself. You were exactly the same as him, only worse.'

They looked each other in the eye.

'Do I need to be afraid of you?' he asked.

He had no feeling of fear. Not yet, at least. Lothar posed no threat to him. On the contrary, Lothar already appeared to be wondering what to do about Emil lying on the floor in his own blood. Lothar had not attacked him. He had not even taken the spade from him. For some absurd reason he was still holding the spade.

'No,' Lothar said. 'You don't need to be afraid of me.'

'How can I be sure?'

'I'm telling you.'

'I can't trust anyone,' he said. 'You ought to know that. You taught me that.'

'You must get out of here and try to forget this,' Lothar said as he took hold of the spade's shaft. 'Don't ask me why. I'll take care of Emil. Don't go and do anything stupid like calling the police. Forget it. Like it never happened. Don't do anything stupid.'

'Why? What are you helping me for? I thought—'

'Don't think anything,' Lothar interrupted him. 'Go away and never mention this to anyone. It's nothing to do with you.'

They stood facing each other. Lothar gripped the spade tighter.

'Of course it's something to do with me!'

'No,' Lothar said firmly. 'Forget it.'

'What did you mean by what you just said?'

'What was that?' Lothar asked.

'How I knew about him. How I tracked him down. Has he been living here long?'

'Here in Iceland? No.'

'What's going on? What are you doing together? What's all this equipment in this shed? What are those photographs on the bench?'

Lothar kept hold of the shovel's shaft, trying to disarm him, but he held on grimly and did not let go.

'What was Emil doing here?' he asked. 'I thought he was living abroad. In East Germany. That he had never come back after university.'

Lothar was still a riddle to him, more so now than ever before. Who was this man? Had he been wrong about Lothar all the time, or was he the same arrogant and treacherous beast he had been in Leipzig?

'Go back home,' Lothar said. 'Don't think about it any more. It's nothing to do with you. What happened in Leipzig isn't connected with this.'

He did not believe him.

'What happened there? What happened in Leipzig? Tell me. What did they do to Ilona?'

Lothar cursed.

'We've been trying to get you Icelanders to work for us,' he said after a while. 'It hasn't worked. You all inform on us. Two of our men were arrested a few years ago and deported after they tried to get someone from Reykjavík to take photographs.'

'Photographs?'

'Of military installations in Iceland. No one wants to work for us. So we got Emil to.'

'Emil?'

'He didn't have a problem with it.'

Seeing the look of disbelief on his face, Lothar started to tell him about Emil. It was as if Lothar was trying to convince him that he could trust him, that he had changed.

'We provided him with a job that allowed him to travel around the country without arousing suspicion,' Lothar said. 'He was very interested. He felt like a genuine spy.'

Lothar cast a glance down at Emil's body.

'Maybe he was.'

'And he was supposed to photograph American military installations?'

'Yes, and even work temporarily at places near them, like the base at Heidarfjall on Langanes or Stokksnes near Höfn. And in Hvalfjördur, where the oil depot is. Straumsnesfjall in the west fjords. He worked in Keflavík and took listening devices with him. He sold agricultural machinery so he always had a reason for being somewhere. We had an even bigger role lined up for him in the future,' Lothar said.

'Like what?'

'The possibilities are endless,' Lothar replied.

'What about you? Why are you telling me all this? Aren't you one of them?'

'Yes,' Lothar said. 'I'm one of them. I'll take care of Emil. Forget all this and never mention it to anyone. Understood?! Never.'

'Wasn't there a risk that he'd be found out?'

'He set up a cover,' Lothar said. 'We told him it was unnecessary, but he wanted to use a fake identity and so on. If anyone recognised him as Emil he was going to say he was on a quick visit home, but otherwise he called himself Leopold. I don't know where he dreamt up that name. Emil enjoyed deceiving people. He took a perverse pleasure in pretending to be someone else.'

'What are you going to do with him?'

'Sometimes we dispose of rubbish in a little lake south-west of the city. It shouldn't be a problem.'

'I've hated you for years, Lothar. Did you know that?'

'To tell the truth I'd forgotten you, Tómas. Ilona was a problem and she would have been found out sooner or later. What I did is irrelevant. Totally irrelevant.'

'How do you know I won't go straight to the police?'

'Because you don't feel guilty about him. That's why you should forget it. That's why it never happened. I won't say what happened and you'll forget that I ever existed.'

'But . . .'

'But what? Are you going to confess to committing murder? Don't be so childish!'

'We were just children, just kids. How did it end up like this?'

'We try to get by,' Lothar said. 'That's all we can do.'

'What are you going to tell them? About Emil? What will you say happened?'

'I'll tell them I found him like this and don't know what the hell happened. But the main thing is to get rid of him. They understand that. Now go away! Get out of here before I change my mind!'

'Do you know what happened to Ilona?' he asked. 'Can you tell me what happened to her?'

He had gone to the door of the shed when he turned round and asked the question that had long tormented him. As if the answer might help him to accept those irreversible events.

'I don't know much,' Lothar said. 'I heard that she tried to escape. She was taken to hospital and that's all I know.'

'But why was she arrested?'

'You know that perfectly well,' Lothar said. 'She took a risk; she knew the stakes. She was dangerous. She incited revolt. She worked against them. They had experience from the 1953 uprising. They weren't going to let that repeat itself.'

'But . . .'

'She knew the risks she was taking.'

'What happened to her?'

'Stop this and get out!'

'Did she die?'

'She must have,' Lothar said, looking thoughtfully at the black box with the broken dials. He glanced at the bench and noticed the car keys. A Ford logo was on the ring.

'We'll make the police think he drove out of town,' he said, almost to himself. 'I have to persuade my men. That could prove difficult. They hardly believe a word I tell them any more.'

'Why not?' he asked. 'Why don't they believe you?'

Lothar smiled.

'I've been a bit naughty,' Lothar said. 'And I think they know.'

36

Erlendur stood in the garage in Kópavogur, looking at the Ford Falcon. Holding the hubcap, he bent down and attached it to one of the front wheels. It fitted perfectly. The woman had been rather surprised to see Erlendur again, but let him into the garage and helped him to pull the heavy canvas sheet off the car. Erlendur stood looking at the streamlining, the shiny black paint, round rear lights, white upholstery, the big, delicate steering wheel and the old hubcap that was back in place after all those years, and suddenly he was seized by a powerful urge. He had not felt such a longing for anything in a very long time.

'Is that the original hubcap?' the woman asked.

'Yes,' Erlendur said, 'we found it.'

'That's quite an achievement,' the woman said.

'Do you think it's still roadworthy?' Erlendur asked.

'It was, the last time I knew,' the woman said. 'Why do you ask?'

'It's rather a special car,' Erlendur said. 'I was wondering . . . if it's for sale . . .'

'For sale?' the woman said. 'I've been trying to get rid of it ever since my husband died but no one's shown any interest. I even tried advertising it but the only calls I got were from old nutters who weren't prepared to pay. Just wanted me to give it them. I'll be damned if I'd give them that car!'

'How much do you want for it?' Erlendur asked.

'Don't you need to check whether it starts first and that sort of stuff?' the woman asked. 'You're welcome to have it for a couple of days. I need to talk to my boys. They know more about these matters than I do. I don't know the first thing about cars. All I know is that I wouldn't dream of giving that car away. I want a decent price for it.'

Erlendur's thoughts turned to his old Japanese banger, crumbling from rust. He had never cared for possessions, did not see the point in accumulating lifeless objects, but there was something about the Falcon that kindled his interest. Perhaps it was the car's history and its connection with a mysterious, decades-old case of a missing person. For some reason, Erlendur felt he had to own that car.

Sigurdur Óli had trouble concealing his astonishment when Erlendur collected him at lunchtime the following day. The Ford was entirely roadworthy. The woman said that her sons came to Kópavogur regularly to make sure it was still running smoothly. Erlendur had gone straight to a Ford garage where the car was checked, lubricated and rustproofed and the electrics were fixed. He was told that the car was as good as new, the seats showed little sign of wear, all the instruments were working and the engine was in reasonable condition despite hardly having been used.

'Where's your head at?' Sigurdur Óli asked as he got into the passenger seat.

'Where's my head at?'

'What are you planning to do with this car?'

'Drive it,' Erlendur said.

'Are you allowed to? Isn't it evidence?'

'We'll find out.'

They were going to see one of the students from Leipzig, Tómas, whom Hannes had told them about. Erlendur had visited Marion that morning. The patient was back on form, asking about the Kleifarvatn case and Eva Lind.

'Have you found your daughter yet?' his old boss asked him.

'No,' Erlendur said. 'I don't know anything about her.'

Sigurdur Óli told Erlendur that he had been looking into the Stasi's activities on the Internet. East Germany had come the closest of any country to almost total surveillance of its citizens. The security police had headquarters in 41 buildings, the use of 1,181 houses for its agents, 305 summer holiday houses, 98 sports halls, 18,000 flats for spy meetings and 97,000 employees, of whom 2,171 worked on reading mail, 1,486 on bugging telephones and 8,426 on listening to telephone calls and radio broadcasts. The Stasi had more than 100,000 active but unofficial collaborators; 1,000,000 people provided the police with occasional information; reports had been compiled on 6,000,000 persons and one department of the Stasi had the sole function of watching over other security police members.

Sigurdur Óli finished spouting his figures just as he and Erlendur reached the door of Tómas's house. It was a small bungalow with a basement, in need of repair. There were blotches in the paint on the corrugated-iron roof, which was rusted down to the gutters. There were cracks in the walls, which had not been painted for a long time, and the garden was overgrown. The house was well located, overlooking the shore in the westernmost part of Reykjavík, and Erlendur admired the view out to sea. Sigurdur Óli rang the doorbell for the third time. No one appeared to be at home.

Erlendur saw a ship on the horizon. A man and a woman walked quickly along the pavement outside the house. The man took wide strides and was slightly ahead of the woman, who did her best to keep up with him. They were talking, the man over his shoulder and the woman in a raised voice so that he could hear her. Neither noticed the two police officers at the house.

'So does this mean that Emil and Leopold were the same person?' Sigurdur Óli said as he rang the bell again. Erlendur had told him about his discovery at the brothers' farm near Mosfellsbaer.

'It looks that way,' Erlendur said.

'Is he the man in the lake?'

'Conceivably.'

Tómas was in the basement when he heard the bell. He knew it was the police. Through the basement window he had seen two men get out of an old black car. It was purely by chance that they happened to call at precisely that moment. He had been waiting for them since the spring, all summer long, and by now autumn had arrived. He knew they would come in the end. He knew that if they had any talent at all they would eventually be standing at his front door, waiting for him to answer.

He looked out of the basement window and thought about Ilona. They had once stood beneath Bach's statue next to Thomaskirche. It was a beautiful summer's day and they had their arms around each other. All around them were pedestrians, trams and cars, yet they were alone in the world.

He held the pistol. It was British, from the Second World War. His father had owned it, a gift from a British soldier, and he had given it to his son, along with some ammunition. He had lubricated, polished and cleaned it, and a few days earlier he had gone to Heidmörk nature reserve to test whether it still worked. There was one bullet left in it. He raised his arm and put the muzzle to his temple.

Ilona looked up the façade of the church to the steeple.

'You're my Tómas,' she said, and kissed him.

Bach was above them, silent as the grave, and he felt that a smile played across the statue's lips.

'For ever,' he said. 'I'll always be your Tómas.'

'Who is this man?' Sigurdur Óli asked, standing with Erlendur on the doorstep. 'Does he matter?'

'I only know what Hannes told us,' Erlendur replied. 'He was in Leipzig and had a girlfriend there.'

He rang the bell again. They stood and waited.

It was hardly the sound of a shot that reached their ears. More like a slight thud from inside the house. Like a hammer tapping on a wall. Erlendur looked at Sigurdur Óli.

'Did you hear that?'

'There's someone inside,' Sigurdur Óli said.

Erlendur knocked on the door and turned the handle. It was not locked. They stepped inside and called out but received no reply. They noticed the door and the steps down to the basement. Erlendur walked cautiously down the steps and saw a man lying on the floor with an antiquated pistol by his side.

'There's an envelope here addressed to us,' Sigurdur Óli said as he came down the steps. He was holding a thick yellow envelope marked 'Police'.

'Oh,' he said when he saw the man on the floor.

'Why did you do this?' Erlendur said, as if to himself.

He walked over to the body and stared down at Tómas.

'Why?' he whispered.

Erlendur visited the girlfriend of the man who called himself Leopold but whose name was Emil. He told her that the skeleton from Kleifarvatn was indeed the earthly remains of the person she had once loved and who then vanished without a trace from her life. He spent a long time sitting in the living room telling her about the account that Tómas had written and left behind before he went down to the basement, and he answered her questions as best he could. She took the news calmly. Her expression remained unchanged when Erlendur told her that Emil had conceivably been working undercover for the East Germans.

Although his story surprised her, Erlendur knew that it was not the question of what Emil did, or who he was, that she would mull over when towards evening he finally took his leave. He could not answer the question that he knew gnawed at her more than any other. Did he love her? Or had he simply used her as an alibi?

She tried to put the question into words before he left. He could tell how difficult she found it and halfway through he put his arm around her. She was fighting back the tears.

'You know that,' he said. 'You know that yourself, don't you?'

One day shortly afterwards, Sigurdur Óli returned home from work to find Bergthóra standing confused and helpless in the living room, looking at him through broken eyes. He realised at once what had happened. He ran over to her and tried to console her, but she burst into an uncontrollable fit of tears that made her whole body shake and tremble. The signature tune for the evening news was playing on the radio. The police had reported a middle-aged man missing. The announcement was followed by a brief description of him. In his mind's eye Sigurdur Óli suddenly saw a woman in a shop, holding a punnet of fresh strawberries.

37

When winter had descended, bringing piercing northerly winds and swirling snow, Erlendur drove out to the lake where Emil's skeleton had been found that spring. It was morning and there was little traffic around the lake. Erlendur parked the Ford Falcon by the side of the road and walked down to the water's edge. He had read in the newspapers that the lake had stopped draining and was beginning to fill again. Experts from the Energy Authority predicted that it would eventually reach its former size. Erlendur looked over to the nearby pool of Lambhagatjörn, which had dried up to reveal a red muddy bed. He looked at Sydri-Stapi, a bluff protruding into the lake, and at the encircling range of mountains, and felt astonished that this peaceful lake could have been the setting for espionage in Iceland.

He watched the lake rippling in the northerly wind and thought to himself that everything would return to normal here. Maybe providence had determined it all. Maybe the draining lake's sole purpose had been to reveal this old crime. Soon it would be deep and cold again at the spot where a skeleton had once lain, preserving a story of love and betrayal in a distant country.

He had read and reread the account written and left by Tómas before he took his life. He read about Lothar and Emil and the Icelandic students, and the system that they encountered – inhumane and incomprehensible and doomed to crumble and vanish. He read Tómas's reflections on Ilona and their short time together, on his love for her and on the child they were expecting but he would never see. He felt a profound sympathy for this man whom he had never met, just found lying in his own blood with an old pistol beside him. Perhaps that had been the only way out for Tómas.

It turned out that no one missed Emil except for the woman who knew him as Leopold. Emil was an only child with few relatives. He had corresponded very sporadically from Leipzig with a cousin until the mid-1960s. The cousin had almost forgotten that Emil existed when Erlendur began inquiring about him.

The American embassy supplied a photograph of Lothar from the time he had served as an attaché in Norway. Emil's girlfriend did not recall having seen the man on the photograph. The German embassy in Reykjavík also provided old photographs of him and it was revealed that he was a suspected double agent who had probably died in a prison outside Dresden some time before 1978.

'It's coming back,' Erlendur heard a voice say behind him, and he turned round. A woman he vaguely recognised was smiling at him. She was wearing a thick anorak and a cap.

'Excuse me . . . ?'

'Sunna,' she said. 'The hydrologist. I found the skeleton in the spring – maybe you don't remember me.'

'Oh yes, I remember you.'

'Where's the other guy who was with you?' she asked, looking all around.

'Sigurdur Óli, you mean. I think he's at work.'

'Have you found out who it was?'

'More or less,' Erlendur said.

'I haven't seen it in the news.'

'No, we haven't made the announcement yet,' Erlendur said. 'How are you keeping?'

'Fine, thanks.'

'Is he with you?' Erlendur asked, looking along the shore at a man skimming stones along the surface of the lake.

'Yes,' Sunna said. 'I met him in the summer. So who was it? In the lake?'

'It's a long story,' Erlendur said.

'Maybe I'll read about it in the papers.'

'Maybe.'

'Well, see you round.'

'Goodbye,' Erlendur said, with a smile.

He watched Sunna as she went over to the man; they walked hand in hand to a car parked by the roadside and drove off in the direction of Reykjavík.

Erlendur wrapped his coat tightly around him and looked across the lake. His thoughts turned to Tómas's namesake in the Gospel of St John. When the other apostles told him that they had seen Jesus risen from the dead, Thomas replied: 'Except I shall see in his hands the print of the nails, and put my finger into the print of the nails, and thrust my hand into his side, I will not believe.'

Tómas had seen the print of the nails and had thrust his hand into the wounds, but, unlike his biblical namesake, he had lost his faith in the act of discovery.

'Blessed are they that have not seen, and yet have believed,' Erlendur whispered, and his words were taken by the northerly wind across the lake.